202

10/24

OTHER BOOKS BY BRETT JAMES

The Deadfall Project

The Drift Wars

Tangent

Lies and Silence

*Toothpaste and Teflon:
Things to Pack in Your Time Machine*

TUNNEL

BOOK ONE OF
THE SUBTERRANEAN TRILOGY

BRETT JAMES

FALLACY PUBLICATIONS  OAKLAND

This is a work of fiction. Names, characters, places, and incidents either are the product of the author's imagination or are used fictitiously, and any resemblance to actual persons, living or dead or halfway between, business establishments, events, or locales is entirely coincidental.

Copyright © 2020 Brett James

Fallacy Publications

http://fallacypublications.com

ISBN 978-1-6799479-1-9

KDP Edition

1 2 3 4 5 6 7 8 9 0

Cover art by Andrew Leung
Book design by MobiHue
Set in Garamond & Franklin Gothic

*For my father, who insisted
I keep shooting until I made it.*

Après nous, le déluge.
Madame de Pompadour

ONE

THE BOWELS OF THE earth are a dark and lonely place. Cut off from the sun, one need travel only a few yards deep before the ground becomes cold and lifeless. Soon thereafter, the dirt gives way first to clay and then to rock. Few things venture to these depths: spiders, beetles, crustaceans, a few blind amphibians, and one species of mammal.

"Help me!"

A child's voice echoed through the dark, cutting through the still air. Then another sound: ticking.

A full minute passed before the child repeated his plea. This time something stirred. Gravel scratched rhythmically against stone, growing louder, closer. A pinprick of light appeared in the distance, moved back and forth, then fizzled into nothing.

"Help!" the child called again. The scratching drew closer, and the light returned, flickering through a veil of smoke. The smoke cast shadows down the rippled rock of a long volcanic tube, whose porous black walls were as rough as sandpaper.

The light disappeared and the scratching resumed, crawling closer.

"Is anybody there?" the child called, his strained voice seeming to come from everywhere at once.

A dark outline crawled up the lava tube, growing to fill it. Light flared with a sharp crack, and a white-hot fire burned frantically, hissing and popping. Acrid smoke filled the air as a flare waved back and forth, illuminating both the lava tube and the face of Julie Porter.

Julie's face was chiseled, with angular planes that seemed at odds with her soft, youthful skin. Green eyes sparkled below a shock-white spray of hair that arced off her forehead. The rest of her hair was short and spiked. A trickle of blood ran down from her scalp, diverted along her eyebrow, and continued down her cheek.

Julie wore a sleeveless lycra shirt and shorts that, once white, were now stained and torn. Her muscles were thick and alive, like a cage fighter's, and her skin was crosshatched with lacerations. Lying prone, she took quick, shallow breaths, keeping her oxygen level up. She moved the sputtering flare as she studied the tube in front of her.

The passage forked, with one way heading down and to the right while the other went up and to the left. She ground the flare out and slid forward, pressing her forehead to the stone in the center of the split. She took a deep breath and held it, then closed her eyes and listened. The ticking, barely louder than her own pulse, sounded the same in both directions. But then:

"Over here! I'm hurt!"

Julie cocked her head; the child's voice was much clearer to the left.

"Almost there," Julie whispered, cupping her hand over the mic of her radio headset.

"Already?" blurted a voice in her ear.

"Shhh," Julie said. She crawled forward, walking on the

leather pads that protected her elbows and knees from the coarse rock. A cylindrical first aid kit bounced after her, tethered to her ankle.

Julie advanced through the dark, slowly circling her outstretched hands. Her finger jammed against something hard and unexpectedly close. Her hand curled in pain.

"Stupid," she chided herself. The voice in her ear started to speak, but she cut it off, saying, "No comments."

"Are you already at the second junction?" the voice asked. This was a different voice, Eric's. He spoke with a faint German accent.

Julie didn't answer. She flexed her fingers, squeaking her leather gloves. Two of the glove's fingertips had been cut away, allowing for a better sense of feel, and Eric had warned her to keep those fingers curled in when she was moving blindly.

Warned me like six times, dumb ass, she thought, pulling out another flare—her third from last—and sparking it.

Ahead of her, a smooth rock emerged from the floor, narrowing the passage until it was just a thin crescent-shaped gap between rock and ceiling. She reached past the rock and felt the passage widen again on the other side. She spread her fingers to measure the height of the gap; it was thin, maybe too thin. But she could hear the ticking on the other side. She was close.

If he can do it..., Julie thought to herself, dropping the flare and crawling forward. She angled her head and shoved it into the gap, the coarse stone ceiling grating along her cheek. She placed a foot on either wall and pushed with her legs, which were as thick and toned as a gymnast's. Her ribs flattened as they passed over rising rock and she exhaled, making herself as thin as possible. The roof scraped along her back, reopening scabs, but then her ribs passed over the hump and popped back into shape. The rock pressed against her stomach and pushed against the inside of her hip bones, but her head was all the way through. She curled an arm back to her waist, drawing out another flare.

"Somebody help me!" the child cried.

His voice was close, and the ticking was loud, but when Julie fired the flare, she saw a thick stalactite blocking the way. It hung from the ceiling and melded with the floor, all but filling the passage. This was a dead end.

"Pain in my ass," Julie said. She shoved at the stalactite, but it was solid.

"Patience," Eric's voice said in her ear.

Patience my ass, Julie thought, but she held her tongue. His advice was sound, even if his timing was terrible.

She reached to her belt for a small, aluminum-handled pickax and chipped away at the base of the stalactite, where it was the thinnest. It was slow work, and the ticking seemed to grow louder. She was losing precious time; she needed a faster solution.

She curled her arm around the stalactite and hammered the back, chipping out a small hole.

"It hurts!" the child called, desperate.

"Hold your horses, sweetheart," Julie muttered.

She dropped the ax and pulled a metal cigar tube from her pouch, sliding out a short, thin stick of dynamite. It was a crudely made, wrapped in brown kraft, its ends twisted like candy wrappers. *PELIGRO! EXPLOSIVO!* was stamped in red on the side. She uncoiled the fuse and lit it with the flare, then reached around the stalactite and pressed it into the hole she had made. Dropping the flare, she pushed backward, but the base of her rib cage caught against the rock, spreading wider the harder she pushed. She was stuck.

This'll be something, she thought, covering her face with her arms and angling herself as far away as possible.

The explosion clapped like thunder, echoing down the narrow cave. Shards of rock dug into her bare arms, and smoke burned her lungs. She coughed hoarsely, the bulging rock clamping her stomach.

Her ears rang and her vision was blurred. Someone was yelling over the radio, sounding anxious and confused, but she ignored them, focusing on the twin circles of fuzzy light that hovered in front of her. They merged, sharpening, becoming her flare. It had been blown several yards forward, through the newly formed gap in the stalactite. The gap looked wide enough to pass.

She slapped at the smoldering rock, knocking away a few jagged chunks, then pushed forward. Her head slipped through, but a hot shard caught her shoulder, digging into the muscle. She tried to shift sideways to get around it, but her skin was hooked, stretching painfully. She gritted her teeth and shoved forward; the rock sliced down her back as she passed through the broken stalactite.

On the other side, the passage sloped down sharply. Her momentum carried her forward, and she had to shift her hands, walking on her palms just to keep her chin up. She was almost to the flare when her hands came down on nothing. She jerked back, but too late. She tumbled, dropping through a hole.

Her scream echoed back at her as she fell headfirst through the empty dark. She flailed her arms, finding nothing but air. Then something grabbed her leg, jerking her to a stop—the first aid kit had snagged on something, holding her upside down by the tether on her ankle.

"Are you okay, Julie?" Eric asked over the radio. He sounded frantic. "Julie!" he yelled when she didn't reply.

"Just peachy," Julie said, swinging in the dark. Bile dribbled up her throat, and her head swelled with blood.

The cut on her back burned hideously, and blood flowed down her shoulder and along her neck. "But suffering a minor setback," she added.

"Where are you?" Eric asked, but then another voice said, "Give me that." The radio was jostled loudly and the new voice asked, "What is your status, Ms. Porter?"

"Help me!" the child called.

"I'm close," Julie said.

"What the hell does *close* mean? What was that noise?"

"Shhh!" Julie said.

The ticking was loud, urgent. Julie tried to hold still and gauge its direction, but the voice in her ear persisted.

"Don't tell me to—"

"Radio trouble," Julie said, pulling it from her ear and letting it drop. She heard it splash below her, into what sounded like water. She sparked her final flare.

She was hanging inside a tall cavern, twenty feet above a shallow pool of water. It was maybe six feet around and ringed in jagged rocks. The blood dripping from her shoulder made red clouds in the clear water. Her head was directly above the sharp rocks on the lip of the pool.

She dropped the flare into the water. It sunk about three feet and hit the bottom. The water diffused the light, bathing the room in a soft glow.

Julie curled up at the waist, moving slowly so as not to dislodge the first aid kit from whatever was holding it, and drew a flat knife from a plastic sheath between her thighs. She set the blade against the nylon tether that was holding her by the ankle.

Watching the pool below, she swung gently back and forth, aiming for the center. On the third swing, she sliced the tether.

As she fell, she kicked her legs, leveling herself

horizontally, and spread her arms. Her whole body slapped against the water, churning it and darkening it with blood. She sprang to her feet but then collapsed backward, overcome by laughter.

"Hell fucking yes!" she yelled, slapping the water with joy.

"Over here!" the child said, his voice quivering with fear.

"Oh," Julie said. "Right."

The cavern turned a dark red as Julie's blood obscured the flare. She clicked on a small penlight and aimed it toward the sound of ticking. A small head with curly blond hair stared at her, its blue eyes blazing in the light.

"Is anybody out there?" it called.

Julie slogged through the waist-deep pool and vaulted over the jagged edge. She started toward the child but slipped on the slick mud. She fell forward, and when she looked up, her face was coated in green slime.

Julie sputtered her lips to clear them, then wiped the flashlight on the back of her shirt. Rising to her hands and knees, she slithered across the mud as quickly as she could.

"Help!" the child yelled.

Julie lunged forward, her arm stretched toward the child. She grabbed the stopwatch hanging from the child's neck and pressed the button on top. The ticking stopped.

"I got it!" she yelled, then remembered she no longer had a radio.

A hissing noise filled the cave. Julie rolled onto her back and saw lights descending from the dark heights. The coiled ends of ropes hit the floor as a half dozen people repelled down on all sides, surrounding her, their heavy boots sinking into the mud. The newcomers wore hardhats, headlamps, and bright red vests labeled *ERI Training—Search and Rescue*.

A woman spotted Julie.

"Over there," she barked, and two others raced across the cavern with a basket stretcher between them, the sort used to transport the severely injured. Julie sat up and waved them off.

"I'm fine," she said, grinning. "And so is this guy," she added, hefting the child up by the hair.

The woman stared at Julie, her look of concern turning to rage.

"Somebody help—" the child called, but the woman jerked him from Julie's hands and flipped a switch on his back. He stared blankly, a plastic doll. The woman let it drop to the mud.

"So that was fast, right?" Julie asked, retrieving the stopwatch from the doll.

"What the hell did you do to this place?" the woman demanded.

TWO

"Explain to me again why we're suddenly leaving in the morning."

"I had the fastest time in the history of the course," Julie said.

"They don't mention that part," Eric said, inspecting the sheet of paper in his hand.

Eric was tall and thin, with shoulders like a coat hanger. He had an Amish-style beard, deep wrinkles around his eyes, and a pony tail of silver hair that reached the small of his back. He read the paper through glasses thick enough to be bullet-proof.

The two of them sat at a table made from the weathered remains of a giant wooden spool, the sort used for power line. They were in a clearing beside a semipermanent campsite that consisted of aged canvas tents and unpainted plywood cabins. A man sat between them, his face buried among the half-dozen empty liquor bottles on the table, snoring loudly.

The night was warm, and Julie's skin glowed alabaster in the moonlight. She still wore her tattered spandex caving outfit, but it had been cut open when Eric stitched her wound, leaving a string of butterfly bandages down the heavy muscle of her back.

"...will leave of her own recognizance by 11 a.m.," Eric read, his German accent thickened by alcohol, "or face legal action for willfully endangering the lives of others, and for the unlicensed use of explosives."

"Boilerplate," Julie said, shaking the last drops from a clear bottle of tequila. The bottle had no label, and its contents smelled more like gas than alcohol. "It's not like they have cops out here."

She divided the remains of the bottle between two glasses, a drip for her, a drip for Eric.

"It's well past midnight," she said, looking expectantly at Eric.

"And something about a $1,500 charge for damage to the course," Eric said, still reading.

"That's my problem," Julie said.

"It's on my credit card."

"And I'll pay you back."

"This was meant to be your birthday present," Eric said. "From your mother and myself."

"Mom wanted me to go to Tibet."

"And I can see why."

"Let's not inner peace this time, okay?"

"Of course not," Eric said dryly. "Why spoil the mood."

"You're the one who said spelunking would help me focus my negative energies."

"I said *harness* your energies. We've only been in Mexico for three days. How did you manage to get hold of explosives?"

Julie shrugged innocently, then slid one of the glasses toward Eric. "It's midnight," she said. "Aren't you going to wish me happy birthday?"

Eric eyed the glass as though it were sinister. "I think I've had enough."

"This'll help," she said, grabbing a lime from the table.

She searched among the empty bottles, then said, "Loan me your knife."

"I already loaned you my knife."

"Then loan me Alejandro's knife."

Eric stared at her, then sighed. He jerked a knife off the belt of the snoring man.

"I'm already covered," Alejandro murmured, then returned to snoring. Julie cut the lime and squeezed half into each drink.

"You did this same course?"

"Twenty years ago," Eric said.

"But you remember it?"

"Yes," Eric said. "It is one of my fondest memories, which was why I thought bringing you here—"

"So how did you do it?" Julie asked. "What did you do at the fork?"

"I took the lower path, of course."

"Just like that?"

"No," Eric said. "The upper path seems shorter. It's meant to lure you in."

"So you went that way and then...?"

"When I saw it was impossible, I backed up and took the lower route."

"You backed up!" Julie said, slapping the table so hard the bottles rattled. "I knew it."

"There is nothing wrong with backing up," Eric said. "Spelunking is as much a test of your intellect as your physique. You have to think, probe, test, think. That's the important part. Thinking."

"That's the boring part," Julie said, frowning at the drinks, which were small and mostly lime juice. "Hand me another bottle."

"There is a tremendously giantly huge middle ground

between dangerous and boring," Eric said. "You could quite easily fit the entire continent of Asia inside it."

"When you're done speaking weird," Julie said, "I still need another bottle."

"What if you had injured yourself?" Eric said. "We're hundreds of miles from the nearest hospital."

"Then it's a good thing I brought my own doctor," Julie said.

"I'm a PhD—"

"Do you hear that?" Julie asked, perking up and looking over her shoulder.

"What if the cave collapsed?" Eric continued. "You'd have been trapped or killed."

Julie was looking over her shoulder, but her hand was outstretched to Eric.

"If I was trapped or killed," she said, "then I wouldn't need another bottle."

Eric glared, but Julie wasn't looking. With a sigh, he reached into a faded plastic rack—the kind used to transport soda bottles—and pulled out a full bottle of tequila. Before handing it to Julie, he gently scooped a bug from the side, cradling it in his hand.

"You have a sighing problem," Julie said, turning to him. She yanked the stained cork and upending the bottle. Tequila glugged out, splashing into the glasses and over the table. Eric retrieved a book from his canvas satchel and flipped through it, comparing the bug in his hand with a photograph.

"What is that?" Julie asked.

"It's a *Neoxabea bipunctata*," Eric said. "A spotted tree cricket. According to this, you don't usually see them at night."

"It's morning," Julie said, jerking a thumb at the bright pink horizon. "And I meant the book."

"It's a guidebook."

"There's a guidebook for nowhere?"

"There's a guidebook for everywhere."

"Hrm," Julie said. "Maybe I'll become an astronaut."

She inspected the drinks. The glasses were nearly full, but now the liquid was as clear as water. She sniffed one and frowned, picking up another lime. "Loan me your knife."

"To attract a mate," Eric read, "the male *bipunctata* will chew a hole in a leaf, then use it as a baffle to amplify its mating call."

"Your knife," Julie said, holding out her hand.

Eric looked up from the book, disappointed that Julie was uninterested. He leaned across the table and grabbed Alejandro's knife—which was right in front of Julie—and put it in her hand. She cut the lime in half, then set the knife down—missing the table by inches. It dropped to the dirt, landing beside two other knives.

"The complicated nature of the *bipunctata*'s behavior," Eric read, "is often cited in debates over the nature of intelligence, specifically in how to distinguish it from genetic preprogramming. Nature versus nurture." Eric snapped the book shut.

"That's the exact question I find myself asking right now," Julie said, carefully sliding a glass to Eric, the tequila flat to the brim. "If you can still read, then you haven't had enough to drink."

Eric smiled at her, then blew gently on the cricket until it flew away. He raised his glass and said, "Happy birthday, Julie,"

"Thank you, Dad," Julie said.

"Step-dad."

"I'm not after your money," Julie said.

"Would that there were any," Eric said.

They tapped glasses. Eric took a sip and Julie poured the entire glass down her throat.

"Who needs a refill?" she asked with a burp. She dumped tequila into her glass, grabbed a lime, and started looking for a knife. But then she stopped—the noise she had heard earlier, a dull thudding, was suddenly very loud and very close.

"What the...?" she said, hopping to her feet. Instantly sober, she dashed into the forest, chasing the noise.

"Julie!" Eric yelled.

"I haven't seen her," Alejandro mumbled.

Eric rose unsteadily and followed her.

Eric emerged from the woods into a wide canyon, its walls rich red in the morning light. Julie stood frozen, staring at a brown cloud of dust, the lime still clutched in her hand. An enormous pair of helicopter rotors cut slowly through the dusty haze, which slowly cleared to reveal the wide body of an Athenian V-47 helicopter that had landed in the middle of the canyon.

Like the V-22 Osprey, the Athenian was a plane-shaped aircraft with pivoting engines that allowed for vertical takeoff. But the Athenian was significantly larger than its cousin, more like a medium-sized cargo plane, and was designed to haul a full company as well as heavy equipment. Its landing gear held it a couple of yards off the ground, and it seemed to float on the billowing dust. Eric felt the beat of the rotors against his chest.

Dark forms appeared in the haze, then two men emerged in full combat gear, seemingly miniature against the towering aircraft. The men spread out, flanking Julie and Eric, aiming husky rifles at them.

"Mexican army?" Eric asked, squinting into the dust.

Julie didn't answer. Her fingers punctured the skin of the lime, and juice drizzled from her hand.

A third soldier appeared between the other two, a lieutenant. He had a pistol on his belt and a bright American flag sewn over the breast pocket of his jacket.

"Shit," Julie said.

THREE

The sweeping hills of Arlington National Cemetery served as the final resting place for hundreds of thousands of veterans from every branch of the military, ranging as far back as the Revolutionary War to as recently as this white winter morning. Nestled among its seemingly endless markers was a small cluster of mourners, mostly civilians, gathered in the snow around a flag-draped casket. At the head of the open grave stood eight soldiers in full dress, with raked green berets dark enough to be taken for black. They wore no designation of their division, designation, name, or rank besides a small golden pin on their berets that was embossed with a shield and the characters *D5*. At the front left of the soldiers stood Lieutenant Brian Simms, who, beneath a row of ribbons, wore on his chest two bronze medals, the twice-earned cross for distinguished service.

Simms was smaller than the other men, fit and lean, and he had an earnest, youthful bearing showing just the first cracks of age. He stared stiffly ahead, self-conscious about the gaudy display on his chest. He rarely wore a dress uniform—his and those of his men had been shipped up from Fort Bragg solely for this funeral—and he felt inappropriately flamboyant for the occasion. All the more so because he was standing opposite the widow, whose swollen, red-rimmed eyes bore into him.

Carla? Simms thought, searching his memory. *No, Charlene.*

Maybe.

She was a small woman with a cherubic face who couldn't be much older than twenty. She wore a simple black dress that, like her makeup, was in disarray from several bouts of crying. And she looked on the verge of crying again. She had an arm over each of her two children, whose names Simms had never learned; the deceased, Lieutenant Weaver, had joined D-5 only two weeks earlier.

Lieutenant Weaver had been an on-station replacement for Lieutenant Perez, who had been an on-station replacement for Lieutenant Roth, who himself had joined them only eight months back, the night before they shipped out to Qumar. They had all been a string of poor choices: college boys, ROTC graduates. They were brave enough and they certainly had brains, but that hadn't been enough.

D-5's charter differed from the rest of the Special Forces' in that it forwent any specific requirements regarding age, years of service, or even physical fitness. Its qualifications were nebulous, a you'll-know-it-when-you-see-it thing. The idea was to create a more adaptable unit, one capable of self-direction when the need arose. It looked good on paper, but in Simms's experience, those who did well in D-5 had already distinguished themselves in other branches of the army. The colonel, however, continued to insist that the position of second lieutenant be filled by someone "uncorrupted" by experience.

"There's no point in applying a second brain to a problem," he would say, "if it thinks the same way as the first."

Unfortunately, Simms thought, *thinking differently hadn't proved to be much of an asset.*

The minister finished his sermon. The flag was snapped off the casket and folded with the care of a religious artifact. They presented the flag to the widow, but she didn't take it. She bowed over, her face melting, letting out a low moan.

"What sort of monster would do this?" she yelled, suddenly pushing through the men and throwing herself on the casket and fumbling with the clasp. Two of the pallbearers pulled her back before she could get it open, which was a relief because there wasn't much of Lieutenant Weaver inside. Certainly not enough for an open casket, and even the casket itself was an exaggeration—large enough to drape a flag over, but all but empty inside.

"What sort of monster?" his wife repeated, howling to the sky.

Monsters, Simms thought. He remembered when he saw the world that way. But there were no monsters out there. No matter how dirty the fight, you were still only fighting other men. Men with wives and children, just like yourself.

Weaver's son, who looked to be about five, came forward and took his mother's hand. She grew still at his touch, and he led her to a chair.

He's strong, Simms thought, wondering how his own son would fare. And his wife. He suddenly felt an overwhelming urge to see them.

It had been eight months since he had seen his family in the flesh, since he had held them in his arms, and that was far from the record. D-5 was one of the most active units in the entire army, and even the greenest man in his unit had seen more action than most double enlistees.

North Carolina was tantalizingly close, and he longed to jump a plane for home, to be with his family for just one night, but he knew it was impossible. D-5 hadn't been rushed back from Arabia for R&R. They had a priority mission, and he had already stretched his authority by attending this funeral.

But we must honor our fallen in person whenever possible, he reminded himself. *The war is far away, and those who haven't seen it personally can never truly understand the real cost.*

Simms's phone vibrated inside his coat. He backed out of the line and put a dozen paces between himself and the ceremony before he drew it out.

The phone was a plastic brick, thick and heavy, but it offered full encryption on any cellular network in the world, and where none was available, it would switch to satellite. It was an expensive piece of equipment, even by military standards, and D-5 was one of the few units that carried them. The name Lieutenant Hiller flashed on the screen—the latest replacement.

"Simms," he said, cupping the mic.

"Hiller, sir," the second lieutenant said. "We've got her."

"Good work," Simms said, glancing at his watch. It seemed that the colonel hadn't been exaggerating when he said he knew exactly where to find her. Simms hadn't believed him, and he was now running late as a result.

"The colonel is already on location," Simms continued. "Proceed there and wait for me."

"Roger wilco, sir."

I guess we're leaving early, Simms thought, hanging up. A sudden noise brought his attention to the tall iron fence at the edge of the cemetery, where a small crowd of protesters had gathered. One held a sign that said *No War for Oil*; another said *USA Out of Arabia*. Their shouts were distant but continuous. Several focused on Simms, their insults rising above the din.

Simms scowled, subconsciously fingering the thumb break on his holster.

No, he decided. *I'll go ahead alone. The others will stay for the rest of the service.*

A sharp noise cracked through the air; seven guns fired three times. The protesters' shouts rose in response. Simms put his back to them and returned to the funeral. Dark clouds loomed above the gravestone-covered hills, and the wind brought the crisp smell of incoming snow.

FOUR

Julie sat on the edge of the bed in her childhood room. She couldn't tell which room—there had been so many—but the drapes had a pink floral pattern, and there were painted ponies on the bookshelf, so this was sometime during the short period when she had submitted to her mother's tastes. She was twenty years too old for this room, and her father, sitting in a chair opposite her, appeared to be in his twenties, an age that she had only ever seen him at photographs.

He wore black fatigues, an outfit he had favored his whole life, but they seemed more appropriate at this age. His hands gripped his knees as he told her they were going to have to move. His voice sounded distant and tinny, like a bad recording. Someone was lying on the bed beside Julie, fully dressed but without shoes. Out of the corner of her eye, Julie could see blue stockings over thin, fragile legs. Something was dripping onto the floor, but she didn't want to look.

Move again? she protested, her voice a child's. *We're always moving*, she complained. *I never have time to make friends.*

You'll make new friends, her father assured her, calling her sweetheart, calling her *Jules*, and patting her wet cheek. *You always do.*

Something dark flowed across the carpet, soaking into her socks, warm and cold at the same time. She turned to look at the stockinged legs, unable to stop herself. Her eyes traveled past calf, thigh, waist.

Her father was shouting now, his hands on her cheeks, trying to turn her away from the body beside her. But he could no more stop her than she could stop herself. His hands went slack and his voice faded as Julie's gaze reached the pillow, where they gazed one last time at the ruined face atop that lifeless body...

"Mother fuck—" Julie said, jerking awake as the aircraft hit a pocket of air. The plane plunged and then caught itself, throwing her against the restraining belt. The belt bit into the wound on her shoulder. She traced her fingers along her shoulder and back, checking for fresh blood, then took in the aircraft around her.

The interior of the aircraft was painted green and was bare to the ribs. She sat on a bench that ran the length of one wall, sharing a wool blanket with Eric, who was curled up, sleeping through the turbulence. The only light came from a small heater overhead, dim and orange, keeping the air above freezing.

The bulk of the plane was filled by a wide stack of metal crates that bounced and jiggled in front of her, held down by a web of strapping. In front of that, by the cockpit door, the kid in the lieutenant's uniform stood with two other soldiers. Seeing she was awake, he started toward her, balancing himself with a steel cable that was strung along the ceiling. Julie glared to ward him off, but he was occupied with keeping his balance as the aircraft bounced under his feet.

He stopped a few paces from Julie, straightening his back and pushing out his chest as if ticking off a checklist. A brass-colored plastic name tag on his jacket read *Lieutenant Thomas Hiller,* and an American flag on his breast was bright and stiff, as if sewn on that morning. He had the same blue eyes and sandy-blond hair as the rescue doll.

"I apologize for the ride, ma'am," Hiller said. "We've hit some weather off the coast."

Julie glanced at her watch; they had been in the air for eight hours. She knew that the Athenian traveled at speeds comparable to those of a prop jet thanks to its retractable rotors, but on such a long journey it would have made more sense to transfer to a faster plane. Unless, of course, you were trying to avoid attention.

"Off the coast of what?" Julie asked.

"Our destination is classified."

"So you've said. But you will let me know we get there, right?"

"I believe somebody will," Hiller said, missing Julie's sarcastic tone.

Eric groaned sleepily, wresting the blanket from Julie as he curled up to face the hull, rattling the handcuffs that held his wrist to the bench. Back in Mexico, he had protested Julie's rights insistently, a quaint gesture that, unfortunately though unsurprisingly, had earned handcuffs for the both of them. He cracked his eyes open, noticed the lieutenant, and shut them again with an even louder groan.

"He had a little too much last night," Julie said.

"I'm sorry for the early hour of our arrival," Hiller said. "My orders were to be expeditious."

"And your orders were to bring both of us?"

"My orders were to bring you and any potential accomplices."

"Accomplices?" Julie asked. "To what?"

"I've not been briefed on that."

"So you walked all the way over here just to show off your ignorance?"

"Sorry, I meant to offer…" Hiller said, motioning one of the soldiers over. "Specialist Petty is a medic, if you'd like him to examine your shoulder."

Specialist Petty was short and strong—a soccer player's build—with bronze skin, dark eyes, and dark curly hair trimmed to his scalp. He was roughly Hiller's age but seemed decades wiser. He moved easily across the unstable aircraft and planted his feet in a surfer's stance. Eric cracked an eye open.

"A specialist in medicine?" he asked.

"Specialist is a rank," Julie said.

"Just above private," Hiller said, then, as if reading from an invisible textbook. "Private, specialist, corporal, sergeant, and lieutenant." He ended by tapping the plastic badge on his chest.

"Don't forget colonel," Julie said.

"A colonel is significantly superior," Hiller said.

"That depends on what you're measuring," Julie said.

Petty motioned for Julie to turn.

"If you would, ma'am," he said.

"No, thank you," Julie said, hiking her thumb at Eric. "I brought my own doctor."

"PhD," Eric mumbled, closing his eyes again.

"I'd feel better if—" Hiller said.

"Is this about your feelings, then?" Julie asked. "Because *I'd* feel better if you returned to your end of the plane."

"It's a helicopter, ma'am," Hiller said. "It only looks like a plane because—"

"She knows what this is, sir," Petty said as Julie smirked.

A buzzer sounded and a red light blinked above the cockpit door. Hiller looked at it, confused.

"We'd better be seated, sir," Petty offered. "We're about to land."

Hiller nodded, motioning Petty ahead.

"Carry on, Lieutenant," Julie said, giving him a limp salute.

Hiller raised his hand to return the salute, but thought better of it. He followed Petty to the front of the aircraft, clutching the cable as the aircraft banked and descended.

"You better wake up," Julie said, nudging Eric. "Things are about to get rough."

Thick flurries of snow swirled in the fierce wind of the harbor. The Athenian stayed low, skimming the surging water as it pushed through the storm. It was heading east, its tail to the orange twilight. As it approached an island, its nose angled up and its rotors extended to full length. Its engines rotated until they were vertical, and the craft descended onto a parking lot buried by a foot and a half of snow.

Two soldiers rushed toward the helicopter, following a path carved through the snow. They each carried a door-sized plexiglas shield, and just before they reached the descending aircraft, they planted the shields side by side, blocking the path. They ducked behind the plexiglas, bracing the shields with their shoulders as the Athenian's giant rotors kicked up a flurry of white. The asphalt beneath the helicopter was blown clean, creating a wall of snow in the shape of a figure eight. Once the craft had landed, the soldiers kicked their shields loose, exposing a gap in the wall between the path and the aircraft. Several servicemen ran down the path, chocking the giant helicopter's wheels.

The Athenian's side door opened and Hiller leaned out, shouting down to one of the soldiers. The soldier raised a hand to his ear and Hiller repeated himself, but between the wind and the rotors, there was too much noise. The ground was eight feet down, so he grabbed the door sill and lowered himself, dropping the last two feet. He cupped his mouth to the soldier's ear as he spoke, and the soldier pointed an arm south, at the faint lights of an approaching helicopter. Hiller nodded his thanks and turned back to the Athenian. The door was too high to reach.

After several jumps, he caught hold of the door sill and pulled himself up, squirming back inside. Petty shook his head, then came over and helped Hiller to his feet.

"Thank you, Specialist," Hiller said. As he shut the door, the huge loading ramp at the back of the aircraft lowered to ground.

Cold air swirled through the hold as a soldier shifted Eric's handcuffs, linking them behind his back, and wrapped him in a blanket. They tried to do the same to Julie, but she strode down the ramp the moment they unlocked her from the bench. Halfway down, she stopped and looked around, the blanket on her shoulders catching the wind and whipping like a cape. Through a break in the tress she saw the vigilant gaze of the Statue of Liberty rising above the harbor.

"New York City is a classified location?" Eric asked, walking up behind her and shouting over the wind.

"This isn't where I expected," Julie said.

"You had an expectation?" Eric asked. "Fill me in anytime you like."

"It's not funny. Why would they bring us here?"

"I wasn't trying to be funny," Eric said. "Why would

they bring us anywhere? And who, for that matter, are they anyway?"

Julie frowned and walked to a sign half buried in the snow. She wiped it clear and saw the words *Governors Island* carved into a plank of wood. A flash of light caught her eye, and she turned to see another helicopter landing across the parking lot. It was a single-rotor Lakota, and it looked minuscule compared to the Athenian.

The Lakota's thin rails sunk into the snow, and two officers in full dress stepped out, a corporal and a lieutenant. The corporal unloaded three duffels and the Lakota took off again, returning to the south. Hiller pushed eagerly through the snow and saluted the lieutenant, who was a grade above him.

"Lieutenant Simms, sir," Hiller said between breaths. "I can't tell you what an honor this is."

"So I see," Simms said, his eyes crinkling distastefully at the junior officer's name tag.

Hiller presented his identification and his transfer orders. Simms flipped through them, then held them over his shoulder; the corporal behind him took the orders and placed a beret in Simms's hand. Simms extended the beret to Hiller, who gazed at it admiringly.

"Allow me," Simms said, taking the hat from Hiller's head and discarding it in the snow. He stepped close, fastidiously adjusting the rake of the new beret, whose golden pin gleamed in the floodlights. Satisfied, Simms stepped back and saluted. "Welcome to D-5, lieutenant," he said.

"Thank you, sir," Hiller said, returning the salute with such vigor that he seemed to chop his own forehead.

"You got them both?" Simms asked, inclining his head across the snowy lot, toward Julie and Eric.

"He practically insisted, sir," Hiller said.

This pleased Simms, but his face hardened as Julie approached.

"The detainee, sir," Hiller said, presenting her.

"Yes, the detainee—" Julie said sarcastically, but stopped short when she noticed his new beret. She turned to the other officers, seeing that they wore the same pin. A gust of wind tugged her blanket away, but she didn't seem to notice.

"Sergeant Porter," Simms said, giving her a dismissive salute.

Simms appeared to be the same age as herself, though he carried himself as someone older. He was lean, almost waifish, with strong cheekbones, a hint of gray over the ears, and an irritating cleft in his chin. Other than his hair, which was slightly long for regulation, he could have stepped right out of a recruitment poster.

"Not anymore," Julie replied.

"Not for long, anyway," Simms said. He motioned Hiller toward the Athenian. "Secure the aircraft, Lieutenant," he ordered. "No one gets aboard. Anyone tries to pull rank, refer them to the colonel." He checked his watch. "The rest of the unit will arrive by 2200. Wait for them before you unload. Corporal Orton will fill you in."

"Sir," Hiller said, saluting again. Simms motioned to Orton, who took two of the duffels and followed Hiller to the aircraft. Simms chewed his lip as he watched Hiller scurry away.

"Eager," Julie said, motioning at the second lieutenant. "West Point?"

"Yeah," Simms said.

"Not that I'm surprised to find D-5 at the end of this rainbow, but isn't there a war in Qumar right now?"

"I don't choose my orders," Simms said, giving Julie the once-over. His eyes lingered on the fresh, burgundy scar that curved back over her shoulder, then on a very different scar on her bicep—the white ghost of a tattoo now removed. She had the mien of a sergeant, but a defiant, undisciplined glint in her eye. Snow collected in her spiked, bleached hair, and she was shivering—but given the temperature and her thin spandex outfit, not as much as he would have expected.

"You're cold," Simms said, pulling a jacket from his duffel—desert camo—and offering it to her.

Julie fingered the jacket's sleeve, staring at it like an old photograph, then waved it away.

"Just take me to him," she said.

Simms led Julie and Eric along a shoveled path, leaning into the wind and walking with forceful strides. Julie, almost a foot shorter, had to jog to keep up, her hands balled up to keep her fingers from freezing. She knew she had been pigheaded to refuse Simms's jacket, but knowing it didn't change it.

They followed a flagstone path cut between shallow hills, then crossed a snow-filled moat and passed through a wide, arched tunnel in a brick-and-stone wall. A plaque above the tunnel stated this was Fort Columbus, built during the American Revolution and turned over to the National Park Service in 2001. But, judging by the level of activity inside, it looked as though the army was moving back in.

They rose into an expansive courtyard, bounded on all sides by two-story, colonial-style buildings fronted with tall, white columns. Nearly all the windows were lit, and inside uniformed men and women worked with frenetic energy. In the middle of the courtyard, army technicians wired up a bank of electrical generators while a nearby group assembled a satellite dish large enough to hold King Henry's feast. Everyone, inside and out, was Special Forces Group Five—Green Berets—and all of them made way for Simms. A captain even led his entourage into the snow to allow them to pass.

"Expecting an invasion?" Julie asked, but Simms ignored her, turning into a passage cut through the center of the northernmost building. The passage ended at two ironclad doors, with an armed guard on either side. Though they obviously recognized Simms, the guards leveled their automatic rifles as they approached. Simms went to a third soldier, who was seated at a portable table, huddled up to a small propane heater.

"Welcome home, sir," the soldier said. He took the plastic badge Simms offered and swiped it through a reader built into his laptop.

"Nice weather you're having, Bennett," Simms replied.

"We can't all be sunbathing in Qumar, sir," the soldier said, rubbing his hands in front of the heater. His laptop beeped approvingly, and Bennett raised a green-faced electronic pad. Simms spread his hand over the pad and the laptop beeped again.

"All clear, sir," Bennett said. "Two visitors?"

"Unofficial," Simms replied.

"I never saw them, sir." Bennett motioned to the guards at the door. They lowered their weapons and one of them tugged on the heavy door, opening it just enough to slip through.

Out in the cold, Julie had tensed up and hunched over, but she forced herself to relax and straighten up as she entered the hallway, which was mercifully warm. Her skin burned as its nerves came back to life.

The hallway sloped down, harshly lit by a line of exposed bulbs hung from rusted sockets along the ceiling. The passage opened into a square room, where space heaters melted the snow on their clothing. The air was humid, and Julie could feel the weight of the walls and of the earth around her.

"Armory," she said.

"Dungeon," Eric replied.

"They didn't have those in the revolution."

"No," Eric agreed. "Not back then."

Empty shipping cases with custom foam linings were stacked against one wall, and opposite them, a pair of thick metal doors opened to a second room, this one draped in clear plastic—on the walls, the floor, and the ceiling.

Inside the plastic-draped room, people in lab coats operated elaborate machinery, mostly medical. Several scientists were clustered around a table, engrossed in something Julie couldn't see. Off to the side, two more were heatedly arguing, seemingly for the benefit of the military officer who stood with them. Simms knocked on the door frame, and the officer broke away from the scientists and headed over.

Any camouflage offered by Colonel Edmond Porter's black fatigues was spoiled by a square foot of bright decorations, whose weight pulled his jacket down on one side, making him appear to be leaning. The combat uniform hung loosely on his frail body, and it was only the combination of his bright green eyes, his upturned mustache, and the exaggerated straightness of his back that kept him from looking completely absurd. He wore the same dark beret as Simms, though his was decorated with the silver eagle of his rank.

He walked toward them in long strides, bobbing

a maplewood cane in his hand as if conducting his own movements.

"Scientists," he confided to Simms, using the lieutenant's shoulder for support as he stepped down into the room, "will argue over the wetness of water." Then he turned to Julie and brightened.

"Jules!" he exclaimed, throwing his arms open. "How wonderful to see you."

Julie turned sideways, thwarting his embrace.

"Father," she said. Her tone was derisive, but the colonel didn't seem to notice.

"She looks very fit, doesn't she?" he said to Simms, beaming. Then, to Julie, "You've been working out?"

"Takes my mind off killing you."

The colonel laughed gently, as if it was a familiar joke.

"I knew you wouldn't be happy about this, Jules," he said, walking past and drawing her attention away from the plastic-lined room. "But this isn't a reunion. Your country needs your help."

"My what needs my what?"

"Your country, dearest daughter," the colonel said. "What are these? Handcuffs? Simms!"

"Yes, sir," the lieutenant said, the keys already in his hand. He removed Julie's dangling cuff and both of Eric's.

"America is still your country," the colonel continued, "no matter how far you stray. And it needs you."

"Tell it I'm not available."

"No, you're on summer break in Mexico playing with"—the colonel inspected Eric, frowning—"your mother's friends."

Eric rubbed his wrists absentmindedly as he stared into the plastic-strewn room. One of the scientists was examining what looked like a plastic stick with a frilled tip. Eric stepped in that direction, but the colonel called out to him.

"Doctor Kirsch, right?" the colonel asked. "I don't believe we've actually met."

"And I'd always hoped we never would," Eric said, his eyes still on the scientist.

The colonel watched Eric, as if trying to figure something out. Despite their dress and grooming, and the colonel's being thirty years Eric's senior, the two men looked oddly similar.

"Simms," the colonel said, "get this man out of here."

Simms stepped forward, but Julie moved protectively in between him and Eric.

"So what brings D-5 to New York, anyway?" she asked. "Clearing terrorists bunkers in Bed-Stuy?"

Simms looked to the colonel, but the colonel was still studying Eric.

"D-5?" Eric asked, turning to Julie. "But they were disbanded."

"As far as the public is concerned, yes," the colonel said. "The embassy fiasco was regrettable, so we had to do something to appease—"

"Regrettable?" Julie swung to the colonel and raised her fingers to his face, counting. "One botched operation deteriorates into—Two—a firefight with over a hundred casualties, which results in—Three—*a war*, which ends in—Four—a never-ending occupation. And you call that *regrettable*?"

"I fought in that war," the colonel said, unwavering as Julie flicked her fingers inches from his face. "So don't lecture me."

He waited for Julie to drop her hand and then continued.

"You seem to have changed your politics," he said. "I imagine it's the company you keep."

"More like I'm finally learning my true nature."

"Your nature? I shouldn't think—" The colonel stopped himself, turning to Eric as though suddenly remembering him. "D-5, you will find," he told Eric, "is still quite operational. We just don't advertise. The public doesn't always see the need for things they find distasteful."

"And the army sometimes forgets that it's not above the law," Eric snarled.

"Yes," the colonel said, twisting his mustache thoughtfully. "Sometimes. But we do the best we can. Lieutenant, if you would."

The colonel motioned at the plastic-lined room. Simms kept his eyes on Julie as he circled around and closed the door. He stationed himself in front of it.

"The thing is," the colonel said, leaning toward Julie conspiratorially, "we need someone with experience on the Atargis."

"Of which there must be hundreds," Julie said.

"It's been three years since they canceled the program. Very few of the original trainees are still enlisted."

"Including me."

"You're a deserter, Julie. You remain active until sentenced and discharged."

Eric stiffened—this was news to him. He shot her a questioning look, but she was focused on her father.

"And that's your excuse to hunt me down and drag me here?" she asked.

"Hunt you down?" the colonel said, amused. "We never lost track of you. Considering your security clearance, it took some effort on my part to keep them from declaring you a traitor. Not that my efforts are appreciated."

"And what were these efforts?" Julie asked. "Tapping my phone? Reading my emails?"

"I let the NSA handle the details," the colonel said with a shrug. "As long as they knew where to find you."

"For this?"

"For something. We've invested heavily in your training, Jules. You don't get to throw that away. But enough about that. Let me show you what *this* is." The colonel started up the slope. Julie looked confused.

"What about the Einstein convention back there?" she asked, nodding at the closed door.

"Oh, that's nothing for you to worry about," the colonel said. Then, to Eric, "You might as well come, too, Doctor Kirsch. As long as you're here."

Julie looked again at the door, and at Simms guarding it. She shook her head and followed the colonel out.

FIVE

The elevator had glass doors, but all Julie could see through them was the chiseled rock of the shaft walls as they descended beneath Governors island. The elevator moved smoothly, but Julie could tell they were traveling fast, going deep. Eric nudged her.

"Deserted?" he mouthed, clearly bothered by this.

"Later," she mouthed back, looking away.

Light rose up through the elevator as they descended into a stadium-sized, man-made cavern. In the center of the cavern, lit by a battery of floodlights, a giant train-like machine rested on widely spaced train tracks.

The machine was red, with gleaming chrome panels and a core of four locomotive engines, two wide by two deep. A yard-wide shaft ran from the engines to a massive steel disc at the front of the machine. The disc was thirty feet in diameter, with spiral pattern of beaked teeth across the surface. This was a boring machine, meant for drilling tunnels like the towering, three-story tall one in the far wall.

As the elevator descended down the cavern wall, the colonel produced a remote—nothing more exotic than what might control a television, but old, its plastic yellowed. He pointed the remote toward the tunnel and, squinting at its three large buttons, pressed the top one with the firm ceremony of someone who viewed the operation of electronics as a combination of determination and luck. Very old holophane lights, mounted along the tunnel's ceiling, jittered to life, revealing square, rough-hewn walls. Wide train tracks ran down the center of the tunnel, stretching out toward infinity. If Julie had her bearings, the tunnel was heading straight east, underneath the ocean.

"How the hell have you kept this thing a secret?" she asked.

"We're better at it than you think," the colonel replied, pride in his voice.

"No joke," Julie agreed, wishing she weren't impressed. "So what is it?"

"New York City water pipe number 3. It's meant to relieve pressure on water pipe number 2, and to expand the flow of water to Manhattan, Brooklyn, and Queens. Authorized in 1954, and under construction since 1970."

"New York City is that way," Julie said, pointing behind them.

The elevator arrived at a glass-lined room that was held above the cavern floor by twenty-foot stilts. Inside was a command center, like those used by NASA during the Saturn missions. The room was abandoned, the air musky and stale. The windows were fogged with green mildew, except for two large, bay windows at the front. These looked out on the machine boring the tunnel beyond, and they were clean to the point of invisibility.

"The water pipe project has suffered decades of delays and cost overruns," the colonel said, leading them into the room, "but this is mainly because the Pentagon was quietly funneling its money and equipment into this tunnel. It's what we call a piggyback project."

Eric picked up the receiver of an olive-green bakelite telephone. He stuck his finger in the rotor and spun it, delighted by the noise as it rolled back to zero. Simms took the phone from Eric's hand and hung it up.

"So what is it really?" Julie asked, looking down the endless tunnel.

"It's the Dwight D. Eisenhower Atlantic Tunnel project," the colonel said. "A railroad to connect New York to Lisbon, which is the westernmost point in Europe, a mere three thousand miles away. It is the most ambitious project ever undertaken by man."

"They said that about the bomb," Eric injected.

"And they were right, at the time," the colonel agreed. "But you can't rest on your laurels."

"How far did they get?" Julie asked.

The colonel squinted at the tunnel, as if peering to the end.

"Maybe a hundred miles," he said. "The Army Corps of Engineers worked on it for almost thirty years."

"Before they realized it couldn't be done."

"Oh, I doubt anyone ever thought it could. It's just one of those things that gets slipped into the budget and then kept there year after year, because it creates jobs and because some politician was whimsical enough to fight for it. Most of your tax money is spent that way, and, all things considered, this one wasn't that expensive. I mean, consider universal health care."

"You're really going to compare this to—" Eric said, but Julie shouldered him.

"You didn't bring us here just to show off some canceled military pork barrel," she said.

"Who said it was canceled?" the colonel said. "Far from it. That enormous and costly boring machine you see down there was installed only two years ago. State of the art, fully robotized. You could run it from a laptop in Minnesota. And look over there. Earth movers, boring machines, backhoes. All completely automated, including the machines that repair and maintain them."

The colonel hit another button on the remote, lighting a different part of the room, where quarter-scale earth movers buzzed between tall piles of gravel. Julie studied the robots, and the colonel watched her with anticipation.

After a minute, Julie frowned. The machines were working in a circle; the gravel was shifted from one pile to the next and then back again.

"They're not doing anything," Julie said.

"No," the colonel said.

"So what's the catch?" she asked.

"The catch, as you say, is that it can't be done. Back in the fifties, the tunnel was pitched as a high-speed, submarine-proof way to get American troops and equipment to Europe in the event of another world war. Later, the claim was it would link the Western world together economically, to better compete with the rising power of Asia. Both are fine ideas, but even our most modern equipment can only dig so fast. Add in the complexities of working two miles underwater, and, practically speaking, we might as well try to dig a tunnel to the moon."

"Okay, but...?"

"But it turns out that we've found a better use for at least part of the tunnel. Come look at this little gem."

The colonel motioned Julie to a diorama of the ocean floor. It seemed to be made of papier-mâché and had a row of flashlight bulbs leading from America to Europe.

"We're here," he said, tapping Governors Island. "This is

the dig in Portugal, heading back toward New York, and right here, between the two, is the Mid-Atlantic Ridge."

The colonel ran his finger along a mountain range that, judging by the color of the paint, was underwater but for the tips of the tallest peaks. He fingered those peaks.

"The Azores archipelago. Islands as seen from the surface, but actually extremely tall mountains that rise up all the way from the ocean floor. When the Army Corps decided to add a third dig site, to speed up the tunnel project, the Azores were the perfect location. The islands offered a staging area from which materials and equipment could be shuttled down by diving bell, not to mention that this tapering mountainside here was the ideal place to dig an access shaft. Working two miles underwater was impractical, given the equipment at the time, so they started a hallway, dug a mile-deep shaft through the bedrock, and started the new section of the tunnel here."

"The tunnel that nobody wants," Julie said.

"The tunnel, no, but this also just happens to be the perfect location to launch and maintain a fleet of underwater drones."

The colonel motioned to Simms, who laid a large tablet computer beside the diorama, displaying a topographic map of the Atlantic Ocean. Yellow and green dots were spread out in a line across the middle, running north to south.

"An impenetrable net of detection and reaction," the colonel said. "We'll be able to track the movement of any known submarines in the Atlantic, as well discover any new ones. This technology has been in the works for years now, but it became quite urgent after the Russians announced their super-torpedo. You've heard of it? A weapon that can travel undetected through the water, then pop up and destroy the coastal city of their choice?"

Julie shook her head noncommittally.

"Our drone network could detect these torpedoes and stop them, but this base is the key, allowing us to service and supply them at depth, to keep them hidden from our enemy's satellites. Patrol and response drones are refueled and rearmed on location by a convoy of supply drones, so they can maintain continuous operation. It's a beautiful system."

"Rearmed?" Eric asked. "You're putting weaponized drones into the ocean?"

"Nothing too powerful, unfortunately," the colonel said. "Long-distance communication is difficult in the water. We've designed an ad hoc network, but it's still impossible to maintain the command and control we enjoy with our aerial drones. As such, the men upstairs have limited their firepower, to avoid any potential embarrassments. We're working to improve the system, of course, but these things don't happen overnight."

"And all this?" Julie asked, waving her arm at the cavern and the machines shifting gravel.

"Budgetary camouflage," the colonel. "The funding for the Atlantic tunnel is hidden inside a municipal project, and the funding for the drone base is hidden inside the tunnel's budget."

"So now your piggyback project has a piggyback project?" Eric asked.

"We're recycling an old project to make a new one," the colonel said. "I would think your type would find that appealing. And, just for the heck of it, we're still moving forward with the tunnel project. Or, at least, we were."

"Trouble?" Julie asked.

"I'm afraid so," the colonel said, his voice dropping to a somber tone. "A few days ago, we lost contact with the central dig." He tapped the mountains in the middle of the ocean. "The timing is suspicious, but the Pentagon suspects nothing more than an accident. It's a large facility, with a staff of three dozen, and so they've called on us to mount a rescue operation."

"And suddenly D-5 is in the rescue business?"

"From what I hear, you're the one trying her hand at the rescue business," the colonel said. Then, giving Eric a knowing glance, "And how did that little experiment go?"

"Well—" Eric started.

"Don't answer that," Julie said. Then, to the colonel, "All bullshit aside, why me? And why the Atargis?"

"The navy has already attempted to enter the base, but the outer hatch won't respond. Their subs have been unable to dock."

"So cut it open."

The colonel motioned to Simms.

"Harder than it sounds," the lieutenant said. "It's two miles underwater, which is a lot of pressure. One wrong move and the whole base will implode. There's a hatch for emergency access, but we're not entirely sure where."

"Classified?" Julie said. She wasn't being sarcastic; she had grown up in the military, and so she had heard dumber.

"Lost," Simms said. "It was installed more than thirty years ago, when all the records were kept on paper. It's certain the plans still exist, somewhere, but lives are at stake so we don't have time to wait for someone to find them.

"What we do know is that the engineers considered the hatch a security liability and so didn't want it in plain sight. There is a cave adjacent to the docking area, at the highest section of the base, and we suspect they installed the access hatch somewhere inside."

"So you need someone to drive an Atargis into the cave and find it?"

"Exactly."

"Well, good luck with that."

"This is precisely what we trained you for," the colonel said. "It had crossed my mind that you might put the needs of others over your own."

"I'm not buying this," Julie said. "This is all just another one of your games."

"You know me better than that."

"I know you better than anyone," Julie said. "You'd do anything to rope me in except say you're sorry."

"And would you forgive me?" the colonel asked.

"I'd enjoy hearing you ask."

"Well, forgive me or not," the colonel said, "people's lives are at stake."

"And you're putting their needs over your own?"

"I'm a soldier," the colonel said. "It's my job."

"Well, it's not mine. Not anymore."

"These people are trapped. Helpless."

"You don't need me," Julie said. "No one else in the entire army would have tapped me for this job." Turning to Simms, she asked, "Would you?"

"I won't order you to go, Jules," the colonel said before Simms could answer. "Or even threaten you with court martial—though no one would blame me. You and I may have our disagreements, but you're my daughter and I love you. And with that in mind, you may, if you choose, serve the remainder of your enlistment—four days, if I remember correctly—in the stockade. You'll be dishonorably discharged, of course, but that can't be helped."

"I'm overwhelmed," Julie said. "Really."

"I'm offering you a chance to make amends," the colonel said. "To make good on your debt to your country, with which you have a contract. You might at least show some appreciation."

Julie stared at the colonel, her face hard.

"This is a critical mission," he continued, "and everyone must be 100 percent onboard, not just tagging along in order to get their military benefits restored. Nor should they do this simply to honor the sacrifices of their father—"

"Shut up!" Julie yelled, her hand shooting out and clamping over the colonel's mouth. He jerked back, teetering, and Simms stepped up, catching the colonel before he fell. Simms shoved Julie back with his shoulder and she dropped into a crouch, growling, her legs coiled to charge. Keeping a hand on the colonel, Simms drew his sidearm.

"Lieutenant," the colonel said, his voice trembling. His confidence had dissolved, leaving him old and frail. Simms turned his back to Julie and helped the colonel into a chair.

"Good man," the colonel said, patting Simms's shoulder. He pulled a small oxygen bottle from his jacket pocket and pressed the mask to his face. His labored breathing filled the room.

"I see you haven't lost your way with people, Jules," the colonel said finally. "You're welcome to hate me, for whatever reason you choose. You can even hate the entire army, but the people trapped down there are civilians. They need your help."

"I'm sure your boys are more than capable of handling it."

"You're their best chance. This is a rescue operation, and one that fits your unique training. Do this and you'll receive a full pardon and an honorable discharge. That's quite generous."

Julie shook her head.

"Okay," the colonel said, resigned. "You win."

He took another drag of oxygen and stared at the floor.

"So I'm free to go?" Julie asked.

"You're free to go," the colonel said, batting at the air without looking up.

"Thank you," Julie said. She grabbed Eric's arm and led him toward the elevator.

"But not him."

"What?"

"This project is top secret," the colonel said. "You may have the proper clearance, but he doesn't. He'll have to be debriefed."

"No," Julie said.

"We'll need a full background check, which will take at least a month."

"Don't do this…"

"I've already had Homeland Security pull his file—and it's quite impressive. Protesting, insurrection, and conspiracy. Your friend even plotted to overthrow the government. Didn't you, Doctor Kirsch?"

"That was just an opinion piece," Eric said. "For a newspaper."

"Be that as it may, the sad truth is that if we can't clear you, we'll be forced to detain you until the tunnel is declassified. But that's only been, what? Fifty years so far?"

"You piece of shit," Julie said.

"I don't doubt, Jules, that if anyone but me asked, you would see that joining this mission was the right thing to do. But here's the deal: you get my men into that base and I'll see that your mother gets her boyfriend back. Otherwise…" The colonel drew his arm out slowly, indicating a very long time.

Julie flushed with anger. She stomped to the window and cocked her fist at the glass. But she held it back, staring down the long tunnel.

"Fine," she said, dropping her arm and walking to the elevator. "Let's go."

SIX

A TUGBOAT CHUGGED ACROSS the dark harbor, teetering over seven-foot swells as it pressed through the driven snow. It hauled behind it a wide, flat barge that was laden with garbage. The garbage had been collected in Newark for delivery in Connecticut, but the tug was taking a circuitous route, first traveling due east, then circling around Staten Island and heading for an abandoned pier on the dark side of Governors Island. The tug's crew secured the barge with long lengths of lumber, leaving a fifteen-foot gap between it and the dock.

An aged green pickup drove down the dock, and a park ranger got out and tossed five bags of trash from the truck bed onto the barge, where it was lost among the tonnage already aboard. He called to the crew, inviting them back to his office for coffee, and they hopped into the back of the pickup. The truck drove off, leaving the dock empty and still.

A few minutes later, three jeeps approached from the opposite direction. They drove in a tight line, headlights off, navigating by yellow fog lights. This was the remainder of D-5, those who had stayed in Virginia for the entirety of the funeral.

The lead jeep was driven by Sergeant Cutter, who was tall

and fit and, despite the winter weather, wore a quilted camo vest that left his arms bare. The chevrons of his rank—master sergeant—were tattooed on his bicep, all but hidden by his dark skin. Cutter was the oldest member of the unit, and his short, gray-speckled hair could to have been drawn on his scalp. He was reclined in his seat, steering with one hand and sneering at nothing in particular.

When they reached the water, he motioned for the other jeeps to stop. He raced down the dock, his tires rattling over the wooden planks, and jerked to a stop beside the barge. Specialist Wolf, sitting beside him, stood up and scanned the harbor with large, boxy binoculars.

Though a few inches shorter, Wolf had the same build as Cutter, and while the master sergeant's skin was dark, Wolf's was midnight. He had inch-long, pencil-thick dreads and fatigues that fit as though tailored. A steel-gray patch on his sleeve featured a scuba mask crossed with long knives—the insignia of a Special Operations deep-water diver.

Wolf moved the binoculars with slow patience, thumbing a dial on the side to switch between low-light and infrared mode. He lingered on every ship in the harbor, then finally lowered the binoculars and gave Cutter a nod.

Cutter grabbed an egg-shaped device from the jeep's dash and walked to the gap between dock and barge. He turned the top of the device, and it started to vibrate—not steadily, but in code. He lowered the device into the water by the attached cord until it came to rest against something solid. Thirty seconds later, the water began to boil.

Cutter reeled the device up and stepped back as a black metal hump rose from the water, the tip of a submarine. A hatch swung open with a clang, a ladder rose out, and Captain Sullivan climbed out. Ignoring Cutter's extended hand, she hopped to the dock.

Captain Sullivan was in her early fifties, thin but fit, with high cheekbones and a nose like an eagle's beak. She wore a black turtleneck and straight-legged gabardine pants, and her flax-gray hair was pulled into a tight knot below her hat.

She gave Cutter a quick salute but was looking past him, peering at the other jeeps.

"He's on his way," Cutter said. "But we're supposed to start loading."

The captain frowned. She turned to Cutter and inspected him from hair to boots.

"Right," she said, drawing a slim radio from her belt and speaking into it. "Bring her up."

The rest of the submarine had emerged, filling into the space between the barge and the dock. It was the size of a small commercial jet but thinner and taller, shaped like a fish with a hump on its forehead. Its tail was ringed with fins, which surrounded a propeller large enough for an aircraft carrier.

The cargo door near the back of submarine was open, and Wolf—driving the barge's crane—maneuvered a refrigerator-sized crate inside. The barge and the submarine rolled in the waves, out of sync, and the crate swung wildly. Sergeant Cutter stood atop the submarine, his legs wide, yelling instructions. The wind was howling, and one side of his body was caked in snow.

A dark sedan drove up along the coast of Governors Island and stopped at the foot of the dock. The chauffeur—a private—hustled around to open the back door. The colonel took the chauffeur's hand and let himself be pulled to his feet, then made a show of jerking his arm away, making it clear he hadn't needed the help. He buttoned his thick wool overcoat up to the neck; it made his head seem small and shriveled. Julie and Eric emerged behind the colonel, and he led them down the dock.

"The Navy Explorer," the colonel said, waving at the boat. "The first of a new breed of submarines, capable of traveling at great speed and to previously unimaginable depths."

"But still appropriately phallic," Eric said.

"Nature's perfect design," the colonel said, motioning them to the hatch at the front.

Cutter's eyes went wide when he caught sight of Julie. He motioned for Wolf to stop the crane as he jumped over to the barge.

"What the fuck is she doing here?" he asked, leaning into the crane's cabin.

Wolf glanced at Julie and shrugged. Both men watched her hop onto the swaying ladder. Cutter shook his head with disbelief.

"What the hell, amigo?" Specialist Serio yelled, his head appearing through the bay doors.

Serio was big, muscular in a professional-wrestling way, with olive-skin and bright green eyes. He had numerous tattoos, and his short black hair was shaved to imply a mohawk. He motioned impatiently to the swinging crate but then saw Cutter's gaze. He followed it to Julie.

"Dat the new señor?" he called out. His accent was unbelievably thick.

"Specialist!" Cutter barked, motioning to the colonel.

"Sorry, Sergeant," Serio said, his hispanic accent replaced by one that belonged in the American Southwest. "Just asking if that was the new lieutenant, Sergeant?"

"No, specialist," Cutter said. "*Dat's* the old girl."

"Girl?" Serio squinted through the snow, not quiet believing him. "That's one tough-looking señorita."

"Yeah," Cutter said to himself, "she is at that." He motioned Serio back into the hold and hopped back over to the submarine, watching Julie descend inside.

SEVEN

"Julie?" Cutter asked, pushing back the wave of black hair that crashed down over his eyes. "What kind of name is that?"

"A woman's name," Julie said, leaning forward and squinting, as if Cutter were out of focus. "You do know what *those* are, don't you?"

Cutter drew out a comb and preened himself. His hair was lye-straightened, glossy, and, except for the bangs, glued tightly to his scalp. He swung his hips as he turned to Corporal Marson, who was both his tutor and babysitter.

"A little girl," he said with the well-practiced contempt of a teenager.

"Colonel Porter has requested that I tutor Julie in addition to yourself," Marson said apologetically, "and your father agreed."

"My father?" Cutter sneered. He turned to Julie, who was studying him intently. She was short, no taller than his stomach, with shoulder-length, sandy-blond hair, bright green eyes, and a cherubic face. "How old are you, anyway?" he asked. "Eight?"

"Try fourteen," Julie said.

"Really?"

"In two weeks."

"Julie's father has just taken command of the base," Corporal Marson added, "and she hasn't had the chance to meet anyone yet. I was hoping you might encourage the other kids to throw her a birthday party."

"Ugh," Cutter said.

"Don't worry about him," Julie said to Cutter, tilting her head at Marson. "He works for my father."

"He works for *my* father," Cutter said.

"Either way, he's just staff," Julie said. "We can ignore him. Want to race?"

"With those short legs?" Cutter asked.

"Up a tree."

"I don't think that's a good idea, Nigel," the corporal said.

"Nigel?" Julie asked.

Cutter looked from the Julie to the corporal and back again.

"You're on," he said, sprinting for the tall tree at the front of the post office.

EIGHT

THE INTERIOR OF THE Navy Explorer was appreciably bigger than could be seen from the surface, in part because of the space set aside for equipment that hadn't yet been installed. The bridge looked temporary, no more than raised platform at the front of the main cabin. The rest of the cabin was empty beyond three rows of temporary, airplane-style seating added for the soldiers. Behind the main cabin was the cargo bay, where the men were loading their equipment, and behind that were several small rooms, including sleeping quarters and a pool room that opened to the ocean. Lastly, there was an airlock connected to the submarine's side hatch, allowing the ship to dock while underwater.

Julie and Eric climbed down the exterior ladder into the main cabin, which was a spartan room with metal walls and an open-grate floor. But after the storm outside, it felt cozy and warm. Captain Sullivan hailed them from the raised bridge, slid smoothly down runners of a six-foot ladder, and met them in the middle of the room. Colonel Porter descended the exterior ladder just far enough to get his head inside, and the two exchanged salutes.

"Captain Sullivan!" the colonel called out. "I believe you know our dive specialist."

The captain gave Julie a warm smile, extending a hand as though to touch her, but hovering it just over her shoulder.

"I don't know if you remember me," she said, shifting the hand to waist height. "You were only this tall the last time we saw each other. Back when your father was stationed at San Jose."

"I'm sorry, I . . ." Julie said, searching for any memory of this woman.

"Call me Rachael, please," Sullivan said, offering her hand. Julie didn't like what was happening to her, but the captain seemed sincere and probably didn't have anything to do with it, so she shook her hand and returned the smile.

"You and your assistant can ride up on the bridge with me," Sullivan continued. Eric opened his mouth to protest, but Julie nudged his ribs. The captain turned to the colonel.

"Looks like we're on schedule," she said. "We should reach the base at roughly 23:30."

"Very good," the colonel said.

"Tonight?" Eric blurted.

"Yes, Doctor Kirsch," Sullivan said. "Tonight."

Eric checked his watch, then whispered to Julie, "Five hours to the middle of the Atlantic?"

The submarine had again submerged until only the top hatch was visible. The dock was abandoned except for Simms and the colonel, who stood close to each other, speaking quietly in the billowing wind.

"I know it doesn't make sense to you," the colonel said, "but there are aspects to this mission that I cannot, for matters of the highest security, disclose to you right now. I do not enjoy skullduggery, so I will ask you, rather than order you, to do as I request."

The colonel extended a small fabric pouch to Simms, who was doing his best to look impassive. Simms hesitated, then took the pouch and put it in his pocket.

"Thank you, Brian," the colonel said. "One last thing."

"Sir?"

"As I cannot be there myself, I need you be my ambassador. You must do more than just follow orders. You must defend Sergeant Porter's presence on this mission. We can't allow anyone's personal feelings, including your own, to endanger our success."

"Understood, sir, but what about the professor? It would be easier to detain him here—"

"Doctor Kirsch is a real bonus," the colonel said impatiently, shivering beneath his wool coat. "He's a top mind in genetics, and despite his age he's probably one of the few scientists in his field who can handle the physical requirements of this mission. My ex-wife couldn't have chosen us a better man if I'd ordered her to."

"I can't see him choosing to help us," Simms said.

"Scientists are scientists. Put something interesting in front of him and he'll have it halfway apart before he even remembers his so-called ethics. Use him as you can, and we'll worry about his discretion later."

Headlights approached from the island—the tugboat's crew was returning. Simms saluted, then hustled down the ladder. The hatch closed and the water swallowed it.

The colonel remained still as the submarine disappeared, his head hung toward the empty water. The bouncing light of the ranger's truck broke his trance. He pulled his face into a smile, as if to cheer himself, then leaned heavily on his cane and hobbled back to the sedan.

NINE

IN THE MAIN CABIN of the submarine, the fifteen members of D-5 were buckled into three rows of airplane-style seats, facing the empty wall below the bridge. The submarine was lit in muted red, and Simms held a flashlight in his mouth, studying the contents of a manila folder, which had been stamped *TOP SECRET*. He held a pair of eyeglasses in one hand, raising them up to inspect a photograph. He passed the photograph to Cutter, who looked at it and let out an appreciative whistle.

"This is big trouble, isn't it?" he asked. Simms only shrugged.

"Does anyone know where we're going?" Hiller asked from the back row.

"Aren't *you* the lieutenant?" Serio asked, turning to face him. Serio was so big that the whole row of seats bent under his movements.

"The sacrificial lamb," Cutter called over his shoulder.

"I'm sorry?" Hiller asked.

"Ignore him," Orton said. Orton was the corporal who had arrived with Simms in the helicopter. He was short and lean, of indeterminable Asian stock, and wore a pencil mustache that made him look even younger than he was. As usual, Orton had inherited the job of babysitting the newest junior lieutenant. "Whenever you can," he added.

"You're the new guy?" Serio asked again

"Lieutenant Hiller," Hiller said, offering his hand.

"I can read," Serio said. "You get that name tag at the cadet factory?"

"He's all right," Petty injected. "I rode in with him."

"One out of one pale-faced medics agree," Serio said, saluting like a Native American—given Serio's complexion, it seemed like a natural gesture. Turning forward, he called to Cutter.

"Hey, Sarge," he said. "The second lieutenant would like to know the purpose of this mission."

"Underwater A-rabs," Cutter called back. "Al Qaeda's bombing the American spermback whale, the only mammal God saw fit to decorate with white stars on its beautiful blue body."

Simms grinned.

"You could give him a chance, you know," he said.

"The new lieutenant, sir?" Cutter asked. "Wouldn't want him to start giving orders, sir. Never know who'll get killed."

"Why is it that the only time you call me sir," Simms asked, "is when you're undermining my authority?"

"Any insolence is unintended, sir," Cutter said.

"I bet," Simms said. "Tell me again how many of your teeth have been broken?"

"What's important is how many I got left," Cutter said, giving him a white grin. His few real teeth were obvious by their yellowish hue.

Eric looked down at D-5 from the bridge.

"That is some boy's club," he said. "I can see why you chose not to stay."

"It's a boy's club because I didn't stay," Julie replied. She wore a blue sweatshirt with Captain Sullivan's name embroidered on the left breast. The fabric was tight to her chest, and the sleeves were stretched as thin as paint on her muscular arms. She was inspecting the bridge, which had a semicircle of video monitors lined up like the windows of a cockpit. The monitors displayed a computer-generated view of the topography around them, as well as their depth and clearance. The submarine was keeping itself directly below the barge as it crept out to sea. The barge, Sullivan had explained, was their cover against satellite surveillance, which could otherwise penetrate the shallow waters of the New York harbor.

"I wouldn't want to stay myself," Eric said quietly, checking to make sure the captain was out of earshot. "But to desert?"

"I don't want to talk about it."

"And with only four days left in your enlistment?"

"Three."

"Even worse," Eric said. "Was it because of—"

Julie turned sharply to Eric, raising a finger in warning.

"I'm sorry," he said. "I know it's not my place to ask."

Julie frowned. Eric's apologies always made *her* feel guilty.

"It's complicated," she said. Then, after some thought, added, "I'm sorry you got dragged into this."

"I'm glad to be here," Eric said. "Your mother would never forgive me if anything happened to you."

"Listen," Julie said, taking his hands and looking into his eyes. "I don't know what this is really about, but you don't know these people the way I do. They're trained to kill, not to think, and they're dangerous in ways you can't even imagine."

"Them," Eric said. "But not you?"

"I've changed."

"Your father doesn't seem to think—"

"I've changed," Julie said, squeezing Eric's hands a little too hard, making him wince. "Just stick close to the captain and stay as invisible as possible. This is my mess, and I'll clean it up."

Eric nodded and Julie released his hands.

"Depth is one hundred," the helmsman said. "We're safe from satellite detection."

"Move us out from cover and bring us to fourteen knots," Sullivan said. Though the submarine was designed for a crew of eight, it was only her and the helmsman. The boat was highly classified, so few people even knew of its existence, much less were trained in its operation. The small crew meant relying heavily on automation, which was fine so long as everything went smoothly, but it put Sullivan on edge. "Hug the bottom until we hit one fifty," she said.

"Aye, aye," the helmsman said, pushing down on the wheel. The submarine angled into a dive, and for a few minutes the only sound was the hum of machinery and the chatter drifting up from Delta Force Group 5.

"One-fifty," the helmsman said.

"Fire the cavitator," the captain said.

The helmsman threw a switch, and somewhere deep in the submarine a throbbing electric motor started to whir, rising to blender speed.

"This boat uses supercavitation," the captain told Julie, shouting over the noise. "Simply put, it creates a tunnel in the water in front of us, reducing our friction to practical zero."

"Cavitation at full," the helmsman said.

"Bring us to three-quarters."

The helmsman eased the throttle forward, and the main engine fired up, rumbling deeply.

"Hang on," the captain said as the engine grew louder, shaking the entire cabin. The boat shot forward as if from a gun, pressing everyone to their seats.

A hundred miles off the coast of New York was the Hudson Canyon, a wide scar in the continental shelf where the ocean's depth dropped from a few hundred feet to three-quarters of a mile.

The Navy Explorer raced toward the canyon, skimming the seafloor. It was enveloped in a shimmering pocket of air that originated from a screw-type propeller on its nose. The oversized propeller at the back of the submarine was a blur, the force of its wake pulling the sand from the ocean floor and spinning it as if there were a tornado growing out of its tail.

The Explorer shot off the continental shelf and faded into the dark depths of the canyon.

"Three-quarters," the helmsman said. The engine still roared, but the force of acceleration had tapered off.

"Steady as she goes," the captain said. "Ship to all clear."

White lights came on throughout the submarine, replacing the red. Down in the main cabin, D-5 unbuckled and filed purposely through the back door, heading for the cargo hold.

"I'm gonna take a look around," Julie said, watching them leave.

"Happy where I am," Eric said, stretching out his legs.

"Good man," Julie said, patting his knee. She climbed down from the bridge and followed the men out.

The cargo hold was the same size as the main room, and

it was filled with crates—the same crates Julie had seen on the Athenian helicopter. Simms and Cutter were using one as a table, spreading out a map and studying it intently. Seeing Julie approach, Cutter folded the map over.

"I am on your side, you know," Julie said.

"Good news for the enemy," Cutter replied

"And they are...?"

"Privileged information."

"Everyone will be briefed," Simms said. "If you'll excuse us, Sergeant Porter."

"Sure," Julie said, continuing on. Cutter shouldered her as she passed, and she shoved back with her own.

"Something I need to know?" Simms asked after she had gone.

"Yeah," Cutter said. "This is total bullshit."

"We need her for the mission."

"Wolf can drive the Atargis," Cutter said. "Better than she can."

"Not according to the colonel," Simms said.

"Yeah, he *never* says that. 'Have you met my daughter? She's amazing at everythi—'"

"Sergeant," Simms barked, and Cutter's mouth snapped shut. "The colonel gave his orders. It is our duty to follow them."

"Yes, sir," Cutter said, flipping the map back open. "But you better have Wolf ready as a backup."

"Hrm," Simms said, chewing on the arm of his glasses. "She did at least *train* on the Atargis?"

"That's what I heard," Cutter said with a shrug. "But that wasn't long before she up and left."

"Okay," Simms said, taking a deep breath. "I guess we'll see what happens."

TEN

"You really think you can get the car?" Julie asked.

"I'm *certain*," Cutter said between huffing breaths. He was following Julie up a seemingly endless steel ladder that hung seemingly in midair, between the legs of a massive water tower.

The water tower was the tallest structure on the base. Its enormous tank, shaped like a flattened sphere, rose high above the low buildings and sprawling pine forests. They were five stories up—about halfway—and already had an uninterrupted view of the low hills lit by a hazy quarter moon.

The rusty ladder was attached at only three points—the top of the tower, the bottom, and a crossbeam about forty feet off the ground. They were well above the crossbeam, and the ladder shook and rattled with every movement. Julie didn't seem to notice, scurrying quickly up the ladder while Cutter, following, rose slowly and methodically, firmly grasping each rung and keeping his eyes in front of him. He was sweating, and his long bangs had deflated over his face.

"Your dad is away?" Julie asked.

"My dad is always away."

"And your mom?"

"You've met her."

"Barely," Julie said.

"Trust me, she won't be a problem."

"Okay, I'll trust you," Julie said. "Watch out for this rung. It's loose."

Cutter frowned when he reached the rung; it had rusted to the thickness of a pencil and had broken free of one of the runners. He stretched an arm up, reaching past it, grabbing the next rung up so hard that his knuckles turned pale. He closed his eyes, took a deep breath, and pulled himself up.

"Maybe we shouldn't be doing this," he said, locking his elbow over the rung and panting.

"It'll be fine," Julie said.

"Until it's not."

"Trust me," Julie said. "I'm trusting you."

"I don't think you are, and anyway those are two completely different types of trust—"

"Shit!" Julie yelled as a rung broke loose in her hand. Her feet slipped and she dropped. Hanging by one hand, she swung out into the air.

"Julie!" Cutter said, climbing rapidly, reaching her just as she got a foot back on the ladder.

"I found another loose rung," she said, tossing the rusted bar over her shoulder.

"Are you okay?"

"I might have shit myself," she said. "It feels a little squishy down there. Sometimes that's just sweat, though."

"This is really great," Cutter said. "Thank you for bringing me up here."

"It's your birthday," Julie said.

"Tomorrow," Cutter said. "If I live that long."

"Hurry up," she said, climbing. "It's almost midnight."

Five minutes later, they reached the steel-grated catwalk that encircled the water tank. Julie peeked down the back of her pants and announced she was "all clear," then the two of them strolled around the catwalk, taking in the lights below.

"How far do you think we can see?" Julie asked.

"I bet that's Raleigh," Cutter said, pointing at a glow on the horizon.

"What's Raleigh?"

"The state capital," Cutter said sarcastically.

"I'm not from around here," Julie said.

"Yeah," Cutter said. "Where *are* you from?"

"Oklahoma, I think," Julie said. "Or Virginia, or California, or Maine, or Texas."

"How can you not know?"

"I know I'm from America."

"What about your birth certificate?"

"What about it?"

"Doesn't that say where you were born?"

"What do you care?"

"I'm curious."

"You usually aren't."

"No?"

"No," Julie said. "You are specifically never curious. That's why you suck at school."

"That's my dad's fault. He's smart, but he married someone stupid."

"Which makes you half-smart?"

"I guess."

"I always wondered what that meant," Julie said. "My mom is smart."

"And your dad?"

"*Very* smart. And very busy. Always off doing his duty."

"Which is?"

"Stopping bad people from being bad," Julie said.

"How does he do that?"

"Bullets," Julie said. "Bombs."

"He's some sort of war hero, right?"

"He's won several of them," Julie said. "I plan to, too. When I'm old enough."

The two of them gazed at the distant lights.

"My mom works near Raleigh somewhere," Julie said. "At some university developing army technology. She's the military *liaison*, which sounds fancier than it is. She says it's boring, but she goes to the university almost every day, even on weekends. And she often doesn't get back until late."

Cutter worked his bangs with a comb as Julie gazed at the distant glow, deep in thought.

"You're sure you can get the car?" she asked.

"Didn't we just talk about trust?"

"You shouldn't call your mom stupid," Julie said.

"Even if she is?" Cutter asked, spitting on his comb and working it into his hair. "She asked me the other day if we were having sex."

"Us?" Julie asked. "What did you say?"

"No," Cutter said. "Obviously."

"I read that men lie about these things," Julie said. "To impress their friends."

"You're my only friend."

"And you're mine," Julie said, looking up at him and smiling. She leaned forward, closing her eyes and rising onto her toes. It took Cutter a moment to catch on; he pocketed the comb, put his hands on Julie's waist, and bent his lips toward hers. Just before they kissed, her eyes popped open and she looked at her watch.

"Oh," she said, deflating. "It's too late."

Cutter looked at his own watch.

"It's midnight," he said, confused.

"You're sixteen now," she said. "But I'm only fifteen. It would be illegal for us to have sex."

"'Illegal,' she said, after we broke in, entered, trespassed, and—wait, did we come up here for sex?"

"Well," Julie said, "sexy stuff, anyway. As a birthday present."

"I…"

"Also, I bought you a knife," Julie said. "With a light on it."

Cutter could only gape, dumbfounded.

"Anyway, we're not at the top yet," Julie said, climbing a rung ladder that curved up the water tank. "There's a radio tower at the center. It goes up another thirty feet."

"There is?" Cutter asked. "Oh, good."

ELEVEN

Julie found Corporal Orton at the back of the cramped cargo hold, working with Specialist Boxx.

Boxx was old for his rank, tall and wiry, and a walking display of tools and electronics. He had large, low-slung glasses and a screwdriver tucked behind his ear.

The two soldiers were setting a wide, flat aluminum case onto a crate. Orton—despite having a higher rank—took his cues from Boxx, springing the clasps and pulling off the cover. Inside, lying on a bed of carved foam, was a drone shaped like a carbon-fiber manta ray.

There was a foot-wide hole through the middle of the drone, housing a large propeller. Four smaller propellers were set in each corner, and a white stencil on the side said *MACARTHUR*.

Boxx lifted the drone and cradled it like a baby as Orton closed the lid. He set it on the case and inspected the rotors and the flaps, then drew a device from his pocket—a remote control that resembled a portable game system.

"I'm going to run a couple tests without the main motor," Boxx told Orton. He thumbed the sticks on the remote, and the smaller propellers began to spin, first one at a time and then in matched pairs.

"That's new," Julie said.

Boxx looked up from the remote and inspected her.

"You're shorter than your reputation led me to believe," he said finally. He continued to study her, but, finding nothing to add, turned back to the drone.

"We're doing a flight check," Orton volunteered. "It moves too fast for anyone—"

"*He* moves too fast," Boxx interrupted, his eyes on the remote. "Main propeller coming online."

The large propeller spun up, moving so fast that it disappeared. It made a noise somewhere between a fan and a snake's hiss.

"Too fast to control," Orton said, raising his voice over the motor. "So it has to be programmed—"

"*He* has to be programmed," Boxx corrected. "Lift him."

"Right," Orton said. "He."

The corporal lifted the drone and then lowered his hands. It hovered in place.

"That's enough," Boxx said cutting the motor as Orton put his hands back under the drone. "I don't want to drain the battery."

Boxx crouched down, looking underneath the drone. He tapped the handle of the screwdriver against his cheek and pumped his lips, making a sound like dripping water. Something at the bottom of the drone seemed to concern him, but then he shook his head dismissively. He straightened up and turned to Julie.

"MacArthur moves too quickly for me to control," he said. "For anyone to control. So he's programmed with sequences and has a limited form of AI. I give him a destination and he handles the details. But it only works if he's perfectly tuned. He has to be able to compensate for any interference."

"Interference?" Julie asked.

"Wind, walls, people, bullets, explosions..." Boxx slipped the screwdriver behind his ear and laid a piece of thick velvet over the drone's case, tucking the edges like a bedsheet. "This is all highly confidential, of course, should you choose to go AWOL again."

Julie bristled, but felt no anger; Boxx had spoken without malice.

"It's clever," she said.

"Clever?" Boxx sneered, taking the drone from Orton and setting it gently on the velvet. "MacArthur is a tactically autonomous combatant. He's not *clever*. He's a work of art."

"Oh," Julie said. Boxx circled the drone, putting his back to Julie as he fiddled with a propeller.

"That's TAC for short," Orton said. "TACs aren't in widespread use, but we've already got two of them."

"Combat robots," Julie said. "As in, 'autonomous kill'?"

"MacArthur isn't armed," Orton said. "He's just a scout. He's a prototype—Boxx helped with design. But Patton, our other TAC, is a whole different story. It was built by General Dynamics, the same guys who make the M1 Abrams tank."

Boxx snorted but made no further comment. Julie looked around, trying to find the other robot.

"Over there," Orton said, pointing at a refrigerator-sized crate.

"But this is just a rescue mission." Julie said.

"We bring them everywhere," Orton said. "You never know, right?"

"Playing with your toy again, Boxx?" Cutter asked loudly, shoving into the tight space. "You treat that thing like a woman."

Boxx ignored him.

"Sleeps with it in his bunk," he whispered with mock confidentially, then he burst into laughter. No one else did.

"Lieutenant wants us for briefing," he continued, clearing his throat and jerking his thumb at the main room. He followed the other soldiers to the door, then turned back to Julie. "I guess he wants you too."

The interior of the submarine had grown colder as it descended, and its hull pinged softly as it compressed from the rising pressure. Most of D-5 was already seated when Julie arrived, and Simms was taping a map of the ocean floor to the wall in front of them.

"Sergeant Major," Hiller said, approaching Cutter just as he was about to sit.

"Sir?" Cutter said, straightening up.

"I haven't had a chance to introduce myself," Hiller said, extending a hand. "Lieutenant Hiller."

"Sir," Cutter said, giving him a quick salute and trying again for his chair. Hiller blocked him.

"I just thought that, since we were going to be working together, we should probably—"

The young lieutenant backed up a step as Cutter let out a deep, animal groan.

Great, Cutter thought. *First Porter and now this overeager lieutenant. As if this mission wasn't trouble enough to begin with.* The lieutenant, at least, he knew how to handle.

For years now—and for reasons beyond his own comprehension—the colonel had insisted that D-5's junior lieutenant be some variety of overschooled pencil neck with his nose so deep in the manual that he'd walk straight over a land mine. It fell on Cutter, as the senior noncom, to keep these buck lieutenants—and everyone in their general proximity—alive. And for this, he had developed his own version of an officer training program. Well, less of a training program, he admitted, than an un-training program.

And, he thought wearily, *I might as well get started.*

"May I see that, sir?" he asked, pointing at Hiller's plastic name tag.

"Of course," Hiller said, unpinning it. "Please."

Cutter held the name tag close to his face, as though scrutinizing every detail.

"Lieutenant Thomas Hiller," he read.

"Yes, that's my name," Hiller said with a smile. "Don't wear it—"

"And you've had a chance to meet everyone on the team, sir?"

"Yes, Sergeant, I have, thank you." Hiller straightened up, suddenly conscious of Cutter's height. "It's an honor to be—"

"Then seeing as how everyone already knows you, sir, you won't be needing this anymore." Cutter slipped the name tag into his pocket.

"I guess not, but—" Hiller said, his eyes following the disappearing name tag.

"May I ask you a question, sir?" Cutter asked.

"Certainly, Sergeant."

"Do you agree with Rommel, sir, that mortal danger is an effective antidote to fixed ideas?"

"I, um, sure," Hiller said. "Did *he* say that?"

"Indeed he did, sir. We'd better find our seats, sir. The briefing is about to start." Cutter dropped into his seat, leaving Hiller staring at nothing. Hiller started to speak, then thought better of it. He moved to the back row and took a seat.

Julie was just taking her own seat when Eric joined her.

"Go back to the bridge," she said.

"I can't see the map from up there," Eric said.

"And you need a mission briefing?"

"I'm curious."

"Don't be curious," Julie said, shoving him toward the bridge. "This is no place to be curious." But then Simms called for attention, and Eric used it as an excuse to sit down.

"Still no word from the base," Simms said, addressing the group. "So we'll assume the presence of hostile forces."

"By which you mean—" Orton said.

"Yes," Simms said, cutting him off. "Exactly that. But we should be prepared for anything."

"CATs?" Serio asked.

"Unlikely," Simms said, "But we won't know until we're inside."

"CATs?" Julie asked, leaning over to Orton.

"Chinese, Axis of Evil, and Terrorists," Orton replied. "The standard enemy."

"The standard...?" Eric blurted, incredulously.

"Most of us don't have deep-water training," Simms continued, raising his voice over the interruption. "But the interior of the base is sealed and pressurized. Once the dock is operational, we'll enter directly from the sub. Which brings me to Sergeant Julie Porter. Her job is to get us inside. She used to be one of..."

Simms trailed off, changing his mind.

"She's already familiar with our signals and methods," he said. "But, to be clear, she holds no official rank in this unit."

Several soldiers looked in her direction. Julie nodded, but only Wolf nodded back.

"Our way inside is somewhere in this cave," Simms told Julie, drawing a circle on the map. "There's an emergency access hatch, but we don't know exactly where. We also don't know how deep, or how complex, these caves are. But the hatch should be obvious—it'll be the only thing in there made of steel. The hatch leads to the docks, which is just a long hallway with a dome on one end and the docking arm on the other. The dock is completely flooded, so it should be secure. Once inside, you'll flush the water and—"

"Secure from what?" Julie asked.

"You flush the water," Simms continued, "so that we can attach the docking arm to the sub and enter the base. After that, your work is done. We'll meet you inside and take it from there."

Simms waited. When Julie nodded, he shifted to a diagram of the tunnel that was taped up beside the map.

"This is the central dig, two miles underwater. Back when the Army Corps started construction, their equipment couldn't stand up to that much pressure, so they built the dock a mile down the mountainside and ran an elevator the rest of the way.

"The elevator takes us to the operations room, which is a new addition to the base. It's a dome exposed to the ocean floor, allowing for communication with the underwater drones as well as with the surface. It also houses the main power generator and serves as staff quarters. This is the first place we can expect to find base personnel.

"We secure the operations room, restore power to the base, and evacuate anyone we find back to the sub. That accomplished, we descend into the transfer station, which is a *very* large room. It was built to store trains and their cargo, back when that was the purpose of this facility. The station runs a mile and a half from the operations room to where the tunnel itself starts. That's a long walk, so pack your canteens."

Simms traced his finger all the way across the diagram.

"We won't have to go far into the tunnel before we

reach the drone maintenance and deployment area. This is the other place we can expect to find base personnel, and it's also our point of extraction. It has an airlock that opens right to the ocean floor and that is large enough to fit this entire submarine inside."

Simms turned halfway to the seated men, moving his hand along the diagram.

"So," he said, "step one is Sergeant Porter gets us into the docking station up here. Step two, we descend by elevator to the operations room. We secure the personnel there, then take this ladder down to the transfer station, where, step three, we cross to the tunnel and reach the drone base. Step four, open the airlock to let the submarine in, load up the survivors, and head for home. There are exactly three dozen people on the base's staff, all civilian. We don't pull out until we have a full account. Any questions?"

"If the power is out," Hiller said, "how can we use the elevator?"

"Right to the point," Cutter said, smiling. Hiller took it for a compliment.

"I believe Specialist Boxx has a plan for that contingency," Simms said.

"Absolutely, sir," Boxx said, twirling his screwdriver as he cast a mischievous glance at Hiller.

"What are those red lines?" Julie asked, pointing to the middle of the transfer station, where jagged lines weaved through the rock like the veins of a bloodshot eyeball.

"Caves of some sort," Simms said.

"The Azores Fracture Zone?" Eric asked, perking up.

"Yes," Simms said, reading the label on the map. "What is it?"

"The meeting point of the earth's three largest tectonic plates," Eric said, brimming with excitement. "A thousand miles of caves and fractures, bigger and more complex than anything you'll find on the surface. And that's just the first few hundred yards, what little we've been able to discover using sounding techniques. We have no idea of how deep they actually go. Nobody's ever been inside."

"And you find that interesting, Fritz?" Cutter asked.

"It could be," Simms said, motioning to Cutter for silence. "We brought along your spelunking gear, if you'd like to take a look."

Eric's face lit up, but Julie shook her head.

"No," she said. "I just want to do my part and leave."

"As you like," Simms said. "Any other questions?"

Orton opened his mouth, but Captain Sullivan called down from the bridge, "We're coming in!"

"Too late," Simms said. "Remember, there's no clock on this one. Move with caution and stay vigilant. Hiller and Orton, prep our guest for her dive. Everyone else, gear up."

TWELVE

THE WATER WAS TOO deep for the sunlight to penetrate, and the two floodlights mounted on the Navy Explorer cut through the pure black waters, sweeping back and forth as the submarine navigated a rocky pass along the ocean floor. Towering overhead was the Mid-Atlantic Ridge, the earth's tallest mountain range, rising two miles before its jagged points punctured the surface, creating an archipelago whose islands covered nine hundred square miles.

Simms stood on the submarine's bridge, watching the narrow pass slip by on the monitors. Visibility was only a few hundred yards, and the pass's rocky walls seemed to roll into existence right in front of him. The submarine reached the end of the pass and steered left, the floodlights glinting off two large square doors embedded in a mound of rock and shale.

"That's the big airlock," Sullivan said, tapping the screen, "where the drone base is."

"And this is where you found the sample?" Simms asked.

"Over there," Sullivan said, pointing to a pile of rocks. "You saw it?"

"Before we left. They flew it in."

"Anyone figure it out?"

"Not that I know," Simms said with a shrug. "Not that they'd tell me, and not that I'd understand if they did."

"I hear you," the captain said, running her gaze across the semicircle of monitors. "Everything out there looks pretty much the same as when we left."

"How long ago was that?"

"Twelve hours and fourteen minutes," the captain said, checking the clock. "That tell you anything?"

"Not yet," Simms said.

"You boys are just flying in the dark, aren't you?"

"That's why they call it recon, ma'am," Simms said. "Someone always has to go in first."

"Someone, yes," she said. "One other thing you should see. Bring us to twenty-two-five." The last she directed at the helmsman, who swung the submarine to the right and eased it forward. He directed the spotlights at a mangled metal hull several times larger than the submarine. Cutter whistled in appreciation.

"Is that the other submarine?" Simms asked.

"It's called bathyscaphe, but yes, more or less," Sullivan replied. "It is, or I should say, it *was* a modern version of a diving bell. They used it to shuttle men and equipment from the surface."

"Any idea what happened to it?"

"Most of the damage is from water pressure, but something had to trigger the initial failure. Something powerful. Its hull is eighteen inches thick."

"Casualties?"

"We sent the ROV in," Sullivan said, "didn't find any bodies."

The three of them stared at the ruined hulk in silence, then Sullivan said, "Let's get on with it. The entrance is right up the side of the mountain."

The helmsman took her words as an order, turning the submarine and climbing up the steep slope. The climb took about twenty minutes, not because of the distance but the depth. Even the most advanced submarines had to be wary of rapid pressure changes.

Finally, the slope leveled out, and they traveled across a flat rock shelf that eventually led to the lip of a wide chasm, deeper and wider than the throw of the floodlights. Heading out over the chasm, they were surrounded by dark, featureless water. The submarine circled back to face the sheer chasm wall, its lights centering on a square pocket cut into the cliff face, inside of which was a small steel dome. An enclosed gangway extended from the dome, similar to what was used at airports but made from thick steel and capped with a sealed hatch. The gangway drooped down, resting on the floor of the rocky shelf.

"Can't we just drill a hole and pump air in?" Cutter asked.

"That's plan B," Simms said. "Or maybe C. It would be a delicate operation. One wrong move and we'd flood the entire base."

"Delicate," Cutter said, "which is why you're sending *her* in. I know you've never had the pleasure of seeing her in action, but—"

"We already discussed this, Sergeant."

"Yes, sir," Cutter said.

"All Porter has to do is get inside and pull a handle," Simms said. "The system is fully automatic."

"Yes, sir," Cutter repeated, dubious.

"That's where she's going in," the captain said, pointing to the left of the dome. "Archie, bring us in line with it."

"Aye, aye," the helmsman said, turning. The floodlights came to rest on a dark hole in the cliff wall.

TUNNEL

The pool room was small and cramped, barely large enough to hold the Atargis deep-water diving suit that hung from a chain hoist in the center.

The suit was a hulking, human-shaped form made from sculpted aluminum that had been cut into thin, horizontal slices, as if run through a bread slicer. The pieces were painted black and then sandwiched between thick rubber that stretched and compressed as Julie moved inside. The suit was twice her size, making her head appear tiny as she peered over its collar.

"This is the same suit you trained on," Orton said, buffing a deep gouge along the side of the helmet. There were more scrapes along the suit's chest and back. "I upgraded the valves for the COBAL rebreather," he continued, "and replaced the halogen lights with LEDs. Some people say they spoil the mood, but they're a lot brighter and use a lot less power. Speaking of power, I couldn't find a replacement battery on short notice. The one in there is four years old now, so don't expect it to last as long as it once did."

Hiller hefted up the suit's right arm and slid it over Julie's. It was a tight fit; she'd added a lot of muscle over the last few years. Hiller used a whirring pneumatic wrench to tighten the bolts that held the arm to the chest plate. He reached for the other arm, but Orton stopped him.

"Hang on," Orton said. "First you have to hook up the ballast hose. There are air bladders spread throughout the suit, allowing for a full range of roll, pitch, and yaw. Let me show you."

He picked up the suit's left glove and opened the wrist. Inside was a pistol grip with several buttons along the side and a thumb-sized joystick at the top. He slipped the glove on and held it up for Julie to see.

"Give it a flick," he said, waving his arm. The glove slid forward, freeing Orton's fingers, and the pistol grip snapped into his palm. Orton demonstrated: "Up-down, tilt forward, tilt back."

"You've driven one of these before?" Julie asked.

"I read the manual," Orton said.

"Then tell him," she said, motioning to Hiller, "because I have."

"Yes, ma'am," Orton said, embarrassed. He pulled the glove off and installed it on Julie's hand. "Should we test the propulsors?" he asked her, motioning to quart-sized bulges on the back of her calves. They were teardrop shaped, with rectangular intakes at the top and circular propellers at the bottom.

"Nah," Julie said, curling her arm. The suit was heavier than she remembered, making her movements sluggish, but she was giddy at the prospect of driving it again.

"How do you even stand up in that thing?" Eric asked. He was perched on a pile of hoses off to the side of the room, cramped against the low ceiling.

"It's easier when you're in the water."

"But how can you even bend your legs?"

"It's not that bad," she said. "You should try it."

"You want me to try a machine of death and destruction."

"You see a gun anywhere?" Julie asked, spreading her arms. Eric only grunted. "There's an extra suit, isn't there, corporal?"

She winked at Orton, but he was slow on the uptake.

"That suit is custom fit to Wolf, so... Oh, yes. Of course. Would you like to try it out, sir?"

"Don't sir me," Eric said, getting to his feet. "I'm nothing to do with your army."

"Eric, wait," Julie said, but he was heading for the exit, ducking along the edge of the room to give the servicemen a wide berth. "Eric," Julie called after him, struggling to move, but he was gone. "Crap," she said.

Orton worked in silence for a minute, then said, "I apologize if I—"

"It's me," Julie said, cutting him off. *Just go to the bridge, Eric,* she thought. *Go to the bridge and stay there.*

"I don't understand why the lieutenant brought him along," Hiller said.

"It wasn't Simms's decision," Julie said. "You can be sure of that."

"The colonel?" Orton asked. Julie nodded.

"The colonel," Orton said to Hiller, as if that was important information.

"Oh," Hiller said. "That doesn't actually explain why he's here."

"No," Orton agreed. He hefted up a two-cylinder air tank and showed it to Julie. "You've used the COBAL rebreather before?" he asked Julie.

She shook her head no.

"It uses a ceramic scrubber instead of a chemical one. It's very efficient and operates in a wide range of temperatures, but it does take a little more effort to breath. The good news, however, is that the COBOL is a closed loop, so no bubbles."

"None at all?"

"None. It recycles 100 percent of your air. You won't run out of air, only oxygen." Orton pointed at a luminous display on her wrist, which read one hundred and fifty. "When the oxygen concentration drops below twenty, your air is no longer safe. At that level, the concentration of CO_2

in the system will reduce your neural activity, impairing your balance and judgment. As it drops lower, you'll start to feel drunk, disoriented, and confused. Eventually you'll forget you're even in danger."

"And after that?"

"Death, I think," Orton said. "The manual didn't specify."

"So, basically, don't let the gauge drop below twenty."

"Don't let it even get close. Ninety-eight is your midway point, and the number will drop faster as it gets lower. Feel free to head back early. We've got three dozen tanks onboard, so we can always send you out again."

Orton walked behind her and attached the tank, raising it over his head and sliding it down slots on the suit's back. He attached the air hoses to nubs on the suit's neck.

"Do you want to do the belt?" he asked Hiller, who picked up a rubber strap and wrapped it around the suit's waist.

"Tools, glow sticks, and explosives," Hiller said, pointing to the belt's pouches. He pulled a hefty block of plastique from the last one. "You've had demolitions training?"

"I'm more of a hobbyist."

"This is C4 enhanced with HMX. It's got a 1.73 RE and a velocity of eighty-four hundred."

"Eh-ha," Julie said. "Not that much of a hobbyist."

"The whole brick is about eighteen sticks of dynamite," Hiller said, "but the pressure at this depth will cut that."

"How much?"

"I don't know," Hiller said. He looked to Orton, who shrugged. "The shockwave is your biggest concerned. Tear off only what you need and don't detonate anywhere that has a direct line of sight to the base's exterior wall. You could implode the whole structure."

"So how much do I use?"

"Start small," Hiller said. "Marble to golf-ball."

"And watch out for shrapnel," Orton added. "At this depth, get even the smallest tear in the suit's rubber and the pressure will crush you like a walnut."

"Walnut?" Julie asked. "Was that in the manual?"

"Actually, I think it was hot dog," Orton said. "Squeezed by a giant fist—"

"Okay," Julie interrupted. "You're funny, but you're not the one going out there."

Simms entered, trailed by Cutter. Both men wore shiny black body armor made from epoxy-hardened kevlar scales. The scales overlapped like the skin of a snake, and dull ceramic plates had been added to protect parts of their chest, arms, and legs.

"Time?" Simms demanded.

"Five minutes, sir," Orton said.

Simms handed Julie a small red book with a plastic seal. "This is the code for the hatch. It's top secret, so don't break the seal unless you actually find—"

Julie ripped the book open. "91-864-382-1," she read. "Got it." She slipped the book into the pouch with the explosives and turned back to Simms. "You were saying?"

Simms gave her a tight smile, digging for patience.

"Corporal Orton has emphasized that you're not to take unnecessary risks?" he asked.

"Corporal Orton has."

"We have plenty of oxygen, and if you call ahead, Wolf can be outside to refit you, to save time."

"Got it."

"You have a sidearm?"

"Why would I have a sidearm?" Julie asked.

Simms held out his hand and Cutter slapped a pistol into it.

"This is a tight-bore nine millimeter loaded with mixed rounds," Simms said. "Three armor-piercing followed by one hollow point, eight shots total. The casings are sealed, so the gun can fire underwater."

Simms offered the gun, but as Julie reached for it, he pulled it back.

"It's expensive," he said. "Even by military standards."

He set the gun in Julie's hand. It was large but surprisingly light—aluminum except for the steel-lined barrel. All of the joints were sealed with rubber. Julie looked down the sights; she hadn't held a firearm since...

"You said the dock was secure," she said. The gun suddenly felt heavy.

"It should be."

Julie held the pistol out. "Then I won't need this."

"It'd be better if you had it."

"I don't want it," Julie said, her voice rising sharply.

The change in her voice caused Simms to step back in alarm. He snatched the gun from her hand.

"Suit yourself," he said. Then, to Orton, "Send her out as soon as she's ready. We're wasting time."

Simms left, but Cutter remained, staring at Julie.

"What?" she asked.

Cutter pointed a finger at her and gave it a firm shake, then he turned and left.

"Whatever," she said.

THIRTEEN

"WE SHOULD GO TO that university," Julie said. "My mom says there's a good pizza joint near there."

"It's over a hundred miles away," Cutter said, fighting to keep the thirty-year-old Charger on the narrow country road. The steering wheel was loose, and the car continually drifted out of the lane. "Besides, what do moms know about pizza?"

"Mine's only thirty-five," Julie said. "We could pass as sisters."

"Could not."

"She was only nineteen when I was born, so most people assume we are. Not with my dad, though. He's so old, he can't even pass as my father."

Cutter nodded, but his focus was on the road. As he turned into a curve, the steering wheel stabilized and he pressed on the gas. He felt the powerful engine rumble, and the acceleration pushed him against his seat. But then came a chirping noise as the rear wheels started to slide. He hit the brakes, too hard.

"Careful," Julie said, almost dropping the knife in her hands as she was thrown forward. The knife was her birthday gift to Cutter—a gaudy variation of a Ka-Bar combat knife, matte black with red trim. The blade had a serrated back that could supposedly cut through barbed wire, and a light in the guard that shined down the edge.

"Totally under control," Cutter said, easing off the brake and accelerating again.

"Yeah," Julie said, leaning against his shoulder and closing her eyes. "I can't believe your mom let you use this car."

"Yeah," Cutter said, his eyes flicking between the road and a bright chrome speedometer that jutted from the dash. Sweat beaded on his brow.

"Your dad said it was okay?"

"That's what I told her. Said it was a present."

"And she bought that?"

"She said, 'Present for what?'"

"I don't believe you," Julie said. "She's your mother. She knows it's your birthday."

"Believe me," Cutter said, wishing he hadn't brought it up.

He had made Julie wait outside when they went to his house for the car. It was nearly afternoon, but his mother was still in her bathrobe. She wasn't much older than Julie's mother, but she looked it. Once upon a time, she had been Miss North Carolina, but these days her face was mottled with red, her cheeks drooped like a hound's, and her hips were great mounds atop the fleshy trunks of her legs. The latter description had been provided by Cutter's father, who, on the rare occasions he stopped by the house, was certain to comment on his mother's weight. Usually right before he left again.

Cutter's mom had nodded absently as he fed her the story about his dad letting him use the car. He talked continuously as he retrieved the Charger's keys from the kitchen hook, his mother growing more anxious, nervously fingering her chemical-blond hair. When she spotted Julie waiting out front, her eyes went wide with fear. She pumped her lips, and Cutter was sure she was about to object, but then she dashed from the room—something that jarred him as much as the china on the shelves. He slipped into the garage and had the car started by the time she caught up to him.

"Use these," she said, leaning into the car and pressing a wad of condoms into his hand. "Don't make the same mistake I did, Nigel." This close, her breath smelled of rotten fruit.

Cutter mumbled a thank-you and backed the car out of the garage, stashing the condoms under the seat. It was these condoms he thought about now, as Julie snuggled up against him.

"You should drive faster," Julie said, stretching her arm across his waist. "It's a long trip."

"Let's just cruise around," Cutter said. "Tour the countryside. We can get pizza anywhere."

"This place is supposed to be the best. And I'm buying."

"Fine," Cutter said. "Just continue straight?"

"Straight, yes," Julie said. "But faster."

It was two hours later when they pulled into the small university town. Cutter was exhausted and his hands ached from gripping the wheel. Adults, he decided, made driving look much easier than it really was.

Julie, on the other hand, had pretended to nap the whole time, her head against his side and her feet sticking out the open window. Cutter knew she was pretending because every time he spoke, she threw it right back at him. Now she stretched and yawned, as if waking up.

They found the restaurant among the brick-fronted buildings of the small downtown. Cutter went to park along the curb, but the Charger was both long and pristine, so he had Julie jump out to guide him. It still took five minutes. Cutter got out and rubbed his back, then used the side-view mirror to fix his hair, which was tussled from the wind.

"You shouldn't be embarrassed by your mom," Julie said, grabbing her clutch from the back seat and slamming the door. "She's a part of you."

"Yeah," Cutter said. "The dumb part."

"She's got really big breasts," Julie said, considering her own. "I'm told that counts."

"Not to me," Cutter said, working the comb through a snag.

"They have to matter," Julie said, pushing her chest out and gauging the result. "Otherwise why would so many people talk about them?"

"Don't ask me," Cutter said.

Julie turned, still posing, and saw that Cutter was focused on the mirror.

"Someone needs to save you from your hair," she said.

"What?" Cutter asked, looking up.

"Come on," Julie said. "I'm starving."

"Me too," Cutter said, pocketing the comb. The two of them walked down the sidewalk.

"Put your hand there," Julie said, pointing to the back pocket of her jeans, the one farthest from him. He shoved his hand in, pulling their hips together. "Good," she said, smiling up at him. "Let's make them put candles on your pizza."

As they approached the restaurant, the front door opened. Cutter stepped forward to grab it, but Julie jerked him back, pulling him into the neighboring doorway. Her mother stepped from the restaurant.

Julie's mother was as short as she was, with the same sandy-blond hair and green eyes. She had changed her outfit since Julie had seen her this morning, exchanging her lieutenant's uniform for a simple, peach-colored dress. She wore a carefree smile that Julie had never seen before.

"If she saw us off base...," Cutter whispered, but Julie punched his chest and motioned for silence. A man stepped out behind her mother, tall with long gray hair, an Amish-style beard, and thick glasses. The two of them exchanged words and then kissed deeply. The man leaned over and whispered in her mother's ear. She shook her head, smiling mischievously. He bit the lobe of her ear, and she laughed—a child's laugh. He kissed his way down her neck and around to her chest. She shoved him back, flush, but she looked at her watch and nodded. The man took her hand and led her to his car—a small thing, old and foreign. He fired its throaty motor and they drove off.

"Who was...?"

"They're getting away," Julie said, dragging Cutter back to his car.

They caught up with the small car and followed it to the outskirts of the university, into a neighborhood with big lawns and small houses. The man parked at one of the houses, and Cutter drove past, pulling over farther down the block. Julie told him to stay and crept back. She watched her mother enter the house, then she circled around to the back, where she heard noises coming from one of the windows. Adult noises. Julie slumped below the window and listened to the whole thing.

It was a full hour before Julie returned to the Charger. Cutter was chewing a golf ball-sized wad of assorted gum, maintaining its flavor with a box of small mints. These were all he could find in the glove box.

"Let's go," Julie said, dropping into the passenger seat. There were stains on her cheeks, dirt and water.

"Pizza?" Cutter asked hopefully.

"Home," Julie said.

"You're not going to tell your dad."

"I have to."

"You don't."

"He trusts her, and she's... she's betrayed him."

"She's your mother."

"He's my father."

"You shouldn't mess with adult stuff."

"I don't have a choice."

Cutter regarded her for a long minute, then nodded and started the car.

Julie's father took her report calmly and asked no questions. That night he ate dinner at home, which was unusual, and sent Julie up to bed early. His calm behavior filled Julie with dread, and, unable to sleep, she sat on the floor of her bedroom with her ear pressed to the door. She heard nothing but the clicks and pops of the wood-framed house as it settled for the night.

She drifted off, waking to the sound of her mother's car in the driveway. She heard her father walk across the house to meet her at the front door. They exchanged a few quiet words and then retreated to his office, closing the door behind them. After that, nothing.

The silence roared through the house. Julie's mind churned, imagining her mother dead at her father's hands. She crept into the hall and over to the top of the steps, hugging the wall to avoid loose floorboards. She was relieved by the faint sound of voices; her parents were having an angry discussion, but not nearly as angry as she would have expected.

"I only agreed to this on the condition that you would be discreet."

"I was three hours away, John. I can't get much more goddamn discreet."

"Language."

"So how did she get there?"

"A friend of hers drove."

"She snuck off base?"

"More or less," her father said. "Her friend took a pass from his father's office."

"We can't let her do those things, John. She needs discipline."

"Don't talk to me about discipline, Caroline."

"Why talk to you at all? You never listen. You give Julie anything she wants, then blame me when she gets in trouble."

"We're not talking about Julie," the colonel said. "We're talking about you."

Something in her father's voice sent a chill down Julie's spine. Her mother seemed to feel it too.

"What is it?" she asked quietly.

"I think it's time you requested a transfer to another base."

"A transfer?" Julie's mother said. There was a long pause, and when she spoke again, her voice was trembling. "But she's my daughter."

"She's my daughter too."

"Don't you dare," she said, anger flaring, "I've done everything you asked of me, but if you take her away—"

"You'll do nothing," her father said, his anger matching hers. "You'll do this voluntarily, or..."

Her father trailed off. A moment later, Julie heard papers ruffling. "These are your orders," he said calmly.

"California?"

"There's a promotion too. First lieutenant."

"I don't want a promotion," Julie's mother said. "Discharge me."

"Difficult to arrange," her father said. "And it'll draw unwanted attention."

"I don't care," Julie's mother said, raising her voice. "California is too far away."

"There's a good college there, with several DARPA contracts. I can arrange a position there, for you and...him."

"I won't live that far away from my daughter," her mother said firmly. "I'll move to the university and take her on weekends."

"That is not possible," he said. "That contract is already terminated. We can work out something regarding visitation later, but our first job is to minimize the damage."

"John, please don't do this."

"It's done," the colonel said. "Take these and go."

There was a long pause, then a sharp sound, like a slap.

"You're a monster," her mother hissed.

The office door banged open, and someone stomped across the living room. Julie, still at the top of the stairs, retreated into the shadows as her mother appeared. Her mother clutched the banister and pressed her head into the crook of her arm, crying quietly. An inch-thick stack of papers was bent in her grip.

Julie watched, willing with all her might for her mother to look up, to see her, yet afraid to move, to draw attention to herself. Whatever had happened between her parents, it was far more terrible than she could understand.

Her mother put a foot on the staircase to climb it, but changed her mind. She walked out the front door, leaving it open behind her. Her car backed out of the driveway, and its wheels squealed sharply as she turned and drove away.

Her father moved silently to the door and watched the taillights disappear before he closed it.

"Go to bed, Julie," he said without looking at her.

Everything that had anything to do with Julie's mother was gone when Julie returned from school the next day. Her father offered no explanation, and she didn't dare ask.

FOURTEEN

ORTON WORKED THE CHAIN HOIST by hand, lowering Julie into the water-filled diving chamber until the water was up to her neck. He grabbed her helmet—a round metal bubble with three vertical panes of glass as a visor. He bent down to install it but hesitated when he saw Julie's vacant stare.

"If you can see the sub, we can see you," Orton said. "So if you lose audio and you're in trouble, motion like this." He made a chopping motion with his hand.

Julie didn't look at him, lost in her own thoughts.

"Can you hear me?" Orton asked.

Julie finally looked up. She seemed disoriented, but after a moment she nodded. Orton slipped the helmet over her head, and there was a loud *prrrrrt* as he tightened the bolts. She heard the chain rattle as the blue water rose up to engulf her. The rattling grew dull and distant, and the sound of her own breathing filled the helmet, each breath punctuated by the click of the air valve.

She gazed at the smooth, featureless wall of the diving chamber, taking a deep breath and releasing it slowly. The gun Simms had offered triggered memories from which she though herself immune, and being in this suit was making those memories resonate. She felt an urgency bordering on panic, mentally preparing herself for events that had, in reality, run their course long ago.

She focused on each breath, trying to fix her thoughts to the present. One of the most critical aspects of diving was conserving oxygen, and she had to be as relaxed as possible.

Her feet landed on the chamber floor and the rattling stopped. She swept an arm over her head, finding the chain and unhooking it. She held it clear of the suit and gave it a shake. It was pulled up and away.

"You read me?" she asked.

"Five by five," Orton replied. He had moved to a small room near the pool, where he had set up mobile comm station consisting of a radio and a video monitor. The monitor's display was divided to show the feed from three cameras: one pointed at Julie's face, one peering out of her visor—showing what she saw—and one mounted on the submarine's exterior. "Close the hatch," he called to Hiller, who was still beside the pool. Hiller slid the chain hoist aside and swung the hatch down.

Julie grabbed the metal handles on either side of the diving chamber as a deep clang vibrated through the suit. Everything went black, and she heard a squeak overhead as the latch tightened. With a whir, the floor slid open, revealing a circle of hazy water beneath her feet. The water was crystal clear, glowing in the submarine's floods. Her body tingled with something like fear, but far more rarefied. She released the handles and dropped out into the endless ocean.

Julie had forgotten to adjust her buoyancy, so she plunged, the water quickly growing dark, the submarine above her shrinking away.

She flicked her arm frantically, trying to slide the glove forward to get at the suit's controls, but her movements were dulled by the water, and it took several tries. The pistol grip popped into her hand, and she engaged the propulsors on her calves to arrest her descent, but only the left one fired. She cartwheeled over, spiraling out of control as she was driven even deeper.

She cut the throttle and jabbed the autostabilization button. The suit's ballasts filled with a hiss, and she jerked to a halt. She floated upside down, catching her breath.

"I've done better," she muttered.

"Come again?" Orton asked.

"Nothing," Julie said, switching off the radio. She looked up between her feet at the distant columns of light lancing off the bow of the submarine. They were the only feature in her black surroundings, and she had no idea how far she had dropped.

Maybe two hundred feet, she thought. *Not that a few more atmospheres of pressure matter at this depth.*

She ran her fingers over the controls, touching each button and reminding herself what it did. *No more fuckups*, she told herself, pressing the button that enabled the suit's right propulsor, feeling the tingle of its haptic feedback. She double-checked that the left propulsor was still engaged, then switched the suit back to manual control. She bent her knees behind her and, tapping the throttle, rotated until she her head was aimed at the tip of the submarine's floodlights, where she would find the entrance to the cave.

"No more fuckups, Porter," she repeated out loud. She eased down on the throttle.

Cutter and Simms stood on the bridge, watching Julie rise, weaving, out of the dark depths. Cutter wanted to comment, but he couldn't find the words; his slackened jaw twitched with false starts. Captain Sullivan loomed behind them.

"What I think, Sergeant," Simms said, frowning at the video screen, "is that the new lieutenant might need some supervision down at the comm station."

"I think you might be right, sir," Cutter said, stepping to the ladder and sliding down it. He raced across the main room, hand clamped over his mouth to hold back the laughter.

Simms continued to watch Julie. She was halfway to the cave when Captain Sullivan stepped up beside him.

"The colonel is a fool to send her," she said.

"She's the best person for the job," he replied.

"Yeah," Sullivan said. "I can see that."

"I'm just following orders."

"You should be giving them," the captain said. "Anyone can see this isn't going to work."

"Sergeant Porter is out of practice. That doesn't jeopardize the mission."

"The *rescue* mission," Sullivan corrected. "And when she finds out the truth?"

"That's not my problem."

"Oh, I'd say it is. She's a liability—a major one—and the colonel is too wrapped up in his own machinations to see that."

"This mission is important. Critical. He wouldn't take a risk like that."

"And what risk is he taking," Sullivan asked, "sitting back in his office?"

"He would be here if he could."

Something flashed on the screen—Julie's suit glinting in the floodlights.

"The great Colonel Porter," Sullivan said, "who three

times refused generalship so he could 'stay in the fight.' And now that they're no longer asking, his old man's hubris demands an heir to his legacy. But he's wrong to think that's his daughter. He should have given up on her years ago."

"She's talented," Simms said. "I've seen her file."

"Hrmph," Captain Sullivan said. "Did the colonel give you his 'ambassador' speech?"

Simms looked away.

"A neat piece of psychology," she continued. "It keeps you too busy defending something to see that it's wrong."

"This is all very interesting, but—"

"You really think your team is down here because you're the best people for the job?" Sullivan cut in. "We have SEALs, you know? People who are actually trained for this sort of mission."

"But we have that," Simms said, pointing at the deep-water suit on the video screen. "And the reason we do is that because the navy didn't want it."

"We have underwater drones," Sullivan said.

"People are trapped in there, and time is of the essence. The Pentagon called us in because they considered us the best option."

"The Pentagon is just giving an old war horse one last victory lap before they put him out to pasture. His retirement party is already scheduled, whether or not he wants it."

"That doesn't mean we can't handle this mission."

"Suit yourself." Captain Sullivan tapped the screen, which showed Julie easing toward the cave in painfully short spurts. "If that's the best Colonel Porter can do, then I doubt you'll even get inside."

"I've had about enough of this," Simms said, turning to face her. "I'm sorry if you feel that we're stepping on your toes, but keep your bullshit opinions about the colonel to yourself."

"Mind yourself, Lieutenant," the captain snapped. "*I* can say what I like on my own boat."

Simms swallowed back his fury, slowly regaining his self-control.

"It is not my intention to slander the colonel," Sullivan added. "I'm simply trying to help you."

"And how does this help?"

"You don't belong here. This is a navy job. Abort the mission and I'll have a properly equipped, properly trained team here in forty-eight hours."

"And in the meantime?"

"The base is intact and the situation is stable. They didn't even launch the emergency beacon."

"Maybe they couldn't."

"Whatever happened down there, rushing in with your cocks out will only make it worse."

"Your assessment, ma'am. But Colonel Porter disagrees."

"Colonel Porter is a religion with you Deltas, but he's not the man he used to be. Maybe he never was. He's a gifted politician, and he's been around long enough to write his own history."

"I'll note your concern, ma'am," Simms said.

"You do that," Sullivan said, turning back to the screen. Julie had reached the cave and was hovering just outside its mouth. "Are you leaving her on my boat?" she asked.

"My orders are to bring her along," Simms said.

"Hrm," Sullivan said pointedly. "And the hippie?"

"Him too. The colonel thinks he might be useful."

"Well, God bless you," Sullivan said, shaking her head.

Julie gave the propulsor a quick jab, floating into the

cave. She emptied the suit's ballasts and landed gently on her feet. Her training was coming back to her, and she was maneuvering without having to think about it.

The mouth of the cave was a wide, horizontal tear in the cliff's face, devoid of life, plant or otherwise. She stepped deeper inside and saw that the cave angled down, dropping into darkness. She turned on her helmet light, but it didn't even register against the submarine's floodlights. All she could tell was that the cave narrowed fast.

"Everything okay?" Orton asked.

Julie was startled; she had left the radio off, but apparently the corporal could override that. She wondered who else was listening.

"Checking for eels," she said.

"Not this deep," Orton said. "And too far out for giant squid. Three known species of fish: the black swallower, the anglerfish, and the tripod. All harmless."

"Yeah," Julie muttered. "Fascinating."

She pulled a small device from her belt and nestled it between two rocks. It was a relay, to extend the range of her radio and video transmissions; radio waves could barely penetrate water, much less rock. She pointed its tiny antenna at the submarine, then plugged in a microthin wire that was spooled up on her belt, no thicker than fishing line.

"Copy?" she asked.

"Solid copy," came the reply. It was Hiller this time.

Julie walked down the slope until she was out of the submarine's sight. There she leaned forward and adjusted her balance until she was floating horizontally. She pressed lightly on the throttle, then, growing more confident, slowly accelerated, the wire unspooling behind her.

Hiller sat beside Orton at the comm station, watching the feed from Julie's helmet. She had stopped at a shallow point in the cave and was measuring it by stacking her hands.

"Dead end," Orton said.

"Not for her," Eric said, standing a few feet behind them. He had come uninvited to watch Julie's progress.

"That's only like sixteen inches tall," Orton protested.

"Twenty-two," Eric said. "See her hands?"

"Still," Orton replied. "Too tight."

"Are you a gambler, Corporal?"

Orton held his hands like Julie's and inspected them.

"Why not?" he said, pulling a bill from his shirt pocket, folded and ready. "Twenty?"

The video onscreen shook violently, and the image was reduced to large blocks of color. Orton pounded the edge of the monitor, then slid off his chair and under the table, checking the connections. He found nothing wrong, and a few seconds later the image resolved itself. Julie's air tank floated in the empty water, its disconnected hoses curling off it like snakes.

Eric leaned into the monitor, searching for any sign of Julie. Orton pushed him gently out of the way and returned to his seat.

Julie's hand appeared at the edge of the screen, grabbing the hoses and reattaching them to her neck. She shoved the air tank forward, through the gap, then started after it. The suit was too thick, catching at the top and bottom, so she drew back and slammed herself forward. Chunks of rock broke off the walls and dribbled past her visor.

"Shiest!" Orton said as Julie slammed forward again, filling the water with milky silt. The silk cleared as she pushed into the gap, coming out the far side and racing onward. "Hard core," Orton said.

Eric leaned back against a crate, unclenching his fists and jaw.

"What are you so worried about, Fritz?" Cutter asked, appearing at the doorway. "Don't you know that Sergeant Porter can handle anything?"

Eric stood up as Cutter approached. The sergeant walked right toward him, pressing his chest against Eric's. Eric stood his ground for a moment, then threw his hands into the air.

"Fine," he said, circling around Cutter and leaving the room.

"Nazi hippie," Cutter said. "We really should have given Germany to the Russians." He turned to Hiller. "You got that squawk box figured? Orton needs to prep Wolf's Atargis, on the slim chance Junior Porter gets inside."

"You think she will?" Orton asked.

Cutter cocked his head, eyes drawn to something beside Orton. He leaned over the corporal, straddling him with his arms, and rested his hands on the table.

"I do," he said with great sincerity. "I really do. So much so that I'll give you twenty bucks if she doesn't." Cutter straightened up, holding Orton's twenty in his hand. "Now go prep Wolf," he said, tucking the bill into his pocket.

"Yes, Sergeant," Orton said, knowing better than to protest. "Sir," he said, saluting Hiller. Hiller saluted back and Orton left.

"Second Lieutenant," Cutter said, giving a half-hearted salute as he dropped into the vacant seat. Then he jerked upright, his eyes bugging out at the monitor. "Now what the hell is she doing?" he asked.

FIFTEEN

THE MOST NOTICEABLE CHANGE in Julie's life was that instead of having dull dinners at home with her mom, she was now having even duller dinners at the officer's club with her dad. Like her mom, her dad usually worked through dinner, his nose buried in paperwork. He rarely spoke to her, and sometimes he left to converse with other officers. But she didn't mind either of those as much as when he invited other officers to join them, to engage in banter so boring that Julie could feel her brain shrivel. On such occasions, her dad instructed her to smile and to give the appearance of an earnest listener. *Most importantly*, he told her, *you must always seem enthusiastic about your future in the army. You do not want to ask for help*, he said. *You want people to ask to give it.*

Tonight her father was especially concerned with her behavior, because they were dining with some bigwig from the Pentagon. He was an air force general supervising the development advanced military technology, which, her father told her, was the future of soldiering. Her father had even bought Julie a dress and had a seamstress come to the house to tailor it. This general, he told her, could have a very positive effect on her future.

The general was maybe half her father's age, but when he

arrived at the club, her father popped out of his chair to salute him. It was the first time Julie had met someone whom her father considered more important than himself, and someone who treated her father with the same disregard that he did with others. The general didn't salute back, and he interrupted her father's overtures to ask about dinner.

Her dad had booked a private booth, where he pitched his idea of a new military unit—small but elite—to test the vanguard of military technology right in the field. The general nodded and grunted, often through a full mouth, and he made Julie's father repeat his questions several times before he bothered to answer. It was only after he had finished eating, leaving his expensive steak in tatters, that he seemed to acknowledge her father at all.

"It's not that I don't agree with you," the general said, leaning back and interlocking his short, thick fingers over his expansive belly, "but the Atargis is a navy project."

"I hear they've cut it out of next year's budget," her father replied.

"They extended it another two years, but they no longer anticipate much use for it."

"All the more reason you should give it to the army."

"To you, you mean," the general said.

"You've spent $5 billion, and haven't even got a prototype," Julie's father said. "That's a black mark for you. But give it to me and I'll see it through to live testing. I'll make it look like money well spent."

"It's a diving suit," the general said. "A little outside the army's purview."

"It's an armored suit for a soldier. Nothing could be more army than that."

Their private booth was at the far end of the dining room, with a wall extending out to block them from view. The two men sat opposite each other, with Julie in the middle. The general turned to her.

"What do you think of all this, little girl?" the general asked, pushing his plate back and trimming a cigar.

"I think this suit sounds amazing," Julie said. "I want to try it."

"And how long until you're old enough to enlist?"

"I'm fifteen, sir," Julie said.

"Almost sixteen," her father added.

"Almost sixteen," the general said, glancing at the colonel, but keeping his attention on Julie. "And you'll go to West Point?"

"No, sir," Julie said. "I want to follow in my father's footsteps. To be a soldier before I'm an officer."

"Very noble," the general said, patronizingly.

"Besides," Julie added mischievously, "my father says I'm not ready to swim with any sharks."

"Does he now?" the general asked, laughing.

"Julie," her father said sternly.

"It's quite all right, John," the general said. "From the mouths of babes." The general patted Julie's knee as he spoke, and left his hand resting on it.

"I'm sending her to cadet camp this summer," her father said, "and hope to send her to North Ridge in the fall."

"North Ridge?" the general said, eyeing Julie with appreciation. "I'm sending my own daughter there. I'm on the academy's board, you know." This he emphasized by squeezing Julie's knee. Julie felt sudden alarm. She looked to her father, and he gave her a knowing nod. He slipped his phone out, looked at it, and frowned.

"If you'll pardon me, Carl, I have to take this."

The general nodded and Julie's father walked off, talking

into his phone. The general turned his body toward Julie and smiled, his small, thick hand kneading her leg.

The general talked for some length, but the words didn't register. Julie nodded frequently—not trusting herself to speak—and tried to maintain a steady smile as the general's hand worked its way up the inside of her thigh. Looking around, her eyes locked on the steak knife beside her dinner plate. Its blade was pinkish with juice and speckled with white globs of fat.

"And do you think you'd like to work at the Pentagon one day?" the general asked, shifting his hips back as he fiddled with his belt buckle.

"I don't know much about it," Julie said evenly, her teeth clenched in a wide, unnatural smile. She swept her fingers through her hair, the way she had seen some women do, as she slipped her other hand over the steak knife.

Julie knew a lot about knives—unlike guns, she was allowed to handle them without supervision—so she knew this one wasn't much of a weapon. The handle was too small, and the blade made from thin, cheap steel. But she only intended to use it as a threat. *This is a test*, she decided, *to see if I can handle myself.* It wouldn't be the first.

She kept her eyes on the general, still smiling, deathly afraid he would notice her easing the knife off the table.

"The most important thing about working at the Pentagon," the general said, leaning so close that his hot breath was panting down the front of her dress, "is knowing how to keep a secret."

The general was grimacing now, and one hand was moving vigorously inside his pants. The other hand, already on Julie's leg, rose suddenly to her groin. A shock ran through her body, as if she had touched a wall socket, and, without thinking, she stabbed him.

Julie put too much force into it; the knife punched through the general's hand and drove an inch into her own thigh.

The general hopped to his feet, howling with pain. Julie's leg, attached to the general's hand, came up with him. She tumbled back, knocking over the table as the general's pants fell to his ankles. He pulled the hand from his underwear and pressed it to Julie's leg, trying to free himself. But the knife was stuck; it sliced though his hand from the middle of the palm to the edge of the knuckle.

The ruckus drew a pair of waiters, whose concern turned instantly to horror. The general yanked the knife out just as Julie's father appeared.

"I...," the general said, shoving his injured hand into his jacket pocket. "She's hurt herself." He motioned to Julie, then scurried for the bathroom.

Julie's father took in the scene, a shade of disappointment on his face. But when he saw the blood on Julie's dress, he quickly grabbed a clean napkin off a nearby table and pressed it to her wound.

"Hold that tight," her father said, replacing his hand with Julie's and checking her over. "Anywhere else?"

Julie shook her head. He father looked her over a second time, then laughed with relief. He hugged her to him.

"I did okay?" Julie asked weakly.

"Very much so, daughter. Dear daughter. I'm very proud of you."

"I didn't mean to hurt him."

"That wasn't my plan, either," her father said, "but I can work with it. This little incident will be difficult to cover up, for which the general will owe me—owe us—a big favor. What is it?"

Julie was crying.

"Why?" she asked.

Her father sat beside her and wrapped an arm over her shoulders.

"Because we need things. You need things. While I am respected, the general has influence. Not the least of which is that he's on the board at North Ridge academy. North Ridge is attended by all of the top officers' children, and the connections you make there will serve your entire career. It is *very* exclusive, but you have, quite literally, cut through the red tape."

The colonel smiled at his own joke, then turned serious again.

"Someday you will see how critical this sort of influence is, Jules. You will face challenges like this one your entire life, and not just because you're a woman. In the army, it isn't enough to just be a good soldier. Being a good soldier won't replace obsolete equipment or get you air support when you're pinned down. It's life and death out on the battlefield, and who you know—and who owes you—will make all the difference. For you and your men."

Julie nodded, though she didn't understand.

"Having a general in your pocket is power, Jules," he continued. "Enjoy it. You've earned it."

"I did?" she asked.

"Very much so, daughter," the colonel said with a warm smile. "Now run on home and bandage yourself while I finish with the general."

SIXTEEN

Julie raced through the cave at full throttle. She had a handful of glow sticks, which she tossed over her shoulder at regular intervals, leaving a floating trail. Her air tank—clipped to her waist—banged against the suit as she moved through the water. Her oxygen gauge read 130, which gave her about fifteen minutes before she'd have to turn back. She pressed harder on the throttle, trying to eke out more speed.

The cave curved sharply, but Julie kept the throttle down. She banked at the last minute, grabbing the wall as she slammed into it, throwing herself in the direction of the turn. She giggled loudly—she had lost contact with the submarine ten minutes earlier and so was free to enjoy herself. She had also turned so many times that she'd lost all sense of direction, but so far there had only been one way to go.

She sped around another corner, and the cave came suddenly to a dead end. She flipped over, aiming the calf-mounted propulsors in front of her. The propulsors howled, fighting to slow her down. Her boots hit the wall so hard her teeth rattled, but this too made her laugh. She shoved back from the wall and used her ballasts to straighten up and bring her feet to the ground. She walked back up the cave, searching for a way forward.

A few paces back she found a small passage just above the floor. Since it was impossible to bend the waist of the giant metal suit, she rose up, tilted herself horizontally, then lowered down to the ground to peer inside. The narrow passage ran straight for maybe forty feet before curving out of sight. It was tight, but as far as she could tell, there were no obstructions. She unclipped her oxygen tank and, holding it in front, drove in.

She moved slowly now, the suit's shoulders and arms scraping against the rough walls. When she reached the bend, she rolled onto her side and bent as much as the suit would allow. It took some maneuvering, but she squeezed through. The passage continued another twenty feet, then turned again.

The second turn was tighter than the first, and halfway through she jerked to a stop with a loud crunch. The suit was wedged between the walls.

She pressed the throttle and the suit slid forward, the rock scraping across the metal, but after a few inches, it again stopped. She pushed the throttle harder, bringing it all the way to full, but the suit didn't move. With a sigh, she threw the throttle into reverse, but she *still* didn't move. She was stuck.

The suit was too bulky to see around, so she snaked her arm down to her waist and felt around the walls with her thick metal gloves. As best as she could tell, she was caught just below the hips—meaning she was more than halfway through—so she decided to push ahead. Besides, even if she did back all the way to the main cave, she'd still have to find a way forward.

She wormed her arm back to the front, grabbed the walls, and pulled. At first, she thought she was moving but then realized she was only stretching the suit's rubber seals. She looked around for more options, but didn't see any. Then she thought of a trick Eric had taught her.

She closed her eyes and counted to twenty, to clear her mind, to make room for new ideas. She counted slowly at first, about once a second, but then sped up impatiently.

"Twenty," she said, opening her eyes expectantly. Everything looked the same as before.

"Buddhist crap," she said.

She pulled hard on the walls again, feeling the suit's seals stretch along her torso, and tried not to think about what would happen if one of them tore.

Leaving the comm station, Eric had returned to the bridge, the only other place on the submarine where he could watch the feed from Julie's helmet. Captain Sullivan gave him a cold reception, but she seemed preoccupied with Lieutenant Simms. Simms was sitting with his feet on the last-available chair. He lifted his feet when Eric arrived, but only to readjust them. Eric retreated to the corner and tried to be invisible.

The mood on the bridge darkened even further when Julie cut the line to her comm. When she reached the end of the spool of comm wire, she had given the camera a quick thumbs-up as she jerked it from its socket. Simms had yelled at the monitor, but the signal was already gone. The captain had a smug look on her face, obviously having won an argument.

With Julie's feed dead, the pilot switched the screen back to the submarine's exterior. The view was as still as an empty aquarium, and there was nothing but a dull hiss from Julie's audio feed. The hiss seemed to grow louder over the next ten minutes.

"If you're going to pace," Captain Sullivan said, "please do so downstairs."

Eric hadn't realized that he was. He retreated to the

corner, but Simms made a brushing motion, directing him to the ladder, his other hand shifting to the butt of his pistol.

"Go ahead," Sullivan said to Eric. "I'll let you know when we hear from her."

Eric climbed reluctantly down. When he was gone, the captain turned to Simms.

"How much longer do we wait?" she asked.

"Are you in a hurry?"

"I suppose not," Sullivan said. "But do you honestly think she still has a chance?"

"I don't know," Simms said. "She was handling the suit okay, even if she was a little, I don't know..."

"Reckless?"

"Suicidal."

"After what the colonel did to her," Sullivan said, "I can't say I'm surprised."

"And what did he do to her?"

"Not my place to say," Sullivan said, "but I wouldn't forgive him, either."

The main room was lit in dim red, an aspect of high alert that struck Eric as more dramatic than practical. He circled the room, dragging his hand along the wall. He was worried about Julie, and also worried what Caroline—his wife and Julie's mother—would say about him letting their daughter get dragged into this.

Their daughter, Eric thought. Julie wasn't his, not biologically, but how else could he describe her if not as his daughter.

When they had first started dating, back in North Carolina, Caroline was still married to the colonel. She told Eric the marriage was nothing more than a business arrangement, that her pregnancy with Julie would have cost her career were it not for the colonel's position and influence. Eric had found that difficult to trust, but he loved Caroline and so took her husband and daughter as part of the package.

Unfortunately, something went wrong with the arrangement and Caroline was shipped off to California. The colonel made generous accommodations—Caroline was promoted to captain, and Eric was enticed to join her. He was offered a tenured position at Berkeley University, where his research budget was tripled.

But the price for all this had been Julie. The colonel took full custody, cutting Caroline off completely. Caroline tried to fight it, but the colonel was just too powerful. The loss took a heavy toll. Caroline pined for her absent daughter, praying nightly for her return. This went on for nearly a decade, until, three years ago, Julie appeared on their doorstep.

She arrived in the middle of the night, looking like something out of Dante. Her hair was spiked black, a cigarette drooped from her mouth, and one eye was swollen shut by a yellow-green bruise.

The colonel demanded that Julie return to the base, and even sent soldiers to collect her, but Julie was too old for custody now, and Caroline, no longer in the army, had become an influential woman—an esteemed member of the Berkeley town council and heir apparent to the mayor's office. She batted aside the colonel's demands, and Julie moved in permanently. This was both the most upsetting and the most fulfilling thing to happen in Eric's life.

His first encounter with adult Julie—drunk and leaning on his doorbell—gave Eric little cause for optimism. And nothing about their first weeks living together changed that.

Julie was a screaming, foulmouthed, hotheaded young woman who burst into a fit at the drop of a hat. Eric tried his best to maintain his calm—he could only imagine what horrors the woman had endured—but he simply wasn't strong enough. Julie threw things, broke things, and put her fists through walls. When she went out at night, it was invariably to drink and fight, ending, more often than not, with him retrieving her from jail. The worst, however, was just when Eric felt that he couldn't take any more, she broke down, begging for forgiveness.

Caroline also begged for forgiveness, and for patience; she blamed herself for Julie's condition, which Eric found absurd. But he kept trying and somehow stuck with it long enough to grow fond of her. Julie was a surging geyser of frantic, irrational emotion—as opposite from Eric as anyone he had ever met—and so no one was more surprised to discover, one day, that he loved her like his own child.

Eric was an avid outdoorsman, and they had their first connection when he took her rock climbing. She took to it immediately, at first simply infuriated that he was better at it, but soon genuinely enjoying herself. She immersed herself in the sport like it was rehab.

Already fit, Julie trained obsessively, transforming into something Olympian. Though she still had dark moments, it appeared that her edge had finally dulled. But now, back with her old unit, playing with her old weapons of war, Eric feared that the old Julie was resurfacing.

Disconnecting the video signal was her way of showing off, which was something she'd been doing from the moment the army had turned up in Mexico that morning. And she was only getting more reckless. Though Eric couldn't think how he might have possibly stopped her—from getting on this submarine or from going out there—he couldn't shake the feeling that it was all his fault.

There is no logic to it, Eric thought, dropping into a seat, *but you always feel guilty when someone you love is in danger.*

He pressed his fingers to his temples, accidentally knocking a folder off the armrest. He bent to pick it up and saw it was labeled *TOP SECRET*. This was the folder Simms had been reading on the journey here.

Eric inspected the folder, fooling himself that he was weighing his options. Then he untied the flap, pulling out a report titled *INITIAL EVALUATION OF THE BIOLOGICAL SPECIMEN RECOVERED FROM THE MID-ATLANTIC BASE*.

He started to read.

The suit's rubber seals made a sucking sound as the glue separated from the metal ribs, and just when Julie was certain she wouldn't pull free of the rock, she did. She shot forward, her helmet ramming into her floating air tank, producing a clang that speared her eardrums. Tendrils of brown silt swirled off the ground as she flopped down, her head spinning.

The suit's buoyancy had been thrown out of whack, and it took Julie several tries to get herself right-side up and level. She heard a faint hiss, but, feeling around the suit as best she could, she couldn't find anything wrong.

"Okay, then," she said, grabbing the air tank and continuing on. The passage widened as she came to another corner, and, rounding it, she saw light up ahead.

She killed her headlamp and the suit's propulsors, letting her momentum carry her quietly forward. She tried to remember whether Simms had said that the base's power was out or just that it *might* be. As she drew closer to the light, she saw it was nothing more than a glow stick. They were strung out in an adjoining passage. She had circled back to her own trail.

"Crap!" she yelled, slapping at the water.

The oxygen gauge on her wrist read 87, which was just below half. Irritated, she clipped the tank back onto her waist, turned down the wide cave, and headed back to the submarine.

She had the suit's throttle at full, but the batteries were running low, and she was moving markedly slower. Her oxygen dropped steadily, fast enough that she decided to radio ahead—as soon as she reached the transmission wire—to have Wolf meet her with a fresh tank. Maybe she'd give him a shot at looking around too. She'd been up and down this cave, with no sign of this supposed hatch. And it wasn't like Simms would take her word that it wasn't there.

Five minutes later—just as her oxygen hit 45—she rounded a corner to a dead end.

"What the...?" she said, releasing the throttle. She was too stunned to react as she thudded against the end of the passage. She looked at the trail of glow sticks behind her, then up at the narrow passage she had taken last time she was here, just below the ceiling.

Why is it up there? she wondered. She tapped the valve on her neck, releasing a short stream of bubbles. They floated down, pooling on the floor.

Fuck, she thought. *I'm upside down.*

Hiller sat at the comm station, attentively watching as static danced on the video screen in front of him. His finger rested on the Transmit button, and he pressed it at fifteen-second intervals.

"Porter, this is Explorer, come back," he said flatly, then waited for a reply. Cutter, sitting beside him, drummed his fingers. He winced when Hiller spoke.

"Porter, this is Explor—"

"So you went to West Point?" Cutter interrupted.

"Yes, Sergeant," Hiller said, eyes trained on the static. He was about to press the Transmit button again, but Cutter cut him off.

"The long gray line?" he asked.

"Yes, Sergeant."

"You don't have to call me sergeant," Cutter said.

"What should I call you?"

"Um...Sarge?"

"Yes, Sarge."

"Yeah, that doesn't sound much better."

"No, Sarge," Hiller said, then, into the mic, "Porter, this is Explor—"

"Stop!" Cutter yelled, jerking Hiller's hand off the button.

"Sarge?"

"She'll call in," Cutter said. "Trust me."

"Yes, Sarge." Hiller fell silent, eyes on the screen. Cutter started to drum his fingers again. The minutes passed like hours.

"Sarge?" Hiller asked, breaking the silence.

"Yeah?"

"You've been in this unit longer than anyone, right?"

"So?"

"So you knew Sergeant Porter back before she was..."

"Angry?"

"Yes."

"So?"

"So what was she like?" Hiller asked.

"Shorter."

"She must have been something, though. I heard she made staff sergeant by the time she was nineteen."

"That don't count," Cutter said. "That was just Neppo... Neppotastic... Neppotestostero—it was because of her father," he blurted finally.

"But still," Hiller pressed, "she must have been—"

"Spoiled?"

Hiller bit his lip, nodded.

"So why *did* she leave?" he asked.

"You know what?" Cutter said. "I've got some really important thinking to do right now, so let's just you and me keep quiet." Cutter tossed his feet onto a crate and leaned his head back, closing his eyes.

Hiller gazed at the sergeant.

"Her loss, huh?" he asked.

"You better believe it," Cutter said.

Hiller turned back to the screen, growing anxious as the minutes passed. He peered at Cutter; he appeared to be sleeping. His finger crept to the Transmit button and pressed it gently.

"Porter," he whispered, "this is Explorer, come ba—"

"Goddamn it!" Cutter yelled, grabbing the lieutenant's hand in a crushing grip.

"Sergeant?" Orton said, appearing in the doorway.

"What?!" Cutter barked, wheeling toward him.

"I need the other valve adapter," Orton said. Then, to Cutter's blank stare, "For the rebreather."

"Oh," Cutter said. "It's in my duffel. In the front room."

Orton turned to leave.

"Wait," Cutter said, releasing Hiller's hand. "I'll get it. You stay here."

Julie turned around and pressed the throttle to full, heading back toward the submarine. She kicked her legs to go faster but only wasted energy fighting the suit's thick shell. The oxygen gauge on her wrist flickered red, fluctuating between 20 and 21. Beside it, the *battery low* indicator glowed steadily.

Against her instincts, she lowered the throttle to one-third, moving slower to stretch out what was left of the batteries. She might be low on oxygen, but it would go a lot faster if she had to walk.

She looked from the oxygen gauge to the battery light, knowing that it wasn't going to add up, that it wouldn't even be close. She switched off her headlamp to save a little power and followed the trail of glow sticks through the dark.

A minute later, her propulsors started to sputter. Julie tweaked the throttle, then switched off the left propulsor, centering her body in front of her right leg. It was precarious, like balancing on a log in water, and she soon lost control. She clipped the ceiling, flipping head over heels and crashing into the wall. She got to her feet, so light-headed that she had to work just to balance herself. She leaned forward and pressed on the throttle, but the propulsors barely turned. She started walking.

She drew deep, unsatisfying breaths, the dirty air burning her lungs. The glow sticks had seemed tightly spaced before, but it took an eternity to reach the next one. She counted at least ten more ahead, fading into the darkness. But she kept walking. There was nothing else to do.

Her foot caught on a rock and she stumbled. She grabbed the wall to keep from falling and switched on her helmet light, which was so dim that she could barely see her own hands. *The glow stick*, she thought, walking back to grab it, but as she approached, there seemed to be two of them floating in the water. She shook her head, trying to resolve them, but they remained separate. She looked from the lower one to the upper one and was surprised to see her own face staring down at her, reflected by a shimmering pocket of air.

She stepped back until she could see both walls at once, and held perfectly still.

She felt herself slouching over as the glow stick pulsed and grew fuzzy. She straightened up and blinked, clearing them just in time to see a tiny bubble bounce up the wall and disappear into the air pocket. She traced back along the bubble's path and found a crack in the rock wall. She pressed her visor to it, and her headlamp reflected off a thousand pearls of air clinging inside. Beyond them, at the very limit of the light, was a hint of red paint. She had found the hatch.

She took the block of explosive from its pouch, tearing off hunks and pressing them into the crack. She meant to use half the block—an appropriate level of overkill—but soon found herself shoving in the last piece.

Too late now, she decided, stabbing a meat thermometer–shaped igniter into the explosive putty, which was so thick it looked like she was trying to patch the wall. She pressed the button on top of the igniter twice, setting the timer to thirty seconds, then decided to add another fifteen. That done, she held the button down until the numbers started to drop, then turned and ran. Shoving the heavy suit through the water, she didn't get very far.

The explosion shook the cave, throwing Julie forward and pelting her with fist-sized rocks. She clamped her hands to her helmet, a vain attempt to protect her ears from the deafening shock wave. She slammed against the far wall, scratching deep grooves across her visor, then she fell onto her back. A cloud of dust enveloped her, darkening the water as she lost consciousness.

Julie woke to the sound of her own labored breath. She was floating in the middle of the dim cave, her carbon dioxide–poisoned body jerking and twitching involuntarily. Her skin was sticky with sweat and her head felt hollow. She curled up as much as the suit would allow, heaving dryly.

She forced in deep breaths of air, relaxing her stomach, then found the suit's controls and lifted herself onto her feet. As she tilted upright, yellowish globs slid down the inside of her visor, cutting streaks through the frost. Between the frost on the inside and the scratches on the outside, it was difficult to see.

The cave was dimly lit by the red glow of the suit's warning lights, and also by the remains of the glow stick, which were smeared on the wall behind her like an absurdist painting. In front of her, the explosives had made a hole large enough to walk through, exposing the steel wall behind it.

The wall was dented and crinkled from the explosion, its oval hatch crimped in along one edge. Most of the red paint had been blasted off; chips of it floated in the water like snow in a globe.

She walked unsteadily across the rubble and slumped against the metal wall for support. There was a small panel beside the hatch. She unclasped the lid and saw a soot-covered keypad inside. She waved her hand, clearing it, but she continued to wave, forgetting why she had started. She watched her hand move back and forth.

"Wake up, stupid!" she yelled, pounding a fist into the wall and sending a deep gong through the water. She reached for the codebook, but the pouch—the same one that had held the explosives—was empty.

She bent down and started to dig through the rubble, but there was too much of it. She straightened back up and, steadying her hand, keyed in *864-3*. After a moment, she added an *8*.

There were more numbers, a lot more. She searched her memory as she stared at the keypad, worms dancing across her eyes. She bent over, eyelids drooping.

She jerked back up, then turned and dropped to her knees, digging frantically through the fresh pile of stones, searching for the codebook. After a moment, she changed her mind again, pulling herself back up to the keypad. She added *31* to what was already there and jabbed the enter button. The screen blinked *INCOR*.

Two, Julie suddenly remembered, the codebook appearing in her mind's eye. She quickly punched it in: *864-382-1*.

"INCOR"

"It is two!" she yelled, slapping the keypad, filling the screen with numbers. Calming herself, she cleared the screen and tried the code again, pressing each number carefully. It still didn't work.

What if he gave me the wrong codebook? she thought.

She punched keys frantically, first switching the numbers around, then picking them at random. Again and again she tried, codes streaming from her subconscious. None worked. Her legs buckled. She dropped to her knees, then onto her back. Her head rolled to the side and she stared at the long trail of glow sticks that led back to the submarine.

"January 17th at 14:00R," Eric read, "engineers in the

Azores Drone Base responded to multiple self-diagnosed problems reported by the automated equipment. The initial error was received from the boring machine, which halted with an unknown code. Within minutes, the support machinery had also failed. Unable to raise the video feed, Operations dispatched a team to investigate onsite. They found extensive damage to the equipment and reported that, while acknowledging the great improbability of such an occurrence, it could have only been the result of intentional sabotage.

"Operations requested additional information, but received no further contact from the onsite team, and they did not return. A second team was dispatched, and also disappeared without trace. Minutes later, communication was lost with the base itself.

"The Navy Explorer Mark I was dispatched with all haste, arriving at 20:30R. It reported that the base's main airlock was inoperable. The Explorer, still in the early testing phase, isn't equipped for external operations at that depth and also had no way to attempt at forced entry. The crew made several attempts to hail the base, from locations near the drone base, the operations room, and the old dock. They broadcast on UQC, Low, and Ultra-Low radio frequencies, but they received no response. Surveying the area, they discovered the base's diving bell, which had been severely damaged, and, by all appearances, rendered inoperable.

"At 01:30R on January 18th, the Explorer discovered one additional irregularity: an unidentified specimen, which they collected by ROV and sent to the surface by capsule. The capsule was retrieved by support personnel from the nearby island of Pico and was delivered by priority aircraft to the NYC facility for analysis. A preliminary assessment of the specimen is detailed in the attached report."

Eric turned the page to a large photograph, but before he could see what it was, a shadow fell across the report.

"You finding that interesting, perffessor?" Cutter asked from the doorway.

Julie lay still, not bothering to struggle. *This is a dumb way to die*, she decided. Not that she had a choice in the matter. Or that she even expected to care in a few minutes. But right now, it was really pissing her off. Rather than the peace and acceptance she had been told to expect, all she could think about was how stupid she felt.

With monumental effort, she raised her wrist and looked at the oxygen gauge, but it was too dim and fuzzy to read. Then she remembered her flashlight. Fumbling with her thick gloves, she pulled the small light from her belt and twisted it on. The gauge said 11. She lay back and groaned. Her oxygen had dropped so quickly before, when it mattered, but now, in the endgame, it was taking an eternity.

Maybe I should stand up, she thought. *Jog in place.*

The idea made her laugh, and she twirled the flashlight around, its light glittering off the floating flakes of red paint. The flakes hung in the water, slowly rising toward the ceiling.

She pushed up to a seated position, her muscles feeling like she had run back-to-back triathlons. Her movement stirred the flakes, and she waved her arms through them. She scooped up a large flake and shooed it into the air. But it wasn't paint, she realized. It was the codebook. She grabbed at it, but it shot out of her closing fist.

She extended a hand, palm up, and eased it beneath the codebook, concentrating so hard it made her ears ring. When her hand reached the codebook, she trapped it with a single finger, then flipped it open.

"Son of a..." she said. She had remembered the code correctly, except she had had forgot the first two digits.

She shoved painfully to her knees, gripping the keypad housing and pulling herself up. She typed *91-864-382-1*.

There was a whir followed by a thunk, but nothing moved. She dug her fingers into the hatch's thick rubber seal and pulled. It swung open, and she flopped inside.

She was in a narrow passage of white-painted steel, crowded with pipes. She grabbed one of the pipes and tried to pull herself up to her feet, but she was too weak.

"Duh," she said, flipping out her glove and raising the suit's buoyancy until she was standing upright. She pulled the hatch shut behind her and pressed the large red button beside it, hearing the latch slide into place. She pulled herself along the pipes, barely walking, and arrived at a hallway. The hallway led in both directions and, having no idea which way led to the dock, she took a right.

Her buoyancy was set too high, and every step sent her bounding through the water. *Like being on the moon*, she thought, pushing herself higher, giggling as she bounded along.

She landed on the edge of her boot, lost her balance, and the heavy suit tipped over. She dropped gently on the floor, laughing so hard her chest hurt. She gasped frantically for air, but still couldn't stop laughing. She rolled onto her back, cackling, drawing pictures on the ceiling with her flashlight. But then the flashlight faded.

She turned the flashlight toward her. The bulb was still burning; the change was the water itself, which was growing brighter. There was another light in the hallway, just around the bend.

It's beautiful, she thought, *like a blue sunrise*. But then she saw a circle of light on the wall, moving back and forth. There was someone in here, and they were heading her way.

Julie twisted off the flashlight and shoved to her feet, backing away. After a few steps, something slapped against her back.

She whirled around, raising the tiny flashlight like a weapon, but it was only a lever jutting out from the wall. The lever was for the emergency water flush system, which was exactly what she had been sent in here to find. The protective glass was broken away and the system was already primed. All she had to do was raise the lever. She planted her feet and pressed up on it, but couldn't get it to move.

The room grew brighter and the light appeared around the corner, a blazing blue ring, searching from side to side, moving right toward her. She jammed her shoulder under the lever, clamped it there with her hand, and hit the emergency ascent button on her suit's control panel. A charge fired in the suit, vacating all its ballasts instantly. The light swung in her direction, blinding her, but then, with a loud snap, the lever slid up.

Air boiled up through the steel grating on the floor, clouding the water and roaring in her ears. She was slammed up against the ceiling and then fell back, bobbing on the surface of the rapidly draining water.

A high-pitched buzz rose above the roar of the bubbles, like the sound of an outboard motor at full speed. The blue light raced toward her, just below the surface.

Julie rolled to the side, but it shifted, too, slamming into her visor with a terrible crunch. She was thrown back, clanging against the wall as the shadow of a man passed beneath her, a blur in the bubbling white water. The dark blur disappeared down the hall as the water drained away, depositing Julie, comatose, on the floor.

SEVENTEEN

"I was just...," Eric trailed off, unable to invent an excuse for the top secret report in his hand.

"Just nosing around," Cutter offered. He drew his sidearm as he advanced on Eric, setting it on a chair. He tightened his fists, knuckles cracking. "Did you happen to notice that stamp on the cover?" he asked. "The one that says *Classified*?"

"I...," Eric stuttered, stumbling back against the wall. Cutter towered over him, smiling perversely.

"I have orders to keep that file a secret," Cutter said, clamping a thick hand on Eric's jaw and cocking his fist. "That no living soul is to read it."

"Cutter," Simms called, sliding down the ladder from the bridge. He hesitated, noticing Eric.

"He was reading the file," Cutter explained.

"I see," Simms said, frowning. "We'll deal with him later. The air tanks just blew in the gangway. Looks like she got in."

Eric collapsed with relief, dropping into a nearby seat. He forgot about the report until it was yanked from his hands.

"We'll discuss this," Cutter said, stashing the envelope under his arm. He retrieved his pistol as he followed Simms toward the back of the submarine.

The Navy Explorer eased toward the docks, then turned to present its side hatch to the enclosed gangway. The gangway, filled with air, had risen up and leveled out.

The hatch at the bottom of the submarine opened, and a larger, better-preserved Atargis diving suit dropped into the water, steering expertly toward the dome. Wolf's face peered through the visor, inspected the gangway as he traversed its length. He landed beside the dome and turned a crank, angling the gangway to point at the submarine's side hatch. Next he drove to the tip of the gangway, cranking a wheel to extend the docking skirt, whose foot-thick rubber seal molded around the submarine's hull, pulled into place by powerful magnets.

Wolf circled the skirt, checking the seal, then stepped off into the water. He let himself sink below the submarine, then drove back in through the bottom hatch.

Half of D-5 was grouped at the airlock inside the submarine's side hatch, wearing black-scaled armor and kevlar helmets. They were all armed with a compact version of the M4 carbine except for Serio, who carried the larger AR-15, and Petty, who had a light rifle slung over his back and a hefty medical kit in his hands. Besides their size, they were practically indistinguishable beyond the names stenciled on their backs. Simms was at the head of the group, next to the hatch.

"Still nothing?" he asked, speaking into a thin microphone built in his helmet. Up on the bridge, the helmsman tried to raise Julie one last time, then confirmed that she didn't respond.

"Okay," Simms said. "Open the door."

The light above the hatch went from green to red. There was a deep clunk, and the hatch slid open, dumping five hundred gallons of seawater on the soldiers' legs. A few feet beyond the submarine's hatch was the one that led into the gangway. Simms stepped up to it, lifted his helmet, and pressed his ear to the metal. He listened for a full minute, then extended an arm to Cutter, who handed him a foot-long wrench.

Simms banged the wrench against the hatch, and the metal rang sharply; the other side was dry. He returned the wrench, which Cutter used to turn a valve in the center of the hatch. Air hissed as the pressure equalized between the submarine and the gangway. Cutter tightened the valve again and the men moved into position. Cutter pressed down on the hatch's long metal handle; it resisted at first but swung down when he put his full weight on it. The inner seals crackled as the door swung inward. The other side was pitch black.

Simms shined a light into the gap between the hinges, checking behind the door, then motioned to Cutter, who leaned in and clipped a floodlight over of the doorway. Pale light filled the empty gangway, sparkling off several inches of water that covered the floor. Gun forward, Simms stepped over the threshold and led the men inside.

They took shallow steps, keeping their feet below the water so as not to splash. They flattened to the inside wall as they approached the bend. Simms peered around it and saw Julie lying face up, motionless.

Simms continued forward in measured steps, giving Julie no more than a quick glance as he stepped over her. The light over the doorway behind them tapered off past the bend, leaving the rest of the gangway dark. Simms peered through his rifle's light-enhancing scope, but nothing registered.

He motioned Cutter and Serio ahead, and once they had passed he turned back to look at Julie.

There was a giant dent in her helmet and a jagged hole in its inch-thick visor. Julie's eyes were closed and a thick cake of blood obscured the left half of her face. Simms crouched down and raised his flashlight to her face. Her eyes fluttered beneath their lids.

"This suit is a lot heavier than I remember," she said hoarsely.

Simms, caught off guard, laughed. "So I hear," he whispered.

Julie's eyes popped open.

"Oh," she said, frowning. "It's you."

Simms raised a finger to his lips, and Julie nodded. He motioned Petty and Orton over to her, then joined the other men. He clipped his flashlight to the barrel of his gun and waited while the others did the same. They advanced down the gangway, fading into the dark.

Petty replaced his armored gloves with blue nitrile ones, opened his medical kit, and reached through Julie's broken visor to inspect the gash on her face.

"How do you feel?" he asked quietly.

"Like I look," Julie replied.

"You think you broke anything?"

"My face?" she asked.

Petty and Orton reached underneath the arms of her suit and eased her up to sit against the wall. Petty unpacked his medical kit while Orton used a hex key to remove Julie's helmet.

"So how did you crack this thing?" Orton asked. "That glass is rated at 300 atmospheres."

"Then whatever hit me must be stronger," Julie said.

Both men froze.

"What did you say?" Orton asked.

"I said, whatever ran into me must be stronger than a three hundred—"

"Shit," Petty said, lowering the mic in his helmet.

"Hold up, sir," he whispered, "possible hostiles." He angled the mic toward Julie and asked, "What was it?"

"I didn't get a good look," Julie said, leaning toward the mic. "Something fast."

It was a moment before Simms replied.

"Looks clear so far," he whispered into the radio. "But you two come forward. Wolf, you out of that suit yet?"

Petty moved away before Julie could hear Wolf's reply. A moment later, the floodlight mounted on the submarine hatch switched off with a resounding click. As the light faded, Petty and Orton unslung their rifles and advanced, abandoning the medical kit, leaving Julie alone in the dark.

Petty and Orton caught up to the others, who were lined up at the end of the gangway. The hatch into the dome was halfway open, hanging by the bent remains of its hinges. The hatch had no lock but had been ripped off rather than simply opened.

The only light was cupped in Cutter's hand, who had his fingers spread just enough to illuminate a baseball-sized device in Simms's hands. Simms pressed various buttons on the device and then motioned for Cutter to kill the light. He felt for the door in the dark, then he reached around it and threw the device upward into the dome, flicking his wrist to give it a spin. He flattened to the wall, clutching his gun and waiting.

The small device arced through the room, firing bright flashes in every direction as a dozen embedded cameras recorded the results.

Sitting at the comm station, Boxx tapped his screwdriver against the side of the monitor impatiently, waiting while the pictures were downloaded and stitched together.

A few seconds later, a panorama of the dome's interior appeared on the screen. Boxx ran his fingers over the touch screen, spinning the view, then zooming in to inspect the broken door and open-platform elevator opposite it. He finished up by checking the floor and the ceiling.

"No sign of intelligent life," he said into the radio.

Julie sat in the dark, pinned down by the weight of her diving suit, aware of nothing but the sound of her own breath. She had hoped that her eyes would adjust, that some detail of her surroundings would emerge, but all she saw were hazy prickles of color, the faint memories of past light.

Orton had left her a hex key, and she used it to remove one of the suit's gloves. She felt around in the shallow water for her flashlight. She wouldn't use it, but it would be reassuring to have. She was fingering the floor's metal grating, trying to decide if the flashlight could have fallen through, when a sharp noise echoed through the gangway, like metal striking metal.

She looked straight ahead, putting one ear in either

direction, but there were no more sounds. She forced herself to relax, to breath, but just then there was a splash in the water beside her. She gasped, recoiling as something whistled past her ear, but it was only Wolf, cracking a glow stick and shaking it to life.

He stood a foot away, with the second half of D-5 lined up behind him. He had a long, thick metal tube strapped to his face—an extremely sensitive night-vision scope. There was a minuscule LED mounted on the tip of the scope, barely visible, casting just enough light for the scope's sensitive optics. Wolf bent down and offered Julie the glow stick. She mouthed a thank-you.

Wolf nodded, then continued down the hall. There were pinprick LEDs mounted at the back of each of his shoulders, allowing the other men to follow him. They stepped over Julie in single file and disappeared down the hall. Try as she could, Julie couldn't make out the sound of their footsteps.

Wolf brought his team up behind the rest of D-5, and at Simms's signal the whole of them advanced into the dome. They spread out as they crossed the room, guns aimed up, down, and to every side. The men moved in perfect synchronization, except for Hiller, who, unfamiliar with their tactics, had to be nudged along by Serio.

At the far side of the dome was an elevator platform. It had an open ceiling, and a couple of men aimed their bayonet lights up the shaft, checking around the cables and behind the motor.

Simms motioned to the trapdoor in the middle of the elevator's floor and Cutter drew a short crowbar from his belt and wedged the tip in. He waited for Serio, who took up position behind him, then pried it open.

The trapdoor opened with a slurp, and the water on the floor started to drain away. Cutter flipped the door all the way back as Serio and Simms advanced, guns pointed into the shaft below.

The water poured through the trapdoor, creating a square tunnel that slowly dissolved to mist. Simms sparked a flare and let it drop. It sailed down the shaft, casting a ring of light on the walls. The ring shrunk into the distance and the flare disappeared. They waited but heard no sound of impact.

"Clear," Simms said.

He stationed Serio at the trapdoor, ordered Hiller to get the submarine unloaded, and motioned for Petty to follow him back up the gangway.

"Let's go check on our diver," he said.

EIGHTEEN

Julie was tucked into a cot in the main room of the submarine. Her diving suit was piled in the corner, and Eric sat at her side, using the submarine's medical kit to stitch the gash in her cheek.

"It's going to leave a scar," Eric said apologetically.

"Good," Julie said. "Nothing like a good facial scar."

Eric frowned.

"You do know I was quite worried," he said, pinching her skin roughly as he pushed the needle through. "I wish you would take more care."

"I know what I'm doing," Julie said, wincing.

"It's not that," Eric said. "It's just... promise me you won't take any unnecessary risks."

"I will not."

"Then at least try not to be so—"

"Are we having this conversation again?"

"I wouldn't say it if it wasn't true," Eric said, tying off the stitch and rethreading the needle.

"Thinking it doesn't make it true. You call it reckless, I call it confidence."

"Just don't get yourself killed."

"Okay," Julie said, smiling. "But only because you said so."

Eric shook his head. "What am I going to tell your mother?"

"Nothing, I expect," Julie said. "This is all classified."

"I can't even imagine what she'll say to *that*," Eric said. "Speaking of classified, I came across something while you were out there…"

He trailed off as Simms entered, followed by Cutter and Petty, the latter carrying his medical kit.

"How are you feeling?" Simms asked.

"Crowded," Julie said.

"Tell me about this thing you saw."

"I didn't see much. It could have been a man."

"And he was underwater?"

"I think so."

"Out of ten?"

"Eight. Is that important?"

"But it wasn't a fish?" Simms asked. "Or a shark?"

"It had a flashlight."

"What about the glowy thing?" Cutter said, holding his arm as if it extended from his forehead and waggling his hand.

The others stared blankly.

"You know," he said. "That glowy thing those deep-water fish have. To attract prey."

"I know *what* you're talking about," Simms said.

"Hey, now," Cutter protested. "No wrong answers in brainstorming."

"It wasn't a fish," Julie said. "Ten out of ten."

The soldiers looked at one another.

"Fuck you," Julie said. "I'm not lying."

"You could have been hallucinating," Petty said.

"I wasn't—"

"You were breathing pure carbon dioxide," Petty continued, looking to Eric for support. "Hallucinations are a common side effect."

Eric nodded reluctantly. "It's true," he said. "I'm sorry, Julie."

"Sorry, Julie," Cutter said, mockingly.

"Arrggggh!" Julie yelled. She raised her arm straight into the air and then swung it down, finger extended to her helmet. It looked like it had been struck by an ax.

"Plenty of ways to bang your head," Simms said, chewing it over. "But that doesn't make you wrong." He motioned the soldiers out. "We'll keep our eyes open."

"Dumbasses," Julie said, watching them leave. Eric raised the suturing needle, but Julie slapped his hand away. "And you?" she asked accusingly.

Eric shrugged.

"Okay, whatever," Julie said, motioning for him to continue. "Hurry up. Looks like you're gonna see that stupid fracture zone after all."

"They're *both* coming?" Cutter asked.

"I'm as surprised as you are," Simms replied. The two men stood at the comm station, the screen behind them showing several views of the gangway, where D-5 was hauling equipment from the submarine to the elevator platform.

"*Surprised* is not the word."

"My orders are to bring them along," Simms said. "The only change is that they're volunteering."

"So we're babysitting," Cutter said.

"Personal feelings aside?"

Cutter snorted, but he thought it over. "Lord knows

she's combat ready," he said finally. "But to her, we're just an extension of her father."

"What's their story?" Simms asked.

"Be out of line for me to say, sir."

"It could be important."

"I understand that, sir."

"Okay," Simms said. "Then I guess we'll just see."

"And what about the perfessor poking his nose into our files?"

"Doctor Kirsch isn't going anywhere," Simms said. "Besides, the colonel thinks he'll be useful."

Cutter opened his mouth to disagree, but the video monitor caught his attention: under Hiller's direction, four men were struggling to shove a refrigerator-sized crate labeled *PATTON* through the gangway's broken door.

"If you'll excuse me, sir," Cutter said, irritated, "I've got to go straighten out the new lieutenant."

NINETEEN

Julie stood at the entrance to the dome, which, owing to its thick walls, was much smaller than it had looked from the outside. She inspected the hinges of the damaged door; they had been rent by a tremendous force.

She had refused offers of D-5's clothing and instead wore a pair of the captain's sweatpants—a tight fit—and a fur-lined sheepskin jacket loaned to her by the helmsman. Eric had borrowed a heavy camouflage jacket from Serio, and it hung from his shoulders like an oversized nightgown. He watched the men pile crates onto the elevator platform.

"You think they're bringing enough?" Eric asked scornfully.

"Be prepared for anything," Julie said.

"That sounds like your father."

"My father is an asshole, not an idiot. We don't know what to expect down there."

"But at least we'll be able to shoot it," Eric said, forcing out a laugh, but Julie wasn't listening. She fingered the bandage on her cheek.

"Just stand in the middle of the doorway," Cutter said, shoving between them. "It's helpful."

Hiller, trailing him, gave Julie an apologetic shrug.

"It still doesn't make sense," he said, catching up to Cutter. "How could someone ride the elevator all the way up here and then just disappear?"

"I'm sure they just climbed back down the shaft," Cutter said.

"Climbed down?" Hiller said, flabbergasted. "A whole mile?"

"It's good exercise," Cutter said. Then, struck by a thought, said, "But you know what? You should really bring this to the lieutenant's attention."

"I should?"

"Oh, yes. He's certain to be interested."

"Thank you, Sarge. If you'll excuse me?"

"You outrank me," Cutter said.

"Yes. Right." Hiller gave a quick salute and, spotting Simms, hustled over to him.

"No moss growing on the new lieutenant," Cutter said, heading to Boxx, who was on a step ladder in the middle of the elevator, running a flashlight over the large, dusty motor and its yards-wide fly wheel.

"What's it look like?" Cutter asked.

"High tech," Boxx said, "for World War II."

"Will it work?"

"Cable is rusted solid, and the motor isn't worth the bother. I had Orton bring a couple winches from the sub, but they're only a couple hundred feet long, so if we went that route, we'd have to use them in stages."

"I wasn't asking about that," Cutter said.

"Ah," Boxx said. "We're doing that, are we?" He swung his flashlight to a metal box in the corner of the elevator and peered up at it. "There's nothing wrong with the brakes."

"First good news I've had all morning," Cutter said. He

called the men over, then yelled to Simms, who was across the dome, fending off Hiller's verbal barrage.

"Loaded and ready, sir," Cutter called out. "And *exactly* as expected."

Simms gave him a nod, raising a hand to cover his smile. He led Hiller to the elevator, did a quick inspection of the equipment, and took his place among the men. Everyone was armed as before, except for Wolf and Serio, who had upgraded their rifles to miniguns.

The miniguns were too heavy to carry by hand, so the men had donned exoskeletons—passive hydraulic frames that were strapped to their legs and supported by aluminum harnesses around their torsos. A spring-loaded arm extended from each harness, taking the weight of the guns, and curving plastic tracks guided bullets from their backpacks to their guns. Serio tested his gun's balance by raising and lowering it, and swinging it side to side. The gun moved easily in his hulking arms.

"Comm cable," Cutter reminded Hiller.

"Sorry, Sergeant," Hiller said, grabbing a spool of signal cable the size of a barrel. The cable ran down the hall and back into the submarine. He hugged the spool to his chest, turning it awkwardly as he walked to unwind the cable.

"Handles," Cutter said, pointing to a rod that ran through the center of the spool. Hiller shifted his grip and moved quickly into position.

"All ready, sir," Cutter said.

"Proceed," Simms replied.

Cutter pressed the Down button, but nothing happened. He pressed it again.

"Elevator isn't working, sir," Cutter said.

"Must be the power, sir," Boxx added.

"Well," Simms said, "that *is* a good question. Any ideas, Second Lieutenant?"

"We could use the hatch, sir," Hiller said, perking up, happy to be consulted. "Or run power from the sub."

Simms nodded, as if considering these options.

"Too slow," he said, peering up at the elevator's mechanicals. He drew his sidearm and fired. The bullet sparked off the elevator's thick cable, jostling the platform beneath their feet. Hiller's jaw dropped. He looked at Simms like he was insane, but Simms only winked and fired again. This shot sheared the cable, and the elevator dropped.

Julie was jarred by the sudden weightlessness. She reached out to balance herself, but the elevator had no walls and her hand touched the bare shaft, which was racing past. She pulled back, more startled than hurt. Cutter smiled at her, and to her surprise she smiled back. The drop was making her pleasantly light-headed. She spread her legs for balance and angled her face into the wind as it whistled through the elevator.

The rapidly unspooling signal cable leaped from Hiller's grip and bounced across the floor. He chased after it, making a clumsy grab.

"Trouble, sir?" Cutter asked, folding a stick of gum into his mouth. The men laughed, and Julie did too.

Fingers dug into Julie's arm; Eric was sheet-white, clutching a crate for balance. Julie's mood soured.

"What the hell is this?" she hissed at Cutter.

"Just relax, J. P.," Cutter said. He elbowed Simms, getting a grin.

"The elevator is designed to survive a fall," Orton whispered to Julie. "It has mechanical brakes that will engage when we reach the bottom, even if the power is out. But *he* doesn't know that." Orton nodded at Hiller, who was hopping around, chasing the spool of cable—it was unwinding so fast that it floated in the air. The second lieutenant was sweating, and not just from the effort.

"You're hazing him?" Julie asked, incredulous. "In the middle of a high-priority mission?"

"Where else?" Orton said with a shrug, then turned to share a joke with Serio. The men of D-5 wouldn't have been more relaxed around a keg of beer. Julie squeezed Eric's hand, reassuring him as the elevator screamed down the shaft, free-falling into the depths of the earth.

The operations room was a metal dome several times larger than the one up at the dock, and the inside was laid out like an air-traffic control tower. Archaic computer terminals ringed the walls, linked to banks of massive reel-to-reel tape readers, their wide spools dormant and dusty. There were three metal tables in the middle of the dome, holding modern laptops and stacks of paperwork. The only light came from the pulsing LEDs of the sleeping laptops, and the only sound was the distant drip of water.

A whistle rose in the distance like an incoming artillery shell. The room began to tremble as the whistle came to a head. The elevator doors bucked as something shot past, spraying light and sparks through the seam between them. The sparks bounced across the floor and faded, and the room was again silent.

A small motor whirred and the light rose gently up behind the doors. It bounced several times, then settled. A conical flame shot out of the seam between the doors, first at the top and then at the bottom, cutting its latches. Two crowbars crunched through the seam, and the light switched off as the doors were pried open. The crowbars made a small gap and then were replaced by metal hooks, which dragged the doors apart, their motors whining in protest. The only thing visible inside the elevator was the stacks of equipment.

A high-speed fan whirred and twin lights rose unsteadily into the air like floating eyes. The manta-ray shape of MacArthur tilted forward, flying into the dome.

MacArthur swept the room, first circling it, then dropping low to check under tables and behind the computer banks. Its lights revealed the disarray that had been cloaked by the dark; paper was scattered, monitors were smashed, and headphones dangled from their wires. Something unpleasant had happened here.

Its sweep complete, MacArthur landed on one of the tables and grew still.

"All clear," Boxx said.

"Move," Simms said.

Shadows rose behind the crates, and bayonet lights cut through the cold, damp air like white blades. Simms led half of D-5 to one side of the dome, while Cutter led the rest to the other. The men hugged the walls as they circumnavigated the room, using the ancient computer equipment as cover. Their thick kevlar armor creaked and their breath puffed like steam, rising to the peaked dome.

The dome had two exits: a sliding steel door on one side and an arched hallway opposite. Simms led his team to the door. He tried the button on the door, but nothing happened. He motioned to Orton, who knelt by the door frame and unrolled his tools. He unscrewed a panel, exposing a circuit board, and began probing it with a multimeter. He tested it in several places, then looked up at Simms and shook his head.

Cutter led his team to arched hallway, easing up to the edge and detaching his bayonet light. He poked the light around the corner and quickly pulled it back. Nothing happened. He poked the light out again, a little slower, then did it a third time. Shifting his chewing gum to the other side of his mouth, he peeked around the corner. Ahead of him was a wide hallway, chiseled through gray rock, with a floor of smooth cement. The hallway looked empty, but the end was beyond the reach of his small light.

Cutter reattached the light to his rifle, then motioned to Serio; the two stepped out and advanced down the hallway, sweeping their guns back and forth. The others fell in behind them.

Condensation trickled down the walls, and a low mist clung to the floor, swallowing Cutter's calves and swirling as he walked through it. The end of the hall appeared, and his light glinted off something just above the floor. He motioned at the men to stop, then crouched low and crept forward, his head seeming to float, disembodied, above the mist. A manhole-sized pipe appeared in front of him, rising two feet out of the floor.

Cutter reversed the bayonet light on his gun, aiming it along the barrel, then he clipped a small mirror beside it. He rolled onto his back and scooted up to the pipe, raising the mirror over the lip and looking inside.

The pipe descended maybe thirty feet and ended in water. There was a metal-rung ladder welded down one side, but besides that it was empty.

Cutter motioned Serio over, then rolled up into a crouch. The two of them leaned forward in unison, pointing their guns into the pipe. They held there for a minute, but the pipe remained empty.

"Water?" Serio asked.

Cutter shrugged. "Pipe is clear," he said into the radio, "but it looks like the basement is flooded."

"Copy," Simms replied. "Secure it and return."

Cutter took a small device from his belt—a motion sensor—and pulled the gum from his mouth. He pressed the gum to the sensor and the sensor to the inside of the pipe, pointing down. The sensor clicked softly, and a watch-like device on Cutter's wrist blinked in unison.

Cutter swept his arms, directing the men back to the dome, and strolled along behind them.

Back in the dome, Boxx popped open a case of electric lanterns. He flipped one over and raised it to the metal ceiling, where its magnetic base snapped into place. He motioned for Julie and Eric to help, and the three of them spread lights throughout the room.

Simms unspooled a couple of extra yards of the signal wire that Hiller had strung down the elevator shaft and pressed it into a slot at the back of a large radio, where small blades dug through the wire's sheathing and connected to the copper inside.

"Explorer, do you copy?"

"Solid copy," Captain Sullivan replied.

"We've secured the operations room. No sign of survivors. We'll attempt to restore power and then proceed down to the drone base."

"Holding here," replied the captain.

Simms signed off, leaving the radio on the table. He poked through the scattered paperwork, which was reports and specifications on the base's construction, then inspected the laptops. The back of one was covered with stickers for skateboarding products and another had a small koala clipped to the bezel. All their screens were locked, and he hadn't been provided the passwords.

"Vasquez," he said to a nearby soldier, "secure these computers."

"Sir," Vasquez replied, stacking the laptops and loading them into one of the crates in the elevator. Simms then returned to Orton, who sat cross-legged at the door, facing a diagram he had taped to its frame. Orton was drilling holes, as indicated by the diagram, through both the paper and the metal behind.

"Time?" Simms asked.

"Twenty-five seconds."

"What's through there," Julie asked, attaching a light over Orton's head.

"I ordered you to remain in the elevator until we secured the area," Simms said.

"This isn't secure?" Julie swept her arm around the room: Cutter and Serio were chatting at the entrance to the hallway, and the rest of D-5 was clustered idly in the center of the dome.

"Follow orders, or I'll have you escorted back to the sub."

"Orders?"

"Orders. You don't get any special treatment because of your father."

"Then why am I here?" Julie asked.

"Not because of me," Simms said. He raised his arm and pointed. "Elevator."

"Sir, yes, sir," Julie said, giving him a limp salute. She turned halfway, then said, "Before I go..."

"Staff quarters," Simms grumbled, "food stores, and the electrical generator. The doors are sealed, so there could be survivors inside."

"Survivors of what?"

"Ready, sir," Orton said.

"Good work," Simms said. "Hiller, Vasquez, and Wolf—you're with me." He waved Julie back, and she led Eric to the elevator.

Orton used a hook the size of a crochet needle to extract a wire from each of the two holes he had drilled in the doorframe. He cut the wires and stripped the ends, then unclipped the lid on a small waterproof case, inside of which was a battery about the size of a motorcycle's. He attached the wires to the battery and, at Simms's command, turned a switch. The door slid slowly open, and light from the dome crept into the dark room on the other side.

The men stood in the doorway, lit from behind, their shadows falling on a pair of sofas in front of a TV. Movies and video games were piled on the end tables, and a half-full bowl of popcorn was balanced on top. This could have been any rec room in any army barrack anywhere in the world. Simms swept the room with his bayonet light as he stepped inside.

The room was wide and deep, its walls the same chiseled stone as the hallway behind them. Plastic panels had been installed along one wall, creating a row of small bedrooms, and on the opposite side were two bathrooms and an open kitchen. Food was laid out on the counter, and there were dirty plates on the table and a stack of pots in the sink, its faucet dripped steadily. In the middle of the room, and filling the bulk of it, was a tall maze made from stacked gray plastic crates, each labeled as food, supplies, or other equipment.

Simms checked the bathrooms first, easing the doors open and sweeping his gun-mounted flashlight inside. Next he crossed to the row of bedrooms, motioning Hiller to follow. Wolf took up station in the middle of the doorway, his minigun balanced on the jutting arm of the exoskeleton.

Simms sent Hiller into the stacks of the crates while he worked along the bedrooms, searching each in turn. Each small room contained two bunks, and he traced his light over the sparse decorations, everything from framed pictures of family to pinups to small plants.

The room grew darker the farther in Simms went, and the path that Hiller was following twisted and turned, separating the men. Simms checked the last bedroom, then turned into the stacked crates, which towered over his head. He moved carefully, checking every gap, and caught an occasional glimpse of Hiller's light, several rows over.

Simms heard a scraping noise ahead. He passed his hand back and forth over his light, catching Hiller's attention through a gap in the crate wall. He tapped his ear, but Hiller shook his head—he couldn't hear it. Simms suddenly wished he'd picked someone else for this.

He looked back in the direction of the door but couldn't see Wolf through the stacks. He made a pinching gesture to Hiller, and the two men continued forward, weaving through the crates to tighten the gap between them.

Simms's path ended at the back wall. He turned around but heard the scraping again, louder, coming from the wall of crates beside him. There was a slurping noise, too, like a straw working the bottom of a milkshake.

Hiller also heard the scraping. It was somewhere between himself and Simms. Crouching down, he peered between two crates. There was movement, but he couldn't tell what. He lowered his mic to his mouth but decided not to speak. He eased the barrel of his gun between the crates and levered them apart. Standing before him was a beetle the size of a rottweiler.

The beetle had a humped, reddish-brown shell, with three rows of silver-tipped spikes along the top. Its head was wide and flat, with large black eyes and thin antennae like jointed toothbrushes. But its most striking feature was its mandibles: eighteen inches of gleaming silver that curved like a jawbone. There were knife-like serrations along the mandibles' inner edges, and spikes jutting from their tips.

The beetle looked unwieldy on its thin legs, the front two of which were shorter than the rest. It was holding a hunk of raw meat between these shorter legs, rotating it to carve off slices with its mandibles, then extending its mouth to suck the slices away.

Hiller jerked back, gasping, toppling the crates behind him. The crates scattered across the floor, and Hiller stumbled over them.

The creature's head snapped up, its jet-black eyes locking on Hiller. Its shell swelled and then deflated with a click, turning the beetle to face Hiller. It leaped at him, shoving through the crates, mandibles wide.

Hiller threw himself flat on his back, and the beetle flew over him, its legs scraping the armored plate on his chest. The beetle clicked again, turning toward him in midair, and it was already running toward him when it landed. But its legs slid over the smooth floor, its momentum carrying it backward. It skittered helplessly as it slammed into the far wall.

The beetle recovered instantly, leaping again at Hiller. Hiller raised his rifle and emptied the clip, shattering the beetle in midair. It splattered against his chest like a giant egg.

A wall of crates tumbled as Simms burst through. He raced to Hiller and kicked the carcass away. Hiller's face and chest were coated in thick, yellow-blue goo that was flecked with chunks of black shell.

"Lieutenant?" Simms asked.

"I'm okay," Hiller replied, scooping the goo from his eyes. Simms offered him a bandana.

Wolf appeared among the stacks, followed by Cutter and Julie. Simms kicked a crate over, blocking Julie's view of the dead beetle and, in the process, exposed the half-eaten remains of a man.

The man was missing an arm, his chest was excavated, and his head had been chewed down to a stump. He wore a pair of blue coveralls with the navy logo on the sleeve.

Cutter raised a hand, shielding his eyes from the gore.

"Shiest," he said. "I hope that was nobody I know."

"What the hell did that?" Julie asked, moving to the body.

"Get her out of here," Simms ordered. Cutter grabbed Julie's shoulder and jerked her back. She whirled around, driving her fist at his face but stopping it an inch away. He glared down at her, a head taller, half again her weight, and armored in kevlar.

"Poof," Julie said, splaying her fingers.

Cutter frowned, jerking his thumb at the door.

"Just leaving," Julie said, ducking under his arm.

Simms knelt by the corpse and searched its pockets, finding nothing. A shadow approached him from behind, creeping along the fallen crates, its silver mandibles glinting in the light.

"Lieutenant!" Hiller called, catching sight of the beetle. He raised his gun, but it only clicked, empty.

Cutter spun, bringing his gun up alongside Wolf's, but Simms was blocking their shot. The beetle leaped.

Simms rolled onto his side and tried to raise his rifle, but its strap was caught underneath him. He tried to push backward, but his boots slipped on the smooth floor. The beetle clamped onto his leg, its mandibles slicing into the armored plate on his thigh. It gnawed furiously, cracking the plate in half, and digging into the kevlar underneath.

Simms planted his foot on the beetle's head and shoved, flipping it onto its back.

The beetle clicked its shell, righting itself, then leaped at Simms's head.

Simms yanked on his rifle, but couldn't free the strap. The beetle landed beside him, its mandibles closing around his neck, but he was suddenly jerked back.

Julie had circled around the room, sneaking back to see whatever it was Simms didn't want her to. When the beetle landed beside Simms, she had raced out, grabbed him by the collar, and dragged him away.

She pulled him across the floor as the beetle leaped after them, its mandibles snapping, slicing the heel off Simms's boot. The beetle planted its feet and leaped again. Julie zigzagged as Simms threw up his forearm, deflecting the mandibles with the ceramic plate on his forearm.

"Somebody fucking do something!" Julie yelled.

The barrel on Wolf's gun was spinning, its electric motor vibrating, but he didn't have a clear shot. Cutter sprinted to the side, trying for a better angle.

The beetle leaped again, this time aiming for Julie. She twisted away, but it turned it with her, and the barbs on its legs dug into her jacket. It thrust its mandibles forward, closing them around her neck. Wolf fired.

The minigun in Wolf's hands could fire a thousand bullets a second, enough to cut through a tree as smoothly as a chainsaw, but he only tapped the trigger, thumping out a single bullet. The bullet sliced through the Julie's right triceps and hit the beetle in the face, knocking it back across the room. It lay still, its head caved.

It took Julie a moment to register that she wasn't dead.

"Fuck," she said, inspecting the bullet wound on her arm. "Nice shot," she said, impressed, but Wolf wasn't listening. He was sweeping his gun back and forth, searching the shadows.

Simms hopped to his feet, and he and Cutter pushed through the crates, knocking them over and checking every inch of the room. There were no more beetles, and no way for them to get in.

"Boxx, I need some light in here," Simms barked into his headset. Then, to Julie, "Thank you."

"So what the fuck is that?" Julie asked, pointing at the dead beetle.

"It's classified," Simms replied.

"No," Julie said, shoving Simms and sending him sprawling. She pointed at the beetle again. "What the fuck is that?" she asked.

Cutter came up behind Julie, clamping his hands to her biceps. "Not now, J. P.," he started, but she cut him off, ramming her elbow back, right into his exposed throat.

Cutter staggered back as Julie spun around, swinging a roundhouse at his jaw. But he recovered in time, deflecting the blow and jabbing a fist into her stomach. The blow bent Julie over, but she quickly straightened up, raising her forearms and blocking Cutter's next two blows. In between, she punched at Cutter's face—the only part of him that wasn't armored—but he kept his right arm up to protect it.

Cutter pulled a switch, trying to surprise her with a hard right, but Julie caught his wrist in midswing. She jerked him forward, pulling herself into the air. She put all her weight behind her fist as she drove it into his temple. He toppled.

Julie landed in a crouch, arm cocked, fist aimed at Cutter's face. Simms shoved between them.

"Stand down," he roared. "Both of you!"

Cutter raised his hands, palms out, to indicate he was done. Julie stepped back and bent at the waist, catching her breath and inspecting her fist. It had already started to swell. She kissed it lovingly, then blew the kiss to Cutter. He shook his head, sneering. He pushed to his feet and walked off, probing the damage to his head.

"You were saying," Julie said to Simms.

It took everything Simms had not to hit Julie himself.

"Petty," he said into his radio, "bring Doctor Kirsch in here." He waited until Eric appeared at the door.

"It's a bug," he said.

"Obvious," Julie replied.

"It's an overgrown tiger beetle," Simms said loudly, looking at Eric.

"How big do they usually grow?" Julie asked.

Simms held his fingers a half inch apart.

"Shit," she said. "And they live down here?"

"That's what we're here to find out."

"But you *knew* they were here?"

"We were briefed," Simms said.

"Must be nice."

"You made your choice."

"There was only one choice."

"And how exactly did you know they would be here?" Eric asked. He was staring, entranced by the beetle's carcass.

"You can't imagine how highly classified this is," Simms warned.

"The colonel made it quite clear what I may expect when we return," Eric said. He pointed at the beetle. "May I?"

"Yes," Simms said, leading them over. Cutter stood nearby, inspecting the messy remains of the man in the blue coveralls. He had found a tube of crackers in a nearby crate and ate noisily, dribbling crumbs on the corpse.

"The Navy Explorer found one of these bugs outside of the disposal tube," Simms said. "It was dead. Shot, we think, by base personnel."

"And you said 'tiger beetle'?" Eric asked.

"The report said they are similar in appearance, minus their size, but their DNA didn't match. They could be cousins, or maybe they just grow bigger down here. There's a lot of radiation in the earth's core."

"We're still quite far from the core," Eric said, kneeling on the floor and leaning over the beetle.

"Not my department," Simms replied. "But I know these caves run deep."

"Radiation would never account for it," Eric said. "Exoskeletal creatures—at least as we know them—would collapse under the weight of their own shells at one-eighth of this size. And, incidentally, this isn't a tiger beetle."

"You know about bugs?"

"You don't have to know much. The tiger beetle is famous. It's the fastest creature alive, if you account for its size. It's light and aerodynamic, whereas this beetle is quite bulky. And its legs are too short."

"I won't argue," Simms said patronizingly, "but we've got the country's top scientists on this."

"What you have in New York could be a tiger beetle," Eric agreed, "but this one isn't the same. The other one had long, frilly antennae. This one's are so small that they're practically ornamental."

"You know," Cutter said, cracking open a can of soda, "whenever someone seems to know everything, I figure it's because they don't know anything."

"Eric does his own thinking," Julie said. "You should try it."

Cutter sliced his hand across his throat, and Julie mocked fright. Cutter smiled.

"Shouldn't you be at your post, Sergeant?" Simms asked.

"Sir," Cutter said, grabbing a second tube of crackers as he left. "Back to our posts," he said to Serio, who had just returned with Boxx, carrying a carton of lights. Serio set the lights down and followed Cutter out.

"Boxx," Simms said. "Check on the generator. Wolf, cover him. Petty, take Hiller to the kitchen and get him cleaned up."

Simms waited until the other soldiers were gone, then motioned to the beetle. "So what do *you* think it is?" he asked.

"Judging by the shape," Eric said, "I'd say it's a common stag beetle, though it seems improbable that we'd find one all the way down here."

"That's the part you find improbable?" Simms asked sardonically. Eric didn't notice.

He grabbed a mandible and, with some effort, twisted it loose from the beetle's head. He rubbed the surface, tested its weight, and ran a finger along its sharp edge. "This isn't the same material as the rest of the shell," he said, handing the mandible to Simms.

"Feels like glass," Simms said. "But it's too light."

"I don't think it's organic," Eric said. "It could be prosthetic."

"Meaning?"

"It may have been grafted on. Surgically."

"Oh," Simms said, examining the mandible and wondering how Eric could tell.

"I'd need lab equipment to be sure," Eric said, bending down to sniff the goo that seeped from the beetle's shell.

"Yeah, turns out we might have brought some," Simms said. "I'll have someone get it for you."

"Sucker punched," Cutter said, draining the crumbs from the tube of crackers.

"And that makes you what?" Serio asked.

"Angry."

Cutter and Serio were posted at the hallway but were facing the storage room, trying to see inside.

"I'm just esorry I missed dat," Serio said, slipping into his fake hispanic accent. "A little señorita kicking your a—"

"Sucker punched," Cutter asserted. "Don't even pretend otherwise."

"You shouldn't have been messing with her," Serio said. "She's tough, like some sort of Camo Barbie."

"More like Bitter Barbie," Cutter said.

"That's right, you two go back. Ever date?"

"No," Cutter said sharply.

"Really? Because it seems like—"

"What are the chances you're gonna shut up?" Cutter asked.

"Not too good," Serio said, shaking his head remorsefully. "Frankly, not too good at all."

Cutter opened his mouth to reply, but the device on his wrist buzzed—the LED was blinking red. He and Serio turned to the hall, to a pipe that rose from the floor.

"Incoming!" Cutter shouted as both men leveled their guns.

TWENTY

"MOVEMENT IN THE PIPE," Cutter said, meeting Simms as he entered from the storage room.

"Wolf and Boxx, get back to the dome," Simms said into his headset. "Everyone prepare a reception, guests arriving from the hallway." The men sprang into action, organizing their defenses with smooth military precision.

Portable barricades—kevlar stretched over carbon-fiber frames—were unfolded and arranged in a semicircle facing the hallway. Serio and Wolf mounted their miniguns on tripods at either end, and the rest of D-5 filled in between them, two to a barricade, their rifles peering over the top. Hiller looked lost, so Orton waved him over to his barricade. Boxx used a remote control to turn off the overhead lights, and to switch on a stand that held four large floodlights, which were aimed down the hallway at the pipe at the far end. Not a word was spoken. The men were ready in under a minute.

Simms took his place at the barricade in the center, motioning for Julie and Eric to stay back in the storage room.

Everything was still. All eyes watched the pipe that jutted out of the low mist. A clicking noise echoed through the hallway. Faintly at first, but growing louder, coming closer.

Simms raised his hand, giving the hold signal. The clicking reached the very top of the pipe and stopped.

Cutter adjusted and readjusted his grip, arms straining as they pressed his rifle to his shoulder. Serio looked over and gave him a nudge.

"They should be scared of us, amigo," he said with a wink. Cutter smiled, relaxing.

"You said it, brother," he said.

Julie and Eric stood in the doorway to the storage room. As the clicking approached, Julie put a hand on Eric's shoulder and tried to pull him behind the wall, but he wouldn't budge. He was fixated on the pipe.

Hiller raised his arm, blotting his forehead with his sleeve, as a beetle popped out of the pipe, balancing on the rim with long, impossibly thin legs.

This beetle was different from those in the storage room. It was flat and thin, white with a brown stripe down the middle and large, mirror-silver eyes that dominated its seashell-shaped head. The beetle rotated on its perch, searching, flicking antennae with tips frilled like feathers.

"There's your tiger beetle," Eric whispered. Julie pressed a finger to his lips, keeping her eyes on the pipe.

The soldiers were motionless, guns trained on the beetle, waiting for Simms's signal. The fog of their breath swirled in the floodlights as it drifted down the hallway.

Suddenly, the beetle's antennae began to vibrate. It turned sharply toward the men as a thunderous noise rose from the pipe—the clicking of a thousand feet.

The tiger beetle leaped to the floor, disappearing into the mist as a swarm of beetles shot from the pipe. They poured onto the floor, clearing the mist, spreading like a dark puddle.

Hiller's jaw unhinged. His finger tightened on the

trigger, but he didn't fire. The other men remained calm, picking a target and tracking it patiently, waiting for the order.

Beetles continued to flow from the pipe, their gleaming silver mandibles shining in the floodlights. Soon their mass spanned the floor. A final beetle sprung from the pipe, scrambling comically over the others and then dropping into a gap.

"Mother of…" Simms muttered, trying to guess their number.

The tiger beetle hopped back up to the lip of the pipe and others formed into rows on the floor below it, facing the men. The room was quiet but for the faucet dripping in the storage room.

Nobody moved until, acting on some unseen signal, the beetles charged.

The rows of charging beetles stretched across the floor and rose halfway up either wall, their feet clinging easily to the coarse rock.

"Go!" Simms yelled, dropping his hand. Gunfire erupted.

The first wave of beetles shattered, but was immediately overrun by the next. And the next.

Hiller emptied his entire clip, waving his gun back and forth, then loaded another, his last; he hadn't thought to replace the one he had used in the storage room.

Beside him, Orton took careful aim, double-tapped his trigger, then moved to his next target. Seeing this, Hiller did the same.

Wolf made short strafes with his minigun, firing only on the beetles that crossed the threshold into the dome. But soon entire rows were getting through; he fired rapidly, draining his ammo belt.

Cutter emptied his second clip and let it drop to the floor, loading his third and final. He glanced at the elevator, to the ammunition stores. They needed the ammo, but they couldn't spare anyone from the fight.

Fuck this, he thought. He hopped up to a crouch, dropped his rifle onto his knees, and pulled two grenades from a pouch in his belt. Crossing his hands, he hooked a finger through their pins and pulled, chucking the grenades into the hoard of beetles that poured into the dome.

"Heads!" Cutter yelled. He flicked his knees, tossing his gun back into his hands, and fired off two shots before ducking behind his barricade.

Julie was halfway to the elevator, heading for the ammunition, but turned back when Cutter yelled. She sprinted at Eric, who stood in the doorway, and knocked him down just as twin explosions erupted. The noise, amplified by the metal dome, was deafening. Shrapnel whistled through the room.

Cutter jerked back from his barricade as a silver mandible sliced through the kevlar, stopping an inch from his face. He aimed his gun at it, but it didn't move; it was just a mandible, disembodied. He burst out laughing.

"What's funny?" Serio demanded. He was sweating, nearly out of bullets.

"Bugs, man," Cutter said. "It's a goddamn bug hunt." He stood up and stepped over the barricade, striding toward the beetles and shooting at the nearest.

"Fuck a duck," Orton said. "I hate when he does this." He took a deep breath and rose to his feet. "Let's go," he said, tossing Hiller his spare clip.

One by one, the men stood up and advanced. The mass

of beetles was shrinking, but there were still dozens left. And suddenly they stopped advancing.

The tiger beetle, still on the lip of the pipe, turned around and leaped inside. The remaining beetles broke rank, racing back for the pipe. The soldiers gave chase, cutting them apart. Cutter was in the lead, chasing a straggler. He fired, but his rifle only clicked, empty. He tossed it aside and drew his sidearm, firing rapidly.

"Goddamn it!" he yelled, his first two shots missing completely. He clipped a leg with his third shot, slowing the beetle enough for him to overrun it. He pressed his gun to its shell and drove four bullets into its neck.

Simms and Wolf ran past, crunching through the thick paste of shattered beetles. They swung their guns down the pipe, but it was empty—nothing but the water at the bottom. Simms patted the inner wall. It was dry.

"All clear," Simms called. "Pull back and check yourselves. Hiller, ammo. Immediately."

Serio shouldered his gun and turned in a circle while Simms checked him over. Then Simms spun for Serio.

Simms tossed his rifle to Cutter, motioning for him to guard the pipe, and walked back up the hallway.

"Nice eshooting, amigo," Serio said as Cutter joined him.

"Thank y—Shut up!"

Simms moved through his men, watching as they inspected each other. No one was hurt.

"You know the drill, Porter," he said when he'd reached the storeroom.

"Whatever," Julie said.

"Do I have to order you not to?"

Julie sighed, then motioned for Eric to turn around.

"Sometimes in the heat of battle," she told him, "you don't realize that you've been hit. My father always insisted on checking."

"He still does," Simms said. "Now you."

Julie walked to Simms and shucked off her sheepskin jacket. The jacket's white lining was stained red, and her tank top was soaked with blood. She lifted her burly arms, flinching slightly at the pain, and turned, displaying the wounds on her back, her ribs, and her arm.

"You're going to need more stitchwork," Simms said. "And if you want something clean, we have some spare wetsuits."

"I don't want your—"

"They're black," Simms cut in. "No insignia."

Julie started to protest, but didn't.

"Thank you," she said.

"You're welcome," Simms said, turning to leave.

"I'd take that gun now, Lieutenant," Julie said. "If you're still offering."

"Here," he said, drawing his sidearm and extending it to her.

She hesitated, then took the gun, gripping it firmly and sliding the chamber back to check inside. An unfired bullet popped out, catching her just below the eye.

"We keep them loaded," Simms said, "as I'm sure you remember."

"Yeah," Julie said, rubbing her cheek. "It just came back to me."

Simms splashed away, barking orders: "Hiller, where's that ammo? Vasquez, relieve Cutter and send him to me. Boxx, get that power on. And Orton, figure out where the hell all this water is coming from." Two inches of water coated the floor.

"What a charmer," Eric said, watching Simms.

"He's all right," Julie said. "For a robot."

"And now you need a gun?"

"I do," Julie said, walking away. "Unless you think these clowns are gonna protect us."

She headed for Hiller, who was distributing clips from a green ammo box.

TWENTY ONE

Orton led Simms to a hairline crack in the dome's ten-inch-thick metal wall, where water sprayed out in a thin, jagged fan. Simms reached for it, but Orton put a hand on his arm.

"Careful, sir," Orton said. "There's 7,000 PSI behind that. He eased a pencil into the stream of water. The wood disintegrated, leaving the tip as smooth as if it had been sanded. Simms nodded, impressed.

"Can we fix it?"

"No way to clamp it," Orton replied. "And welding would only weaken the metal."

"Will it get worse?"

Orton shrugged. "Don't know," he said, "but we should lay off the grenades."

"Yeah," Simms said, giving the water leak a wide berth. "Dealing with that next."

Cutter and Serio were lowering a crate to the floor. Cutter released his side as his hands neared in the goo-tainted water, but only caused the water to splash over his legs.

"Ugh," he said. "This place is nasty."

"It wasn't before you got here," Serio replied.

"Hardy-ho. You know why you're not as funny as me?"

"Because ugly people have to be funny?"

"Because—"

"Because people just laugh at you anyway?"

"Because—"

"Cutter!" Simms said, splashing up. "What the hell are you doing with grenades?"

"Saving our lives, sir," Cutter said.

"My orders were clear!" Simms yelled, pressing his chest to Cutter's and looking up at his face. "Where did you get them?"

"Sorry, sir," Cutter said, stiffening, locking his eyes straight ahead. "They must have been left over from the previous mission, sir."

Simms waited, glaring.

"It won't happen again, sir," Cutter added.

"See that it doesn't," Simms said. He glared at Cutter for a moment longer, then left.

Once Simms out was out of earshot, Cutter added, "I only had those two, anyway."

"That's not cool," Serio said.

"You asking for push-ups, *Specialist?*" Cutter asked, pointing at the mucky water.

"Like I'm disrespecting you?" Serio retorted. "You're disrespecting the lieutenant. That's out of line."

"I know what I'm doing," Cutter said. "I was in officer training myself, you know."

"He was," Julie said, walking up in a black wetsuit. "For three whole days."

"Shit," Cutter said, looking away.

"He ever tell you about that?" Julie asked Serio. "Got himself kicked out for fighting."

"For drinking," Cutter objected. "This the army. No one gets in trouble for fighting."

"You're a sterling example for these boys," Julie said with mock approval. Then, quietly, "A word?"

"Not if you were...," Cutter started, but changed his mind. "Yea-ah," he said. "The specialist was just leaving."

Shaking his head, Serio hefted an ammo box onto each shoulder and headed back to his minigun.

"I see you've still got the knife," Julie said, moving close as she drew the combat knife from his belt. She switched on the light. "Fresh batteries."

"It's useful," Cutter said, swiping the knife back. "So what's with the suit?" The neoprene was tight to Julie's body, and she had put on a lot of muscle since he'd last had a good look at her. Her chest was broad, her arms heavy and sculpted. Her stomach was thin and flat, emphasizing the broad curve of her hips. The muscles on her short legs were as thick as a bull's, tapering down to thin ankles. Cutter's body stirred, and he hated himself for it. "Going for a swim?" he asked.

"What's your take on Simms?"

"Good man. Decent officer. Big fan of your pop. You gonna ask him out?"

"I wouldn't want to step on your toes."

"If you're done with the buttering...," Cutter said, walking away.

"One more question."

"Yeah?"

"Any harm in me knowing a little more about this mission?"

TUNNEL

Cutter raised his eyebrows, checked if anyone was nearby, then leaned back against a crate.

"Now that *is* a good question," he said.

TWENTY TWO

Julie, who had never been to Cadet Training Camp, was unbearably enthusiastic on the ride in. Cutter, on the other hand, was serving his third sentence.

As far as he knew, he was the only repeat attendee in the camp's history. Surely all the other parents, upon collecting their children at the end of the summer, had been too horrified at their condition to ever consider sending them back. Cutter's father, however, had always been absent when Cutter came home, and his mother had been too drunk to notice that he'd left in the first place.

This year was different; Cutter's father had provided a limousine for the eight-hour trip to camp, though Cutter knew more than to think it had anything to do with him. It was a gesture to Julie's father, who seemed to carry more weight than most generals.

Cadet Training Camp was a privately run venture that advertised itself as "a fun-time boot camp for kids." The campus was set up like a bantam army base, with musty surplus tents arranged around a dusty parade ground, and rusting army equipment littered throughout like discarded statues. The decor was to meant to leverage the nostalgia of those who had—given a decade or two to forget the details—glorified their own stint in the service and now wanted their children, or grandchildren, to have the same experience.

The little camp was a thrill for the uninitiated, but Cutter, who'd spent his entire life on the real thing, was unimpressed. And even though he hadn't said as much, the camp's staff resented him anyway, seeing him as a threat to their authority. This was particularly true of the "base commander," who was himself a veteran of many years—though he had never enjoyed anything close to the rank he now claimed in his private show. The base commander encouraged his staff to embarrass Cutter at every turn, and Cutter was all too aware that his arrival by military limousine would only make things worse.

He had been relieved when Julie decided to join him, seeing her as someone to commiserate with, but she was dismissive of Cutter's cautionary tales, and as the car turned down the long, dirt road that led to camp, she pressed her face to the window to gawk at the dilapidated military paraphernalia decorating the unkempt grass.

Still, he figured her enthusiasm would dampen once the program began—once she saw this was just a fake version of basic training, with a lot of yelling and muddy push-ups. But this only seemed to spur her on.

Though staffed by real veterans, the camp took its cues more from the movies than real life. Starting on day one, the kids were woken at 5 a.m. by bugles and banging trash cans. They were lined up in their underwear on the cheap, pallet-wood tent floors, doing their best to stand at attention while the base commander walked down the line, peppering them with tired insults. Cutter had cut his hair this year, but the commander reaffirmed his nickname of Rooster, telling the other kids that Cutter was the only student in the camp's history who had failed to graduate—as if there were such a thing—for two years in a row.

After this "inspection," the kids were chased into the yard for several hours of calisthenics. In the afternoon, they had drill practice and marching, and the evening was capped off with after-dinner activities such as night hikes in the nearby hills or moonlight swims in an icy lake that left most of the kids in near-hypothermic states. At the end of this eighteen-hour daily routine, they were sent to their bunks, tired and hungry, but well aware that complaints would only make it worse.

Cutter saw very little of Julie for the first three weeks—the handful of girls who attended the camp were kept in a separate tent, and they dined at their own table. The girls were also kept to the side during exercises, watched over by the "first lieutenant"—the base commander's wife, whose only experience with an army base was waitressing near one.

When Cutter did catch sight of Julie, she seemed unaffected by the routine. She looked fresh every morning and was still energetic by dinnertime. If they happened to catch sight of each other, she would wax him with one-handed push-ups or by hiking at double time. Cutter suspected that he had grown to hate her, but between the physical exhaustion and the sleep deprivation, he couldn't be sure of anything.

Every Saturday the kids were allowed a full eight hours of sleep, and it was on one of those, halfway through the summer and halfway through the night, that Julie woke him. If she hadn't had the foresight to roust him by shaking his foot, he probably would have punched her. He jerked up, angry, but she only smiled excitedly, motioning him out of bed.

Cutter flopped back down with a groan, instantly asleep again. Julie shook him side to side.

"Come on," she whispered.

"Fuck off," Cutter mumbled.

"Exactly," Julie said, leaning so close that he felt her warm breath in his ear. "It's my birthday."

Julie winked at him, then raced from the tent, giggling. Cutter shook his head and lay back down, but a second later his eyes popped open. He stared at the canvas ceiling, wondering if he was dreaming, and deciding not to risk it. He threw back the covers, grabbed his clothes and boots, and raced after her.

Julie was waiting outside the tent, but she raced into the forest before he could reach her, following the dusty road they used for long hikes. Cutter pulled on his clothing as he chased her, tripping several times. Julie paused to let him catch up, laughing, but stayed just out of reach.

The road rose along a steep hill. At the top, Julie scrambled onto a wide, flat rock and waited for him. They stood side by side, staring out at the valley below, which was illuminated by the bright moon. Cutter reached tentatively for Julie's hand. She grabbed his and squeezed.

"Happy birthday," he said.

"Five more minutes," she said.

They stood there quietly, facing the valley.

"So when we...?" Cutter asked. "How do we do this?

"First, you should kiss me," Julie said.

"Now?"

Julie checked her watch. "Sure," she said. "Why not."

Cutter leaned down and they pressed their lips together, sliding them back and forth, working their jaws as if eating. After a minute of this unsatisfying mimicry, Julie grabbed the back of Cutter's head and drove her tongue into his mouth. He jerked away, startled.

"Sorry," she said. "I don't think I did that right."

"I won't complain," Cutter said.

"Here," Julie said, lifting her shirt and turning. "Unclasp my bra."

Cutter leaned close and, squinting in the moonlight, twisted the small hooks until they popped free. Julie let her shirt drop and slipped her bra out from underneath. She put her lips to Cutter's and they kissed again, already better for the practice. He slipped a hand up her stomach and cautiously cupped her breast. The stiffness in his pants grew painful; he pressed it to Julie's thigh.

"Oh," she said, grabbing him through the fabric of his pants and sending an ache rippling through his body. He staggered, and Julie grabbed his shoulders to keep him from falling.

"I wanna see it," she said, probing the bulge in his pants. "I've only ever seen photos."

"What do they look like in photos?" Cutter asked, undoing his belt with one hand, keeping the other cemented to her breast.

"Huge," Julie said.

"Huge?"

"Like a throbbing, bloated earthworm the size of your forearm."

"I, um," Cutter said, softening at the thought. His hand dropped from his belt. "No need to rush."

"Okay," Julie said. She looked down at the hand on her breast. "Am I supposed to enjoy that?"

"I am."

"Maybe try your mouth," she said, pulling off her shirt and tossing it to the ground. Her skin was the color of moonlight and the pink tips of her breasts crinkled in the night air. Cutter dropped to a knee and clamped his mouth to her breast, tasting the sweet oil of her skin. Julie moaned, clamping her hands to his head.

Neither of them heard the jeep arrive. Its headlights penetrated Julie's eyelids moments before the WW II–era vehicle skidded to a stop on the gravel. She pushed Cutter's head back as the base commander and the first lieutenant started toward them, the man smug, the woman boiling with rage. Cutter, engrossed, put his mouth back on Julie's breast, but she forced his head around until he saw them.

"No," Cutter said, sagging over, shaking his head.

TWENTY THREE

AT THE BACK CORNER of the supply room, a yard-thick pipe rose from the floor, feeding through a massive, stainless steel-clad turbine before continuing up through the ceiling. The turbine, which spun the steam heated deep in the earth, was connected to an electrical generator the size of a bus. This was the base's main power source, connected to inch-thick cables that disappeared back into the floor. But the generator wasn't turning, because there was a five-inch-wide hole melted in its side. Simms shined his flashlight into the hole, seeing the wall on the other side.

"That's ten solid feet of steel and copper," Boxx said, standing beside him. "And the hole cuts right through the center shaft. The whole machine's a wipe."

"Was it the base's engineers?" Simms asked.

"No. They don't have anything that could do this."

"What could?"

"A laser," Boxx said, shrugging. "But it would have to be a big one."

"How big?"

"Using the most efficient technology that I've got the clearance to know about," Boxx said. "You'd need a battleship to carry it."

Simms inspected the hole again. "I want complete photos," he said. "On the double."

"Yes, sir," Boxx said.

Two soldiers rolled what appeared to be a portable biology lab into the supply room. They positioned it beside Eric, who sat beside the carcass of a mandible beetle wearing latex gloves and working to separate the beetle's head from its body.

"The army thinks they're just bugs," Julie said, squatting down beside him. "That the drilling crew stumbled onto their nest."

"Hold that up for me," Eric said.

Julie cupped the beetle's head in her hands. It was cold and heavy, like a river rock. Eric grabbed a scalpel, shoved his arm into the shell up to his elbow, and began to saw in earnest.

"These are not just bugs," he said. "They are evolutionarily extraordinary—if they indeed evolved. Look at this." Eric handed her a fragment of a beetle's shell, which was honey-combed with the precision of an aircraft's wing. "Nature does wondrous things, but this..."

"You think they were engineered? Genetically modified?"

"Look at the DNA report from the army's scientists," Eric said, handing her a thick, spiral-bound book filled with multicolor squiggles. Julie reached for it and found it covered in cold goo.

"Sorry about that," Eric said, wiping the report with a towel that wasn't much cleaner, "but look at this pattern." He traced his finger along a squiggling blue line; it could have been the measure of a heartbeat. Julie studied it without comprehension.

"What about it?" she asked.

"It's perfect," Eric said.

"So?"

"So genetics are never perfect. There's defects, junk DNA and the like. It's only natural."

"And you're saying these bugs aren't."

"Well, not entirely, anyway. I'm trying to keep an open mind here, but—"

"Hold off on your studies, Kirsch," Simms said, striding up. "Specialist Bell, get that bug bagged. We're taking it topside. Orton, get those winches hooked up to the elevator."

"We're leaving?" Julie asked.

"You're leaving," Simms said. "We're checking in, which means a ride back to the surface. In ten," he emphasized to Specialist Bell, who was trying to slip a large duffel around the beetle's carcass.

"What about the survivors?" Julie asked.

Simms took the mandible from Eric's hand and held it up to the light, marveling at it.

"My orders are to gather intelligence about what happened here," he said.

"You haven't even gone into the tunnel yet," Julie said, "much less the drone base."

"To gather evidence and return with it," Simms said, tossing the mandible to Specialist Bell. Then, to Eric, "We'll make room for your lab in the submarine, if you'd like to continue your work."

Eric started to answer, but gunshots rang out from the operations room.

Cutter sat for a long time after Julie had left, his mind chewing over things long past and not much caring for it.

"Why couldn't you have just stayed gone, Porter," he said to himself. Then, as if in reply, the motion sensor on his wrist buzzed. He tapped it, confused, but it kept buzzing. He walked to the hallway.

"Hey, Vasquez!" he yelled. "You seeing anything...?"

Cutter trailed off. Two soldiers lay beside the pipe, motionless, the water around them red with blood. The tiger beetle stood beside them; it looked at Cutter with its large, silver eyes.

"The fuck?" Cutter said, drawing his sidearm and firing. The beetle hopped up to the pipe and then down inside.

"Stations, everyone," Cutter called, sidestepping to the kevlar barriers, keeping his gun trained on the pipe. "Serio," he called, "bring me my rifle."

The men reacted instantly, fanning out behind the barriers. Serio, who was helping Wolf load his minigun, jogged back to his own. He tossed Cutter a rifle as he passed.

"The bug with the eyes," Cutter said as Simms approached, motioning to the dead men. Simms nodded, checked that everyone was in position, then took his own.

Julie ran to the elevator and searched the crates, digging for the flak jackets she had seen earlier. By the time she had found two of them, the click of approaching beetles filled the room. She turned and started back for the storage room, running into Eric. He had followed her into the dome.

"Wolf," Simms ordered, "shoot whatever comes out. The rest of you shoot anything he misses."

Julie looked to the storage room; it was far.

"Put this on," she said, thrusting a flak jacket into Eric's hand. She kicked a table over and pulled him down behind it.

TWENTY FOUR

Beetles poured from the pipe. Wolf fired his minigun continuously, sweeping back and forth, cutting them apart as fast as they appeared. But it was only seconds before he saw a green tracer sail from his barrel, indicating that he was three-quarters of the way through his gun belt. He switched to shorter bursts, and some of the beetles slipped past. Serio tried to pick up the slack, but he didn't have Wolf's aim. Three of the beetles reached the ground and charged.

"What the fuck are they?" Cutter asked.

The new beetles were strikingly different; they barely looked like insects at all. Their cone-shaped bodies were apple-red, and they had stubby back legs and overlong front ones. Their necks were ringed with silver quills, like a porcupine's but slanted forward. The beetles formed into a line, spread their legs to brace themselves, and jerked their heads back into their bodies, sending a dozen quills whistling across the room.

Simms ducked behind his barricade as the silvery tip of a quill punched through the kevlar. He fingered the sharp point, jerking back as several more punched through around it.

"This just keeps getting better," he muttered. He rose to his knee and fired half his clip, shattering all three beetles. But a half dozen arrived to replace them, and there were more of them every second. The quills came as fast as rain, shredding the barricades. The floodlight shattered, spraying glass, and the room went black. By the time Boxx had switched the overhead lanterns on, the beetles had advanced up the hallway and into the room.

"This ain't working!" Cutter yelled. Simms didn't need to be convinced.

"Storage room," he called. "Staged retreat. Right crosses left. Orton: door. Go!"

Hiller and Orton went first, moving straight back from their barricade before circling behind the others, keeping low. Once they were clear, Orton sprinted for the door. He slid up to it on his knees and yanked the wires from the battery, reversing the connection. Hiller crouched behind him, shielding him, facing the incoming beetles.

Boxx went next, heading first to the elevator to grab a long, flat case that he dragged behind him as he raced for the storage room.

"Come with me!" he yelled at Julie and Eric as he passed.

Eric stood to follow but lurched back as a quill sailed by his face. He lost his balance and started to fall. Julie locked an arm around his waist and hefted him onto her shoulder. She hustled after Boxx.

The beetles lined up in V-shaped rows, like migrating birds. They advanced as the men retreated, firing in waves. One soldier fell, a quill jutting out of his forehead. The soldier beside him was thrown forward by the barrage, but his armor held. He scrambled for the door.

"Everyone go," Simms called. "Now!" The remaining men backed toward the storage room, with Simms bringing up the rear.

A beetle shoved through the barricades and shot a

half-dozen quills into Petty's leg. The medic fell, his head catching the doorframe and knocking him cold.

Wolf drew his sidearm and fired, shattering the beetle, then grabbed the back of Petty's collar and dragged him into the storage room. More beetles appeared through the barriers.

Simms lined up beside Serio, Cutter, and Hiller, all protecting Orton, who twisted the final wire into place. The door started to close. Simms emptied his clip into the approaching beetles and grabbed another from Cutter's belt. Reloading, he ordered everyone else inside.

The barricades collapsed, trampled by a phalanx of beetles. Simms was completely exposed, but they didn't fire. Then the tiger beetle appeared, hopping onto a table and fixing its silver eyes on him. The beetles fired in unison. Simms dove through the closing door.

"Smokers!" he yelled as he rolled across the floor; two of the men pitched smoke grenades into the dome. Simms looked back, meeting the tiger beetle's gaze as it faded behind the rising smoke. The door closed and quills rattled against it like hail on a tin roof. There was another round, then silence. Simms lay still, gazing at the door.

"Are you okay, sir?" Hiller asked.

"Yeah," he said. "It's just..."

"Sir?"

"They're just bugs," Simms said, shaking his head.

"And they've got us trapped," Julie reminded him.

"Boxx," Simms called, "remind me why I bring you on these field trips."

"Working on it, sir," Boxx replied. He and Cutter hefted the long case onto a couple of gray plastic crates, creating a makeshift desk. Cutter popped the lid as Boxx crouched in front of it. Inside were two separate control panels.

The control panel on the left was fairly minimal, a few

buttons beside a swelling mass of electronics that resembled the base of an oversized blender. Boxx went to the other side, flipping up a monitor and throwing a power switch on the side. He typed furiously on the keyboard.

Wolf and Orton laid the unconscious Petty on a blanket, pulling off his helmet and stripping the armor from his injured leg. Eric came over, sweaty, shaking.

"May I?" he asked.

"Please," Orton said, making room. Eric pulled back Petty's eyelids, then fingered the gash on his head. He bobbed his head noncommittally, then shifted over to finger one of the quills in Petty's leg.

"Into the bone," he said. "Do you have any pliers?"

"Yes, sir," Orton said, heading for the same tools Eric had used to dissect the beetle.

The video monitor in front of Boxx showed a curved steel wall, monochrome and grainy. As he typed on the keyboard, the view rose unsteadily, rotating to face the center of the dome. It was the video feed from MacArthur, the aerial drone.

"What are they," Cutter asked, pointing at a quilled beetle on the screen. The beetle fired, but MacArthur rolled sideways, dodging with blinding speed.

"I can't read the label from here," Boxx replied, typing more instructions. MacArthur shot toward the elevator. "Let's just call them bug number three."

"Of bug how many?"

"That would be your department."

MacArthur dropped down among the crates, hovering beside the refrigerator-sized one labeled *PATTON*. Boxx switched the drone to manual and, flying it with a joy stick, maneuvered MacArthur over the clasp at the top. With great care, he slipped the drone's wing under the clasp, then angled it to the side, prying at the clasp. The wing slipped loose, and the drone spun away.

"Gah!" Boxx yelled, slapping the Autopilot button. The drone stabilized itself. He switched back to manual and tried again.

"Come on, baby," Boxx said, his hand white on the joystick. MacArthur's wing thrust under the clasp, and the drone rolled, popping it open. The side of the crate fell away.

"I told them he needs a claw," Boxx said, landing the drone on a nearby crate. The monitor dimmed as the drone's lights faded. "You know how hard it is to fix scratches in carbon fiber?"

"You also said he needed a laser," Cutter said.

"He still does," Boxx said, shifting to the other end of the control panel, which had nothing but a short row of buttons. Boxx interlocked his fingers, and, pushing his hands out, cracked them. He punched the button labeled *ON*.

Patton's crate, seen on MacArthur's display, began to shake. A low rumble came through the wall to the supply room, and a pair of lights snapped on inside of the crate, appearing on the monitor as burning white spots.

The swell of electronics in front of Boxx began to glow, and a three-dimensional display appeared, floating in thin air. The view was from inside the crate, looking out at the dome.

"Patton is online," Boxx called out.

"Put him to work," Simms said, coming over to watch. Men crowded around the display.

Boxx picked up the control stick—a short, wireless rod with spherical sensors on either end—and tilted it forward. The rumbling noise grew louder as Patton's engine came up to speed. Boxx reached a hand to the other end of the control panel, typing a command that sent MacArthur high in the air, giving him a full view of the dome.

Patton rolled out of the crate on steel-belted treads, its squat body resembling a small tank with a mast rising from its center. The mast tapered like the wing of an airplane, and it was capped with a disc-shaped head. Its head bulged out on either side, housing a pair of lights and an array of cameras behind thick glass.

Patton had been secured by straps, but these stretched and snapped as it rolled into the dome. The beetles showered it with quills, but they bounced harmlessly away.

Transparent quills shot at Boxx's face as he leaned into the three-dimensional display, searching. He rotated the control stick, turning Patton's head.

"Orton," he called over his shoulder. "Where the hell is Patton's gun?"

Orton was beside Julie, helping hold Petty's leg as Eric tugged at the quill in his shinbone. "Left of the elevator," he said. "Near the oxygen."

Boxx steered Patton to a stack of air tanks, beside which was a yard-long fiberglass tube. "Got it," he said. When Patton reached the tube, Boxx dipped the control stick, extending a double-jointed arm from the robot's body.

"You look ridiculous," Cutter said as Boxx leaned forward, stretching his arm to extend Patton's. Boxx twisted the stick—locking Patton's arm to the metal plate on the top of the tube—then sat back down. The robot rolled backward, withdrawing a gun from the tube.

The gun was huge. It had an inch-wide barrel with howitzer flashing, and a coil of bullets the size of a banker's cigar. Patton leveled the gun, sweeping it back and forth, its head moving in sync with the barrel.

"Authorization to engage, sir?" Boxx asked.

"Authorized," Simms replied.

Boxx set the control stick down and reached for two wide buttons on the control panel. The top one, green, was lit. Boxx lifted the cover for the red one and placed his finger on it.

"God have mercy on my enemies," he said ceremoniously, "because I won't."

He pressed the button.

Patton's motor revved up to high speed as the robot spun to face the beetles. It fired a single shot, its massive barrel recoiling a full foot. The report shook the walls. One of the beetles vaporized, leaving nothing but a stain on the floor.

Patton swung the gun at another beetle and then another, firing rapidly. The machine's aim was perfect—one shot per beetle. The men warmed at the sight, jostling each other and cheering. Boxx leaned back, arms folded in satisfaction.

Drawn by the noise, Julie pushed through the soldiers. "Holy shit," she said, catching sight of Patton on the black-and-white display. "When did you get that thing?"

"That's classified," Simms replied. "Officially, that robot doesn't even exist."

Patton splattered three beetles as they clamored up the

side of the dome, his bullets pounding large dents in the wall behind the men. Julie ducked instinctively, then laughed.

"And what exactly have you been saving it for?" she asked, admiring the dents.

"Patton can't distinguish targets," Boxx said. "He kills anything that moves."

Patton dispatched several more beetles. Julie whistled with admiration.

"Yeah," Cutter said, agreeing with her. "We should start using him at protests."

Julie spun on Cutter, who snapped his fists up defensively, but she only jabbed his arm. "Good one," she said, not meaning it. She looked past him to Eric, who was stitching Petty's leg.

"They're retreating," Boxx said.

"Follow them," Simms said. "Find out where they're going."

"Yes, sir." Boxx slid over to MacArthur's control panel and typed.

A dozen quill beetles raced down the hallway. Patton chased after them, picking off several, but the rest outpaced him and escaped down the pipe.

MacArthur sailed overhead, angling down over the pipe and watching the beetles descend. The beetles reached the end of the pipe and rolled over the lip—which was above the waterline—and disappeared. MacArthur flattened out and cut its main rotor, dropping like a plate down the center of the pipe. Its rotor spun back up when it reached the bottom, and it dashed after the beetles.

Patton rolled back to the dome and circled it, sweeping

its disc-shaped head back and forth. Finding nothing alive, it pointed its gun at the floor. The red LED on its back turned green, and its engine switched off.

Above Patton's head—and out of its sight—a half-dozen gray, slug-like creatures slithered across the domed roof. They were pear-shaped, with short antenna and beady black eyes. Their bodies were studded with silver dots that spread as their bodies swelled, almost doubling in size, their skin pulling taught.

They dispersed throughout the room. Two of them slipped below the elevator's threshold, heading up the shaft wall.

Hanging from the very peak of the dome, the tiger beetle watched on with large, silver eyes.

TWENTY FIVE

Boxx and Simms watched MacArthur's monitor as the drone chased the beetles along a chiseled stone ceiling, their hind quarters lit by its small lights. They were moving upside down on the ceiling with the same ease they moved across the floor. Below them was the transfer station, a cavernous room that was flooded with a lake's worth of water.

Static danced across the monitor, then the video became distorted and went black. Boxx fussed with the control panel but couldn't restore the picture.

"Lost the signal," he said. "MacArthur's transmission can't penetrate this rock."

"What will it do?" Simms asked.

"He'll chase them as far as he can, until he loses them or his battery runs low. Then he'll come back and we can play the video off his memory."

"Okay, and Patton?"

"Stand-by mode."

"Good work." Simms turned to his men. "Listen up! We're doing an immediate e-vac. It's a long climb, so weapons only. Corporal Orton, get that door open."

Orton started for the door to the dome, but the room

shook from a series of explosions, throwing everyone off balance.

"The hell?" Simms blurted. Boxx scrambled to the control panel, but couldn't bring up Patton's display. "No idea, sir," he said.

"Serio and Wolf, with me," Simms said. He started for the door, but it was bowed inward; it wasn't going to open.

"Blow it," Simms ordered.

Hiller produced four cylindrical charges, each the size of a roll of quarters, and attached them to the door. He set the timer, displayed in red, to fifteen seconds. He looked to Simms for confirmation, then pressed the button. The charges were radio synced, so starting one started them all. They counted down in unison.

The men stepped back, closing their eyes and covering their ears. The explosion was small, controlled. The door teetered, then fell inward, drawing a cloud of smoke from the dome, along with a smell like burnt popcorn.

"Let's go," Simms said, leading his men out.

The floor of the dome had been cleared, the furniture blown to the sides. Burning paper floated in the air, and ash coated the water on the floor. There were several dents in the wall—inward, not out, from the ocean's pressure.

A sheet of water poured down the elevator shaft, gushing into the dome like a river. The spool of signal wire was unwinding rapidly, pulled from the top.

"Cover me!" Simms yelled as he dashed across the room. He leaped for the radio and yelled, "Explorer, do you copy?"

"Lieutenant," replied Captain Sullivan. She was calm, but an alarm was sounding and someone was screaming in pain. "We're taking on water," she said. "I had to blow the tanks. We'll be on the surface in five minutes and I'll radio for—"

The spool ran out and the wire went taught, yanking the radio from Simms's hands. He chased it across the floor and leaped as it bounced up the elevator shaft, but it was too high to reach. It disappeared up the dark shaft. Simms cupped his eyes against the water, peering after it. The empty spool appeared, plummeting out of the water, missing him by inches. It shattered at his feet, a strand of frayed wire hanging from its side.

"Shit!" he yelled. Julie ran up beside him and stopped, gaping at the sight of the broken wire. "Shit!" Simms yelled again, water pouring over him. His voice echoing up the shaft.

TWENTY SIX

Julie and Cutter were no strangers to trouble, but they were to punishment. Back on base, MPs would never risk the ire of their parents, and they were generally just home with a warning.

But the base commander of the cadet academy made it clear that he was not intimated, and, in fact, he seemed driven to make as big a fuss as possible about their nighttime outing. He expelled them both effective immediately and demanded that their parents come retrieve them personally, insisting he couldn't legally release such troublesome children into the hands of a lackey.

Julie was separated from Cutter and locked inside a closet-sized room in the main building with nothing but a cot and a sleeping bag. She was fed leftovers from the mess tent and allowed no shower or change of clothes for the three days before her father arrived to retrieve her. She heard him approach down the hallway, calmly replying to the base commander's heated statements. She braced for his anger, but when the door opened, the first thing he did was apologize for making her wait. He had never before apologized to her for anything.

"It was my fault," Julie burst out. "I woke him up. I dragged him out there."

"Don't be a child," her father said, waving her words away. He closed the door on the base commander and motioned her to the cot. He sat in a chair facing her and set a green duffel between them. He looked weary, which made him look older, and he seemed to be bothered by something much deeper than just her infraction.

"Please don't get him in trouble," Julie said.

"Don't worry about Nigel," her father said. "His father's a major. I couldn't touch him if I wanted to. Neither could that clown who runs this place. No, what I'm worried about is you, Julie. I believe I've made a terrible mistake."

Julie started to speak, but her father looked away, nervously fingering the duffel. Her words sank back into her stomach, and she curled her knees to her chest, her eyes dropping to the floor.

"You are sixteen now," her father said. "If you were a boy, I would have initiated you to adulthood the way my own father did. But you are not a boy, and I have dithered too long, imagining there is some great difference between us, simply because you're a girl. I left you to fumble in the dark, and this incident is my failure, Julie, not yours. I have failed you, my daughter, and I apologize."

Julie nodded, feeling the gravity of his words even if she didn't understand them. She gripped the wooden bar at the edge of the cot as the room tilted sideways. Her father put a hand on her shoulder, as if to steady her.

"It is important that you do this yourself," he said. "Just as my own father insisted, back when it was my time. He gave me the money and dropped me outside, but it was up to me to go through with it.

"It wasn't easy—I must have stood there for an hour,

praying that he would change his mind, that he would return for me. But I finally found the courage to go inside. I can't say that I enjoyed the experience. There were several woman to choose from, but I was too terrified to speak. The one who chose me, she was old enough to be my mother and not at all what you'd call attractive. She had this terrible perfume..."

Her father laughed absently, staring off at the wall. Julie tried to picture him as a teenager; it seemed so long ago as to be in black and white.

"Make a good choice and you will enjoy it more," he said, his focus returning to Julie. "But enjoying it isn't the point. Your body is a liability as well an asset. To be a leader of men, you must first master yourself. You must be a woman, and so we will eliminate these girlish distractions."

Her father reached into the duffel and drew out a set of fatigues. The name tag read *Julie Simmons*, *Private First Class*.

"I know that if you could choose anyone, you would choose Nigel, but that would be shortsighted. A sentimental encounter would create more problems than it would solve. Your pick must be anonymous and forgettable, and it can wait no longer. Change into these and meet me out front."

Her father dropped the fatigues on her lap and left. They were too large, the shirt sloping over her shoulders and reaching down to her thighs. She rolled up the pant cuffs and shirt sleeves and stepped from the room, her steps stiff and self-conscious. Thankfully, she saw no one on her way to the front door.

Her father was waiting in the circular driveway. He stood beside his limo, but motioned her to the humvee parked behind it. She started toward the truck, then faltered. She ran to her father and grabbed his coat.

"Please," she begged, her face suddenly wet. "I'm sorry.

I'll never do anything like that again. I promise. Just please don't—"

His hand cracked across her face. She stepped back, stunned, her cheek pulsing.

"You are my daughter," he said, cold. "Act like it."

Julie backed away, finding the humvee and scrambling inside. The truck's engine rumbled to life, and it followed the limo down the long driveway to the interstate.

The two vehicles drove east for a couple of hours before the limo turned south, back toward the base. The humvee continued straight.

TWENTY SEVEN

The bodies of the three dead soldiers were sealed into black plastic bags and carried into the storage room.

"Take them to the back," Simms ordered. "See if you can't find something to cover them, to keep those things from..."

He didn't finish the thought, but waved the men on and went to check on the fortifications. The kevlar barriers were beyond repair, so the two men were creating a barricade of gray plastic crates from the storage room, stacking them in a semicircle at the entrance to the hallway. Serio and Wolf stood behind this makeshift barricade, their miniguns aimed at the pipe.

Simms passed without comment, moving to the remains of their equipment, which was piled on a table in the center of the dome. Hiller had scavenged what he could from the debris. It wasn't much. Simms grunted at the pile and continued to the elevator shaft.

Orton stood in the middle of the shaft, spotting for Cutter, who was climbing what remained of the ladder. Cutter fought through the streaming water, trying to find a way back up. The dock was a mile above them; Cutter had been at it for thirty minutes and had got no higher than twenty feet.

Simms watched quietly; it had only been two minutes since he had last circled the room, so there was no reason to ask about progress. He felt a sudden chill and looked down to the rising water spilled over the top of his boots.

"I found him," Boxx called from inside the dome, prying back a table that had been thrown flat against the wall. Behind it, Patton was encased in a Patton-shaped dent. Boxx fiddled with a portable remote—the same one he used for MacArthur—and Patton's eyes lit up. Its engine rumbled to life and Boxx drove it into the room.

"Indestructible!" Boxx shouted, his enthusiasm earning him glares from around the room. There was a loud crack as Patton's arm snapped in half, its gun plopping into the water.

"Crap," Boxx said.

"Can you fix him?" Simms asked.

"If I had a TIG welder."

"He's still a pair of eyes," Simms said. "Get him over to the pipe."

Boxx nodded, drove Patton down the hall.

"Hiller!" Simms yelled. "Still waiting on an ammo count."

"Yes, sir," Hiller said, prying the lid from a mutilated container. Simms walked toward the hallway to start his circuit again, but changed his mind and headed for the storage room.

Petty had been moved onto a cot, where he was wrapped in a sleeping bag and fitted with an IV drip. His eyes were closed and his breathing was shallow.

Eric sat by his side but was turned away, reading a book on entomology that had been included with the army's lab equipment. He had dog-eared several pages and was comparing the different drawings to the burnt remains of the quill beetle, which Julie held in her lap. Eric's hands were shaking, and he was dripping sweat.

"How's he doing?" Simms asked. Eric jumped, startled. He wiped a damp palm on his pants and set it on Petty's forehead, checking his temperature.

"His leg is fine, but he took a hard blow to the head," Eric said. "He'll be unconscious for... I don't know."

"Anything we can do?"

"Only wait."

"Okay," Simms said. "And what about that thing?"

"I can't figure it out," Eric said, turning to the beetle. "Not even the genus. These quills are unprecedented."

"I'll take anything you can tell me."

"You don't find this strange?" Julie asked.

"Two days ago," Simms said, "I didn't even know there *were* giant bugs."

"Exactly. Finding even one species of giant bug would be the discovery of a lifetime."

"And?"

"And now we've found three of them," Julie said. "All in one place."

"And not just any bugs," Eric said, flipping through the book. "Exceptional ones. *Lucanidae*, one of the largest beetles on the planet, renowned for its pronounced mandibles. And the *Cicindela eburneola*, the tiger beetle, which might be the fastest thing on six legs. It blinds itself, quite literally, by outrunning the incoming the light. When chasing down its prey, it must stop frequently to allow itself to see."

"The fastest bug on the planet," Simms said, rubbing his eyes. He couldn't imagine how, in normal circumstances, anyone would find that interesting. "How fast?"

"The regular one can travel at four miles an hour. Scaled

to this size, that's 230 miles an hour. Of course, there would be other factors, such as increased wind resistance. Also these antennae aren't what you'd call standard equipment, and also I don't expect—"

"But very fast," Simms cut in.

"Yes," Eric agreed. "Very fast."

"Okay, exceptional bugs, three of them. But wouldn't whatever made one grow big be the same for them all?"

"No," Eric said. "Not three separate species. Evolution doesn't work like that."

"The report ruled out genetic engineering," Simms said. "Said this would be too advanced."

"For us, you mean," Julie said.

"For us, for China, for Russia. Hell, even the Japanese aren't making much headway. So what makes sense is that, for some reason, these bugs just grow really big."

"You make a point," Eric said impatiently. "Occam's razor and all that. And humanity is barely at the forefront of genetic technology, struggling with seeds and cloning. But there is evidence of intelligent design here, not to mention surgical procedures." Eric turned to the beetle beside him. "There's scar tissue here, at the base, which implies the quills were added surgically. Or they replaced what was already there. I found similar scars at the base of the mandibles on the *Lucanidae*, and I suspect we'd see the same around the eyes and antennae of the tiger beetle.

"And let us consider the origins of these insects. Two of them, at least, strongly resemble insects we find on the surface, while the last," Eric said, pointing at the quill beetle, "is completely alien to my experience."

"Yeah, yeah, okay," Simms said, holding up his hands. "Let's say all that is true. How does it help us?"

"Well, it's... it's an important discovery," Eric said.

Simms sighed, closing his eyes and pressing his fist to his forehead.

"Okay," he said finally. "When we get out of here, I'll see that you get proper credit."

Simms walked away, but Julie hopped up, intercepting him.

"There could be more of them," she said. "Species of bugs we haven't encountered yet."

"Also not helpful," Simms replied. "We'll deal with them if and when we come across them. For now, the priority is to get out of here."

"And you have a plan for that?"

"I'm working on it," Simms said, stepping around her. But Cutter appeared in the doorway, soaked, frowning.

"Nothing," Cutter said, squeezing water from his jacket. "The elevator shaft is collapsed about a hundred feet up. No way past."

Simms nodded.

"So what's the plan?" Cutter asked.

"Call everyone together," Simms said, heading into the dome. "I want reports from all quarters."

Cutter watched Simms leave, then turned to Julie.

"What do you think?" he asked.

"I think we've moved beyond all anticipated scenarios," Julie said.

"Which means?"

"Which means that from here on out, you're self-directed. Think your poster-boy lieutenant is up for it?"

"He's run plenty of ops," Cutter said. "And we've all seen a few casualties before."

"I can tell he's got guts, when he's following orders."

"Brains too," Cutter said. "He didn't get *all* his medals for being pretty. Smart and brave, just like your pop."

"My father is a lion in his orders," Julie said, "but none of us are sitting this one out."

"All these metaphors," Cutter said. "Just talk to me like I'm stupid."

"What I'm wondering is," Julie said, "without orders to back him up, does your lieutenant have the balls to do what it takes? Even if that means pushing forward into the unknown?"

"Shiest," Cutter said. "I hope not."

TWENTY EIGHT

IT WAS SEVERAL MORE hours before the humvee reached its destination, which was an army base in Virginia. The driver had printed orders that got him whisked through the front gate, and he drove undirected to a cement-block building somewhere in a maze of older wooden ones. He held the truck door open for Julie, then led her inside.

The foyer was also cement block, painted blue, with the antiseptic smell of a hospital. There was a single metal door to the left and a uniformed receptionist stationed behind reinforced glass in the middle. The driver pushed his orders through an oval slot in the glass, and the man paged through them.

"AWOL, huh?" the receptionist said, eyeing Julie appreciatively and then winking at the driver. He jerked his thumb at the metal door. "Put her in general holding."

There was a buzz, and the driver pulled the metal door open, motioning Julie inside.

"I'll wait out front," the driver said, speaking to her for the first time as he closed the door behind her.

Julie stepped into a hallway that led to a room some twenty feet ahead. She smelled stale smoke and heard a faint, tinny TV. There was an abrupt burst of laughter—what sounded like a group of men. The laughter died off again, leaving only the TV. She stood in the hall for some time, then drew up her courage and marched into the room.

It was a recreation room of sorts. A couple dozen men in white T-shirts lounged on sofas by the TV or played pool or ping-pong. Most of the men were smoking, and a haze hung from the ceiling, obscuring the fluorescents overhead. The men all turned as Julie entered, falling silent. A forgotten ping-pong ball bounced across the room, plinking faster and faster as it settled in the corner.

Finally, one of the men from the sofa stood up and said, "Can I help you, ma'am?" He had dark hair and appeared to be about nineteen. His pale skin was peppered with acne scars.

All the men waited, expectant.

"I just need to use the restroom." Julie said.

"Certainly," said another man, this one short, with dark skin and broad shoulders. "It's only for men, but we'll watch the door for you," he added with a wink.

The men shuffled back, clearing a path to the bathroom.

"Thank you," Julie managed, stepping through the men. Her gait was stiff, as if she had forgotten how to walk.

The men looked her up and down as she passed. One of them hummed noncommittally, and another shrugged his shoulders. She was almost to the bathroom when a man stepped into her path, blocking the way. He had strawberry-blond hair, and his neck was kinked back at his Adam's apple.

"You're not a guard?" he asked.

"Don't be stupid," the short man said. Then, after a moment, asked, "Wait, are you a guard?"

All the men turned to her with renewed interest. Their eyes seemed to press against her body.

"No," Julie said. "I'll...I'll come back later."

"No reason to rush off," the blond said, moving closer. The cluster of men tightened around her.

"I changed my mind," Julie said, pushing through the men and racing down another hall, finding an empty bunk room. She closed the door and, finding no lock, slid a bunk in front of it. She backed away from the door until another bunk caught her behind the knees. She dropped onto its hard mattress, eyes glued on the door.

No one came to the bunk room, but Julie kept her eyes on the door, her knees curled to her chest. After a while, she had the absurd realization that she was hungry. Still, she didn't dare move.

After what felt like hours, she rose quietly and crept across the room. She eased the bunk back, cracked open the door, and peered out. She couldn't see past the hall, but the sounds were as before: TV, pool, ping-pong, and occasional laughter. She slid the bed farther back and slipped into the hall, moving cautiously toward the room, encouraging herself with every step.

Peeking around the corner, she could see a half dozen of the men. Her attention was drawn to a tallish one, with dark skin and thin shoulders that jutted up like folded wings. But then he turned and she saw that his eyes were small and spread disturbingly wide. She pulled back behind the corner.

"Just pick one," she told herself. "It's not going to matter." Straightening, she stepped into the room and cleared her throat.

The men turned to face her, but this time there was no surprise. They formed into a loose group, presenting themselves. A few of them pushed out their chests.

Scanning their faces, Julie's eyes locked with a man in the back. He was older, probably in his midtwenties, with black stubble on his face. His hair, cropped short, still managed to curl. He stared back at Julie, drawing on his cigarette, and there was something in his sneer that reminded her of Cutter. That, at least, was something.

"You," she said, pointing. "Come with me."

He shouldered the other men and followed her to the bunk room, flipping the door shut behind him.

"Well?" he asked.

Julie's heart was pounding so hard that the whole room pulsed. Forcing a smile, she walked to the man, rising onto her toes and bringing her lips to his.

"Not so fast," the man said, putting a hand out to stop her; his breath was burnt and stale. He looked her over, kneading the baggy fatigues that obscured her features. Julie managed to keep the smile plastered on her face as he stretched her shirt collar and peered inside. Dissatisfied, he cupped her crotch roughly, squeezing the fabric in several places.

"Okay," he said, stepping back and sticking a fresh cigarette into his mouth. "How much?"

Julie shook her head, not trusting herself to speak.

"Really?" he asked. "So this is what? Just for the thrill?"

Julie shrugged.

"Well, in that case," the man said, tossing away the unlit cigarette. He jerked his belt open, sliding down his pants and underwear in a single movement. His legs were coated in black hair, and his golden brown skin turned shockingly pale at mid-thigh. There was a tangled nest of dark hair between his legs out of which jutted the tip of his penis, thick and shriveled. Julie gasped, stepping back. The man soured at her reaction, anger covering his embarrassment.

"Get to it," he said, grabbing her hair and pulling her

head down. She smelled the acerbic musk of his crotch two feet before her face reached it.

Julie staggered out into the night air, holding her pants together with a fist, her shirt half-buttoned. She managed three steps before dropping to her knees and vomiting on the sidewalk. Down on all fours, she wretched until there was nothing but bile. Even after the gagging subsided, she didn't trust herself to sit up. After a while, she felt a hand on her shoulder—the driver of the humvee. He helped her up and offered her a towel. He waited with the expression of a mannequin as she wiped her mouth, then took the towel back, folded it, and held out a small white pill.

"The colonel said you should take this in the next twenty-four hours," he said, offering his canteen.

Julie took the pill and dry swallowed it, keeping her eyes locked on the driver, resisting the urge to hit him. She knew he wouldn't fight back; she knew it would change nothing.

"There's a change of clothes in the truck," he said. "And private showers over by—"

"Just take me home," Julie said, her voice worn to gravel.

The man nodded. He opened the truck's rear door for Julie, then set the canteen on the seat beside her. He went around to the driver's side, started the engine, and drove away.

Julie didn't move once the entire journey; she just stared at the road ahead. By the time the truck reached the base, the morning sky was glowing pink. The truck pulled up to her house, and she saw lights on inside. She walked robotically through the front door, directly to her father's office. He was at his desk, thumbing through a thick report and making notes on a yellow legal pad. He worked for several minutes, checked his watch, then looked up.

"Any problems?" he asked, seemingly unmoved by her appearance, or her smell.

"No, Father," Julie said.

"Good," he said. "Were you scared?"

Julie tried to answer, but her voice only squeaked.

"Being scared is natural," her father said. "Only the foolish are fearless. The smart use their fear. They draw strength from it while keeping their mind clear and their judgment sound. One thing I wish *my* father had told me was that sometimes you just have to stare death in the eye and say fuck it."

When Julie said nothing, he added, "If you'll pardon my language."

"Fuck it," Julie repeated, her voice wooden. Her father, suddenly concerned, came around the desk. He put a hand on her shoulder and looked into her eyes.

"I'm very proud of you for what you just did," he said. "It's something that most people twice your age couldn't do. It sets you above them. After this, you will face your darkest fears head-on. You can do anything now. Do you understand?"

"Yes, Father," Julie said. She met his gaze, but her eyes were unfocused.

"My daughter," he said, beaming. "Get yourself cleaned up. Now that you know how to handle yourself, I'm sending you to North Ridge."

TWENTY NINE

D-5 WAS GATHERED TOGETHER in the dome, near enough to the hallway to keep an eye on the pipe to the transfer station. Hiller walked through the men, divvying out ammo from a small box.

"And what about oxygen?" Simms asked.

"Twelve tanks, sir," Hiller said. "Enough for everyone, taking into account..." Hiller trailed off.

"Twelve is plenty, Lieutenant," Simms said. Then, pointing down the hall, "Orton, what would it take to seal that pipe?"

"I can weld something over it with the oxyacetylene torch."

"We can't seal the pipe," Boxx objected. "Not until MacArthur returns—"

"Nobody cares about your stupid hovertoy," Cutter said, waving at their makeshift barricade. "We're low on ammo and we're shielding ourselves with produce. If more bugs show up, we're fucked."

"So you seal the pipe," Julie said. "And then what?"

"And then you shut up," Cutter said. "I know that tone, J. P.. That one when you think you're smarter than—"

"Sergeant," Simms cut in. Then, to the group. "First we

seal the pipe, then we work out a way back to the surface. Step one is to get back up to the docking station."

"Which still leaves us under a mile of water," Julie said.

"But halfway there," Cutter said.

"Halfway to nowhere," Julie said.

"We should blow the place up," Orton said.

"And how does that help?" Serio asked.

"It releases all the air at once," Orton said. "We can ride the air bubble to the surface."

"We're two miles down," Serio said. "It'll take hours to reach the surface."

"That doesn't matter," Orton said. "You enter a state of hypoxia—lack of oxygen—and pass out. The near-freezing temperatures cause severe hypothermia, which preserves your nervous system. You leave your mouth open, so the expanding air doesn't explode your lungs, and you wake up on the surface."

"And you know this how?"

"I read it," Orton said. "In the *emergency evacuation* section of the Explorer's manual."

"Submarines have a manual?" Serio asked

"Everything has a manual."

"You read too much," Cutter said.

"Or not enough," Serio added. "That kind of pressure change will boil your brain fluid. You'd end up dumb as a carrot."

"They didn't mention that part," Orton said, frowning thoughtfully. "Maybe it's classified."

Serio stared at Orton, incredulous, then broke out laughing. One by one, the men all joined in.

"I say we continue down," Julie said as the laughter tapered off. "We head to the drone base."

"I knew it," Cutter said, shaking his head.

"We can't stay here," she said. "This isn't a fortress, and it's quickly becoming an aquarium. Welding the pipe shut will only make that worse."

"So we cut drain holes," Cutter said.

"The tunnel will fill up," Julie said. "It's already halfway there and we've got the whole ocean above us. And we're going to be stuck down here for some time, aren't we, Lieutenant?"

Julie looked at Simms, but he made no response.

"The Explorer's not coming back," Julie continued. "Even if it is still functional, the navy won't risk their billion-dollar prototype over a few grunts. They'll dry-dock it for a full inspection. And you said that the base's bathyscaphe was damaged?"

"Destroyed," Cutter admitted. "So what?"

"So where does that leave us?"

All eyes turned to Simms, waiting. Cutter motioned for him to speak and put a hint of a threat in the gesture.

"It leaves us waiting for another ride," Simms said finally. "Probably a Seawolf outfitted with a submersible. There aren't any in the Atlantic right now, which is why we used the Explorer in the first place. The Russians could reach us faster, but I doubt the colonel would ask. They're the main reason they built this base."

"Agreed," Julie said. "And he won't enlist a private sub because this base is top secret. So we're down here for days, at least, while they fly something in from the Pacific. A full week if they bring it by boat."

"Fuck," Cutter said.

"Either way, the elevator shaft is sealed, with about a billion tons of pressure on top of it, so the only way out of this place is down there, through the drone base's airlock," Julie said.

"Which is all the way across the transfer station," Simms said. "We'd be exposed to attack the whole way."

"We're exposed here," Julie said. "You might as well just put a blanket over your head as seal the pipe. You saw the door up in the docking station."

"Not that you care," Simms said, "but there are men's lives at stake. The prudent move is to hole up here and wait for extraction."

"The pussy move, you mean," Julie said.

"What the fuck is your damage?" Simms said. "We are on a priority military mission for the United States of Americ—"

"You're errand boys," Julie said. "You really think the colonel gives a shit about this mission?"

"You..." Simms said, flabbergasted. "You really think this is all about you?"

"Isn't it?" Julie asked. "I have no doubt that the colonel gave you special orders regarding—"

"I will not have this conversation. We would not be here if it wasn't important."

"Oh, sure," Julie said.

"Sergeant," Simms said, motioning to Cutter, "take this woman to the store room and cuff her to something."

Cutter rose wearily and started toward Julie. She held up a hand, motioning for him to wait, then spoke to Simms. "Just give me two air tanks and you'll never see me again."

"It's tempting," he said.

"You really think we should go down there?" Cutter asked.

"I'm certain of it," Julie said.

"This is not a discussion, Sergeant," Simms said.

"I think maybe it is," Cutter said, turning to face Simms. "Sir."

"I will not have this brat undermine my—"

"She is definitely a brat," Cutter cut in, "but that doesn't make her wrong. You said so yourself, sir: all our lives are at stake. And we've already run through our playbook."

"Yes," Simms said reluctantly. He looked around at his men, who seemed dubious and apprehensive. His gaze stopped at Wolf, who, among all of them, appeared unfazed.

"Well?" he asked.

"She's right," Wolf said. His voice was deep and soft, and the men leaned in to listen. "They'll look for us at the extraction point, at the drone base. That was the plan."

Nods of agreement spread through the room, even from Cutter.

"Okay," Simms said, hands raised. "Looks like we're going down."

THIRTY

Orton worked an oxyacetylene torch under the water, circling the pipe as he cut it at floor level. When he finished, Cutter toppled it with his foot. The water drained so quickly he almost lost balance.

Boxx arrived with Patton, centering the robot in front of the hole. Across the room, Julie sat with Eric, instructing him on the COBAL rebreather.

"Bite gently as you breathe out," she said. "There's a switch in the mouthpiece that opens the valve. Then relax your jaw and draw air in. Easy, huh?"

Eric drew on the mouthpiece, his cheeks sucking in, his face growing purple.

"Release your bite," Julie said. "The tube is still closed."

Eric spit out the mouthpiece, coughing and gasping in air. "I wasn't biting, dammit," he said once he recovered. "*It wasn't working.*"

"You'll get used to it," Julie said.

"I don't see why I have to. What was wrong with the old system?"

"The COBOL system is 20 percent more efficient," Orton said as he and Cutter walked by, rolling the cut section of pipe, pushing it against the stream of water coming down the elevator shaft.

"And no air bubbles," Cutter added. "So they can't hear you coming."

"Who can't hear you coming?" Eric asked, irritated.

"Anyone," Cutter said, "if you do it right." They wedged the pipe against the wall, and Cutter walked away. "Don't worry, Fritz," he called over his shoulder. "You'll figure it out when you have to."

"What's the scale on this," Julie asked, pointing to the tank's pressure gauge.

"PSI," Orton replied.

"Fifteen thousand PSI?" Julie asked, incredulous.

"Yeah," Orton said, following Cutter. "Try not to drop it."

Simms was watching from far side of the dome. He called Julie over, and, reluctantly, she went.

"The rising air pressure is getting to him," Simms said, nodding at Eric. "It's affecting his nervous system."

"I don't need you to tell me that," Julie said.

"I just wanted to be sure you knew."

"I know!" Julie said, her voice unintentionally loud. Everyone in the room turned.

Simms motioned the men back to work, then waited a moment before he continued. "The water leaks are only going to make it worse," he said.

"I know," Julie said quietly, looking at the floor.

"I'm leaving Boxx behind to watch Petty. You want Eric to stay with them?"

"You shouldn't leave Boxx," Julie said. "You shouldn't leave anyone."

"Your friend Doctor Kirsch said moving Petty could be fatal."

"It's a hard choice, which is why they sent along a lieutenant, Lieutenant."

"Thankfully, I don't consider it a choice."

"Okay," Julie said. "I'm just trying to help."

"I wish I could believe that," Simms said. "I find it hard to believe you even value your own life."

"I value his life," Julie said, nodding at Eric.

"That's true," Simms said. "And for what it's worth, you were right. About going down to the drone base."

"I know," Julie said.

"But it doesn't help any of us if you question my authority. You know how this works. When you have an idea, you bring it to me personally."

"I didn't put you in charge," Julie said, then softened. "But you're right. Insurrection won't help anything. Just get us out of here."

"Ma'am," Simms said, giving her a tepid smile. She returned it.

"And thank you for your concern, Lieutenant," Julie said. "About Eric."

"Of course," he said.

Julie returned to Eric, who was hunched over, on the verge of passing out.

"Ready to try again?" she asked.

Eric drew himself up and nodded.

THIRTY ONE

JULIE THREW HER FIST without warning, jabbing at the man's exposed cheek. Sensing a clean hit, she leaned into the punch, putting her weight behind it. But at the last second a black leather pad moved in and took the blow.

"Good," her instructor said. "Again."

They were sparring on the dry October grass of North Ridge Military Academy's south lawn, encircled by fellow students. Julie's class was nicknamed the Latecomers, and consisted of students who had enrolled as upperclassman, and so missed the disciplinary routine offered to the freshmen. The Latecomers were kept separate from the rest of the students, because they had historically been a source of trouble—most of them came from families with enough influence to place them at North Ridge after they'd been kicked out of other academies.

Julie circled the combat instructor, a short, muscular man with a mouthful of metallic crowns and large scars on his face and neck. She shifted her bare fists like a boxer and swept a foot at his knee. He pulled back just before she hit.

"Weak," he said, slapping Julie's cheek with the leather pad strapped to his hand. Julie tried to block his blow but was too slow. The instructor swung again, slapping her other cheek.

"Faster," he said.

Julie brushed the hair from her eyes—she wore it bobbed now—and continued to circle. She made a jab at the instructor's stomach, which he easily blocked as he slapped her again. She tried to punch his face, but he shoved back on her shoulder, pushing her out of reach.

"Focus, Porter," the instructor said.

Julie made another jab, but he beat her back with his open hand. Her cheeks stung and had started to bloat. She snarled in frustration and charged, driving her shoulder at the instructor's chest. He sidestepped easily and pressed his foot to the back of her leg as she passed, shoving her knee to the ground. But Julie had anticipated his attack; as he himself had taught her, she had been lulling him into a false sense of confidence, taking his blows and waiting for him to get sloppy, to provide an opening. She twisted around and grappled the instructor's ankle. Pulling him to her, she drove her head into his stomach.

It was a solid hit, knocking the instructor flat on his back. Julie sprang forward, driving her fist into his jaw. She cocked her arm for another blow, but the instructor grabbed her arms in his thick fingers, immobilizing her.

Several of the other students gasped—in three months, this was the first time any of them had scored a hit on the instructor, much less brought him down. Julie struggled against his grip, sweat dripping from her face. The instructor broke into a deep, rich laugh.

"Good," he said. "Very good."

He released her arms, pushed her to her feet, then held out his hand. Julie was worked up, overwrought, but the instructor's laugh was infectious. She grinned, taking his hand and pulling him up.

"You have a healthy temper," he said, patting her arm. "That's a powerful thing, *if* you can control it." He turned to the group and said, "Pair up for Drill One."

Drill One was a grappling exercise in which one student lay on the ground while another straddled them with their knees, pinning them down. The student on top locked their hands to the lower one's throat, and the lower student's task was to break their grasp and end up on top. The students had learned several methods of both escaping and preventing escape, and the trick was for the trapped student to use a method the other wasn't prepared for.

The only other girl in the Latecomers was Kathlyn, and so Julie was always paired with her for combat. They also roomed together, showered together, and sat with each other at mess. That was more Kathlyn than Julie cared for. Frankly, she'd have been happier if they'd never met.

Kathlyn would have been young for a sophomore but, thanks to her flawless grades, was enrolled as a senior. It didn't hurt that her father was some bigwig in the Pentagon, and that she had been educated at some elite private school in DC. Unlike the rest of them, she was at North Ridge to pad out her résumé before heading to West Point.

Julie stretched out on the ground and Kathlyn straddled her stomach. Kathlyn's long chestnut hair was drawn back in a doll-head pony tail, and her outsized breasts ballooned off her emaciated frame as if glued on as an afterthought. Kathlyn was a head taller, but she was so light that Julie barely felt the knees pressing on her arms.

"Are you ready?" Julie asked, twinkling with anticipation.

"Yes," Kathlyn said. Her voice was deep and lush, the sort of thing men found attractive—especially the older ones.

She wrapped bone-thin fingers timidly around Julie's neck. Julie remained still, waiting while Kathlyn mentally rehearsed possible countermoves as if they were formulas for trigonometry. Kathlyn was at the top of the class in everything but combat, for which she had no aptitude, no instinct, and so little muscle that her father had probably fudged her fitness report.

"I'll do the arm grab," Julie said with a wink, "then trap your leg."

Kathlyn gave a small nod, grateful for the help. She extended her leg to the side, stabilizing herself against Julie's attack.

As if, Julie thought.

"You ready?" she asked.

Kathlyn nodded. Julie looked to the instructor, waiting until he was occupied with another student before making her move.

She slipped her arms free and grabbed one of Kathlyn's arms at both the wrist and the bicep. She hooked her leg around Kathlyn's, bending it as she rolled them both sideways. Kathlyn struggled futilely as Julie, now on top, splayed her against the ground. The final move was for Julie to pin Kathlyn; she rose into a handstand and then drove her knees into Kathlyn's stomach. The younger girl groaned, and as the instructor turned to look, Julie slid her knees to the ground.

"Your turn," Julie said with a grin.

"When are you gonna give me a crack at Kathlyn?" David asked.

"You can have her," Julie said.

Julie, David, and two other boys were walking from the

dining room back to their dorm—but as soon as they were out of sight, they slipped into a nearby patch of woods. There was an hour between dinner and curfew; it was meant for studying, but no one kept tabs.

"Old Scarface would never let me," David said, lighting a cigarette as soon as they reached the cover of the trees. David had been kicked out of three schools in three years and fully expected the same to happen here. But he didn't care because his family was wealthy, and he was already set for life. He was the oldest in their class, almost college age, and his piercing blue eyes projected innocence and sincerity. "I think the old man pops one watching you two wrestle."

"He probably chubs up just thinking about it," added Kevin, the youngest.

"And you probably chub up thinking about him," David said, shoving Kevin forward, then kicking at his feet. "Groping your butthole in the shower."

"So classy," Julie said, but she smiled, amused.

"I like watching you wrestle," George said. George was large, and lumbered alongside Julie with a hulking gait.

"See?" David said, as if this proved his point. "Tell Scarface you and George want to train together. Then he'll have to let me wrestle Kathlyn."

"You're wasting your time," Julie said, taking the cigarette from David and drawing deeply. "She's too proper for that."

"Oh, all you ladies are," David said. "Until you're not. You just need a little warming up."

David grabbed playfully at Julie's breast, but she snatched his wrist and twisted it, spinning him around and locking his arm behind his back in a single, fluid movement. George laughed, deep and dull, as David tried to break free of Julie's grasp.

"Calm down, Porter," David said, and she let go. He

rubbed his wrist, then snatched his cigarette from Julie's mouth. "You should try men sometime," he said. "You might even like it."

"You're sad," Julie said.

"And you're bitter," David said, hopping back as Julie took a swipe at him. "But Kathlyn, she's just shy. Did you see the way she looked at me during dinner tonight?"

"Like she was sick?" Julie asked.

"Lovesick," David said. "And I'm the cure." He pumped his hips, getting a laugh from Kevin.

"Sick for your love," Kevin said, laughing harder, as if he had made it funnier.

"Ugh," Julie said. "You make me gay."

"Oh, I'd be gay for you, Porter," David said, pumping his hips at her. "You just say the word, cowgirl."

"So many boys," Julie said. "Where are the men?"

THIRTY TWO

The water on the floor had drained down to a half inch, but remained at that level, fed by the stream pouring down the elevator shaft. Patton was centered over the pipe, balanced on two planks of wood.

"Watch yourself down there, buddy," Boxx said, patting the robot on its would-be cheek. Serio and Wolf jerked the planks away in unison, and Patton plummeted. Boxx covered his eyes as the robot rattled down the pipe, ricocheting against the walls. It dropped out of the pipe and plunged into the water, sinking beneath the surface.

Boxx fed a wire down the pipe that had a small antenna on the end. When the antenna cleared the pipe, he tied the wire off and plugged the other end into Patton's control panel, which had been moved nearby. He hit the power switch, and Patton's lights turned on, glowing beneath the surface.

"Online," Boxx said, an underwater view rising on the three-dimensional display. He rotated Patton's head—there were walls on three sides, but only darkness on the last. "Visibility maybe twenty feet."

"Advance thirty," Simms said. He sat down beside Boxx and watched the hazy water roll by as the robot moved along the smooth cement floor.

"Hold there," Simms said, and Boxx stopped the robot. "Cutter and Orton, you're up."

Cutter stepped to the edge of the pipe. He had exchanged his armor for a wetsuit and wore the same thick-tubed nightscope that Wolf used when he had first entered the base. His only other equipment was a radio headset and a sidearm. He pulled on neoprene gloves and crouched beside the pipe.

"You be ecareful down there, amigo," Serio said, leaning down to pat Cutter on the cheek.

"Beep boop beep," Cutter replied tenderly.

"Fuck you both," Boxx said.

"Stay frosty," Simms said. "There's still—"

"Don't remind me about the bugs," Cutter said. He rolled into the pipe headfirst, grabbing the top rung and descending the ladder upside down. It was hard work, but Cutter moved ably, barely breaking a sweat.

When Cutter was halfway down, Orton entered the pipe behind him, right-side up, with two pairs of flippers dangling from his waist. Orton stopped when he was chin-level to the floor, and Serio set an air tank on each of his shoulders, wedged between Orton's head and the pipe's walls.

"Don't leave anything alive on my account," Serio said. Orton nodded, smiling, but his hands were trembling. He climbed down after Cutter, the tanks scraping along the walls.

The transfer station was cavernous, five stories tall and twice as wide. A lake of dark water filled the room, rising to within eight feet of the pipe, which itself hung fifteen feet down from the ceiling. The ladder extended less than a foot from the pipe before the steel runners were twisted and broken off. A tube of water flowed from the pipe walls, glowing from the light above, frothing the underground lake and raising an eerie mist.

A shadow appeared inside the watery curtain—a man uncurled, hanging from the pipe by his feet. The curtain was broken by the long lens of a nightscope.

Cutter, hanging upside down, looked left and right, then switched his feet to check behind him. The room looked empty, but it continued on well past what he could see. He clicked the Transmit button on his headset twice.

"Proceed," Simms replied quietly.

Cutter slipped his feet from the ladder's rung, dropping into the water without a splash. He surfaced inside the flowing water, and Orton dropped him a pair of flippers. He pulled them on and kicked hard, rising halfway from the water to grab the air tank that Orton dangled from an extended foot. Cutter strapped the tank on his back and submerged, reappearing outside the tube of water, pistol in hand. He spun around, checking behind him. The air was warm, considerably more so than the operations room, and thickly humid. It felt wrong.

Orton dropped out of the tube, clutching his air tank to his chest as he splashed feet first into the water. He sank below the surface. Cutter swam over and grabbed him by the collar, hauling him up. Orton coughed loudly; it echoed through the transfer station.

"Up my nose," Orton apologized between coughs.

Cutter held Orton as he pulled on his flippers and air tank, then both men adjusted the air in their vests until they were floating on the water. They exchanged thumbs-up, then Cutter clicked his headset twice. Patton's lights, glowing twenty feet beneath the surface, glided forward.

The men followed, swimming quietly into the long darkness.

THIRTY THREE

"Can't that thing go faster?" Simms asked.

"Patton is heavy armor," Boxx said, watching the water move silently past the display, the view sweeping back and forth as the robot swung its head. "He's slow *above* water."

"How long will his battery last?" Julie asked, standing behind them.

"I ran him for forty-six hours once," Boxx said. "He has some sort of high-efficiency fuel cell, but that's all they'll tell me. I shouldn't even know that much, but—"

"What's that?" Simms asked, raising his finger to the screen, where a dark object floated in the water.

Swimming painfully slow, Cutter and Orton were nothing but a dark outline against the glowing water as they followed Patton's submerged lights through the cavernous tunnel. Cutter's gaze circled around the transfer station's walls and arched ceiling, checking every shadow of the coarse rock. Orton trailed behind, checking their rear every few seconds.

The air grew warmer the farther they went and was now bordering on tropical, though the water remained just above freezing. The end of the room was still too far away to see, and the pipe behind them had shrunk to a distant, faint line.

Orton motioned to Cutter, twirling his finger. Cutter nodded in agreement, then shrugged. He, too, would like to move faster, but there was no way to ask without breaking the silence. And if anything was down here, he hoped all it noticed was the robot.

Orton frowned at Cutter, then, looking back, motioned anxiously—they had swum ahead of Patton's lights; the robot had stopped.

"I can't tell," Boxx said, leaning into the floating display and peering at the dark object.

The radio clicked three times—Cutter requesting status. "Hang on," Simms replied absently, his attention on Patton's display.

Boxx eased the robot sideways, shifting the view, but the object remained a dark blur, floating just above the floor. He turned Patton and drove straight at it.

Cutter turned in a circle, jerking his gun back and forth. Orton wore a diving mask and had his face in the water, watching Patton's murky outline recede.

"What the fuck?" Orton mouthed, popping his head up.

Cutter clicked his Transmit button rapidly.

"Hold there," Simms said into the radio, which was clicking wildly. "Boxx is taking a closer look at something."

Patton approached the dark object, circling it, but the radio signal was growing weak. Static swirled through the three-dimensional display like snow.

As Patton swung to the object's profile, they saw it was MacArthur. But half of the drone was missing, as if torn apart lengthwise. Boxx recoiled.

"Did the bugs get him?" Simms asked, but Boxx only stared, too horrified to answer.

"Specialist!" Simms barked.

"Sir?" Boxx asked, dazed. "Sorry, sir," he said. He bent over and fiddling with the control panel, but the image was breaking up, the static growing thicker. "Send Cutter to take a closer look," he said.

Simms gave him a dubious look, but picked up the radio. "Sergeant," he said. "Specialist Boxx requests you to dive down to look at something," he said.

Cutter replied with a single click.

"Order him to," Boxx said.

"It's his butt," Simms said, shaking his head, "so it's his call. We proceed."

Boxx didn't move. Simms took the specialist's hand and placed it on the control stick.

"Proceed," he said.

Reluctantly, Boxx tilted the stick forward. Patton passed the floating remains of MacArthur as he continued down the tunnel.

"You're up, Serio," Simms said.

Serio heaved a large rubber bundle up over his head and started down the pipe. It was a tight squeeze, for both him and the bundle.

Serio hung by one hand from the bottom rung in the pipe, the rubber bundle clamped between his knees. He dug inside, finding a small air tank and turning the valve. He dropped the bundle, which sank into the water and then rose back up, hissing, inflating into a Zodiac-style raft.

He dropped into the water and flipped the raft over, emptying the water, then turned it back upright and pulled himself in. He reached up to the pipe, taking the rifle Hiller extended down to him, then slid to the front of the raft and aimed into the dark tunnel.

Hiller dropped awkwardly into the water and climbed into the raft, positioning himself near the pipe. A metal basket filled with equipment was lowered down. He unloaded it and gave the rope a tug. The basket drew back up and returned with another load.

Above them, in the hallway, two soldiers loaded equipment into the basket while Simms and Boxx squinted at Patton's static-filled display.

The air was stiflingly hot, but the walls had begun to converge, and Cutter could see the far side of the room. They had almost made it.

"We've lost video," Simms said over the radio. "You'll have to drive Patton from your end."

Cutter clicked his headset twice and holstered his gun. He flipped back the nightscope, splashed cool water on his face, and pulled out Patton's remote. The remote was in a plastic case, and its small screen showed nothing but hazy green water. He put his thumbs on the twin control sticks and pressed forward. The robot backed up.

Orton motioned for Cutter to rotate the remote, which he did, but this time Patton veered off to one side. Cutter angled the remote, leaning his body as if to straighten the robot's path, to no effect. He released the controls just before Patton hit the wall and, exasperated, tossed the remote to Orton. Orton grabbed it before it sunk, then worked the controls expertly, turning the robot and driving it forward.

"You should be nearing the end of the transfer station," Simms said, his voice breaking up. "Wait for us there. And see if you can't get Patton out of the water."

The men swam forward in silence. Up ahead, a cement ledge hovered just above the water, jutting out to a rock slope that led up to the far wall. *THIS WAY* had been spray-painted on the wall in bright orange, along with several arrows and a splattered rendering of Kilroy.

Cutter swam faster, home free, outpacing Patton's lights, but then Orton started to click his radio—he had stopped. Cutter motioned him forward, but Orton shook his head, waving him back. Reluctantly, Cutter returned. Orton turned Patton's remote to show Cutter the display. Below them, the floor of the room was blocked by a pile of steel rails, the sort used for trains. The rails were mangled, interwoven as if they were part of a giant bird's nest. Orton drove Patton from one side of the room to the other, but there was no way around it.

"Leave the damn robot," Cutter whispered, looking to the ledge, and to the dry land beyond it. "Let Boxx figure it out."

"We're blind without him," Orton replied, waving at the water.

"Fuck," Cutter said. Orton was right. There was only about fifty yards between them and the end of the tunnel, but they had no idea what might be hidden in or on the other side of the steel pile. Their job was to clear the way, for the safety of the others. "So what do we do?" he asked, but just then Patton's lights faded. Orton held up the remote; the display was blank. He hit every button, but nothing appeared. He looked to Cutter, but it was too dark to see. A light switched on right in front of him, the small LED on Cutter's pistol. It made a white cone in the wet air. Orton drew his own sidearm, and the men swam in a circle, swinging their guns toward every sound, real or imagined.

Cutter looked longingly at the cement ledge, then turned away, motioning downward. Orton nodded.

Cutter pulled on his diving mask, knocking off his nightscope and headset. They sank into the water, forgotten, as the men dove, swimming down to where they had last seen Patton. Their small lights faded beneath the surface.

Simms was in the transfer station, treading water just beneath the pipe. He reached up to help Eric down to the water, then shuttled him to the raft. He returned to help Julie, but she was already swimming over.

The raft was laden with equipment, and the soldiers, of which there were now eleven, were lined up in the water on either side, holding the rope that ran along its tubular hull. Serio was at the back, beside a small motor, and Wolf was the only one aboard, lying across the cargo, his minigun aimed forward.

"Cutter, come back," Simms said into his headset. He listened, then repeated himself. No reply.

"Weapons out," he said. "Let's get moving, Serio."

TUNNEL

The men shifted their rifles forward as Serio twisted the throttle on the electric motor, propelling them through the cavernous room.

THIRTY FOUR

The worst part of being paired with Kathlyn for a report on military history was that she insisted on working every night after dinner, which was when Julie would hang out with her friends in the woods. And it stung all the more so tonight, because David had somehow gotten hold of a bottle of whiskey. He promised to save her some, but she doubted he would.

Julie spent an hour in the library with her face pointed at a book on WW II that, for all she noticed it, could have been upside down or entirely blank. The library was nearly empty and so quiet that she could hear the scratch of Kathlyn's pen as she took notes in her perfect longhand.

"I don't know about using this Rommel quote," Kathlyn said, looking up. "Everybody uses Rommel. Can we can find someone else who spoke on the importance of the radio in the evolution of battlefield tactics? Maybe from Montgomery? Or Eisenhower?"

"Sure," Julie said, flipping through her book as if reading. *Studious Kathlyn,* she thought. *Vestal Kathlyn. Friendless Kathlyn.* The last made Julie laugh; she pretended it was something in her book. "Montgomery was ridiculous."

"He was a genius," Kathlyn said.

"He was a jerk."

"He just didn't concern himself with what people thought of him," Kathlyn said. "That's an important quality for a leader."

"Huh," Julie said, keeping her eyes on the book. Kathlyn had romantic feelings toward several dead generals, and, irritatingly, she assumed that Julie did as well. Kathlyn treated Julie like she was her best friend when nothing could be further from the truth.

When the library finally closed, Julie ducked into the bathroom to avoid walking back to the dorms with Kathlyn. Once the coast was clear, she made her ways for the woods, lighting a crumpled cigarette. She searched for David and the others, but they had already left.

It was almost curfew, so she killed the cigarette with a few long drags, crushed it out, and headed for the dorms. She was rounding a curved hedge when she heard David's voice on the other side.

"I say she's fresh," he said, his speech slurred. "Untouched. Just look at her."

Julie found an opening in the hedges and peered into a circular courtyard. David was standing with an arm draped over Kathlyn's shoulder, his face close to hers. George and Kevin were nearby, leaning unsteadily against each other and watching. This wasn't the first time David had hassled Kathlyn. Julie smiled, expectant.

"I really need to be going," Kathlyn said, cringing from David's breath. Julie noticed the empty bottle lying at David's feet.

Bastard, she thought. *So much for saving some for me.* She started into the courtyard but stopped when David suddenly sprang at Kathlyn. He locked a hand on her neck, chewing her mouth as he groped her breast through her shirt. Kathlyn pushed him back and shot her knee up between his legs, but he grabbed it before it hit home. He spread her leg to the side and shoved his groin against hers, kneading her butt. She writhed, trying to break free, but he was too strong.

Julie took another step and again stopped, unsure what to do. Unsure what she wanted to do. David was her friend. Kathlyn was a nuisance.

David was trying to grab Kathlyn's belt, but every time he took his hand from her leg, she twisted away from him. Frustrated, he shoved her into George's arms.

"Hold her, goddamn it," he said. Kathlyn, trapped in George's thick arms, let out a scream. George clamped a hand over her mouth, and everyone froze, listening as the scream echoed through the still night.

Kevin backed away, wide eyed. He saw Julie across the clearing and motioned for her to do something. Julie shook her head and turned to watch David. He surveyed the nearby dorms, but saw nothing in response to Kathlyn's scream.

"Sounded like an owl to me," David said, retrieving the whiskey bottle. Finding it empty, he chucked it away and returned to Kathlyn. George had one hand clamped over her mouth and the other arm around her waist. Her back was bent at his hip, jutting out her chest. David unbuttoned her shirt casually, like unwrapping a package, then stripped off her bra.

"Glorious," he said, cupping a breast from below, as if testing the weight. "You should be in magazines."

Kathlyn squirmed, helpless.

"Now, where were we?" David asked, unbuckling her belt, and then his own. Kathlyn kicked at him and he grabbed her legs, pulling off her pants, exposing pale, frail legs. "Easy, sweetheart," David said, sliding his pants down to his knees. Kathlyn trembled as if from hypothermia, but she no longer struggled. Her eyes were unfocused. She hung limply in George's arms.

"Much better," David said, stepping forward. "I knew you'd come around."

"Julie!" Kevin shouted, anxious, pleading. David looked sharply at Kevin, then followed his gaze to Julie.

"Porter," David said, relaxing. "Just in time for the fun."

As he turned to face her, she saw his cock was swollen in anticipation. Her anger flared, and she started toward him. There was no mistaking the look on her face. David kicked off his pants and raised his fists.

"Careful," he said, the word scrubbing as Julie drove a fist into his stomach. He doubled over, a wad of vomit flying from his mouth. Julie slammed her elbow down on the back of his neck, flattening him to the ground.

"Get out of here, Kevin," she said, advancing on George, who looked confused by this turn of events. Julie swung a roundhouse at George's face, and he staggered back. He released Kathlyn; she fell to the grass, curling her legs to her chest and weeping.

Julie threw one punch after another, driving George backward. He tried to block her, but, big as he was, he was too slow. His nose flattened with a crunch, and blood poured down his face. Finally, he started to teeter. Julie kicked his leg, toppling him, and hammered her heavy boots into his ribs and face. He coughed, spitting out blood, then teeth.

David rose unsteadily to his feet. Kathlyn gasped, retreating, but he didn't seem to notice her. He was looking at George, whose face was a bloody pulp, and Julie, who was still kicking him. He gaped in horror.

"Julie," he said, pleading, stumbling forward, hand outstretched. "Stop."

Julie turned, seemingly confused to find him there. Then she grinned, balling her fist and cocking back her arm.

"One boy has lost half his teeth," the colonel said. "The other is in intensive care. You almost killed him."

"But I didn't," Julie said.

The two sat in the academy's infirmary. A nurse looked on from across the room, staring at Julie with both scorn and fear. There were thick bandages on Julie's knuckles and a metal brace across three of her toes. It was almost morning—the colonel had arrived by police-escorted motorcade just hours after the incident was reported, followed shortly by Kathlyn's father, who had arrived by helicopter. Kathlyn, who was shaken but unharmed, had been taken elsewhere to meet him. David and George had been taken to the hospital. Kevin was still missing.

"You did this to save that girl?" her father asked.

"No," Julie said.

"Then what were you...?"

The colonel pressed his lips together, then turned to the nurse.

"Would you give us a few minutes?" he asked.

The nurse nodded and left. The colonel turned back to his daughter.

"Do you even know who Kathlyn's father is?" he asked, all but whispering.

Julie looked up, surprised by her father's tone. She shook her head. The colonel smiled broadly.

"Then you have great luck," he said. "Of all the people to have in your debt, she is certainly one of the best."

"Kathlyn?"

"Yes, Kathlyn. When I sent you here, I had hoped the two of you might become close, but this..." Her father smiled, gripping Julie's shoulder in excitement. "Kathlyn's father has the ear of the president himself and is certain to be the next secretary of state. There is no limit to what he can provide us with. My daughter."

The last he said with such delight that Julie felt herself swell. Doubt and regret gave way to pride and satisfaction. She now knew she had done the right thing.

"Take me home," she said. "I don't want to be an officer. I want to be a soldier, like you were."

Her father squeezed her hand in his own, wizened one, and told her she was strong and brave, and that she was the best child a man could ask for. Julie leaned against him, feeling his words gently vibrate in his chest.

There was a knock at the door and a man entered. He was out of uniform, but Julie recognized him immediately.

"Sorry to interrupt," he said.

"Please," her father said, standing quickly and motioning him over. "Julie, you remember General Covington?"

"Call me Carl," the general said. "I wanted to thank you personally for saving my daughter from..."

The general trailed off and looked down at his hands, which fumbled about nervously. The colonel eased Julie toward him.

"Kathlyn is my dearest friend," Julie said. "I would die to protect her."

"Yes," he said, examining her with moist eyes. "I believe you would."

He gazed at Julie for some time, until the colonel cleared his throat.

"My daughter has been through a lot herself," he said apologetically.

"Yes, of course," the general said, moving to the door "You should be proud of that young woman, John. Call me on Monday. We have a lot to discuss."

The colonel said he would and the general turned to Julie, extending his hand. "Thank you," he said.

Julie shook the general's hand, her fingers curling around the scar on the back of it, the same scar she had put there just the previous year.

THIRTY FIVE

Boxx paced the length of the dome, bored and anxious. He went to Petty's cot and checked the IV drip. The bag was half full, as it had been a minute earlier. He walked back to the control panel, but Patton's screen was still blank. He sat down, drummed his fingers, and then stood again. He looked from Petty to the pipe, down to the transfer station, and then back again.

Making a decision, he grabbed an air tank and jogged to the pipe.

The men drove the raft the length of the transfer station, seeing no sign of Cutter or Orton, or anyone else. As they approached the end of the cavernous room, the men peeled off and spread out in the water. Serio continued forward, driving the raft right onto the cement ledge—the water had risen and was now level with the ledge. He spun the raft around so that Wolf and his minigun were aimed back at the water. The other soldiers scrambled up the ledge, forming a rough line, guns pointing in all directions. Simms lit a flare and tossed it high on the rocky slope that led onward, in the direction of the tunnel.

Around the point where the slope crested, the ceiling cracked open into a gaping fissure. Simms walked up the slope, searching the overhead fissure so intently that he nearly stepped into it—the gap continued down through the floor, growing wider as it descended, its walls coated in the rippled black stone of long-cooled lava. It descended beyond the range of Simms's light, and air rose from its depths, furnace-hot, blasting his face.

"The Azores Fracture Zone," Eric said, walking up behind him. "I never thought I'd see it with my own eyes."

"How deep does it go?" Simms asked.

Eric shrugged. "Nothing goes deeper."

"Volcanic?" Julie asked, extending her hand into the hot, dry air.

"Definitely," Eric said. "This is a straight drop to the earth's mantle."

"That's over twenty miles below us," Simms said, incredulous.

"Yes," Eric said gravely. "Watch your step."

In front of him, three planks of wood had been lashed together to form a minimal bridge. Simms tested the wood gingerly, then started across the chasm. By the time he reached the center, the thin planks bounced with every step, their ends rising up and slapping against the ground. He changed his pace, trying to counter the bounce, and took longer, faster steps. He leaped the last yard, and when Julie started after him, he motioned her back.

There were more fractures on this side, all quite deep, though none wider than two feet. Simms hopped over them as he walked to the far wall, looking for a way forward.

"Short tunnel," Julie said, after he returned.

"It's not supposed to be."

"Maybe the rest is under the water," Julie said.

"The whole thing?" Simms asked. "It's a hundred miles long."

"Flashlight," Julie said, holding out her hand. Reluctantly, Simms handed her the light from his gun barrel.

Julie laid down along the edge of the fissure and shined the light inside. There was a perfect circle cut in the far wall, three stories high—the train tunnel, though much more modern than what she had seen under Governors Island. This one was a perfect circle, smooth, machine cut. She slid out over the abyss and angled the light back. She saw the same hole below her, only this side had been entirely filled in.

"The tunnel has been plugged," she said.

"The whole thing?" Simms asked, leaning over to look. The tunnel beneath them had been sealed with what looked like wet, brown cement.

"That's what's keeping the water in," Julie said. "Otherwise it'd drain into the fissure."

"That's a lot of water," Simms said, looking at the flooded transfer station behind him. It held as much water as a small lake. "How thick do you think that plug is?"

"How would I know?" Julie asked.

"Care to take a closer look?"

Julie shot him a withering look.

"Will you anyway?" Simms asked.

"Yeah," she said. "Okay."

Simms walked back down the slope to Hiller, who was on the radio, trying to raise Cutter.

"Nothing, sir," Hiller reported. "Could we have passed them?"

"I don't know," he said. "Keep trying, Lieutenant.

Martin and Chavez, get that raft unloaded. Serio and Wolf, set up a defensive line. The rest of you, help where you can."

"Which way are we defending from?" Serio asked. Simms looked up the slope to the dead end, then to Hiller, calling into his radio.

"That way," he said, pointing at the water.

Boxx's flashlight waved wildly as he struggled to keep his head above the water. He had climbed down the pipe to the transfer station, which was dark and empty, and dropped into the water. He treaded water as he worked along the wall, counting his distance in arm lengths.

"...twenty-three...twenty four..."

Boxx looked back to the pipe, having second thoughts, but it was too late now—the pipe was too high up to reach, so he had no way back up to the operations room. He steeled himself, pulled on his mask, and dove.

Julie dangled from a rope twenty feet down inside the fissure, sweat coating her body and dripping off into the abyss.

Eric held the other end of the rope on the ledge above, sitting with his legs braced against a rock. Though several yards back from the heat of the abyss, he was sweating as well, and short of breath. The rope was wrapped around his waist, and his knuckles were pale where they gripped the rope. Further down the slope, Wolf sat facing the water, aiming his minigun with one hand while the other, unseen by Eric, held the tail end of Julie's rope.

Julie tilted forward, inspecting the brownish cement

that filled the tunnel's thirty-foot diameter. The cement was bumped and pocked irregularly, and still wet despite the hot dry air blowing up from the fissure. She pressed it with a finger, leaving a dent. Her finger came back smelling of mildew and nail polish.

She turned around, looking to the other side of the fissure, where the rest of the tunnel lay. It was dark, but she could see that it continued well past the end of the transfer station.

She pushed off of the wall, swinging toward the open tunnel, but fell as her rope went suddenly slack. She dropped two feet and jerked to a stop.

"Sorry," Eric called from the ledge, his voice uneven.

"Hold tight," Julie said. "I'm coming back up."

She took one last look down the tunnel, then climbed arm-over-arm.

Boxx descended through the water, swimming awkwardly, his flippers fouling against each other. As he neared the floor of the transfer station, the water grew cold and dark. His small flashlight reflected off the haze, blinding him as much as it allowed him to see. Something appeared out of the dark, and Boxx lurched back, batting at it with his flashlight. But it was only the remains of MacArthur, unmoving.

Boxx reached for the drone gently and turned it over. The left half had been melted away, leaving a smooth, semicircular gouge along the middle.

A light appeared in the water, a bright blue halo. Boxx turned and held up the remains of the drone. While he would be in trouble for abandoning Petty, Simms would certainly understand how important it was to recover MacArthur. The drone's video unit was intact, and they could use it to see what had done this to him. He waved the drone at the light, black threads of carbon fiber billowing like hair from its melted edge.

The light drew closer, glowing so bright that Boxx had to shield his eyes. He squinted, trying to see past it. The light was coming from a thick black cylinder with a tube on either side, feeding in blue liquid. It was a device unlike any he had seen before.

Boxx backed away, but the light—and the dark shape behind it—shot forward, focusing into a blue circle on his chest. There was a pistol grip attached to the light, held by a small hand. It was human's hand, but also not. The fingers were too long, too thin. The skin was pink and translucent, revealing the bones beneath.

One of the fingers rested on what could be a trigger.

Hiller was down by the lake, unloading the raft, when a light came racing at him beneath the water.

He whistled sharply, calling attention to it as he threw himself flat on the cement ledge, steadying the barrel of his rifle on the raft. Serio raised his minigun in his bare hands, spinning up the motor. Simms sprinted toward the water, ordering the men to spread out along the rocky slope. The light pushed up to the surface, raising a hump in the water as it sped toward them.

Julie was coiling her climbing rope over by the fissure, but she dropped it and ran to Eric, first gesturing and then shoving him down behind a low stone. Once he was safe, she went to the stack of equipment and dug out a rifle.

The approaching light had nearly reached the shore, a

long, foamy V stretching out behind it. Simms, crouched, had a hand raised in the hold signal. The light leaped from the water, held by something large and dark. It landed in front of Hiller, who almost fired, but it was Cutter.

Cutter crawled straight over Hiller as he scrambled up the slope, then he rolled onto his back and yanked off his flippers. Orton emerged behind him, sitting on the ledge by the water as he removed his own flippers. He was calmer than Cutter but moved with the same urgency.

"The hell...?" Simms asked, but Cutter pushed past, shrugging off his air tank and letting it crash to the ground behind him.

"It got Patton!" he yelled, heading up the slope. Simms grabbed Cutter and spun him around.

"What got Patton?" he asked.

"Something in the water," Cutter said, shaking his head. "It was fast. Came up right behind—"

A loud report echoed through the tunnel, like the pop of a tremendous balloon. Everyone turned toward the water.

"What the...?" Hiller asked.

"No time to talk," Cutter said, pulling loose of Simms's grip. He dashed up the slope, stopping when he saw the far wall.

"What is this?" he asked.

"Dead end," Simms replied.

"Don't say dead," Cutter said. "Where's the tunnel?"

"Down there." Simms pointed at the ground.

"So why are we up here?" Cutter asked.

"It's blocked."

"By what?"

"That's what we're trying to figure out," Simms said. He turned to Julie, who shrugged.

"So we're cornered," Cutter said, looking around frantically.

"Control yourself," Simms ordered.

"We cannot be fucking cornered. Did you see what that thing did to Patton?"

Simms walked up to Cutter and locked his hands onto the sergeant's forearms. "Calm down!" he said.

Cutter tried to wrench free, but Simms slid his hands to the sergeant's wrists, bending them backward, immobilizing his arms.

"Calm. Down."

Cutter struggled half-heartedly, but he had already given up. He took a few snorting breaths and then relaxed. Simms released him.

"Where's my goddamn rifle?" he said, stomping toward the equipment.

Julie went down to the cement ledge, where Orton sat staring at the water.

"What was it?" she asked.

"Something got Patton," Orton said, distant. "He's a total wipe."

"The bugs?"

"No bug did that."

"Orton," Simms said, walking up. "I need to take a look at Patton."

"Are you serious?" Julie asked.

"That's our back," Simms said, pointing at the water. "We keep our back covered."

"We keep going," Julie said, pointing toward the tunnel. "We get the fuck out of here."

"Just let me get a fresh tank, sir," Orton said, scooping up his flippers and heading to the equipment. Cutter was already there, arming himself like a child hoarding toys.

Simms watched Cutter and frowned.

"I'm leaving Hiller in charge," he said to Julie. "It'll be in your best interest to see that he stays there."

"This is a mistake," Julie said. "We're exposed here. Who cares what's back in the water? We're past it, so let's press on. We follow the tunnel to the drone base. It's the only place that's safe."

"You don't know that."

"It has to be better than this."

Simms glared down at her, the muscle in his jaw twitching.

"We're here," he said, "because you suggested it."

"What I suggested was—"

"Serio, you're with me!" Simms yelled, turning away. "Hiller, I want a barricade along this waterline." Simms yanked a battery-powered floodlight from Cutter's hands and tested it, flashing it across the water.

Orton, Simms, and Serio followed the rocky slope as they descended into the water. The slope was steep, dropping forty feet to the cement floor. When they reached the bottom, the entrance to the tunnel loomed over them, its giant circular plug outlined by the darker rock. They swam back toward the operations room, retracing Orton's path.

Simms and Orton took point, skimming across the bottom while Serio watched over them above and behind. Simms aimed the portable floodlight at the floor to keep the reflection off the murky water from blinding him. The light diffused around them, surrounding them with a hazy glow.

The pile of tangled steel appeared, two stories high but still well below the surface. Train rails were twisted and scarred, as if they had been ripped violently from their ties. Interwoven inside was an ancient backhoe, tilted as if trying to escape. Simms hadn't seen the pile when he had passed this way before, in the boat, and he swam in for a closer look.

Buried in the nest of rails was more heavy equipment—the crushed body of a bulldozer to his left, the twisted body of a grader off to his right. The equipment looked decades old, but there was little rust—they hadn't been underwater very long.

He swam up the side of the steel pile, staying as low as he could, the others flanking him. When they crested it, Orton pointed down at the floor on the other side. Patton was a dark shadow, motionless, but there was something else, too, circling the robot. It looked like a man.

Simms handed the floodlight to Orton and motioned for him and Serio toward the wall, as a decoy. He started for the robot, weaving through the warped steel rails, using them as cover. He edged over until Patton was between himself and the other figure, then he swam out on the open floor.

As he approached the robot, he saw that the left side of its disc-shaped head was bent down at nearly a right angle. He slowed his pace as he drew close and at the last minute swung around Patton, gun forward. The water was empty. Simms spun, checking behind him, but saw nothing. He signaled to Orton and Serio; whatever it was, neither had seen it leave.

He motioned for Serio to stay back and waved Orton over. He took back the floodlight and inspected Patton, startled by the five-inch hole in the robot's torso—the same size hole as in the base's electrical generator.

The hole was supernaturally perfect, as if a section of the robot had simply been teleported away. Simms reached inside, feeling the smooth edges. Something sparked, shocking his fingers, and Patton's lights clicked on. The robot stuttered to life.

The robot lurched forward, its half arm flailing. Simms raised the floodlight, but the robot smashed through it, its arm coming down on his head. Blood wafted into the water and Simms went limp, the rifle dropping from his hands.

Orton grabbed Simms's ankle, pulling him back just as Patton swung again. The light on the robot's back flickered, then glowed a steady red. The robot turned its mutilated head toward the retreating men and started after them. Serio, over at the wall, fired, but his bullets plinked uselessly off the robot's armor.

Orton scrambled backward toward the pile of steel, dragging Simms. The lieutenant woke with a start, wide eyed and confused. He jerked free of Orton's grip and floated in the water, disoriented. Patton's dark shadow glided up from behind.

Orton made a grab for Simms, but the lieutenant dodged him. Serio swam toward them, kicking his flippers hard, but he was too far away. Patton, arm raised, rolled up to Simms and swung.

Orton shoved past Simms, thrust his rifle into the hole in Patton's torso, and emptied the clip. The robot's blow came down on Orton's forearm, snapping it in half and folding it back on itself. Orton clutched his arm and thrashed in pain as Patton raised its arm again, aiming for his head. But the robot's movements slowed; its lights dimmed and went black.

Serio swam up behind Simms, wrapping him in his big arms and holding on until Simms recognized him. He tucked Simms under one arm and grabbed the valve of Orton's air tank. He started back, dragging both men with him.

Far behind them, another light appeared in the water, deep blue in color and heading their way.

Back on the shore, the soldiers had constructed a low wall of piled rock halfway up the slope, between the water and fissure. It was a small barricade and D-5 was crowded behind it, their remaining lanterns spaced out around them.

Wolf made himself a separate gunner's nest higher up on the slope, almost to the fissure, and had assembled a makeshift bipod for his minigun from two pipes and some tape. Cutter manned the other minigun at the lower barricade, whipping it left and right as he mumbled to himself.

Julie was on the other side of the fissure. She had found her bag and was buckling her spelunking belt over her wetsuit. She pounded a spike into the ground, tied the rope to it, and lowered herself into the fissure. Peering down the tunnel, she used the laser sight on her rifle and a pair of binoculars to gauge how deep it went.

"There's definitely something up ahead," she said, speaking to Hiller, who stood on the ledge above her. "But I can't tell what. We should go check it out."

"That's the lieutenant's call," Hiller said. "We'll wait for him."

"This is our only path of retreat. We should make sure it's safe."

"You go right ahead," Hiller said. "I've got my orders."

"Another robot," Julie muttered. "This unit is overflowing with initiative."

She slung the rifle over her shoulder and climbed back up the rope.

"So who plugged the tunnel?" Eric asked as Julie pulled herself onto the ledge. "The base personnel?"

"Not them," Julie said, leaving the rope in place and walking back across the narrow plank bridge, timing her steps to reduce the bounce. "Everything else around here is just regular cement," she said. "The stuff in the tunnel is more like rock dust mixed with epoxy."

"Some new military technology?" Eric asked, looking to Hiller.

"Nothing I've heard of," Hiller said.

"We'll ask Corporal Orton when he returns," Eric said. "He's the one who would know."

"Whoever put that plug in," Julie said, "it's meant to dam the water, either to fill this room or keep it out of that fissure. How long since you first lost contact with this base?"

Hiller looked at his watch. "Forty-six hours," he said.

"Hrm," Julie said. The plug was thirty feet in diameter and thick enough to hold back a mile and a half of water. It should have been impossible to make such a thing so quickly. She walked down the slope to the rock barricade and knelt beside Cutter. He was whipping the mini gun back and forth frenetically, sweat rolling down his forehead.

"How's it going, Sarge?" she asked.

"Do *not* distract me, Porter."

"Distract you from what?"

"From that," Cutter said, jerking the gun toward another section of empty water.

"Of course," Julie said, laying her hand on Cutter's forearm, "but maybe you should leave this to the grunts. Maybe you and I should go take a look inside that tunnel?"

Cutter looked at her hand with wild eyes, then shook it off.

"Not me, Porter," he said. "I don't know what you're up to, but—incoming!" Cutter yelled the last word, jabbing a finger at the water. Hiller and Eric rushed to the cover of the barricade as a light appeared beneath the surface.

The soldiers, Julie included, took aim at the light and

Hiller raised his hand in the hold signal. Cutter ignored Hiller, pulling the trigger as Serio broke through the surface. His aim was true, but Julie knocked the barrel upward. Bullets strafed across the ceiling, and shards of rock rained down on the men. Serio didn't notice. He shoved Simms onto the cement ledge—now several inches under water—then crawled up it with Orton over his shoulder.

He set the men into the raft, then dragged it up the slope. Eric went to inspect Simms, whose forehead was split open to the white of his skull, but Simms motioned Eric to Orton.

"Oh, fuck," Cutter said, realizing that he had almost shot Serio. Julie eased the minigun from his hands.

"Serio!" she called. "Get up here and man this weapon."

Serio hesitated, but Simms nodded for him to go.

"All eyes on the water," Simms called out, pulling off his flippers. Just then, the blue light appeared in the distance, just below the surface. It advanced on them in short bursts.

"What is it?" Julie asked, moving over and crouching beside Simms.

"We never got close enough to tell," Simms said, shaking his head. He retrieved Orton's rifle from the raft, pointed it at the ceiling, and opened the breach. Water drained out. He blew into the breach, let it snap closed, and loaded a fresh clip. "From what I could see," he added, "it looked like a man."

Serio hefted up his minigun and moved beside Cutter, who now had a rifle in each hand. Cutter sidled closer to the large man, calmed by his presence.

"Am I fucking glad to see you, brother," Cutter said. Serio grinned, giving him a wink.

The blue light stopped fifty yards from the shore and rose out of the water, reflecting off the surface like a cold sunrise. It swept across the men and stopped at Serio. Its focus tightened, painting a blue circle on Serio's chest.

Serio squinted into the light and Cutter leaned sideways, trying to see past it. Neither noticed the movement behind them. Simms crept up over and placed a hand on Serio's arm.

"Wait for it," he whispered.

Serio turned to give Simms a nod and saw something over the lieutenant's shoulder.

"Oh, shit," he said.

A loud hiss filled the transfer station as a half-dozen quill beetles—lined up directly behind the men—all fired at once.

THIRTY SIX

It was a slaughter.

The beetles, facing down the slope, had a clear line of fire.

Two soldiers had been helping Orton to the barricade when he felt quills thud into his back. The soldiers on either side of him fell dead, and he teetered, confused.

Julie saw the beetles just moments before they fired. She raced toward Eric, but a quill punctured her thigh. She tumbled and fell, landing splayed out in front of the line of quill beetles.

"Take cover!" Simms yelled, and men scrambled to the other side of the barricade, putting their backs to the water.

Orton just stood where he was, his legs ignoring his desire to move. Then he noticed the silver-eyed beetle off to the side, watching and, no doubt, directing the others. He drew his pistol with his left hand, steadied it against his broken forearm, and fired. His shot went high, hitting the slope behind. The silver-eyed beetle turned at the noise, saw Orton, and hopped behind a rock. But before it reached cover, Orton fired again. The beetle flopped over, goo leaking from its shell.

Orton looked to the line of quill beetles. Now that their leader was dead, he expected them to break ranks and retreat, as they had before, but they remained focused on the men, drawing their heads into their bodies and firing off another barrage. A half-dozen quills impaled Orton's chest. He wavered, rolled his eyes up, and fell dead.

Eric dove at Julie as the beetles fired, shielding her body with his own. Quills rained down on the men as Wolf hefted up his minigun and spun toward the beetles. One of the soldiers stepped in front of him, taking the quills that were heading for Wolf. The soldier was thrown back, lifeless, and Wolf opened fire.

Eric hopped up, took Julie in his arms, and ran for the barricade. He dropped her safely behind the rocks, then leaned against them, fully exposed, laughing. The beetles drew back their heads to fire again, but Wolf sliced through the entire row with a single sweep of his minigun.

Throughout all of this, Serio had maintained his position, keeping his back to the beetles and his gun trained on the blue light, which, in turn, was trained on him. The light had started to advance at the same moment the beetles attacked, and Serio opened fire, his bullets splashing into the water. The light flickered and there was a twang like the pluck of a bass string as a translucent blue bolt shot across the water. The bolt hit Serio's minigun, vaporizing both it and his hand, and spraying molten metal across his face. He screamed and then collapsed.

By this time, Wolf had dispatched the beetles, so the remaining men turned and fired on the blue light. The light dropped below the surface and disappeared.

Simms dashed to Orton, checking the corporal's pulse. There was none. He moved to the next soldier and did the same.

Cutter straddled Serio, slapping his ruined face and demanding he wake up. Hiller, rifle in hand, drew back from the water. He bumped into Wolf, and the two men stood back to back, one gun pointed at the land, the other at the water. These four men were all that remained of D-5. The rest had been killed in scant seconds.

"Well, that was something," Eric said, standing up and walking to the remains of the beetles. There were eight of them, the same number that had escaped the battle in the dome.

"Don't!" Julie yelled, leaping after Eric, but she didn't get far. Pain jolted through her leg and she collapsed, clasping the quill in her thigh. Eric bent over to inspect the silver-eyed beetle, prodding it with his finger.

"I really thought this one was the brains," he said. "That killing it would win the battle."

As he turned, Julie saw his back was bright red, peppered with quills. He straightened up and then fell over, dead.

"Eric!" Julie screamed. She lunged over the barricade, propelling herself with her good leg and landing flat on her face. She scrambled forward, clawing up the rocky slope, but Simms grabbed her ankle and pulled her back.

"It's not safe!" he yelled.

"Let me go!" she screamed, kicking, but Simms rolled on top of her, locking her arms behind her back and pinning her down. "Fucking bastard," she said, struggling, but her strength passed quickly. She grew slack, and Simms eased her back behind the barricade, sitting her against the rocks. She stared at Eric's body, lips quivering, tears drawing lines along the dirt on her face.

THIRTY SEVEN

Julie ran down the gravel road at what she estimated was twelve miles an hour. It was hot out, and her olive-green tank top was soaked in sweat. She was exhausted despite the powered exoskeleton, whose hulking metal legs were supposed to be doing all the work.

The exoskeleton, encasing her up to the waist, was a jumble of aluminum tubes with electric motors the size of paint cans jutting from her hips and knees. The machine was supposed to sense the movements of her legs and augment them, but she could feel it straining against its own weight. The gasoline generator strapped to her back was running at full speed, emitting a shrill that was painful even though her thick earmuffs. The sound chased her down the road like some monstrous bee.

Up ahead, a yellow and black pole was strung across the road at chest level. Julie leaned forward, angling toward the ground and pumping her legs faster to maintain her balance. But there was a slight delay in the suit's reaction time—with each step, the legs first resisted her and then jerked forward, shoving her legs from behind. It was all she could do just to stay on her feet, not to mention that the exoskeleton's straps ground into the skin on her thighs, bringing sharp pain with every step. She pushed harder, going faster, and the straps dug deeper.

Her head passed below the pipe with inches to spare, but the generator on her back clipped it, knocking it to the ground.

"Shit," Julie said.

A soft voice in her ear said, "Fourteen point six miles per hour. Slow down as you come into the turn."

"Fuck that," Julie muttered, gritting her teeth and running faster. She leaned the suit so far forward that her hands dangled just off the ground. Her legs shoved against the suit's, forcing them forward. The generator on her back whined horribly, and the smell of burned plastic stung her nose.

She passed an orange cone and banked hard. The exoskeleton's metal boots sank into the gravel as she hooked to her left, leaving deep divots in the road. Halfway through the turn, she bent her waist to use the weight of the generator to pull herself upright, but just then the generator failed, its motor cracking open and spraying out dark oil. The metal legs seized up, and Julie was thrown onto her chest.

She howled and cursed as her skin was scraped across the gravel. The electric motor attached to one knee ripped off with burst of sparks. It bounced down the road, outpacing her, with most of the mechanical leg still attached.

She rolled over onto her back, getting the generator underneath her and her skin off the gravel. Gas poured out, leaving a dark trail behind her. The generator slammed into a rock and came to a jarring stop, but Julie's momentum rolled her head over heels. She landed in the shape of a tripod, formed by her head, an arm, and a frozen leg of the exoskeleton.

"Piece of shit!" she yelled, jerking the straps from her legs. She pulled free of the exoskeleton, stood up, shoved it over, and kicked it away. This wasn't enough, so she drew her sidearm and emptied it into the machine. The generator caught fire. Flames engulfed the device and spread along the line of gas on the road, making the machine look as though it had crashed down from the sky. Julie nodded, satisfied, and limped away. Soldiers rushed in with extinguishers.

She pulled a bandana from her pocket and wiped the blood from her cheek and eyes, then started to dig the gravel from her face, which was covered with lacerations. Several soldiers sat at a portable table beside the road, working on laptops. They buried their faces in their screens as she glared at them.

"That was worth several million dollars," the colonel said, walking up through a path in the tall grass.

"No," Julie said. "That's just what you paid for it."

"What DARPA paid for it," Kathlyn said, appearing behind the colonel, jotting notes on a tablet computer. She wore a slender jumpsuit that emphasized her curves, and her hair was pinned neatly behind her head. The men at the table shifted their eyes, glancing at her as discreetly as they could. "And also what it will cost DARPA to replace it," she added.

"Why would they bother?"

"The goal of these tests," Julie's father said, "is to improve this equipment, not destroy it."

"One improvement would be to strap them to a jeep," Julie said. "They'd move four times as fast with half the noise."

The colonel frowned, but Kathlyn covered her mouth, stifling a laugh.

"Well, Captain Covington?" the colonel asked, turning to Kathlyn. He motioned to the exoskeleton, which smoldered in a haze of extinguisher dust.

"Looks like mechanical failure to me," Kathlyn said, typing on her tablet. "I'm ready to send Wolf on his run."

"Proceed," the colonel said.

"You should go to the infirmary," Kathlyn said, moving close to Julie and gently probing the cuts on her forehead.

"But I'm not going to," Julie replied, pulling back out of reach.

"I know," Kathlyn said. She let her eyes linger on Julie, smiling, then turned and started up the road. "I'll see you this evening."

"She's quite an attractive young woman," the colonel said, admiring Kathlyn from behind.

"Never heard that before," Julie said.

"You know, in the month that she's been here, she's barely even noticed the men."

"And you blame her?" Julie asked. She turned and barked, "Corporal Cutter!"

"Sergeant," Cutter said, standing up from the table. He wore pressed fatigues and well-polished boots. He stepped toward Julie and stood at attention.

"Clear up that mess," Julie said, indicating the exoskeleton. "Wolf is about to start his run."

"Sergeant," Cutter said, saluting and starting away.

"Corporal!" Julie yelled, tossing him a pair of thick silver gloves from the table. "Don't burn yourself."

"Yes, Sergeant," Cutter said, turning just in time to catch them "Thank you, Sergeant."

"And to think you were ready to settle for *that*," the colonel said as they started down the trail.

"He's a good man," Julie said. "He's just more suited for combat than all this high-tech bullshit."

"I imagine you think the same of yourself," the colonel said.

"Well," Julie said. "Those lying liberal newspapers are claiming we're at war in the Middle East..."

"Right now, it's just a bunch of soldiers in the desert practicing their hydration techniques. You may rest assured that we'll be there by the time the shooting starts."

"Weighted down with all the latest DARPA doohickies?"

"*This* exoskeleton may not be ready for combat, but technology is the future of warfare," the colonel said. "And I intend for my men—and my daughter—to have the best available. But in the meantime, we should focus on more immediate opportunities. If you take my meaning."

"I do not."

"Captain Covington won't be joining us overseas."

"You've mentioned this before," Julie said.

"It's your future," the colonel said, "so you must make your own decisions. But it's nothing I haven't done myself."

Julie grunted.

"DARPA has sent us one other toy," the colonel continued. "A deep-water diving suit they developed for the navy. The navy backed out, leaving them with a $5 billion boondoggle. As a personal favor to General Covington, I agreed to oversee the program for a few years, to cushion the fallout."

"So?"

"We'll be testing it at Harvey Point, out on the coast, and I'm sending you and Captain Covington ahead to prepare the facility. The rest of us will join you in a couple of weeks."

"A couple of weeks?"

"I feel the two of you should spend more time together."

"I can't possibly fathom why you would."

"It's not like you've shown much interest in men, either, Jules."

"That doesn't mean—"

"Trust your father," the colonel cut in. "He still has much to teach you."

THIRTY EIGHT

The transfer station was dark and quiet. The water had risen further and now lapped against the bottom of the barricade. The dead remained untouched, and two of the bodies were half submerged. The living remnant of the D-5 was huddled behind the barricade, with Wolf guarding the water in one direction and Hiller guarding the fissure in the other. Cutter sat with his head gripped between his hands, staring at the ground. Simms attended to Julie's thigh, removing the quill and wrapping it with strips of fabric torn from a shirt—their medical kit was in the pile of equipment, halfway up the slope, and the ground between here and there was exposed to the blue light lurking in the water.

Julie seemed oblivious to Simms's ministrations and only stared at Eric's body.

"I'm sorry about Doctor Kirsch," Simms said.

"You didn't even like him," Julie said. Her voice was dull, emotionless.

"He was brave. He gave his life to save yours."

"I wish it had been me. I deserve to die, but my father..."

"Your father couldn't have known this would happen. He wouldn't have sent us down here if he didn't believe we could handle it."

Julie looked over at Simms, confused, then let out a deep laugh. Simms boiled over.

"Stop it," he said loudly, drawing everyone's attention.

"I just realized how funny it all is," Julie said. "All these men slaughtered, just to satisfy—"

"There is nothing funny about this," Simms cut in.

"All to satisfy an old man's ego," Julie finished.

"You're a psychopath," Simms said. "A lunatic. You have no regard for human life, not even your own."

"And how, exactly, do you think I got that way?"

"Only a child blames her father for her problems." Simms said.

"And only a fool worships so blindly. The difference between you and me is that my eyes are wide open. I *know* what the colonel has done, to you, to Eric, to all these men."

"The difference between you and me is everything."

"Yeah?" Julie asked. "Tell me, then, what were your colonel's orders regarding me?"

Simms crossed his arms, fuming.

"He must have wanted something," Julie continued. "He didn't cook up this mission just to get his best men killed. My father doesn't like to waste good resources."

"You spoiled, self-centered, obnoxious!" Simms said, his voice rising to a yell. "Colonel Porter is a great man. An Ameri—"

"*An American hero?*" Julie cut in. "A man you'd follow to the gates of hell?"

"Yes," Simms said firmly.

"Well," Julie said, shrugging, "here we are."

Simms fell quiet. Julie turned to look at the water, curling her leg and testing the bandage.

"Nice work," she said.

Simms grunted.

"Let's go," Julie called out, rolling to her knees.

"Where are we gonna go?" Cutter asked.

"Those bugs came from somewhere."

"Yeah," Cutter said. "A place with more bugs."

"They came from the tunnel," she said. "Or from the fissure."

"Let me know when you find them," Cutter said.

"She has a point," Hiller said. "If there were more bugs, they would have already attacked."

"You want a point?" Cutter said. "How about we should have never left the operations room? How about like I said so in the first place?"

"Well, that didn't happen," Julie said. "You want to sit here and whine about it?"

"Fuck off, Porter," Cutter said. "You're the reason we're down here. Maybe we should just surrender. Beg for mercy."

"Shut up," Wolf said.

"I won't shut up," Cutter said, standing up. "Hey, cock-smoker!" he shouted at the water. "We're trapped and we're stupid, so why don't you just come get us?"

The blue light clicked on, two hundred yards away, drawing a circle on Cutter's chest. He dove back behind the barricade.

"Okay," he said. "Not so smart."

The light swept across the shore and, finding no other target, descended back into the water.

"I'm pressing forward to the airlock at the drone base," Julie said. "If you're smart, you'll come with me."

"The airlock won't protect us," Simms said, pointing at the water. "Not from that."

"And this will?" Julie gestured at the rock barricade.

"This is good ground."

"This is a tomb."

"This is *not* a debate."

"Agreed."

Julie stripped off her wetsuit, down to the torn lycra underneath.

"I cannot allow this," Simms said, starting toward her. Julie drew her sidearm and leveled it at him.

"I personally don't care how you die," Julie said.

Simms drew back, hands out. Keeping the gun up, Julie used her other hand to pull on her spelunking belt. She looked out at the water. It was calm and dark. She dropped down and started to crawl up the slope.

"Stop," Simms ordered. "Come back here."

The light appeared over the water and the blue circle swung toward Julie. She slipped behind a rock the size of a softball, using what little cover it offered.

"You'll get yourself killed!" Simms yelled.

"And you won't?" Julie called back.

Simms fumed. He itched to chase after her, but didn't dare leave the cover of the barricade. "Let her get herself killed," he muttered to himself.

After a moment, the blue light clicked off and Julie continued up the slope.

"If I don't come back," Julie called over her shoulder, "then you'll know I made it."

Slipping behind a large rock near the top of the slope, she took one last look at Eric's body. Then she stood up and raced for the bridge, hobbling on her wounded leg.

She leaped into the fissure just as a circle of blue light appeared on her back. She grabbed the rope as she fell, stopping herself just out of sight.

The light swept back and forth across the far wall, then turned off again. Julie peered up from the fissure and raised a thick fluorescent pen. She caught the men's attention and drew an arrow in the air, pointing down. Simms turned away, but Hiller nodded, hope glimmering in his eyes.

Julie motioned for him to follow, then climbed down toward the tunnel.

THIRTY NINE

Julie swung the rope and leaped into the tunnel. It was a short drop, but her injured leg buckled and she collapsed to the floor. She clutched her leg, taking the pain quietly, her pistol out and aimed down the dark tunnel. The tunnel was a perfect circle wide enough for two trains to pass, and just by sheer size, it had the gravity of a cathedral. Julie felt insignificant inside it.

After the pain passed, she crept to the edge of the fissure, into the dim light coming down from the transfer station. The tunnel floor was the texture of poured cement, with a spiral groove the thickness of a bolt thread left behind as the boring machine had slowly advanced.

Julie set down her pistol and checked her climbing gear, making sure everything was in place and that all the pouches were secured to her belt. She strapped a small diver's knife to the inside of her thigh, just above the knee, and pulled on her gloves. Eric had given her these gloves just the day before, but it might as well have been years ago.

She cupped her headlamp in her hand and turned it on, releasing just a sliver of light, which she aimed at the floor. She held the light out to the side, so that it, not she, would be the target for anything waiting ahead. She picked up the pistol and crept down the tunnel.

The tunnel was broken by dozens of narrow cracks, just like the floor of the transfer station above her. She peered down a two-foot-wide gap, seeing a straight drop into darkness. Julie hopped over the crack and continued forward, sweeping the light back and forth, seeing nothing but smooth walls.

She went another hundred yards before a massive fissure split the tunnel apart, leaving it separated by a twenty-foot-wide chasm. Across the chasm was the remains of some bridgework, destroyed but for a single steel rail that spanned the gap. The rail hung in the air beside Julie, hovering a foot above the floor, and was attached to a single cement tie on the other side. She stepped onto the rail, arms wide for balance, and it wobbled fiercely. She took a step forward, tilting and waving to steady herself, and then took another. The last step brought her out over the chasm, where warm air, heated by the earth's core, blew up from the depths. She raised her foot and eased it forward.

"Bullshit," she said, spinning around and hopping back to the ledge. "Nobody went this way."

She sat down on the ground, only then realizing how tense she was. Her legs felt like gelatin.

As she sat wondering what to do next, she became aware of a faint mechanical noise. She cupped her ears and rotated her head; it was coming from farther down the tunnel, on the other side of the chasm. Peering ahead, she could just make out the faint gleam of electric lights.

She walked along the ledge, but found no other way across the gap. Retracing her steps, she bent down beside the two-foot-wide fissure. Circling her light inside, she noticed scuff marks on the wall; something had passed this way and, by the looks of it, more than once.

She sat down on the edge, dangling her feet inside as she strapped the lamp to her head. She stashed the pistol inside the bandage wrapped around her thigh, putting it between her legs so it wouldn't foul against the rock. She removed her gloves, rubbed chalk on her hands, then pulled them back on. She centered herself over the gap, braced her feet to either side of the fissure, and started to descend. She stopped when she was chest-level to the floor, pulled out the fluorescent pen, and drew an arrow on the wall, pointing down.

The first couple of hundred feet passed effortlessly. The fissure was narrow enough that she could brace with her arms while she lowered her legs, and vice versa. But the gap widened steadily, and soon she was stretched to the very limit, holding herself with her back arched out to one wall and her fingers extended to the other. The fissure continued below her, beyond what she could see, but she could go no further. As she began to climb back up, she noticed a U-shaped piece of metal above her, sticking out of an overhang off to the side, which had blocked it from sight on the way down. It was a rung.

Julie stared at the rung. It made no sense for it to be here, but there it was. *The real question*, she thought, *is, Will it hold my weight?*

She stretched out her foot, but the rung was too far away. She climbed up until her view of the rung was blocked by the outward curve of the rock, then she shifted her position so that her body was extended across the gap, with her hands on one wall and her feet on the other. She carefully turned over until she was facing straight down and reached blindly under the overhang, feeling for the rung. She brushed it with her fingertips. It was close enough to grab, but doing so would commit her—she'd be leaning over too far to get back up.

Something went this way, she assured herself, extending her arm. *And so can I.*

She gripped the rung and let herself drop.

Her arm snapped straight as it took her weight, and she swung back and forth through the dark. The rung held—it was cemented solidly into place—and as her swinging slowed, Julie curled up and threaded her foot through it, hanging by the back of her knee. She shook her arms out, which were sore from the climb down, as she searched around with the headlamp.

Below her, there was nothing. Overhead, the rock curved up and flattening out, creating a high ceiling with a row of rungs down the center. The rungs led to a cave in the wall, maybe thirty feet away. It seemed the obvious way forward, so Julie drew out her florescent pen and circled the rung several times.

She grabbed the rung in her hands and withdrew her leg, then swung forward and back to build momentum before she reached for the next rung. She moved fluidly from rung to rung, doing her best not to think about what was—or rather wasn't—below her.

When she reached the final rung, she stretched her legs forward, getting them thigh-deep into the cave and spreading them out to catch the walls with her feet. She released the rung and curled forward, slipping inside.

The cave was actually an old lava tube, with black pumice walls, rippled and as rough as sandpaper. Julie's gloves had thick leather palms, but her knees were bare. She crawled forward gingerly, the coarse stone biting her skin.

The tube curved to the left, then to the right, but overall it seemed to be heading in the same direction as the tunnel above her. It was large enough that she could move freely, and after what she guessed was a quarter mile, the tube split, with one path going sharply to the right, while the other went down and to the left. She searched for any signs of passage—wear marks or more the scratches she had seen before—but found none. Both tubes were heading in the wrong direction, but the one to the right more so. She drew an arrow to the left tube and followed it down.

The lava tube curved to the side, slowly spiraling downward. The spiral tightened as she descended, and the tube grew so narrow that she had to wriggle like a caterpillar. It was hard work, quickly wearing out her already tired arms. She considered taking a break, but she was feeling isolated, not to mention apprehensive about what might be down here with her. Her plan was to find the tunnel again, but wherever she was going to end up, and however far away that was, she was anxious to get there.

After a while, the tube made a sharp downward turn and then angled back underneath itself. Julie lowered her head through the turn and saw the tube spiraling back in the other direction, curving out of sight. She pulled back to inspect the turn itself. It was tight, and its inner edge was knife sharp. But this was the way forward, so she wiggled down into it.

As she moved through the turn, she bent her body first into an L and then a V, such that were it not for the rock between them, her nose would be touching her knees.

She shimmied farther down until her heels were shoved against the ceiling of the upper tube and the front of her thighs were pressed against the turn's sharp inner edge. She had no way to bend her legs and no room to twist them. Her only option was to bull through, so she found handholds on the walls and pulled.

The rock edge cut through her skin as her legs bowed backward, bending in a way they weren't meant to, but her heels scraped along the ceiling as she pivoted forward. Then, just as she felt the pressure on her legs lessen, her feet caught in a divot in the rippled rock.

She emptied her lungs, making her stomach as thin as possible, and rocked herself forward. That did nothing, so she relaxed, catching her breath. Sweat stung her eyes, but her hands were covered in black grit, so all she could do was try to blink it away. Her headlamp had slipped down the side of her head, and as she adjusted it, she saw a knob of rock hanging from the ceiling in the lower part of the turn. She stretched out her arms and locked her hands around the back.

She moved slowly, wiggling her body from side to side. The rock cut a red streak along the top of her thigh as she inched forward, and she could feel her knees separating as her legs bowed in the wrong direction. Then she was through the worst of it. Her legs straightened, shoving her forward, but she jammed her hands against the walls, stopping herself.

Think, she told herself, looking at Eric's gloves and remembering his words. *Thinking is the important part*, he had said.

What if there was nothing at the end of this passage? Or what if there was no end at all? Eric had said the fracture zone went on for miles, and at the rate she was moving, she could travel for days and find nothing at all. And once she was past this curve, would she have any way to go back?

She remained still for some time, folded painfully, blood swelling in her head.

"Shit," she said.

She reversed her hands, placed her palms against the

knob of rock, and shoved, working herself back into the upper part of the tube. Then she shimmied backward, reversing through the spiral.

It was slow, hateful work, and every time she scraped her bare knees against the course floor or knocked her head against the low ceiling, it was all the more painful because she was in retreat. She stopped twice, changing her mind, deciding to start forward again, but she didn't. It was the colonel's voice telling her that retreat was failure, but it was Eric's voice, the one encouraging her to back up, that was the right one. She was two miles underground. If she got herself stuck, there was no one here to save her.

She backed all the way to where the tube had split, crossed out the arrow she had drawn, and made a new one that pointed to the right. She brushed the grit from her knees and started down the other tube.

The path angled up, growing steadily steeper until she was more climbing than crawling. The cave walls turned white, their rough texture smoothed over with mineral deposits. It also felt better on her knees, but the smooth floor meant more effort for less progress. Finally, the tube leveled off, and she collapsed, panting. She felt a chill run through her stomach, water from the floor soaking through her thin shirt. The water felt strange and made her skin tingle. She rubbed it between her fingers, smelling it, tasting it. It was just water.

It's me, she realized. She was light-headed, her blood sugar dangerously low.

She dug through the pouches on her belt, producing a half-eaten energy bar and a couple of hard caramels. She popped the caramels into her mouth and ground them between her teeth, then gnawed at the stale, rubbery bar. She felt better almost immediately. She rolled onto her back, pulled her shirt up, and twisted it, squeezing a few drops of water into her mouth.

She lay there for some time, enjoying the rush of sugar, but then she realized something was wrong. There was something nearby. She pulled off her headlamp and shined it down the tube behind her. She saw movement, but whatever it was, it seemed to hang just at the edge of her light. She heard feet scurry through the tube, echoing around her such that she couldn't tell if they came from up ahead or behind. Or both.

She pulled her headlamp on, rolled back over, and continued on, fighting against her panic and forcing herself to move slowly. The sugar she'd eaten wouldn't last long, and she had to conserve what energy she could. Whatever was out there—if anything even was out there—she couldn't do anything until it showed itself.

The passageway sloped downward, and a few yards later she came upon the nubby remains of a stalactite. It had been broken off, recently by the looks of it, to clear the passage. There were tracks in the rock dust that surrounded it, but they were messy, and she couldn't tell what kind.

Bugs, she decided, continuing forward. *What else is there at the bottom of the Atlantic?*

She was stiff from the cold, which amplified her aches, but now the floor grew warm, and she felt herself loosen up. She figured she was passing near one of the fissures, and she took a moment to lie down and absorb the heat.

The floor grew steeper, and she felt like she was crawling headfirst down a slide. Her hand came down on a section of floor so searingly hot that she jerked it into the air, losing her grip and tumbling forward.

She slid down the smooth rock, which grew hotter and hotter. She rolled side to side, trying to keep her skin from burning, and she clawed at the walls, trying to slow herself down. Then floor was gone and she was plunging headfirst through the dark.

She clutched at the air, finding nothing. She kicked her legs, flipping herself upright, and the back of her head stuck something hard. Her neck was snapped forward, and then even the black was gone.

The men of D-5 were up to their chests in water, and their rock barricade was nearly submerged. Cutter held the front of his diving mask in the water, watching below, while the others guarded the surface. The situation was bad.

"She's brave," Hiller said.

"She's insane," Cutter said. He swept the mask back and forth, scanning. "But she's not here," he added. "I'll give her that."

"She's probably dead by now," Simms said.

"And we're doing so much better?" Cutter asked.

The blue light rose from the water, no more than twenty yards away. Wolf fired three shots. They rang against something solid, and the light dove back down.

"How's the ammo?" Simms asked.

"Not good," Wolf replied. There were fewer than a dozen bullets on his gun belt.

"It's time to go," Cutter said.

Simms looked at his men and at the rising water.

"Weapons only," he said, turning toward the tunnel. "And anything we can use to climb with."

FORTY

JULIE OPENED HER EYES sluggishly, squinting at the stinging white light. She rolled across the wrinkled sheets and wrapped an arm around Kathlyn's bare torso. She pulled her to her, pressing against her warm flesh. Kathlyn stirred.

"Morning already?" she asked sleepily.

"You used to be such an early riser," Julie said.

"I get up when I have to."

"Well, you have to. The rest of the unit arrives today."

"At noon."

"We have a lot to do," Julie said. "To get ready."

"No, we don't," Kathlyn said. She sat up and looked at Julie. "You're nervous."

"My father," Julie said.

"He doesn't have to know," Kathlyn said.

"He has a way of knowing everything."

"Well, you should have thought of that two weeks ago," Kathlyn said, rolling on top of Julie and kissing her. "Besides, your father would handle this better than mine."

"Religious?" Julie asked.

"The hardest decision of his life was the air force or the seminary."

"Sorry," Julie said.

"I don't care what my father thinks," Kathlyn said. "I've never wanted anyone, or anything, in my entire life as much as I want you."

"You'll be a speechwriter someday."

"Someday," Kathlyn agreed, toying with Julie's short hair. "You ever think about growing it out?"

"When I was a kid," Julie said, rolling away, suddenly distant.

"No, no, no," Kathlyn said, chasing Julie across the bed, wrapping her arms around her and squeezing. "Don't go to that place. Let's change the subject. Or better still, let's not say anything at all."

Julie looked at Kathlyn and nodded.

"I'll tell you someday," she said.

"Someday is fine by me," Kathlyn said. "I trust you, and I... well, you wouldn't believe me. Not yet." Kathlyn laid her head on Julie's chest. "But maybe someday."

Julie stared at the ceiling, feeling Kathlyn rise and fall with every breath. She could not remember feeling so happy, but her every instinct rejected it, told her not to trust it. She hadn't wanted to be with Kathlyn; it was her father who had sent them here. This was his plan, and whatever he had in mind, his goal was not simply for Julie to be happy.

So what had he wanted?

"I...," Julie said, then changed her mind. "This has been really wonderful," she said, but that didn't feel strong enough. Not for what she was feeling. The way she felt was beyond her own understanding. "I never imagined..." she said. "Which isn't to say... I..."

"You'll never be a speechwriter," Kathlyn said.

"No."

"Anyway, what's the rush?" Kathlyn asked, planting small kisses around Julie's neck. "They don't arrive for hours."

"They don't," Julie agreed, pulling Kathlyn's mouth up to hers and sliding her hands down her lithe back.

FORTY ONE

JULIE WOKE WITH A jolt, sitting upright in the dark cave. The movement set off an instant migraine, so she laid back down again. She probed the tender bump on the back of her head, which stuck out like an apple embedded in her skull.

She massaged her temples, but the pain only grew stronger. Her final memory of Kathlyn filled the darkness around her, and Julie shook her head to chase it away. The movement sent white-hot waves of pain rolling through her body. Tears leaked from her eyes as she yelled out, a deep guttural yell that amplified through the dark caves. She yelled until her breath ran out, then she yelled again, harder, her voice cracking, her chin wet from her own spit. She yelled until she could no longer bear the pain in her throat, and then she lay still, listening to it echo back at her.

She wiped a hand across her forehead and wet her lips with the sweat, then she eased up to a seat, found her headlamp, and looked around.

She had fallen into a tall, thin crevice, the base of a crack in the gray bedrock. Cliff walls rose on either side and met below her in a sharp V. Ahead of her, or at least what she thought was ahead of her, the crack was filled in with loose gravel, creating a level surface to walk on. Julie stared down the path, which seemed to stretch onward forever, feeling cold and alone. She *was* alone, as alone as any human had ever been. She was lost in the middle of the planet, with no way to go but forward. So forward she went.

She stood up by walking her hands up one of the sloped walls and started to walk forward unsteadily, too disoriented to know where, too addled to care.

Kathlyn disappeared, without warning or explanation, two weeks after they had begun training on the Atargis. She was called back from the boat one morning, and, by the time Julie returned that evening, her quarters were empty. Julie called her cell phone repeatedly, but there was no answer. Several days passed without word, so she snuck into her father's office and used his rolodex and telephone to call Kathlyn's father's house.

"What is it now, John?" the general answered gruffly.

"It's Julie, sir. I'd like to speak to Kathlyn."

"Sergeant Porter? How dare you…?" The phone slammed down, so loud Julie pulled it from her ear. But the connection hadn't closed; she heard faint voices. A full minute later, a woman's voice came on.

"My daughter doesn't want to talk to you," she said. "Please don't call again."

"Ma'am, I—" Julie said, but she had hung up.

Julie called again the next day, from a pay phone, but no one answered. The day after that, their number was disconnected. With no other options, she asked her father what had happened.

"It would seem that we overplayed our hand," he said

to her over dinner, more interested in his meat than the discussion.

"Overplayed what hand?" Julie asked.

"Our plan," he said, "was to leverage your tryst with Kathlyn for a featured role in the coming war. The Pentagon, you see, has convinced itself that I'm too old for combat, and as such has appointed me head nursemaid of this training facility. General Covington could have changed that, but he turned out to be less open minded than I had expected.

"When I approached him about our mutual problem—you and Captain Covington—he went nuts. He had his daughter discharged, then locked her up in some private facility for the mentally unstable. Pretty uptight behavior, if you ask me, for a man who likes to touch little girls."

"She's gone?"

The colonel looked at Julie with sudden concern.

"Whatever you think you may feel," he said, "you must never believe that people like the Covingtons can have feelings for you. They are rich people, born into power, and with no real understanding of sacrifice. To someone like Captain Covington, you are no more than a toy, a distraction. You and I, we turned that around. *We* took advantage of *her*. I'm certain that she's embarrassed, and if she does turn up again, the only thing she'll have on her mind will be revenge. She'll try to take you down with her, Jules, so don't believe a word she says. Is that clear? Julie?" He added the last when she didn't respond.

"Yes, Father," Julie said dully, staring at the wall.

"Good," he said, turning back to his steak. "Let's hear no more about it."

Julie stumbled through the crevice like a zombie, dragging her hands along the walls and barely noticing the rocks that shifted underfoot and twisted her ankles. Her progress was slow, the silence thick.

Up ahead was a stone the size of a bus, wedged at an angle between the two walls. Ducking down, she saw a low passage beneath it. The rock had probably been stuck there for eons, but she scurried under it as if it might come loose at any second.

There were more such rocks ahead, massive obelisks that had dropped from the unseen heights and been caught between the walls at random angles, like the abandoned toys of a god-sized child. Some were so high she could barely see them, others so low she had to crawl under them on her elbows. The passage below one such rock went on for yards and yards, taking her out of the crevice and into a wide, flat room, barely tall enough to sit up straight.

The ceiling was coated in a white frost, and several chalky stalactites hung down almost to the floor. Water dripped from one, feeding an inch-deep puddle. She crawled over and drank greedily. The water had a salty tang; it was seepage from the ocean above, filtered through the bedrock. She pressed her throbbing head against the cool, wet stalactite and looked down at her reflection in the water.

Her hair was caked with blood and gravel. Her headlamp was dim, its batteries, unreplaced since Mexico, were almost dead. The light was so weak now that she wondered how she could see at all—until she noticed that she was casting a shadow. She turned sharply, seeing a cragged hole in the ceiling. Blue light beamed though the hole, its glow filling the room. She crawled toward it cautiously, digging her pistol out of the bandage on her thigh.

The hole was narrow, bending sharply in one direction

and then the other, such that she couldn't see through it. She heard nothing above her so, centering herself, she stood up slowly, threading through the hole. It was a tight squeeze, but, as her legs straightened out, her head rose into a tall chamber.

The chamber was a perfect cylinder, three stories tall and ten feet in diameter. Its stone walls were as smooth as polished glass, and several mineral veins broke through the surface, wiggling toward the ceiling like long, thick snakes. There was an open gash in the ceiling through which blue light shone, painfully bright, but the room's most striking feature was a quartz helictite that spiraled out of the center of the floor.

The helictite resembled a crystalline tree, with its heavy trunk and thick branches rising high into the air and disappearing into the ceiling. The crystal itself was translucent, a quartz-like mineral left behind by whatever had carved this room from the gray rock. The light from the ceiling spread through it, making it glow from within. Julie had never seen anything like it. She touched one of the low branches, which moved easily, creaking and cracking. Despite its girth, it was too weak and brittle to hold her weight. She circled the room, gazing up at the helictite, wondering what might have cut this circular room from the heavy rock and yet left such a fragile crystal behind.

The light cast shadows around the room and made it difficult to see. Julie cupped her hands around her eyes and scanned the walls, spotting a high passageway just below the ceiling. The passage was smooth and round, like the walls around her, and as best as she could tell, it was wide enough to fit through.

There was something deeply wrong about the passage, and about this whole room. The Azores Fracture Zone stretched out for hundreds of miles; it should be barren and impassable, but someone, or something, had made a path through it. The implications were staggering, but Julie was too tired, and in too much pain, to think about it. At least the choice in front of her was easy—there was no way she was heading up into the glowing gash in the ceiling.

She worked her pistol back into the bandage on her thigh, and, shielding her eyes against the light, she searched the high walls for a way up.

Back in the transfer station, the four men crawled along the narrow bridge that spanned the gaping chasm. They spread out as they reached the other side, forming a row, guns pointed back at the water. Simms climbed down Julie's rope, descending into the fissure and searching the dark tunnel with his bayonet light. Seeing nothing, he dropped inside and motioned for the others to follow. Cutter came next, followed by Hiller. Wolf waited until the blue light rose from the water, then opened fire, emptying the belt on his minigun and chasing it back down one last time. He tossed the minigun into the chasm, then unstrapped a rifle and climbed down after the others.

The men moved slowly down the three-story-wide tunnel, Simms and Cutter circling their flashlights over the walls and the high ceiling while Hiller and Wolf followed behind, walking backward, their guns aimed at the dangling rope behind them.

After the men were gone, the transfer station was quiet. Small waves lapped against the shore, catching the light of the abandoned lanterns. The bodies of the dead had been swallowed by the rising lake.

Some distance from the shore, the blue light emerged from the water. It waited patiently for several minutes, then, when nothing happened, it advanced. It circled to the side, checking behind the submerged rock barricade, then rose onto the shore. The bright light obscured figure that held it, which was roughly the shape of a man, though not half as tall.

FORTY TWO

Julie was splayed against the wall, thirty feet up, clinging to a two-inch-thick mineral vein that snaked up the stone and disappeared into the ceiling. When she had inspected the vein from the ground, it had appeared to pass right beside the high passageway, but as she climbed, it had veered off, leaving her five feet away and with no way across.

Most of her weight was on one bare foot, her toes curled around a crystal extrusion no larger than a peapod. Her other leg, the one that had been injured by the quill, dangled in the air. She held the mineral vein in one hand for balance as she leaned to the side, stretching her other hand toward a crack in the wall. Her fingers got tantalizingly close, but her knee buckled and her foot slipped. Her hand came loose and she fell.

She kicked her legs backward—swinging the top of her body toward the wall—and grabbed the mineral vein in both hands. Her arms snapped straight and she jerked to a stop. There was a flash of white as her face planted into the smooth stone, and she dangled for a moment, waiting for her head to clear. Once she had recovered, she wiggled her toes into a small crack and let her arms relax, shaking them out one at a time.

She had to find a way over to the passage—the climb had been rigorous, and she didn't have enough strength left to start over. Just hanging here was wearing her out, and it was only a matter of time before her body gave out completely.

She looked at the tree-like helictite rising in the center of the room. One of its thick branches stretched right to her, and it was all she could do not to reach for it. No matter how sturdy the helictite looked, she knew it wouldn't hold her weight. Besides, it led straight to the glowing blue gash in the ceiling, which was the last place she wanted to go.

She searched for a handhold, but it was difficult to see. The light, passing through the helictite, filled the room with bright spots and dark shadows. Probing the ceiling, she found a crack not much wider than her fingers. The crack ran straight across the room—directly toward the passage—but also took her far from the safety of the wall. Worst, the crack didn't appear to go the whole way.

And at least it'll get me closer, Julie thought, climbing the mineral vein until her head was bent against the ceiling. *I'll figure out the rest when I get there.*

She jammed a hand into the crack and flexed her fingers, wedging her knuckles against the rock. She leaned out from the wall, testing the hold. It seemed solid. Taking a deep breath, she released the mineral vein and swung away from the wall, her feet dangling three stories above the stone floor.

She rotated her body and jammed her other hand into the far side of the crack, then she kicked back and forth, swinging toward the passage, still several feet away. Her fingers started to slip, peeling the skin from her knuckles, but she flexed them harder, pressing her torn skin into the coarse rock.

The point of her toes brushed the lip of the passage. She was close, but she had to get closer.

She let herself stop swinging, then took her weight on

one hand and slid the other to the very end of the crack, where it was so narrow it pinched her fingers. She slid her other hand beside it, then shifted her weight left and right, working her fingers as deep as she could. She had moved maybe six inches closer to the passage. She started to swing again, flexing her fingers hard—her knuckles were bleeding, and the blood made the rock slippery.

On the third swing, her feet brushed the edge of the passage. On the fourth, her toes caught on the lip, holding her at an angle, her face toward the ceiling. She wiggled her feet in, glancing down at the distant floor and immediately regretting it.

A marble-sized nub of crystal protruded from the ceiling near her chest. She slid a hand from the crack, wiped the blood on the back of her shirt, and clamped a finger around the nub. She locked the finger in place with her thumb, then pulled, her feet sliding farther into the passage. She pulled until her other arm was stretched out and her face was pressed to the ceiling, her breath fogging the polished stone.

She found another crack in the ceiling, down at her waist, but it was too narrow for her fingers. She looked around, but from what little she could see, there were no other holds. Steeling herself, she moved both arms at once—jerking her hand out of the crack as she yanked on the nub, throwing herself into the passage. She was waist-deep when she started to slide back out.

She spread her feet, pressing them to the passage walls, but they found no purchase on the smooth stone. She was falling now, her thighs halfway out of the passage.

With a loud grunt, Julie curled her stomach, bringing her torso all the way up and getting her hands on the lip of the passageway. She held herself there, folded in half, her chest pressed to her legs and her legs pressed to the wall. All her weight was on the last two joints of her fingers, which were bent over the lip of the passage. It wouldn't take much for them to slip.

She spread her legs slowly, until her ankles touched the inside of her wrists, then she twisted to the left, slipping her leg under her wrist and to the outside of her arm. She repeated this on her right, then rotated her legs out, keeping them flat to the wall as she swept them down. Hanging straight down from the passage, she pulled herself slowly up. Her fingers started to tremble, slipping, so she lurched up, getting her chin onto the lip of the passage. She shifted her fingers, getting a better grip, then pulled herself up to her chest and bent into the passage. Bracing her hands against either wall, she wiggled inside. She rolled onto her back, panting, her body tingling.

She peeled the wrapper off the last bite of her energy bar, but, too weak to chew, she just set it in her mouth and let it dissolve. She closed her eyes to stop the passageway from spinning.

Kathlyn reappeared a month later, waiting for Julie when she returned from work one day. Since she'd left, the colonel had the lost the support of her father—DARPA had taken away all his high-tech toys and sent D-5 overseas, to the war in Qumar. But Julie and her father had been left behind, he as the base commander while she was stuck drilling new recruits, something that left her in a perpetual foul mood.

"So you've crawled back," she said, finding Kathlyn at her kitchen table.

"Don't say that," Kathlyn said.

"Even if it's true?"

"My father claims that you tricked me," Kathlyn said, "but I know better. I know you, and you know me, too."

"Do I?"

"I love you, Julie," Kathlyn stood up and took a hesitant step toward Julie. "I would have given my whole life to be with you, but I no longer have one to give. Will you take me anyway?" She continued forward, stopping a few feet away and stretching out a hand.

"I..." Julie said, stepping out of reach.

"I know you love me, too," Kathlyn said, moving close, placing her hand on Julie's cheek. It seemed to burn Julie's skin. Julie grabbed Kathlyn and pulled her to her, kissing her, desperate and hard. It was some time before they released.

Kathlyn laid her head on Julie's chest, and Julie ran her fingers through Kathlyn's hair.

"Come with me," Kathlyn said.

"Where?"

"Anywhere. This is our fathers' world, and they don't want people like us. Let's find somewhere we can be together."

"Quit the army?"

"Yes," Kathlyn said, flushing with excitement. "Quit the army and run away with me."

Julie pulled away. "Is that why you came back?" she asked.

"Yes," Kathlyn said. "I love you."

"To get me to quit?"

"I want to be with you," Kathlyn said. "Now, and for the rest of our lives."

"You want me to desert?" Julie asked. "Go AWOL?"

"It doesn't matter. Your dad will fix it. You know he will."

"My dad will have you arrested."

"I don't care," Kathlyn said. "I love you."

"Stop saying that."

"It's true."

"Liar."

"No."

"My father warned me—"

"Your father is the liar. He set us up, betrayed us, turned my family against me."

Julie stared at Kathlyn, chewing her lip. Beautiful Kathlyn. Perfect Kathlyn. But the woman in front of her was nothing but a shell, hungry for Julie the way a vampire is for blood. Or the devil for a soul.

"I'm sorry about your family," Julie said finally. "But I've still got mine, and I'm not going anywhere."

"But you love—"

"Shut up!" Julie yelled, driving her fist into Kathlyn's chest. Kathlyn flopped to the floor, sitting with her legs splayed. She stared at Julie, then, after a moment, bowed down and started to weep.

"I'm sick of this," Julie said. "Get out of my house."

"I—"

"I said leave," Julie said, turning her back to Kathlyn and stomping from the room. "I never want to see you again."

Julie slammed the door behind her, then leaned against it, panting, listening. After a while, she heard the front door open and close. She went to the bathroom and stared in the mirror, daring herself to cry.

Simms swung in the air, hands clamped to a half-inch-thick rope, his boots locked around a knot at the end. Holding his flashlight in his mouth, he searched the widening crevice for any sign of—or from—Julie.

He had found the arrow drawn on the floor of the tunnel

and had followed it down a narrow crevice, but now the crevice wasn't so narrow. It had spread steadily until he could no longer reach both the walls, and had continued down on this rope. But there were no further markings, and the chasm was seemingly bottomless.

He contemplated going even farther, to dangle from the very end of the rope, but decided against it. The extra few feet were unlikely to reveal anything new, and as tired as he was, he doubted he would be able to climb back if he was hanging by his arms. He spit the flashlight into his hand.

"Can you get me any lower?" he called up the crevice.

"Fucking stop asking that," Cutter called back down. He was twenty feet above Simms, with his feet braced against one wall and his back to the other. The other end of Simms's rope was tied around his waist, and Cutter himself was lashed to Hiller by another rope, a very short one that put the young lieutenant's butt inches from his face.

"How about you stop fucking around and come back up?" Cutter added. Simms ignored him, peering into the darkness below.

Maybe she just fell, he thought, but he didn't believe it. More likely, she had simply kept going, somehow, without even realizing how impossible it would be to follow. Just getting this far had taken everything Simms had.

"Coming up!" he yelled, making one last sweep with the flashlight. Cutter's reply was a string of obscenities, and when he had finished, Simms worked his way back up the rope. He had risen two arm lengths when he saw the overhang. Tightening the focus on his flashlight, he saw Julie's fluorescent markings glimmering around a steel rung that was driven into rock. He traced the light along the overhang, finding another rung and then the whole row of them, leading across the chasm to a small cave on the distant wall.

"How the…?" he said.
"What's that?" Cutter yelled.
"You're gonna *hate* this."

The round passage was as smooth and man-made as the room Julie had just left. She drew a thin cord from her belt, tied it to a crystal jutting from the floor, and cast the other end back into the room. It stretched nearly to the floor. She leaned back into the room and drew an arrow on the wall, pointing to the passage. The pen squeaked against the smooth stone, setting off a chorus of rattles in the glowing gash in the ceiling above her. The blue light flickered as though something passed in front of it. Julie pulled back into the passage, then scurried away as quickly as she could.

The passage grew quickly dark, but she pressed on blindly, more worried about what was behind her than in front. After a few hundred yards, a yellow dot of light appeared up ahead. As she drew closer, she heard the same mechanical drumming as back in the tunnel. The yellow dot grew, becoming the end the passage. Julie found herself looking down at the tunnel from high on its wall. The opposite wall had a string of naked bulbs, filling the tunnel with a dim yellow glow. These were the first working lights—the first working anything—that she had found since arriving at the base.

The string of lights continued to her right, the same direction of the mechanical noise. To the left, the tunnel faded into darkness, and even though she had lost her sense of direction, she was certain that was the way back to the flooded transfer station. She remained still, scanning the tunnel, but the only thing out of the ordinary was that the train tracks were still intact. Unlike every other part of the tunnel, this looked exactly as it should have. She sat on the lip of the passage and pulled on her shoes, then she slipped out, dropping into the tunnel.

Julie dropped about ten feet before the tunnel wall curved out to catch her. She slid down, her good leg extended and her body centered behind it. She hit the floor and tumbled, pulling into a crouch as she stopped. She checked the dark tunnel behind her, then crept toward the mechanical noise, following the train tracks. The rear end of an enormous boring machine—the same type she had seen back in New York—filled the tunnel ahead.

She slid alongside of the large locomotive, eyes on the exposed machineworks. The machine had endless hiding places, but nothing came after her. The thirty-foot grinding disc at the front of the machine blocked the way forward, but a yard-wide hole had been melted through it at ground level, and there was more light on the other side. She approached the hole cautiously, cringing at the smell of freshly burned metal, and peered through.

The tunnel continued on the other side, but it was smaller here, maybe only twenty feet wide, and square—the product of the bygone era of digging and blasting. Up ahead was a large pile of rocks, rising almost to the ceiling, beyond which Julie could hear the thrumming and clanging of machinery. She crouched low and climbed up the pile, crawling the last few feet and peeking over the top.

On the other side of the rock pile, the tunnel opened into a cavernous square room. The room's walls were crenelated, the rock perforated with drills and then broken loose. It was a modern technique, and the work looked recent.

The floor of the room was below that of the tunnel, and therefore hidden from view, but the sound of machinery was loud and crisp, and certainly coming from inside.

Julie straightened her arms, raising her head, and looked down into the room. Her heart froze when she saw movement at the base of the pile—a line of beetles was marching straight for her.

Julie saw Kathlyn one final time, when she returned home the following night. Kathlyn lay on Julie's bed with a pistol in her hand and red fanning out behind her head. There was no note. There was no need.

Julie sat with her for a long while, petting what was left of her hair and making a small sound, like a mouse trapped by the tail. Then she walked out of her house and off the base, and never returned.

Simms and Hiller circled the tall, cylindrical room, inspecting the glowing limbs of the helictite and the bright blue gash in the ceiling. Both men were disheveled, dirty, and bruised.

"Is it some sort of access tunnel?" Hiller asked.

"Maybe," Simms said, fingering the glass-smooth wall. "But it wasn't on the map."

Hiller motioned to the passage near the ceiling and to the arrow Julie had drawn beside it. Simms nodded.

"Let's hope she knows where she's going," he said.

"Goddamn it!" Cutter yelled. He had been crawling into the room through the hole in the floor, but was now stuck, his arms pinned to his side. He grunted and wiggled, but couldn't pull free.

"His armor," Simms said.

"Yeah," Cutter said. "My armor."

The men bent over and loosened the straps on Cutter's chest plate.

Wolf lay prone in the flat cave below, glaring at Cutter's legs, which dangled from the ceiling. There was a lot grunting and kicking, but no progress. He shifted his gun impatiently.

The cave was dark—Cutter's body was blocking the light from above—but then Wolf saw a flash of blue behind him. He drew his legs in and rolled over, leveling his rifle at the approaching light.

Cutter, exhausted and still pinned inside the hole, waited impatiently while Simms and Hiller struggled to free the armor plating from his arms. His chest plate lay on the floor beside his head.

Everyone jumped at the sound of gunfire—a short burst, followed by another—coming from the flat cave below.

Cutter bucked hysterically, trying to break loose. Simms and Hiller grabbed Cutter by the armpits and pulled with everything they had.

Another burst of gunfire. Cutter twisted violently, straining, his face red and bulging.

The gunfire was a steady now; Wolf was emptying his clip.

Cutter's left arm came free and he shoved down on the floor, pushing up one inch, then two, then popping loose. The gunfire ceased as Cutter scrambled across the room and collapsed against the far wall, his chest heaving.

Simms unslung his rifle and dove headfirst into the hole. He spread his legs, catching the rim of the hole with his thighs, and hanging halfway into the cave below. He probed the dark with his bayonet light. Shell casings littered the ground, but Wolf was nowhere to be seen.

He lowered himself to the floor and crawled deeper into the cave.

Several long minutes had passed since Simms had left. Hiller kept his rifle leveled at the hole, but Cutter had given up completely—he lay on the floor, mumble-singing, staring up at the blue gash in the ceiling.

There was a sound from below and Hiller retreated from the hole, the rifle trembling in his hands. Cutter stopping singing and sat up to watch. A moment later Simms hopped up into the room. He backed toward the men, his gun aimed at the hole. Cutter got to his feet, astonished that Simms was alive, and his eyes widened when he saw what Simms held in his hand: the barrel of a gun, mangled as though squeezed by an impossibly powerful fist.

"Wolf's?" Cutter asked.

"Yes," Simms said.

"Bastard," he said, picking up his rifle and checking the clip. "Let's finish this."

He started toward the hole, but Simms put a hand on his shoulder. He motioned to the high passage, and to the cord that hung from it.

"Fine," Cutter said, slinging his rifle.

The cord was too thin to grip, so Cutter cut a length off the end and tied it into a loop. Reaching as high as he could, he wrapped the loop around the cord, feeding it through itself and cinching it tight. He used the loop to pull himself into the air, then, holding on with one hand, he tied another loop, this time in the cord itself, just below the one he was holding. He raised his foot and used his hand to guide it into the bottom loop, then straightened his leg, rising into the air. He slid the top loop up, cinching it as high as he could, and repeated the process. He made slow progress up the wall.

"I'll get your armor," Simms said, grabbing the chest plate on the ground.

"Don't bother," Cutter said without looking. "Won't do no damn good."

By the time Cutter had reached the passage, Hiller had spliced a length of rope to the end of the cord. Cutter pulled up the rope and tied it off. Hiller climbed, and when he was close, Cutter leaned out and hauled him into the passage. Cutter motioned to Simms, but he crouched beside the hole, listening.

"Come on!" Cutter yelled, anxious. His voice set off a loud chattering from the bright gash overhead and his nerve broke. Cutter shoved past Hiller and scurried down the passageway. Hiller watched him go, then leaned back into the room, guarding Simms as he climbed.

"Bring that rope," Cutter said, crawling back up the passage. He seemed a lot calmer than he had just a few minutes earlier. Simms passed him the rope, and Cutter led them to the end of the passage, to where it met with the tunnel. He tied the rope off and rappelled down to the tunnel's floor. He motioned the other men to follow, then put his back to the wall to watch in both directions. Hiller leaned out, marveling at the electric lights.

"She's found it," he said.

Simms urged him down the rope, then followed. When the men reached the ground, they formed into a triangle, with Cutter and Simms out in front and Hiller in the back, keeping an eye on the high passage and on dark tunnel behind them.

They crept past the large boring machine and crawled through the hole in its front plate. They hesitated; the noise and light on the other side was overwhelming after so much time in the deserted base. Then they edged along the tunnel's rough-hewn walls.

They approached the large pile of rocks, staying in its shadow. Cutter and Simms crawled up to the top, the sound of shifting rocks drowned out by the droning machinery, and peered down into a wide, square room—the drone base.

There were floodlights bolted to the ceiling, powered by a large thermoelectric generator. A swarm of robots scurried around the room, carrying rocks to a conveyor belt that crossed the room and ended at a wide fissure.

On the far side of the room was a massive set of doors. This was the inner half of the drone base's airlock, and their extraction point. The doors were slightly ajar, just enough for someone to squeeze through.

"Don't get your hopes up," Julie said.

Simms and Cutter spun. Julie was stretched out above them, in an alcove in the wall.

"Shiest!" Cutter said. "Why do you always have to—?"

"Shhh," Julie said, raising a finger to her lips and winking. Her hair was matted with blood and she had a queer look on her face: detached, amused. The bandage on her thigh had unraveled and a shroud of blood draped down the wall below her.

FORTY THREE

"Do you see it?" Julie asked from her perch. Simms shook his head, and Julie nodded at the sunken room. "What's wrong with this picture?" she asked. Her voice was crusted over, the words hard to understand.

Simms pulled out binoculars and scanned the room. The machines were all missing parts; their claws, scoops, and drills had been ripped off or melted away. Unaware of their own disabilities, they moved at a frantic pace, miming their work.

"They're broken," Simms said.

"And that's not half," Julie said. She swung off her perch and lowered herself with one arm, moving as slow and sure as if she were hydraulic. She dropped the last few feet and landed in a crouch, a spurt of blood shooting from the hole in her leg. She didn't seem to notice.

She strolled up the side of the rock pile with a white metal box swinging in her hand. She stood over Simms, who still lay on the ground, she reached down, and took his binoculars. She scanned the room.

"There," she said, holding the binoculars in place as she stepped back. She motioned Simms up. He rose cautiously, suspicious of Julie's bravado—something was off; her eyes were vacant, unfocused.

He leaned into the binoculars and saw an enlarged view of the airlock. The doors had been forced open—bent outward like the lid of can—creating a foot-wide gap in the middle. Damaged as it was, there was no way the airlock would close, and therefore no way its outer doors would open.

"Down a little," Julie said.

Simms obeyed, aiming the binoculars at the floor, seeing a stream of dots flowing through the gap between the doors. He rolled a switch on the side of the binoculars, magnifying his view tenfold, and the dots became bugs.

These bugs were unlike the others, and appeared to be a cross between an ant and a termite, with six arched legs and sectionalized bodies. The hindmost section was a large, translucent bulb filled with clear liquid.

The bugs formed two lines. The first marched into the airlock, each bug holding a rock in its mandibles. Peering into the airlock, Simms saw the incoming bugs climb a rock wall, press their rock to it, and glue the rock into place with regurgitated brown saliva. The saliva took just moments to set up, after which the bugs joined the outgoing line, returning to the room.

Simms tracked one of the returning bugs, but it disappeared from sight, hidden behind the sunken wall of the drone base. He rose onto his toes, trying see where it had gone, but just then another bug popped up onto the ledge in front of him. Magnified, its head filled his view, its bulging mandibles stretching toward him. He dropped the binoculars and raised his rifle, firing.

Cutter hopped to his feet and, seeing the line of bugs that was coming straight toward them, also fired. They dispatched the closest bugs, but more clambered over the ledge. The newcomers trudged over the shattered remains of their comrades, scrambling up the rock pile, closing on the men. Julie folded her arms, unimpressed.

Both men emptied their clips, backing away. Simms shoved in a fresh clip just as one of the bugs reached him. Simms pressed the barrel to its head, but the bug only clamped its mandibles around a rock at his feet, lifting it, and started back to the airlock.

The next bug did the same, ignoring the men.

"They won't attack you," Julie said. "It's not in their programming."

"Their programming?" Simms asked.

"They're like the construction robots over there, only their job is the opposite—to repair the damage we've done. I wouldn't worry about them."

"I'm worried," Cutter said, still backing up. Hiller had joined them, staring wide eyed at the bugs.

"What you *should* worry about," Julie said, "is whatever is controlling them."

"Shit," Cutter said, whipping around, aiming his gun at the dark tunnel behind them.

"The blue light," Hiller said. "What is it?"

"Well, it isn't the standard enemy."

"An alien?"

"Underneath the ocean?" Julie said. "No, I think it's something from earth. Something that lives down here."

She winced suddenly, grabbing her leg and collapsing to the ground. She threw open the white box—it was a medical kit—and pulled out a vial of clear liquid. She found a syringe and filled it.

"Is that TMB?" Hiller asked, looking at the bottle. "That's for emergency anesthesia. Too much of it will kill you."

Julie waved a hand absently, shooing him away. Simms crouched down beside her.

"And you think the tunnel crew stumbled onto this thing's nest?" he asked.

"Dug right through it is more likely," Julie said. "Or maybe it has something to do with that conveyor belt over there. We always tend to get curious when chunks of rock start dropping out of the sky."

"You're talking about an intelligent species that no one has ever encountered before," Simms said, dubious.

"Nobody's ever been this deep before," Julie said. "You remember what Eric said: the fracture zone descends all the way to the earth's mantle."

"And this... thing. It's never once come to the surface?"

"It'd have as hard a time getting up there as we do coming down. Hell, it probably didn't even think there *was* life on the surface."

"Until now," Cutter said. "Now we both know better."

"An underground monster?" Simms asked, still unconvinced.

"It's more than that, and you know it. These aren't just bugs," Julie said, waving at the line of termites. "They're machines. Same with those that attacked us. Whatever controls them, it sent them in first. The same as you do with MacArthur or Patton."

"It's a soldier," Cutter said. "Like us. Defending its home..." He trailed off, staring at the tunnel behind them.

"Where's Wolf?" Julie asked.

Simms shook his head. "It got him in the caves."

"Just Wolf?"

Simms nodded.

"Why not the rest of you?" Julie asked. "For that matter, where is it now? It knows the layout of this place, knows we've reached a dead end. Why not just finish us off?"

"Sadism," Cutter said.

"It was right on our tail in that cylindrical room," Simms said.

Julie stabbed the syringe into her leg, an inch from the wound, and injected. She closed her eyes, smiling as the warm numbness spread up into her body.

"How much of that are you taking?" Hiller asked.

"It's possible that we've killed all its bugs," she said, speaking to Simms. "What if the story here wasn't that we were cornered, but that it was cut off from its base?"

"We cut *it* off?" Cutter asked, incredulous. "You happen to notice its gun?"

"It's not a magic boom stick, Nigel," Julie said. "And there were four of you against one of it."

"You think that thing is afraid of us?" Simms asked.

"I think it's cautious," Julie said. "No doubt it values its own life."

"Nigel?" Hiller asked Cutter.

"You shut it," Cutter replied, bringing his finger to bear on Hiller.

"Well, it isn't cut off anymore," Simms said to Julie. "So what's it waiting for?"

"What do we always wait for?" Julie asked. She closed the medical kit and stood, testing her leg.

"Reinforcements," Simms said.

"Exactly."

"What was that?" Cutter asked, spinning to Simms. "You did not just say that."

But Cutter didn't wait for an answer. He took off running, heading back the way they came. Halfway to the boring machine, he changed his mind and turned around. He skirted the sunken room, heading deeper into the tunnel. He didn't get far before he changed his mind again.

"Where are you going?" Simms asked as Cutter ran past.

"We've got to get out of here," Cutter said between labored breaths.

"There are several large fissures that way," Julie said. "No way across."

Cutter grunted, turning around yet again.

"And a hundred miles of nothing that way," Julie continued. "Sorry, I mean, 'a hundred miles of the most ambitious project ever undertaken by man.'"

"We have to do something!" Cutter yelled.

"I'm all ears," Simms said.

"We dig that out," Cutter said, pointing at the airlock. "We get one of those dozers working and dig right through the outer doors and escape into the ocean."

"And then we just swim away?" Hiller asked sarcastically.

"Exactly," Cutter said, looking around for tools.

"We have to blow the place up," Julie said quietly. Simms turned to her as the other two squabbled.

"You could always surrender, *Nigel*," Hiller said. "Beg for mercy."

"You think we're gonna kill *that* thing?" Cutter asked. "The three of us and her?"

"Why do you say that?" Simms asked Julie.

"Three soldiers and you," Hiller told Cutter. "A blubbering sack of crybaby, *Sarge*."

"We blow this place up," Julie repeated loudly. "The whole place."

Now everyone turned to her. Cutter's eyes were bulging from his head.

"With what?" Simms asked.

"With that," Julie said, pointing across the sunken room to a twenty-foot shipping container. "There's enough dynamite in there to carve a new Grand Canyon. Good medkit, too."

"You want us to kill ourselves?"

"We die either way," Julie said. "Let's take this thing with us."

"And what does that even accomplish?" Simms asked.

"What does it ever?" Julie asked. "You're soldiers. Killing the enemy is what you do."

Simms rubbed the back of his neck, staring at the shipping container.

"Hiller," he said.

"Sir?"

"Go check on those explosives."

"Yes, sir," Hiller said.

"Show him," Simms barked at Julie. Then, politely, "Please."

"Sure thing, Lieutenant," she said. She led Hiller down into the sunken room and through the spinning, whirring robots. The container door had been pulled open about a foot before it stuck in the accumulated dirt. Hiller peered inside and whistled appreciatively. It was stacked full of crates, all labeled *EXPLOSIVE*.

"They must use them for iron deposits and other things the machine can't drill through," Hiller said.

"Sure," Julie said, shrugging. "But it's enough, right?"

"Oh, yeah," Hiller said. "For anything."

Julie and Hiller returned to find Simms and Cutter in quiet conference. As Julie approached, Simms held up a hand to silence Cutter.

"The explosives will do the job," Hiller reported. "But they'll work better if we can get the container up here, lined up with the tunnel." He motioned to a small, human-operated crane. It looked about five decades old.

"Okay," Simms said. "And how do we detonate?"

Hiller pulled out a pack of four charges, the same type that he had used on the door back in the operations room.

"Good work," Simms said. Then, turning to Julie, "If you'll excuse us?"

"No," Julie said.

"For a moment."

"Not at all."

Simms smiled patiently, rubbing the dark stubble on his cheek, but she wasn't going to leave.

"Fine," he said. Then, to Hiller, "We set the timers immediately and then seal the container. That way it blows no matter what. You and Cutter start back for the operations room while I move the container into place."

"I'm the best with explosives," Hiller said.

"That part will already be done. And Cutter will—"

"Cutter will not be going back into those caves," Cutter cut in. "If I have to fight this thing, I don't want to be crawling on my belly."

"This is not a discussion, Sergeant," Simms said. "One of us needs to get back to the operations room, to take the Atargis diving suit back to the surface and report what we've discovered."

"That's the plan?" Cutter asked.

"That's the plan."

"I can think of three better plans without even thinking about it."

"This is not the time for—"

"What does it even matter?" Julie cut in. "Who cares if you report in?"

"We have orders."

"Ha," Julie said.

"Listen, whatever this thing is out there, it's more than just some aberration, more than some isolated monster. Like you said, it's a soldier, a member of some advanced civilization. I don't know what or where or even how, but this thing didn't just build its own weapons, or teach itself how to control these bugs. There are more of them, maybe a lot more, and someone has to tell the colonel. He'll have to stop this dig and prepare for... for whatever is coming."

"Ah," Julie said. "You're going to save the world."

"We're soldiers," Simms said. "It's what we do."

"So we rendezvous at the operations room?" Hiller asked.

"You and Cutter head to the operations room," Simms said. "I'm staying here and guarding the explosives."

"Now who's suicidal?" Julie asked.

"Just because I'm willing to give my life," Simms said, "doesn't mean I don't value it."

"Hmph."

"Try to see past your own problems, Porter. The world has bigger ones. Hiller! Get those charges in place."

"Sir," Hiller said, turning sharply and walking toward the blue container.

"You're going back, Sergeant," Simms said to Cutter. "Maybe your girlfriend can give you some tips on how to get there."

Simms stomped off. Cutter watched him go, then turned to Julie.

"So, that's it?" he asked. "You're just giving up?"

"There's no point in going back," Julie said. "Turns out that there was no point in coming down here in the first place."

"You were trying to save us," Cutter said. "Well, to save Eric, anyway."

"Yes."

"Everyone who died here—Serio, Orton, the perfessor—they died because of your father. And you're just going to let him get away with it?"

"This isn't a game," Julie said.

"You're damn right," Cutter said. "If you're right about why he sent us down here..."

"Then what?" Julie asked. "What would you want me to do?"

"I'd want you to kill him," Cutter said. "I wish I could kill him myself."

"You?"

"Yeah," Cutter said. "Who wouldn't?"

Julie stared at Cutter, shaking her head.

"I hate you," she said.

"I know it," Cutter said.

Julie turned on her heels and started after Simms, catching up with him among the whirring robots.

"I'm going back," Julie said, shouting over the mechanical din.

"Yahoo," Simms said without looking.

"I mean it," Julie said. "Cutter can stay. I'm going back with Hiller."

Simms stopped and turned.

"With that leg?" he asked.

"With or without it, I've got a better chance in those caves than any of you. And I'm the only one who knows how to drive the Atargis."

"All he has to do is put it on and float to the surface," Simms said.

"But can he put it on?" Julie asked.

"He helped Orton back on the sub."

"Barely."

"Barely will do," Simms said, turning and walking away.

"What were the colonel's orders?" Julie asked.

"I'm busy," he said.

"He ordered you to protect me with your life, didn't he?" Julie asked.

Simms kept walking.

"Didn't he?" Julie asked, grabbing his arm and spinning him around. Simms cocked his arm, his fist aimed at Julie's face.

"Don't flatter yourself," Julie said.

Simms fumed and let his arm drop.

"What were his orders?" she asked.

"You think those matter now?"

"I think you'll follow them."

Simms stared at Julie. When he spoke, it was guttural, like he was trying to prevent the words from escaping.

"Yes," he said. "I am to protect you with my life. And to reinstate you, if you are willing."

Simms pulled a pouch from his pocket and dumped two pins into his hand. One was sergeant's strips, the other D-5's emblem. Julie gazed at the pins, shaking her head.

"That fucker," she said. "I knew it."

"Well?" Simms asked. He extended the pins to Julie, but she only stared at them.

"And what did you tell him?" she asked finally.

Simms shrugged.

"My, you're a loyal soldier," she said.

"Not that loyal," Simms said.

Simms's hand started to close. Julie reached for the pins, but it was too late. He slid them into his pocket.

"I would save the life of any other person in the world before I would save yours," he said.

"But I can make it back," Julie said.

"I don't know that you can."

"I can," Julie said. "If anyone can."

"And if you do?"

"Then I'll report in, just like you want."

"You?"

"Yes."

Simms looked at Julie, sizing her up, his mouth curling to a frown.

Hiller overturned a crate, heaping loose sticks of dynamite onto the other crates. He buried two of the charges into the heap, set the timer to twenty-five minutes, and started the countdown. He brought the remaining two charges to Simms.

Simms checked the countdown and nodded. He put one charge into his pocket and brought the other to Julie, who had a fresh bandage on her thigh and was injecting a large dose of painkiller. The D-5 pin was clipped to the collar of her ragged shirt.

"It's not much time," Simms apologized, offering her the charge.

"It's enough," Julie said.

"You press here to detonate. I don't know what the transmission range is, but if you're close enough, you'll trigger the others as well."

"And if I'm out of range?"

"Hold it here," Simms said, pressing it to the side of his head. "And you'll never know the difference."

"Can I disarm it?"

"Probably," Simms said. "Ask Hiller."

"Okay." Julie stashed the charge into a pouch along with

her pistol, a syringe, and a couple of vials of painkiller. She did a last check to make sure she had everything.

"Get as far as you can," Simms said, motioning at the container. "When that blows—"

"I got that part," Julie said. "Anything else?"

"No."

"Okay, then."

Julie walked to Cutter, who was making a bulwark by clearing a channel in the top of the rock pile.

"You gonna be okay?" she asked.

"I'm fucking gonna die, is what I'm gonna be," Cutter said. "What kind of stupid question is that?"

"Whatever," Julie said.

"Yeah, whatever," Cutter said, turning away. One of the oversized ant-termites walked up and took a rock from the pile. He kicked it, sending it flying back into the sunken room. "You don't have any Raid, do you?"

Julie grabbed Cutter and turned him to her. She smiled up at him, laying a hand on his chest. They stood there for a moment, then Cutter noticed the D-5 pin on her shirt.

"What the hell?" Cutter asked, fingering the pin.

"I'm throwing that away the moment I leave," Julie said.

"Whatever you say, *Sarge*."

"I *will* kill you," Julie said.

"You better hurry."

Julie pressed her other hand to Cutter's stomach, feeling a sudden, urgent need to touch him, to affirm his existence. *It's just the painkiller,* she told herself, but when Cutter leaned down, she drove her mouth up to meet his. They kissed deeply. Julie pressed into him, feeling the warmth of his body against her. When the kiss finally ended, she realized she was shivering.

"About time," Cutter said.

"No shit," Julie said, pushing him back and jerking the knife from his belt. "You mind?"

"You asking?"

"No."

"Then happy birthday."

"What?"

"I remembered," Cutter said. "Just don't forget where you got it from."

"Not fucking likely," Julie said, brushing the back of her hand across her eyes. She gazed at him for a long minute.

"See you in hell," she said finally, starting down the tunnel to Hiller, who stood waiting.

"Not if I see you first!" Cutter yelled after her.

Hiller stood by the rope up to the passageway. When Julie reached him, she turned and called to Simms.

"Sir," she said, the word tasting of rust. "I will get back, sir. And I will report in."

"I know you will, Sergeant," Simms replied, giving her a sharp salute. She snapped her arm up, returning the gesture, then climbed the rope and disappeared into the passage.

"Keep her safe, Lieutenant," Simms said. Hiller saluted, then followed Julie up and out.

When he and Cutter were alone, Simms climbed into the crane. It started with a smoky cough, and he drove it toward the container of explosives.

FORTY FOUR

Hiller coiled up the rope and, ignoring Julie's outstretched hand, slung it over his shoulder. He motioned her aside, so that he could lead. When she didn't move, he pointed to the gold bar on his sleeve and then her sergeant's chevron. She shook her head derisively but moved over and waved him ahead.

Julie stayed tight on Hiller as they crawled down the passageway, hassling him with an occasional hand on his boot. He was blocking her view of the passage, but she caught an occasional glimpse of blue light as they approached the cylindrical room.

Hiller dropped flat, sliding the last few feet on his belly. He peeked down into the room, then slid his shoulders out, rifle in hand, checking to the left and right. He peered behind the crystalline helictite and in every corner of the room.

Julie grew impatient.

She raised herself into the air by straddling the tube walls with her hands and knees. Hovering a foot above Hiller, she crawled forward and looked around. The room was empty, but something had changed since she was last here. She couldn't tell what.

Hiller motioned Julie back, then tied off the rope and

slid down. By the time Julie reached the floor, he was peering into the hole in the floor. He jerked back suddenly, retreating toward Julie. Julie drew her pistol and crouched beside him. They waited.

The next minute was so quiet that Julie could hear Hiller's breath. Even in the blue light, she saw that he was pale and glistening with sweat. She wanted to ask what he had seen, but blue light flashed inside the dark hole.

Hiller motioned Julie back up to the passage, but she shook her head, advancing on the hole. She could see the light moving closer, growing brighter. She leaned into the hole, but Hiller grabbed her arm and pulled her back. He gave her a look of disbelief and then slung her toward the rope. She started back for the hole, but he had already moved in front of her. He dropped to one knee and propped up his gun with an elbow on his thigh, the quintessential army rifleman.

"Shit," Julie muttered. She stowed her pistol and, ignoring the rope hanging down from the passageway, climbed up one of the mineral veins. She moved fast, arm over arm, legs dangling.

Gunfire erupted below her. Light flickered like a strobe, casting confusing shadows through the room, but she kept climbing.

The mineral vein sunk into the smooth wall, emerged again three feet above her, too far to reach. She curled her legs, bringing her feet up just below her hands and clamped them to the vein. Murmuring encouragement to her injured leg, she thrust herself up. Her stronger leg pushed her out at an angle, but she managed to grab the upper vein and pull herself upright. Gripping solidly, she released her feet and continued to climb. Below her, the gunfire paused; Hiller was reloading.

As Julie neared the ceiling, she realized what about this room had changed—the blue gash was glowing much brighter. She had no idea what was up there—and she really didn't want to find out—but it was her only choice. She climbed faster, urged on by the gunfire below.

Her head came up against the ceiling, but the gash was about five feet away, in the center of the room.

The gunfire paused again as Hiller loaded his third and final clip. Julie looked at the crystalline helictite that rose through the middle of the room. It was the only way.

She coiled up and flattened her feet to the wall, aiming her whole body at the helictite.

"Don't go soft on me now," she told herself. She drew a breath and sprang into the air.

Julie dove through the air, arms extended in front of her. Thirty feet below, Hiller was backed against the wall, his face alternating between blue and white with every flash of his muzzle. His finger was tight on the trigger, his face twisted with desperation. A dark form stalked toward him across the floor.

Julie's hands closed around a thick branch of the crystal tree. The branch broke under her weight, but she had already grabbed another, and then another. She scrambled up the helictite as it collapsed underneath her, showering the room with log-sized chunks. The entire tree shattered, but she clamped a hand on the edge of the gash, dangling by one arm.

Somewhere in the cacophony of shattering quartz, Julie heard the pronounced click of an empty rifle.

The gash's jagged rock started to crack in her hand, and she eased herself up slowly, trying not to jar it. She got her other hand on the rock, then curled her legs and threaded them through the hole. A scream of pain filled the room, Hiller's.

Hanging by her hands and legs, Julie straightened her body, pulling up through the gash and into the room above.

She rolled to the side, out of sight, then lay on her back and held her breath.

Heavy footsteps circled the room below her, then stopped. Julie felt eyes peering up at the gash, but then there were more steps, this time moving away. The sound faded. She waited until she could no longer hear them, then sat up and looked around.

This room had the same smooth walls as the one below, but it was short and wide, the bulbous shape of a mushroom or the inside of a diving bell. A forest of translucent helictites filled the room, passing from floor to ceiling, and the entire room glowed blue, as bright as the night under a full moon.

Julie got to her feet but had to crouch beneath the low ceiling. She felt a faint jab of pain in her thigh; the painkiller was wearing off. She was about to sit back down, to medicate herself, when something shifted under her foot—a human thighbone. Dry white bones littered the floor around the gash, broken and scored as though gnawed upon.

She backed away, scanning the room, seeing movement in every shadow, and nearly stepping off a cliff.

FORTY FIVE

THE CHASM WAS DEEPER than sight, a crack in the earth as broad and long as the largest canyon in the world. Julie peered over the edge, the rising heat blowing on her face. She stood atop a sheer cliff, and, leaning forward, she saw an orange glow so faint that it could have been imagined. Very real, however, was the string of blue lights that rose up from the depths, alongside a ladder of steel rungs. The rungs rose all the way to the floor beneath her feet, and the lights, strung on a thick black cable, continued into the room. She turned and followed it.

The cable fed into a box of clear rubber with dark fibers woven through it. A spray of smaller cables sprouted from the other side, each leading to one of a dozen metal spheres—aluminum polished to a mirror shine—spread throughout the room. Each sphere had a belt of glowing blue pods, whose light filled the room.

Julie approached the nearest sphere. It appeared to be some sort of machine, rotating the pods slowly around it. The pods were egg shaped, about two feet tall, and had translucent skins the texture of a dry leaf.

A tube extended from the sphere, and each pod paused as it passed beneath it, receiving a dose of luminous blue liquid. The liquid swirled inside the pod, creating dark eddies in the glowing haze.

Julie approached carefully, checking each step before she took it. The sphere thrummed like a heartbeat, vibrating the floor and the soles of her feet.

At the base of the sphere, a tiny metal chair faced a panel of doll-sized switches and nobs. An array of small lights—no more than pinpricks—flickered wildly.

Julie leaned down, slipping her head between two of the glowing pods and inspected the miniature controls. She extended her finger to the largest button—the size of a pencil eraser—and was about to press it when something slammed against the side of her head. She jerked back, raising her arms defensively.

The blow had been loud, though more startling than painful. It had come from the pod to her right, which was undulating, expanding first on one direction, then in another. Thin shadows scraped along the inside of its skin.

Julie backed away, bumping into another sphere. Its cocoons rattled like a rattlesnake's tail, and she pulled back, her foot landing on the uneven floor. Her ankle twisted, shooting pain up her thigh. She tumbled, grabbing one of the spherical machines, her face knocking against one of the pods. A barbed leg stabbed out from the pod, its pointed tip stopping an inch from her eye. The leg sliced down the pod's skin, fluid pouring out as a beetle pushed its head out.

FORTY SIX

Julie scrambled backward, walking with her arms and dragging her legs behind her, her thigh screaming with pain. She propped herself against the wall and yanked out the syringe from the pouch on her belt, scattering bottles of painkiller across the floor. She grabbed the nearest bottle and jabbed the needle in, but froze when a second beetle appeared, pushing out of a nearby pod. Its enormous mandibles gleamed silver and globs of blue liquid dripped from its shell. It walked straight at Julie, staring into her eyes, but then another beetle tumbled from its pod, knocking against the first. The two beetles faced off, hissing.

Pods were hatching throughout the room, and blue liquid coated the floor, creating a glowing canvas on which dark outlines hissed and sparred. Julie fumbled with the syringe, drawing the plunger back with trembling fingers.

She peeled back the bandage on her thigh and held the needle to the skin beside her wound. But before she could use it, a beetle came galloping at her, its shell apple red, its neck sparkling with silvered quills.

The beetle went right to her thigh, its small antennae quivering. It poked her wound with its foreleg; the pain was terrible. Julie bit her cheek to keep from screaming, and her mouth filled with the metallic taste of blood.

The beetle studied her thigh, probing it in several places, but Julie managed to remain still. Eventually it continued on, scrambling over her leg, its rear legs digging into her wound. Julie clamped her hand over her mouth, and the moment the beetle was gone, she swung the syringe into her leg, jabbing deep and plunging hard.

By now most of the pods had hatched and beetles crowded the small room. They grouped together by type and marched the perimeter in loose formation. Julie sat up and looked around, searching for a way out.

Fifteen feet to her right was a dark patch on the otherwise luminous floor. Using the wall for supported, she pushed to her feet and, keeping her leg straight, hobbled toward it. Halfway there, a pod burst open and a beetle rolled out, stopping directly in her path.

The newborn struggled to its feet, toppling twice before it found an unsteady balance. It shook its head like a wet kitten, flinging away blue goop, then it looked up at Julie with its big, silver eyes.

It was a tiger beetle, full-sized, and it was looking straight at her. She drew a breath and held it, not daring to move.

The beetle rubbed its eyes and then cleaned its antennae by pulling them between its forelegs, first one and then the other. It raised the antennae and wiggled them.

Julie's chest ached, but she held her breath. She glanced past the beetle to the dark patch on the floor, only a few feet away now. It was definitely a hole; blue liquid was pouring over the edge and draining away.

The beetle wiped its eyes one last time, then turned and walked away. Despite the urgency she felt, Julie waited. She exhaled slowly, drew in another breath, then took a step toward the drain hole. The tiger beetle whipped back around, its antennae quivering. It leaped onto a nearby sphere and let out a hiss. The room fell silent as every beetle in it turned to face Julie.

Julie sprung at the tiger beetle, driving her fist into its face and sending it flying. A hundred pairs of eyes tracked the beetle's flight across the room, watched it crunch against the wall, then turned back to Julie. She remained as still as possible, her fist throbbing like she'd punched a rock. Nothing happened for a moment, then another tiger beetle appeared, climbing up the far wall. It hissed at Julie and the beetles attacked. Julie sprinted for the drain.

A beetle sprung at her and she ducked, its mandibles slicing past her head. Another moved right in front of her, and she shoved down on its shell with both hands, leapfrogging over it. Quills whizzed by her head, ricocheted off the nearby helictites and splashed into the blue liquid at her feet. She took several vaulting strides and dove headfirst into the hole in the floor.

She plunged straight down for several seconds, then bounced off something hard. She tumbled forward, landed on an angled floor, and slid along a runnel of blue. She screamed uncontrollably, too frenzied to even realize that she was. She clawed at the smooth walls, trying to stop herself, but only managed to spin herself around.

She slid faster and faster and then the floor dropped away.

The transfer station was dark and silent. The water had risen to cover the barricade, and dim lanterns, abandoned by D-5, rolled back and forth below the surface. Small waves spilled over the edge of the gaping fissure, sending sprays of white mist into its endless depths.

At the other end of the station, the pipe leading up to the operations room hung in darkness, its tip swallowed by the rising lake.

A scream rose in the middle of the room, trumpeting from a hole in the ceiling. The scream turned sharp as Julie dropped into the room, flailing wildly, her body coated in glowing blue.

She fell twenty feet and plunged into the water, and the room was again silent.

A moment later, she popped to the surface, no longer screaming but swimming with all her might. She headed for the pipe, navigating by the glow of her own skin. Beetles dribbled out of the hole in the ceiling, splashed into the water, and chased after her.

Julie gave it everything she had, but she wasn't much of a swimmer. She splashed awkwardly, coughing out water and then sucking in more, the water stinging her lungs.

Behind her, the beetles spread into a wide, dark blanket that rolled over the surface. Their underbellies, stained blue, lit the water beneath them. Julie glanced back, then swam harder.

Her hand slapped against something hard. She pushed back, grabbing for her pistol, but it was only Specialist Boxx. He was dead, a hole burned through his chest. She shoved him aside and swam.

The first wave of beetles scurried over Boxx, their momentum rolling him like a log. They coated him on all sides, devouring him hungrily. The next wave raced over the first, bearing down on Julie.

Julie saw the pipe ahead, a gray line slicing the dark. It was far and the beetles were gaining.

She swam on, gasping for air, her sloppy strokes growing

sloppier as her arms tired. Her hands chopped ineffectively at the water and she felt the beetles closing in, their scrambling mass pressing a wave of water against her back. She gulped in a breath, and, just as the first claw scraped her calf, she dove.

The beetles rolled overhead, covering the surface with glowing blue bellies and squirming legs. A mandible beetle dove at Julie's leg but was pulled back up by its own buoyancy. More beetles dove, but none could reach her. Julie swam through the dark water, heading for the unseen pipe.

A blue light appeared in front of her. She stopped, pushing back, but then realized it was only a reflection. The blue light was behind her, distant but coming fast.

Julie swam hard, frog style, sweeping with her arms and pumping her legs. She fought to hold her breath, but her cheeks puffed out and bubbles leaked from her lips. The blue light cut through the water like a torpedo.

Julie's chest convulsed, desperate for air. Her body was beyond control; her arms thrashed uselessly, her legs hung limp. The blue light bore down on her, just yards away now. She shook her head, but couldn't think beyond the need for air. Then her flailing hand stuck something solid—the pipe.

She reached down, found the lip, and rolled inside.

The water rose several feet inside the pipe. Julie burst through the surface, sucking in air.

Beetles slammed against the outside, scratching the metal with their feet. The sound was loud, the beetles inches away, but she was safe. The tip of the pipe was submerged in the water, too deep for the beetles to reach.

Her skin had lost most of its glow, but she found the ladder and started to climb.

The water below her brightened, but then dimmed again. Halfway up, Julie saw there was something covering the top of the pipe. She couldn't tell what.

The scraping and pounding rose to a deafening pitch and then suddenly stopped. Julie continued to climb, hearing only her labored breath and her hands slapping on the rungs. And then:

Boom!

A hole was punched through the pipe, twelve inches across, just above the water line. Julie gaped at it, climbed faster.

Another boom, and another hole appeared beside the first. Then a third, this one severing the pipe entirely; the bottom fell away, sinking into the water. Beetles poured inside.

Julie reached the top of the pipe and found it capped with a steel plate. She put her shoulder to it, but it didn't budge. She pounded the steel with her fist, yelling with each strike:

"WHAT—THE—FUCK—IS—THIS!"

The beetles thundered up the pipe, shoving against one another, each jockeying to reach her first. A mandible beetle leaped and Julie kicked, catching it in the chin and sending it tumbling back down the pipe. It knocked back several others, but more rushed in to fill the gap. Two beetles attacked in unison.

Julie kicked at one while trying to dodge the other, but there was no room to maneuver—the pipe was no wider than her shoulders. Jagged mandibles closed around her calf, but then a light appeared overhead and she was yanked up and away. Petty grabbed her by the armpits and pulled her from the pipe. He dumped her onto the floor and fired a shotgun into the pipe, three times. He slid an overturned table over the pipe and piled furniture on top.

"I was wondering where you guys went," Petty said. He was dressed in his armor, with the left leg cut away to allow for his bandages. The hallway was well lit and surreally quiet. Julie felt like she had been transported to another world. But then the beetles started pounding against the overturned desk, rattling it and the furniture on top. Julie sprang up and helped toss on more.

"We went to have a look around," she said. Petty looked over at Julie and gawked, seeing for the first time what a mess she was. Her clothing was shredded, her body was covered in lacerations, and her skin was tinted cadaver blue.

"Where is everybody?" he asked.

"I am everybody," Julie replied, taking the chair he held in his hands and tossing it on the pile. "Come on."

Petty didn't move, seemingly confused by her words.

"Come on," Julie repeated, dragging him toward the operations room.

The dome looked much as it had before, except that metal plates had been welded over the elevator doors. Water sprayed through pinprick leaks, but the room was basically dry.

"Any oxygen left?" she asked, looking around. Petty was dazed, his face blank.

"Specialist!" Julie yelled, grabbing him by the collar. "Are there any air tanks left?"

"Yes, ma'am," Petty said, waking up. "Over here."

Petty led her to a small stack of tanks. She shoved one into his hands, then slung another over her back. She tucked an inflatable life vest under her belt, pulled a diving mask onto her forehead, then went to Wolf's Atargis diving suit and hefted up the giant metal torso. Her legs bowed under its weight.

"Arms out," she demanded. Petty did as he was told.

Julie slung the torso over his head and began clasping it down the side.

"You have to be the one to go back," she said, "because I'm the one who knows how this suit goes together. So it'll be up to *you* to tell them about this."

Petty dropped his arms.

"Tell them about what?" he asked.

"About the thing that controls the bugs. I found its lair, or its base of operations, or whatever it was. It definitely lives down here. Tell them that. Tell them to stop digging."

"What are you talking about?" Petty asked. He was at a complete loss.

Julie realized she was babbling. She took a moment to pull her thoughts together, then realized that the pounding had stopped. She looked down the hallway, to the pipe.

Boom!

The pile of furniture jumped several inches into the air. Julie took a step back.

"That," she said.

"What is it?" Petty asked, his voice cracking.

Boom!

The table split in the middle and rose up like a tent. Chairs tumbled away.

"We need to get those elevator doors open," Julie said. "Right now."

"There's no way," Petty said. His mind swimming. This was too much, too fast, for him to process. "I welded them shut."

Boom!

The pile toppled, scattering.

Julie pulled the explosive charge from her pouch and shoved it in Petty's face. The timer read one minute and twenty seconds.

"Listen to me, soldier," she barked. "We have exactly *this long* to get out of here."

Petty didn't respond. Julie slapped him, then held the charge up again, shaking it for emphasis.

"Doors! Now!"

Petty nodded, taking a step toward the elevator, but then stopped, his jaw unhinging.

Mandible beetles swarmed out of the crumbled furniture and spread across the hallway. Petty motioned Julie behind him as he eased his shotgun up, aiming at the center of the swelling horde.

Quill beetles appeared behind the mandible ones, lining up in sharp ranks. The tiger beetle came last, climbing atop the pile to survey its army.

"That one," Julie said, pointing at the tiger beetle. "That's how it sees us."

Petty fired, and the beetle shattered. The other beetles remained still.

"There," Julie shouted as another tiger beetle appeared. Petty fired, but this one dodged, leaping onto the wall. Petty fired again, making the kill, but quills ripped into his arm. His arm went limp and the shotgun clattered to the floor. He stared at the beetles, and they stared back.

"Now what?" he asked, clutching his arm, trying to stem the bleeding.

"I don't know," Julie said.

Blue light glowed inside the furniture pile, streaming through the gaps like searchlights. The pile swelled, then broke in the middle and fell to either side. The bright blue light rose into the room. Hidden behind its glare was a dark form: short, headless, the source of the light in its hand.

The yard-tall shadow cast aside the last remnant of furniture, its arms flexing like thick hose. It trained the blue light on Julie's chest, focused it to a circle, and held it there. Then the light switched off and they saw the creature behind it. It was a machine, dark and brutal.

The machine was an intricate work of metal, comprised of components so small they were like the texture of an irregular fabric. Its arms and legs—identical in all respects—were comprised of short, jointed sections. The limbs were flexible in all directions and moved with hydraulic smoothness.

Its headless torso was a dull black, scratched and worn, with a large, clear gemstone set in the front. The gem had been hollowed out, its thick walls creating a cockpit inside of which was strapped a small man. Or, at least, something that resembled a man.

He was barely a half foot tall, hairless, with worm-colored skin that was transparent to the veins and organs beneath. His head was disproportionately large and supported by a thick, triangular neck. Despite his bantam size, he was muscular and fit.

Eyes the size of quarters dominated his face, filled to the rim with shiny black pupils. He angled his head and made a noise like a curious bird. His outstretched arm was mimicked by that of his robotic powersuit, which lowered the light-emitting device as the man brought his arm to his side. The device resembled a pistol, but with a short, three-inch-thick barrel capped by a glass lens.

The small man threw a switch on a small control panel and beetles parted, clearing a path in front of him. The powersuit walked forward, its whirring legs taking arcing steps, all but twirling through the air. The man inside smiled at Julie with death's-head teeth.

Julie backed away, glancing at the timer on the explosive charge, then lowering the diving mask onto her face. She groped at the air tank on her back, finding the hose and sliding her hand down to the mouthpiece.

"Hold on," she said between her teeth. Petty nodded, bending down to grab the tank at his feet.

The small man stopped a foot from Julie and raised the arm of his robotic suit, its metal hand nothing but a knob with three stubby fingers spaced around it. He pointed a finger at the charge in Julie's hand and motioned for her to show it to him. Julie smiled, friendly, and held it out, getting it as close to the man's protective shell as she could. The timer was ticking off the last ten seconds.

The robotic arm reached for it but stopped as the small man recognized the countdown. He snapped his hand away and stepped back. There were three seconds left.

Julie threw the charge at him and he raised his pistol to shoot it. The gun hummed as a blue ring of light focused on the charge, but the charge exploded before he could fire.

The small man was blown across the room, and Julie and Petty were thrown in the opposite direction, tumbling across the floor. For a moment, everything was still. But then came a distant rumble, like an approaching earthquake. The floor began to vibrate.

Julie shoved the air regulator into her mouth as a two-foot-wide stream of water shot from the pipe and cascaded down the hallway. The floor cracked and the pipe tore loose, launching into the air. Water poured into the operations room.

The dome around them began to warp, its ten inch-thick-metal walls buckling, drooping inward. A crack appeared behind Petty, and the escaping air sucked him back, holding him fast.

Across the dome, the metal powersuit rose out of the

knee-deep water. The small man inspected his gun, frowning as a hunk of the glass lens fell off into the water.

Beetles swirled through the room, floating, tossed about by the churning water. The entire room was shaking, and chunks of the floor blew open as geysers sprang up, bringing even more water. The dome walls collapsed in stages, creaking heavily as they bent two or three feet at a time, bringing the roof down with crushing force.

The small man ignored the chaos, advancing on Julie, disappearing as the rising water engulfed him. Julie ducked below the surface, but couldn't see far through the swirling bubbles. Spotting Petty's air tank, she grabbed it and pushed through the chest-high water to where the specialist was trapped against the wall. She shoved the air regulator into his mouth just as the roiling water engulfed them both.

The force of the escaping air was gone, but Petty had been pulled deep into the crack, and its jagged metal edges had dug into the torso of his diving suit. Julie planted her feet on the wall and tried to pull him loose, but he didn't budge. She started to pop the suit's clasps to free him, but Petty shoved her back, pointing anxiously over her shoulder.

The small man was approaching, walking as easily through the water as he had through air. He raised his power-suit's metal arm, and its fingers retracted into the knobby hand, replaced by three long, gleaming blades. The man smiled as he clicked the blades together, then he drove them at Julie's head.

Julie dodged to the side, slowed by the water, feeling the blades graze her cheek. She pushed the water with open hands, shoving herself away, but she backed right into the wall. She drew her pistol and fired, the bullets tunneling through the water.

The robotic suit dodged the bullets easily, cartwheeling

up the dome wall with impossible speed, its hands and feet clinging like magnets. The clear chamber in its torso rotated, keeping the small man inside level. He leaped at Julie, blades extended.

Julie crouched low, swinging her arm to deflect the blow, but the man changed his attack in midstrike and was suddenly stabbing down at her. Julie twisted back and braced her wrist on her knee, keeping on the dull side of the blades as she took the blow with her forearm. The impact was so hard it rattled her teeth. She was thrown flat on her back. She rolled to the side, escaping under a section of wall that was bent nearly to the floor.

As she rose on the other side, something snapped at her ears. She jerked away as a flailing beetle swept past, its mandibles scissoring as it tried to reach her. The beetle disappeared in the frothing current, and seconds later, the dark powersuit appeared from the same direction, walking calmly toward her.

Julie tried to skirt around him, but there was a heavy groan and the roof drooped down on the other side of her, trapping her in a metal corridor with a wall behind her and the robotic suit in front.

The man advanced, and, absurdly, Julie found herself wondering at his size.

To him, the powersuit was a massive piece of machinery—something he would describe as three stories tall. And the beetles he controlled would be as large to him as an elephant was to her. He was wielding terrible weapons of war, but they wouldn't have been developed to fight humans—the two races had only now learned of each other's existence.

Julie must have seemed a terrifying behemoth to the small man, a veritable Godzilla, but he didn't hesitate in his attack. He backed her to the wall, cocked his arm, and raised his blades for a final, fatal strike. As alien as he was, Julie could see he was pissed.

He stepped forward as he drove the blades at Julie's head, but they stopped short, falling limp. A green plume rose from the shoulder of the powersuit—Petty stood behind it, free from his diving suit, hacking its hydraulic hoses with his knife.

The man scowled when he realized what had happened. Blades slid out of his other hand and he whirled around, driving them deep into the armored plate on Petty's chest and into the man behind it. Petty fell, leaving a trail of red in the water. The man turned back to Julie.

"Motherfucker!" she screamed, her words mixed with bubbles. She fired her gun, but the creature cartwheeled out of the way, rolling up the collapsed roof, its damaged arm swinging freely.

Julie sprang at the small man, but her foot slipped. She tumbled, sprawling out on the floor, her eyes closed. The small man hesitated, but when she didn't move, he thrust his blades at her head. Julie's eyes popped open, and she clamped her hands to his wrist, rolling to the side and using her weight to pull the creature off its feet. It spun through the water, landing on its back.

The robotic suit curled its limbs back, shoving itself upright, but Julie was already on top of it. She pressed her pistol to the glass encasement, aimed it at the small man's head, and fired.

A fifteen-carat chunk of glass broke loose from the encasement, leaving a divot, and a crack spread across the front. The recoil ripped the pistol from Julie's hand, and it disappeared into the swirling water.

The small man was motionless, eyes wide as the crack spread in front of him. Julie drew Cutter's knife and jammed it in, levering it back and forth, prying at the glass.

The man drove his blades at Julie, but she grabbed the mechanical arm in both hands, holding it back. The powersuit's legs grabbed at her with their thick fingers, but she braced her feet to their ankles and shoved them back. The hydraulic motor in the robotic suit whined, straining, but it overpowered Julie, bending her arms and legs, closing its limbs around her.

"You think you're the monster here?" Julie yelled, spitting out the air regulator. "I'll show you a fucking monster!"

She pushed harder, her biceps bulging. The whining motor grew to a scream and the powersuit's limbs started to creak, giving way. The whole machine began to buck, and the motor seized with a pronounced thump. The suit went limp.

Julie smiled maniacally as she shoved the air regulator back into her mouth. She grabbed Cutter's knife and stabbed the glass over and over. The small man flipped switches rapidly. The motor chugged to life, then died again.

A wide grin spread across Julie's face. She swung harder, chipping away at the glass.

The floor broke open beside her and a towering rock the size of an upended eighteen-wheeler shoved through, sliding into the room and crunching against the ceiling. Its tip shattered to boulders, which rained down through the water in slow motion. Air rushed through the new hole in the floor, forcing the water from the room. The boulders came crashing down.

Julie dodged the boulders, only to run into one of the beetles—they were dropping to the floor all around her.

The sudden air was disorienting, and Julie's ears rang as though concussed. She grabbed a melon-sized rock and sprang at the man, hammering the knife into his glass encasement, the noise echoing off the dome walls.

Inside the robotic suit, the small man worked the

controls frantically, trying to bring his machine back to life. But then he stopped, looking at Julie and then past her, a grin spreading across his face. She turned; the beetles had formed into rows and were advancing on all sides.

"Oh, shit," she said. She ducked behind the towering rock just as they launched the first barrage of quills. She barely made it; the painkiller was wearing off again, and her leg was stiff and unresponsive.

A cluster of mandible beetles charged around the rock, but just as they reached Julie the towering rock shifted, first tilting and then rising, propelled by a yards-wide stream of water. The rock ripped through the dome and hurtled out of sight, leaving behind a gaping hole. The air rose in a single, tremendous bubble, hauling Julie, the beetles, and the small man along with it. The lanterns from inside the dome rose up alongside them, surrounding them like bright stars in the black ocean.

The pressure punched at Julie from all sides. She opened her mouth, equalizing the air in her lungs with that around her, but then the giant bubble broke into a million tiny ones, surrounding her in a white haze.

The cloud of bubbles outpaced her, rising overhead, and Julie spotted the powersuit below, coated in a sheen of air. Its arm was raised, its blades spread like a propeller. The suit's motor whined and sputtered, and the blades turned in fits, pushing the suit downward.

Oh, no you don't, Julie thought, flipping over and swimming toward it. The water was heavy, and her legs were stiff and clumsy, but she slowly gained on it.

The small man was pounding on his control panel, panicking, but not because of Julie. He didn't even notice her. She followed his gaze to a cluster of beetles. Goo leaked from their shells, and, one by one, they were exploding into colored wisps, like the smoky clouds of antiaircraft fire.

The powersuit's engine whirred to life, and its blades spun faster and faster until they were nothing but a solid wheel. The suit shot away, but Julie lurched forward, grabbing the suit's dead limb, which trailed behind. She stretched out a hand and locked it to the suit's torso, then scissored her legs, spinning both her and the robotic suit, angling the propeller to the side. The two of them, joined together, started to spin in place. The man angled his wrist, aiming the propeller up, but Julie swung her legs again, this time flipping them all the way over, such that they were heading straight up.

The small man snarled, throwing a switch to form the blades back into a claw. He stabbed at Julie, but she shoved him away, and his blades swished through the water between them. He kicked his legs, trying to flip back over, but to little effect. His suit didn't have the right balance. He stretched his arm backward, switched the blades back to a propeller, and drove toward Julie. He faded into the black water as he drew closer—the lanterns were high overhead, their light dimming. Julie saw the robotic arm swing down, its blades closing on her as everything went dark.

She reached over her shoulder and slung her air tank forward. The blades struck the tank, shoving her back, screeching as they clanged into the metal. The tank shook back and forth as the man tried to free his blades. A blue glow filled the water—lights on the powersuit's shoulders.

Julie drew the small knife from her belt and sliced through the air hose. A stream of air shot out, propelling her—and the small man—with tremendous force. She aimed the hose down and the tank pulled them straight up. They fluttered behind it, facing each other, Julie holding on with all her might while the man bucked and contorted, trying to break free.

The pressure changed rapidly and Julie's vision started to blur. The robotic suit's lights fluttered in and out; either they were dying or she was. A glowing cloud passed them at a distance, heading down. It was the lanterns, she realized, watching them fade.

There was a loud clink, and cracks spread across the small man's encasement, frosting the surface. The glass bulged as the air in the cockpit expanded, and Julie got her arm over her face just as it exploded. Tiny shards speared her skin and, when she opened her eyes, the powersuit hung limply beside her, a hole in the middle where the man had been.

She pulled the air tank to her and got the cut end into her mouth. The air had stopped flowing, but, turning it right side up, she felt fresh air rise into her lungs, cool and calming.

Julie gazed into the endless darkness, wondering how fast she was ascending, and how long it would take to reach the surface. Too long, she knew, but she felt no panic, no alarm. The water was cold and hypothermia had set it, bringing with it peace and contentment. She was dying, but it was a small matter.

Taking another breath of air, she remembered the life vest stashed under her belt. She tugged it out and, holding it tight, yanked on the cord. At this depth, with this much pressure, the vest didn't inflate. She shook it, but it only flapped in the water.

Oh, well, she thought. She held on anyway, taking another hit off the tank. It was the last of the air, so she let the tank drop and the remains of the robotic suit went with it. She released her last bubbles slowly, feeling them tickle up her face, wishing she could see them as they rose above her.

She remembered that she had been shivering, but now

she was not. Her lungs were empty, but she didn't convulse this time. She merely grew still.

Her body spiraled up through the water. Her arm was stretched over her head, pulled by the yellow plastic vest that, still deflated, flapped like the flame of a torch. An occasional bubble escaped her lips as the pressure lessened, and, sometime later, she passed through the thermocline, where the temperature rose sharply from just above freezing to refrigerator cold. More time passed and the vest started to expand. It tried to pull free, but Julie's hand was locked around it, her body all but frozen.

Eventually, the water lightened to the color of iron, then steel, and, finally, deep dark blue. Sunlight glimmered through the waves, high overhead.

The life vest broke through the surface of the ocean, fully inflated, dragging Julie's body behind it. She rolled stiffly on the waves, her eyes closed, her skin glacier blue. She didn't move, not even to breathe.

The air was cool, but the sun was warm, and her body loosened slowly, her limbs flopping in the water. A large wave rolled up, and as she tumbled over the top, the life vest was yanked from her hand. She sank into the water, five feet, ten feet, but then her eyes popped open. She kicked back to the surface, coughing out water and gasping in air.

She scrambled for the life vest, pulling it over her head and strapping it to her waist. Her body ached as though she'd been beaten with a bag of rocks, and each breath brought fresh pain.

She looked around, but couldn't see past the nearest waves. Then a swell rolled up, carrying her to its peak. She turned in a circle, scanning the horizon. There was nothing but ocean in all directions. Just miles and miles of cold, gray Atlantic.

NYC unit

Anney Fresh Ozar • Iris Lassen • Jeff Stark
Paula Z Segal • Jon Gray • Mike Ross • Nicole Whelan
Maureen Flaherty • Jason Engdahl • Rosanna Scimeca
Colleen Mulleedy • Mary Roberts • Shane Gross
Judge Cal • Dan Rabinovitch • Mark Harder • Mike Conner
Sherry Smith • Pablo Morales

Los Angeles unit

Pam Susemiehl • Kyle Kannenberg • Barri Evins
Zenzi Gadson • Elaine Smith • Jason Hoey • Carl Paey
Adam Merims • Laura Rutter • Danielle Lance
Brad Golden • Ted Kamp • Kristen Campbell Taylor
Andrew Leung • Liza Malashenko

North Carolina unit

Jeremy Roth • Donna Bell • Bill Loeb
Ed and Abby Overton • Luis Hernandez
Tom Livers • Randy Hackley • Muriel Williman
Ray and Xenia Bode • Eric Singdahlsen

San Francisco unit

Guy Stilson • Allen White • Mark Rawling
Michelle Morby • Nicholas Sher • Trevor Tuttle

At Large unit

Julie Porter Scott • Elaine Issack • Victoria and Charles Su
Ian Saunders • Alissa Kozuh • Randy Grannovetter
Katrina Krasser • Katie McNiesh • Laura Kozuh • Chad Stutz
Erika Thomas • Alexander Levy • Christine Humphreys

Acknowledgments

This book has been in the works for well north of a decade and owes its existence to a slew of sympathetic folks—too many, I'm afraid, for me to believe that I've captured all of them here. My deepest apologies to anyone that I've overlooked.

First and foremost, I'd like to thank Megan Caper, who was with this tale from the very beginning and has stuck through to the bitter end. I'd also like to thank my editor, Jenna Kamp, who continues to offer her time, her skills, and her invaluable advice no matter how lost the cause may appear. Thank you Donna Bell for not holding the truth back, and Rob Humphreys for, at various points in this project, teaching me what little I can claim to know. Thank you Danielle Hlatky for your continued encouragement and support. Thank you Jeanne and Lance James for nurturing me through all of my unpredictable life choices, many of which ended up more trouble than they were worth, and thank you Jason for plowing ahead and insisting that I tag along

Lastly, thank you to everyone who appears on the opposite page. You deserve more credit than I can possibly express, and I am forever in your debt.

BRETT JAMES HOLDS THE US Army record for the fastest completion of basic training, at just 8 days. Historians have attributed this not to skill, but to his being voted "most likely to shoot a fellow soldier." After basic, James was assigned to activities designed to curb his expansive ego, such as standing in a pit banging a gong (pictured above).

Eventually James was stationed in the basement of an otherwise abandoned building, where he was tasked with the duplication of important memos. At the pinnacle of his career, James attained a typing speed of 17 words a minute using a technique he branded "two roosters fighting over a bug."

Find more by Brett James at
http://brettjames.com

THIS EDITION WAS HANDMADE BY THE AUTHOR.

Made in United States
North Haven, CT
02 May 2024

51972618R00214